OUR FATHER

OUR FATHER

▼

Paul L. Hall

Writer's Showcase
San Jose New York Lincoln Shanghai

Our Father

Writer's Showcase
an imprint of iUniverse.com, Inc.

For information address:
iUniverse.com, Inc.
5220 S 16th, Ste. 200
Lincoln, NE 68512
www.iuniverse.com

This is a work of fiction. All names and characters,
as well as institutions and organizations, are either invented or
used fictitiously. The events described are purely imaginary.

ISBN: 0-595-14970-7

Printed in the United States of America

Every day, every act betrays the ill-concealed deity.

Ralph Waldo Emerson, "Experience"

I imagine, Stephen said, that there is a malevolent reality behind those things I say I fear.

James Joyce, *A Portrait of the Artist as a Young Man*

The gods are what we now call hallucinations.

Julian Jaynes, *The Origin of Consciousness in the Breakdown of the Bicameral Mind*

Contents

CHAPTER I

▼

FARGO, ALMOST TOO FAR GONE

It was the voices that drove me out of academia, out of the English Department at Wayne State University in Detroit, the first modern city wherein democracy had evolved into routine peril.

I shut the book on my academic career. Then I *burned* the books, all 715 of them in my collection. I burned them one at a time in the basement incinerator of the apartment building where I lived and listened to the voices wail in agony. My own personal Final Solution. I'm not proud of this, but the voices are gone. The boisterous larvae of hundreds of narratives, the strafing of critics.

I'd escaped just in time. I had become reduced to a fascination with the minutiae of my profession. I had begun to read only the footnotes, discerning in their marvelous continuity an eternal kibitzing. I thrilled to the incidental biographies of great men—what they ate, the causes of their deaths, how many women they accumulated, and the apocrypha they spawned. I knew that James Joyce liked cheroots, but I couldn't be trusted to buy toothpaste on my own. My colleagues began to look askance at my approach, as if I were some corpse who had misplaced his grave. I had become an intellectual casualty. You can see these walking wounded everywhere, especially on park benches, bribing pigeons with popcorn so that they can lecture them on dissociative sensibility, a topic upon which they are eminently qualified to expound. I don't regret being a refugee. After I escaped academia, my wife escaped from me. She had always wanted to work in the movies, and one day, out of nowhere it seemed, she got a call from a Hollywood film production company offering a job. I didn't blame her. She wanted to follow her dream and I had few prospects. The abruptness of her departure came as a shock, but I should have seen it coming. I should have seen a lot of things coming.

The only aptitude I had was for reading and writing, so I started looking for any kind of job along those lines. But even before I could start my search, a job fell in my lap, or so I thought at the time. The guy who offered me the job ran a private investigation agency. He was an acquaintance of the head of my department and had mentioned the need for a writer. There wasn't the least bit of glamour to the job. The agency investigated insurance claims, for the most part. A staff of investigators would check up on claimants to make sure they weren't trying to defraud the insurance companies that hired the agency. Sometimes the agency did work for lawyers who were defending clients against bodily injury suits, which sometimes were the result of violence, but that's about as spicy as it got. We didn't even do divorce work.

My job was to summarize the reports filed by the agency operatives, to make them concise and coherent. I didn't even actually have to compose them. I just dictated them and the secretaries typed them up. For this I got paid $2,500 per month and all the audiocassette tapes I could steal. What demon had possessed me, I wondered, that I had languished in scholarship for the first thirty years of my life?

Speaking of the secretaries, they alone made the job enjoyable. Rudy Sultana, the guy who owned the agency, liked to surround himself in luxury, and that penchant extended to his female employees. He had one executive assistant and two other secretaries who did nothing but type and file, but as far as looks were concerned, none of them could pull rank on the others. They were all stunning beauties.

The executive assistant's name was Minerva Hewitt and if anyone had the edge in looks, she did. There was something sophisticated about her carriage and demeanor, something refined about even so mundane an activity as applying eyeliner that stirred the blood. At least it stirred my blood, a fluid long sluggish with apathy. I had begun to evolve along a separate relational path from women since my wife had left me. I knew they were out there moving around the terrain like I was, but I didn't know what to do with them. Whenever I did encounter a woman at close quarters, I felt like an animal sharing a water hole. We were not natural enemies, but they had become some parallel species. I had almost grown indifferent to them. Well, Minerva was sure a cure for indifference.

And apparently I wasn't the only male so affected by her, for when I tried, almost in spite of myself, to hit on her (a favorite expression of hers), the cold-blooded, mechanical viciousness of her rejection suggested that she had long ago wearied of propositions from men.

"Why I'd love to," she had said when I had suggested dinner. But already there was something frosty in her inflection, something forced about the smile, something taut about the eyes. I overlooked it. Hell, the way she looked I would have overlooked it if she had responded by discharging her nostrils one at a time in my shirt. I want to make it clear that she was a knockout.

"In fact," she continued, "why don't you drop by early. That way we could fuck for an hour or so before we go out to dinner. Then we won't have to worry about it all through our meal. In fact, then we could each of us just go out and eat by ourselves, or better yet, you could go home and I could *stay* home and we could save ourselves a lot of trouble—and you a lot of money—by eating at home alone."

Clearly, here was a challenge of some sort. At this point I should have said something like, "It's a date then. I'll be over about six." Except that to have done so would have required that I rehinge my jaw. And Minerva wasn't done yet.

"...and you will have accomplished your objective without having gone through some extravagant mating ritual, and I will not have been disappointed to find that your attention had been focused on the culmination of the evening's activities all along. I will not feel like a whore, and you will not have had to pay for it. We'll be just like two dogs that happened to bump into each other. We can blame it all on the biological imperative."

The other two secretaries had apparently witnessed similar scenes before. They busied themselves to conceal their embarrassment. The only gratifying thing about the whole episode was my awareness of their mute sympathy. I glanced at each of them. Neither was about to defend me, but I could see that they both regretted Minerva's rancorous demonstration.

The youngest of my sympathizers was Denise Raccette, a blonde who wore tight Levi's and men's dress shirts, which she never seemed to button above the navel, and which did such a poor job of concealing her small, but, well, I guess you would call them athletic, breasts, that I felt I knew them well enough to greet them each morning on the elevator. The other secretary's name was Helen. Her last name was so full of G's and Z's and W's and K's that it was virtually unpronounceable this side of the Iron Curtain. Everybody simply called her Helen G. And that, to put it mildly, is the first expression that might spring to your lips were you to lay eyes upon her. Her avocation was disco dancing, even after that had already started to decline in popularity, and it looked as if she came directly to work from the disco bars every day. She wore clingy satin dresses that revealed every contour of her body, and believe me, they were very provocative contours. She was younger than Minerva, about twenty-six, and she had smooth, jet-black hair and subtle facial features of an almost Asian cast, which really made you wonder where she came by a last name of nearly nonstop consonants. Like I said, they were all beauties. And they could type like demons.

But I was all business with them after my run-in with Minerva. I might have been womanless at the moment, but I wasn't desperate enough to risk total humiliation. That was no way to start a new life.

Besides the secretaries, Sultana employed six operatives. They were an obscure breed. I only caught rare glimpses of them. Mainly, they seemed to inhabit the office at night, like mice, when nobody else was around.

Every morning I would find half a dozen or so reports in the six-story in-box on my desk testifying to their invisible industry. Each drawer of the in-box had the name of one of the operatives taped to it. That was my most intimate contact with them. That seemed to be the way Sultana wanted it. He was visible enough for all of them put together. He weighed over three hundred pounds, wore $1,500 suits and $200 double-knit Italian shirts. His watch—gold-banded and diamond-encrusted—did everything but sign his checks and the star sapphire on his left pinkie was big enough to stop a wine bottle. He was bald on top and had big gaps between his teeth. He drove a big Lincoln and drank martinis constantly out of ten-ounce tumblers. The guy had a certain style.

Well, I probably could have kept my mouth shut and worked at this cushy job for thirty years or so and retired to a starter's job at a golf course in Florida had I not one day come across the name of Draper Blessing in one of the investigator's reports. The report concerned not Draper, but his son, Victor, who was claiming compensation for an injury he had suffered while employed by one of his father's companies. His father had died about two years prior to the claim, and the claim was being denied by the company, which was now in the control of the major stockholder, Leona Blessing, widow of Draper. There was a good deal of money involved. Draper had made millions on his patent for some laughably minuscule, but essential, part for automatic car transmissions. He had known Henry Ford personally and his name was real big in the city of Detroit. Streets and elementary schools named for him, that sort of thing. I knew all about him. My father had worked in one of his factories for thirty-five years and had cursed him often enough to engrave the name in the doughy headstone that, at the time, was my memory.

The nature of the injury that Victor Blessing had suffered was not clear, but whatever it was, it was supposed to have made it impossible for him to earn a livelihood. Somehow, it didn't figure. You'd think the heir to that kind of money would be exempt from any kind of hazardous occupation. Hell, by rights he shouldn't even have to get his hands dirty. But here he was, filing a claim just like any tool-and-die man who'd gotten his finger flattened in a press. Well, I simply dictated my summary of the report. It was intriguing, but it was none of my business.

In fact, I forgot about it until a couple of days later when I came across the name of another Blessing in the obituaries. The name was Florence Blessing, wife of Victor. That alone was enough to merit notice, I guess, but Florence Blessing was noteworthy in her own right, in the way that wives of corporate executives often are. She presided over more civic organizations and chaired more charity groups than any human being would have the time in several lifespans to ever really be attentive to. I chalked that up to noblesse oblige. The really interesting thing was a rather obscure reference to her will. Apparently she was leaving her considerable fortune to a religious organization headquartered just outside of Washington, D. C. The name of the sect was The Society of Trent. Who or what The Society of Trent worshipped was not clear, but they were about to do it a lot more comfortably. To the tune of two hundred and fifty million dollars.

CHAPTER 2

▼

OCCUPATIONAL HAZARDS

When I arrived at work the day after reading Florence Blessing's obituary, I decided to have another look at the investigator's report on Victor Blessing. I don't know what I expected to find, but it seemed awfully damned funny to me that Florence Blessing was getting the royal treatment in her obit and leaving to an obscure religious group enough money to keep a small country in swimming pools until the middle of the next century, while her husband had to sue his father's company for a paycheck. It was force of habit, I guess. I'd been chasing down textual inconsistencies for so long that I couldn't let them go unresolved.

But first I had to deal with Minerva, who maintained a vigil over the files like a couchant lion on the steps of the public library.

"Miss Hewitt," I said, "I was wondering if I might have a look at that Blessing report that came in a couple of days ago. It just occurred to me that I might have made a small error in my summary. I'd just like to check it out." A Boy Scout asking for a Band-Aid couldn't have been more innocent. I'd resorted to calling her Miss Hewitt immediately after my first confrontation with her. I wanted to make it clear to her that ours was the most formal of relationships. In order to do so, I'd have addressed her by her license plate number, if it came down to that.

She listened to me politely, but it was the kind of transparent, efficient politeness that made you suspect that she had printed circuits for brains.

"Oh, I'm sure your summary was satisfactory," she said after allowing a few seconds for my request to run through her programming. "Mr. Sultana would have called any inaccuracies to my attention immediately. As that has not happened, you can assume the report was acceptable."

I had to remind myself that I was talking to a fellow employee and not to a magistrate who had just finished reviewing my conviction on a murder charge. She raised her left eyebrow as though to ask if there was anything else. I thanked her, said something innocuous about how one couldn't be too careful when it came to matters of such importance, and walked away as nonchalantly as possible, all the while feeling like a blip on somebody's radar screen.

The first thing I did when I got back to my desk was to check the inbox. Apparently, the previous day had been slow. There were only three reports. The most interesting of them concerned a request from the lawyer of an industrial firm that was being sued by one of its employees, who claimed that he had been disabled through the company's negligence. Specifically, the suit charged that the company required that the employees take their lunch breaks in poorly lighted areas, and, as a result, the claimant had eaten half of a bologna and Swiss sandwich before realizing that a can of acetone had been spilled on it. All I could think of was that his wife must have prepared some dandy sandwiches for it to take him that long to realize that there was something wrong. Anyway, he claimed to be bedridden—even partially paralyzed—and he had all sorts of documentation from chiropractors to prove it. The investigator had followed him to Boston, where the plaintiff had said he was going for consultation with an orthopedic surgeon. Instead, the guy had competed in the Boston Marathon, placing fifty-sixth.

The other two reports were more or less routine. I had hoped to see a follow-up report on Blessing. The original report had been written by an investigator named Hugo Demuth. But his was one of the empty trays.

Later on that day, around lunchtime, I stopped at Denise's desk to see if I could get her to lift Blessing's file for me. She was sitting there in all her breathtaking décolletage, spearing away at an avocado salad with her fork and reading one of those fat paperback historical romances with exotic one-word titles and a beautiful woman swooning under the embrace of one of those Heathcliffe types on the cover.

She had to grunt her way through a mouthful of avocado pulp before she was able to answer me. I was beginning to think that nobody around there answered a question straight off.

"I'd like to help you out," she said after a swallow that looked almost painful, "but Minerva has strict rules about the files. Just two months ago I saw her fire a girl just for unlocking one of the cabinets. Her first offense. I need this job too bad."

And I certainly didn't want her to lose this job. I was standing over her as she sat at her desk. I was afraid that if I opened my mouth again I'd propose marriage, or a less formal equivalent. She noticed the direction of my gaze and looked down at her chest. Another woman would have closed up shop, or turned to ice, or at least blushed, but she just looked back at me and smiled as casually as if we were both chance tourists overlooking the Shenandoah Valley.

I left her to her book, her avocado salad, and her unconfined chest and nearly sprinted down to the bar in the lobby of the building, where I ordered an ice cold, very dry martini. I half expected the martini to sizzle as I took my first sip.

Only a few lunch hour patrons sat sparsely distributed throughout the bar. I had the entire length of the bar proper to myself.

I had been in the bar a couple of times before, and the bartender afforded me the sort of casual privilege of someone who worked in the building by hanging around to make small talk. We covered a couple of forgettable topics for a few minutes until I mentioned that I worked for Sultana's agency. The bartender became animated at once.

"As far as I'm concerned," he said, mixing me another martini and waving me off as I started to pull out my wallet, "you couldn't be working for a classier guy. If it wasn't for Rudy, I'd have lost this place a long time ago."

"How's that?" I asked.

The bartender explained that about three years earlier he'd nearly had his license revoked and his place shut down after being accused of attempting to bribe a buildings safety inspector. As he explained it, it was common practice for inspectors to overlook violations in return for a couple of hundreds slipped in an envelope. But apparently there'd been a crackdown just about the time his license had come up for renewal and the bartender had been set up as an example.

Not knowing what to do, the bartender had explained his problem to one of Sultana's operatives who frequented the bar. The operative had promised to speak to Sultana about it. A couple of days later the charges were dropped and the bartender's liquor license was renewed without a subsequent inspection.

"I offered to pay Rudy, but he wouldn't hear of it," said the bartender. "Just show's you what a standup guy he is. Hugo, too."

"Hugo Demuth?"

"Yeah. He's the one who spoke to Rudy for me. Helluva guy."

"I'd like to meet him," I said. "I don't seem to cross paths with the operatives much."

"Well, hell," said the bartender, glad to be of service. "Hugo's in here almost every night. He usually stops in for a drink about nine. I don't see much of the other guys, but Hugo's a regular."

I finished my drink and promised to drop in later to meet Hugo.

The bartender offered to buy me another martini, but I was already getting lightheaded and I'd been gone about an hour. I spent the rest of the afternoon cursing myself for drinking those two martinis.

CHAPTER 3

▼

HOLDING THE PHONE

I got to the bar early—about eight-fifteen. Some instinct told me that these operatives were a jittery species. I wanted to be in the bar when Hugo arrived, rather than walk in on him abruptly. I ordered a beer from my new buddy the bartender and nursed it at the bar for a few minutes. But after a while, it occurred to me that this bartender was a bit too mouthy and that I might be better off not giving him an opportunity to eavesdrop on any conversation Hugo and I might have. I picked up my drink and moved down to one of the tables. But after sitting there for a couple of minutes, I began to think that that, too, was a little too public. So I picked up my beer and moved to one of the heavily padded booths along the wall. When I looked up, the bartender was looking at me suspiciously. I had started off badly. The last thing I wanted to do was attract attention. It seemed to me that the supreme virtue of an operative was his ability to maintain a low profile, and here I was leaping all over this bar like a porpoise at Sea World. I had a momentary urge to bolt. What the hell was I doing there, anyway? What did I care about the Blessings? What did I care about Hugo Demuth? This sort of thing was his job, not mine.

Before I could do anything, a waitress approached me and asked if I would like another beer. Thinking that I would only arouse more suspicion by an abrupt departure, I ordered another beer and resolved to leave as soon as I had finished it.

I distinctly had the sense that I was jeopardizing my job by doing whatever it was that I was doing. The feeling was probably reinforced by the ambiance of the bar, which had a completely different character at night. It was more obscure and sinister. Nobody seemed to be talking directly to anyone else, yet there was a clearly audible murmur swirling about the room. I felt as though I were in the midst of a rendezvous point for conspirators. In a word, I was out of my element.

The waitress returned with my beer and I pulled out my wallet.

"It's on the house," she said, motioning back to the bar. I followed her gesture and saw the bartender smile and nod. I smiled back and gave him a short salute. My anxiety began to wane. Obviously I had not caused the bartender to suspect me after all. I began to feel a lot better. As casually as I could, I pulled out a cigarette and lit it. Damn, it was dark! The match did nothing to dissipate the gloomy atmosphere, and, indeed, seemed to be fighting hard to stay lit. I had been in there twenty minutes and still my eyes hadn't become accustomed to it.

I sat through two more beers before it became obvious to me that Hugo wasn't going to show up. Apparently, this was one of those nights that warranted the bartender's "almost." I thought of speaking to the bartender before I left—he might be expecting some sort of explanation, or perhaps be anxious to offer one. But as I got up and approached the bar, he simply smiled at me again and waved goodbye, so I decided to let it drop. Maybe he had forgotten my purpose for being there. Bartenders, after all, talk to hundreds if people every day. They can't be expected to remember everything.

I had just crawled into bed when the phone rang.

"This is Demuth," said the voice on the other end as soon as I picked up the receiver. "What did you want to talk to me about?"

His abruptness left me speechless. In my rehearsal of the scene I had hoped to approach the subject of Victor Blessing a bit more indirectly over a beer after Hugo and I had been properly introduced. Now I felt like I was being interrogated.

"Well, nothing special," I said. "Certainly nothing *urgent.*"

"My information was that you wanted to talk to me," said Hugo brusquely. Hugo seemed to be a very literal-minded fellow.

"Well," I said, "I just happened to be talking to the bartender today. I work upstairs in the same building, the same place you do as a matter of fact, Sultana Investigatory—"

"I know where you work. And I guess I know where I work," said Demuth. "What did you want to talk about?"

"I don't know," I said. "It just seemed like a shame that we work in the same place and don't even know each other. So I just thought it might be nice to stop in at the bar tonight and intro—"

"That's the way Sultana wants it," said Hugo. "The confidential nature of our work requires our complete independence." He seemed to be taking a great deal of pride in this.

"I don't have anything particular to discuss with you," I said. "Just curious about my fellow employees is all."

"Uh-huh," said Hugo after an extended pause. He followed that with another long pause, as though it took him a while to digest and analyze my remarks. Hugo was beginning to strike me as a very dull fellow indeed. He didn't at all conform to my idea of a detective.

I was just about to put the conversation to a tactful end when he spoke up again.

"According to my information, you been asking questions about one of our clients—Mrs. Leona Blessing."

I waited for him to continue, but all that followed was another of his long pauses. Hugo had no sense of rhythm when it came to conversation. I had the feeling that I was conversing through a translator.

"Well, I was just a little unsure about the accuracy of my summary," I said. "I have this obsession with accuracy."

Pause, followed by another of Hugo's cryptic "Uh-huhs." These were starting to get on my nerves. He uttered the expression with the same inflection that a dentist uses when he examines your teeth. In fact, the whole conversation with Hugo was getting very tedious, and I had just about decided by this time that no mystery was intriguing enough to suffer a conversation with Hugo over. He could make the secret of eternal youth boring.

"I have reviewed your summary personally," said Hugo suddenly. "That's SOP. It was accurate in every detail."

"That's good to know," I said. "Well, I guess that just about does it then. Sorry if I inconvenienced you." But Hugo was no longer there. He had hung up. He had all the social grace of a drill sergeant.

I walked to the refrigerator, got myself a can of beer, sat down at the kitchen table and tried to make some sense of this strange sensitivity to my inquiries about the Blessing case. It didn't seem to me that my curiosity had been devious enough to account for it. Indeed, I had openly requested summaries for review before with nowhere near this much reluctance to cooperate (except from Minerva, but I doubt that her vocabulary included the word *cooperation* or any of its cognates).

I wondered how Hugo knew that I was interested in the Blessing file, since I was sure that I hadn't mentioned it to the bartender. I was still puzzling over this when the phone rang again, equaling in one night (one *hour*, actually) my usual quota for the month.

It was Denise Raccette. There was no doubt about this, since she finally screamed it into my ear after I failed to understand her the first three times she tried to identify herself. Apparently she was in a bar someplace, and apparently the bar had live entertainment, and apparently the bar telephone was located about two feet from one of the amps. I could barely make out what she was saying when she screamed. A rock band was playing behind her at extraordinarily high volume. She was saying something about the Blessing file, but exactly what I couldn't tell. Suddenly, the band's number concluded in a formidable crescendo, followed by hysterical applause and then merciful, relative silence.

Denise, however, was still screaming. I didn't have the heart to tell her at this point that she could lower her voice, so I held the receiver about five inches from my ear.

"I said I stayed after work for a few minutes tonight and looked through the files for the Blessing account that you asked about, but it was gone."

"Gone?"

"What? I can't hear you."

I wasn't surprised.

"Are you sure it was gone?" I screamed. I was beginning to feel as ridiculous about this conversation as I had with Hugo. I was convinced now that no one at the Sultana Investigatory Agency knew how to conduct a civilized conversation.

"Sure I'm sure," said Denise. "There's not a trace of the Blessing family anywhere in the files—no summary, no preliminary reports, no letter of agreement, no invoices—nothing."

Denise was obviously a little drunk. She was slurring her words and her voice was up an octave from what I remembered it.

"Isn't that unusual?" I asked—twice, the second time loud enough, theoretically, to get an answer from my fellow tenant down the hall, a hooker named Yolanda. She was probably in bed, and I hoped that whatever she might be doing was conventional.

"You better believe it," said Denise. "I'd hate to be in Minerva's shoes when Mr. Sultana asks for that file."

I appreciated the ingenuousness of Denise's remark, but I felt certain, although I couldn't say why, that Minerva wasn't going to get into trouble over the missing file. It wasn't the kind of mistake she was likely to make.

In fact, I had the overwhelming feeling that Sultana would never have occasion to consult that file.

Meanwhile, Denise was beginning to ramble.

"I almost forgot all about it until Mona, that's my girlfriend, she's sitting right here with me, mentioned that this guy she's been going out with for the past three months hasn't called her in a week and I mentioned that I had seen Tony, that's his name, I know him pretty well because he used to date my cousin Linda about two years ago, and I could have told Mona this kind of thing would happen, but you can never tell anybody, ya know? Anyway, I had seen him with this other girl at a bar, I think it was the Nauti-Time, and I said hello to him and he got all uptight, see, he knows I know Mona and I could tell by the way he didn't introduce me to the girl he was with that he didn't want me to think that he was with her, some of these guys really make me laugh, they think you're so stupid, so anyway, I told Mona about it and she says 'Well, whoever he was with can have him with my blessings,' and all of a sudden I remembered about the Blessing file and I didn't want to bring it up at work because Minerva might hear, I did try to call you earlier, but there was no answer, I hope I'm not calling too late. Hey, why don't you come down and join Mona and me for a drink. Hello?"

At this point, I felt much like a motorist waiting for a train to go by at a railroad crossing. I was waiting for the end but what was going on in the meantime was not really capturing my imagination. Denise kept telling me to speak up because she couldn't hear me, which didn't surprise me since I wasn't saying anything. I was stalling, trying to think of some diplomatic way of declining her invitation. Actually, I wouldn't have minded joining Denise for just about anything she might suggest. She was the kind of woman that inspired that sort of enthusiasm. When I thought of what she wore to work everyday, I could only imagine what she might wear (or *not* wear) during her leisure hours. But overriding that undeniably alluring prospect was the fact that I'd have to put up with the apocalyptic environment of that bar to enjoy it. I'd long ago lost my fascination for high-decibel entertainment.

"Gee, Denise," I finally screamed. "I'd like to stop by for a drink, but I promised the building manager that I'd keep an eye on the building tonight. His son was on a camping trip with some friends and a snake bit him. He's gonna pull through, though, but the building manager wanted to go up there and be with him in the hospital."

I stopped short, horrified, trying to remember whether there were any species of snake indigenous to Michigan capable of inflicting such an injury. Had I said he was poisoned, or just bitten?

"Maybe another time then," shouted Denise, and punctuating it with a sudden and inappropriate squeal. Was someone feeling her up or something? Then she hung up very unceremoniously. I didn't even have time to finish saying "See you tomorrow." Denise had clicked off into the limbo of dead telephone conversations somewhere in the midst of those three poignant words, or so I thought them. You must understand the spell Denise cast over me. I felt like a sixteen-year-old, for whom those three words constituted a substantial commitment.

But once the conversation was over, I began to think about this whole Blessing affair again. All this sleight-of-hand and evasiveness was either the most inept effort at concealment, or the most awkward of theatrics, or both. Something was irregular about the case. For an unnerving moment, I had the feeling that I was being subtly manipulated by everyone in the office— Sultana, Minerva, Demuth, even Denise, *even* the bartender—but I dismissed that anxiety almost as soon as it invaded my thoughts. I fell asleep resolving to forget the whole Blessing business and instead to devote my energies toward establishing some sort of "meaningful relationship" with Denise. That was what my ex-wife had always said was lacking in our marriage. In fact, she had gone so far as to accuse me repeatedly of being incapable of such a thing. Meaning*less* relationships. That's what I was good at.

CHAPTER 4

▼

VARIOUS FORMS OF EXPOSURE

But in the morning, I found myself less interested, for the time being, in my sexual fulfillment than in the possibilities of a different encounter. It occurred to me to visit that grand old matriarch herself, Mrs. Leona Blessing. Just *why* it should have occurred to me, I can't exactly say, unless I had just been deprived too long of that amorphous condition known as involvement throughout my years as an academic, and was now making up for this deficiency in totally inappropriate ways. At any rate, by the time I had finished off my first cup of coffee, I had convinced myself that I could pull it off.

I called the office to let them know that I wouldn't be coming in. I had an elaborate excuse ready to spring on them, but nobody answered the phone, which was unusual. Minerva was invariably in the office by seven-thirty. But now it was already eight-forty and no one was even answering. Even with the hangover that I could imagine her to have, Denise, too, should have been there by now. Well, at least I had tried. Now I would have time to fabricate an even more precious alibi.

I knew where Leona Blessing lived. Anyone who had lived in the Detroit area for more than two days knew where she lived. She lived in a half-century-old mansion out along the lakeside of Lakeshore Drive in Grosse Pointe Shores. It was one of a generation of grand old houses of automobile titans and other members of the Detroit aristocracy. Many of these old homes had been torn down to make way for condos, their owners realizing the impracticality of trying to maintain those huge monuments to the era of the robber baron under the burden of modern taxes and fuel bills. But Leona Blessing had held out, and presumably *would* hold out until she died.

The fact that my father had worked in an automobile factory rather than owning one didn't mean that I was unfamiliar with Grosse Pointe and its inhabitants. I had spent much of my adolescence and young manhood in the area working for landscaping companies in the summer and chasing the daughters of Grosse Pointe on basically on an open-season basis

But now, as I drove through the winding, Arcadian avenues of Grosse Pointe on my way to the Blessing mansion, I felt abjectly conspicuous. Who was I to drop in unannounced on the idle rich? What the hell was I going to talk to her about, assuming (and this was an unjustified assumption) that she did consent to talk to me?

Before I had time to formulate answers to all of these questions, I was turning the car towards the ample, tree-lined cul-de-sac at the end of which, I knew, stood the Blessing mansion. The huge wrought iron gate at the entrance of the cul-de-sac was open. Just outside and to the left of the gate stood an elaborate, gothic-looking gatekeeper's kiosk. Its shutters were closed and locked with a heavy, rust-colored padlock. I began to feel that all this lack of vigilance over the entrance was an omen of hospitality, and some of my earlier confidence and adventurous spirit of the breakfast table was restored.

I drove past the kiosk and through the gate along the generous breadth of the road that led toward the house. Huge sycamores (at least I *took* them to be sycamores—they might have been *anything*) shaded the driveway except for the occasional brilliant rents in the canopy of foliage through which light seemed to beam with almost divine intention. The slightest of breezes was blowing, just enough to stir random leaves. I had to resist succumbing to the awesome splendor of the place; I felt enchanted by its timeless serenity. But I hadn't been an English major for half my life for nothing. I knew all about pathetic fallacies and things like that.

Besides, if I had felt conspicuous before, driving through the public streets of Grosse Pointe, I now felt about as subtle as a medicine show passing through a funeral as I drove uninvited up the *very* private driveway of one of the richest and most famous families in the city. My car needed a muffler and any number of obscure gaskets. Wind resistance was enough to rip the rust from the cancerous rocker panels. I felt as though I left a wake of dingy confetti wherever I went, and I probably did.

The driveway culminated in a circular piazza, the centerpiece of which was an ornate, but inoperative, fountain. The fountain depicted three life-size figures—two nude men grappling ambiguously with a voluptuous and equally nude woman. I found myself wishing that the thing were in working order so that I might determine where the water issued from. I imagined it streaming from the woman's mouth in a torrent of protest; that speculation wasn't entirely satisfactory, but it was a lot more tasteful than anything else I could imagine. The huge basin beneath the statue had obviously been drained some time ago; brittle leaves were scattered around in it and a gritty residue lay like a film along the bottom.

The house was set back a good fifty yards from the circular drive in the middle of a huge lawn. From where I stood, it looked like a wedding cake in the center of a pool table. I pulled my car up to the sidewalk that led from the driveway to the house. Stationed on either side of this sidewalk were two of those little statues of black porters in their spiffy red and white livery outfits and shiny boots, their right arms extended in an eternal gesture of deference.

I got out of the car and walked self-consciously between those two dwarfish sentries, almost expecting their resentful eyes to swivel after me.

Suddenly, I stopped dead. As frozen as the statues I had just passed. I had been immobilized by the conviction that from somewhere, somebody was watching me. But not *simply* that. Not just the unsettling sensation of feeling the penetration of somebody's stare. This feeling was more profound and much more desperate than that. I felt trapped, scrutinized, analyzed, oppressed. I felt myself observed with utterly malicious intent. I felt the shadow of cross hairs fall over my heart. Never before had I experienced such hopelessness, such isolation. The tide of my own frantic blood roared tumultuously, then subsided, and, abruptly, the feeling vanished.

But I was now trembling uncontrollably, gasping for air, and a great flush of perspiration had sprung from each of my pores. I leaned on one of the statues and tried to steady myself. Maybe that's what they were there for, I thought. To break the falls of latent epileptics and clinical paranoids. The rush of terror had left me debilitated. I had to *leave*. There was *no* wind, now. I had to *breathe*.

I turned and lurched back toward my car, but ran immediately into the rippling pecs of a huge black man. I imagined for an instant that one of the statues had sprouted into a giant. My nosed was pressed right into his solar plexus. Strangely, instead of succumbing to complete shock, I found myself estimating this giant's height judging from my own. I was five-eleven (at least I always had been five-eleven, but I was beginning to feel like Alice in Wonderland), which made this guy no less than seven feet tall. If there was any bright spot in the harrowing confrontation of that moment, it was in my rationalization that this monster's presence and my peripheral awareness of it had been the cause of my panic attack of only seconds before.

I stepped back and looked into his face, only then realizing that he wasn't a black man at all, just very deeply tanned. His features were Hispanic, or perhaps Indian. He was not smiling.

"You're not one of the sandblasters," he finally announced suspiciously. His voice had the incongruous suggestion of a British accent. He was looking at my sports coat and tie. I had made as much of an effort as my wardrobe allowed to look professional, and apparently to some extent I had been successful. Had he been three feet shorter, I would have given this guy an example of my rapier wit by congratulating him on his insight.

"No," I said, trying to regain my composure, which was going to take some doing given the variety of assaults on it over the past few minutes. "I'm an insurance investigator with Sultana Investigatory Agency. My name is Hugo Demuth." I added this reluctantly. I hadn't planned to impersonate Hugo, but then I hadn't planned on a collision with Godzilla, either. But maybe he was accustomed to running into insurance investigators all over the property, because his voice lost some of its menace, if he didn't exactly become cordial.

"Ah, you are you here to see Mrs. Blessing?" he asked, still blocking my retreat in a passive sort of way.

"Well, I don't have an appointment. I was just in the neighborhood and—"

"I'll tell Mrs. Blessing you're here," he said, almost eagerly. "You'll have to go in through the front door, I suppose, with the sandblasting, you understand."

He seemed to regret this, as though it were a serious but unavoidable breach of protocol, as though anyone beneath the rank of duke was *supposed* to enter through the storm cellar and ride the dumbwaiter to the drawing room. I was beginning to wonder if I smelled like the son of a workingman. Maybe I walked around with some congenital musk of the laborer swirling in my wake.

I followed him down the sidewalk in the direction of the house. He kept glancing from right to left over the hedge (which was a good *foot* over *my* head) and I got the feeling he must be the security force. All of it. Certainly one of him was enough. I knew now why the kiosk near the entrance was locked; he could never have fit into it. On the other hand, he certainly wasn't dressed like a security guard, and, in spite of his awesome size and formidable demeanor, he didn't seem to have a security guard's bearing. He wore only jungle fatigues and enormous Army boots and a sweat-stained bandanna around his head. He looked like an overgrown Che Guevara.

He walked up to the portico of the house, which looked more like a state capital building than a place to kick off your shoes, flop on the couch with a beer, and watch reruns of *Gilligan's Island* while the frank odor of stuffed cabbage meandered from room to room. I was out of my element and I began to sense the onslaught of that visceral weightlessness that every impostor must feel when exposure is imminent. But escape was out of the question. The giant next to me could just about stretch his arm from where we were standing to my car.

Some kind of activity was taking place around the side of the house to my left. The sandblasters, no doubt. They had apparently already finished with the marble in front of the house, which shone like a new set of dentures.

My escort ushered me through the door and into a generous foyer where he asked me to wait, then disappeared to announce me to Mrs. Blessing. I recognized my opportunity to sprint to my car, but I was beginning to think that things were going in my favor, despite my earlier crisis. It was almost too easy, but who was I to argue? Besides, the interior of the Blessing mansion was arresting. I was standing in a magnificent mausoleum. It was hard to believe that anyone actually *lived* in the place, and, in fact, it occurred to me that perhaps the house was about to be vacated. Maybe it had been sold. That would explain the fountain that didn't operate and the cosmetic work on the exterior of the building. Certainly the *interior* was anything but cozy. The only light was supplied by two intersecting beams of sunlight that entered the house from very high and very small windows—the kind found in medieval churches. There were no paintings on the walls and the lone piece of furniture in the room—a severe, Shaker-style settle—made you hope that you had the stamina to remain on your feet as long as it took. From what I could see of the great hall into which the foyer led, the atmosphere was just as desolate in there.

After a few minutes, I began to hear, from some distant section of the house, the clean, steady whir of a small electrical motor; it sounded like a kitchen appliance, an electric can opener or something. But the sound grew louder, or clearer—approaching. Behind it now I could hear the heavy footfalls of the big Mexican's army boots. A moment later Mrs. Blessing rode into the room on a motorized wheelchair. The Mexican followed her in and posted himself discreetly just inside the door. He crossed his arms over his massive chest, and his face assumed the nonchalance and menace of a veteran bouncer.

He didn't introduce Mrs. Blessing, but he didn't have to. For her, introductions were redundant. I had seen her face hundreds of times in the newspapers and on television, although over the past decade, as far as I could recall, she had become comparatively reclusive. And although she seemed to have aged considerably during her retirement from society (it was somewhat of a shock, for example, to see that her hair was completely white—she had always been the archetypal raven-haired beauty in her photos), the distinctive features—the serene brow, the large, almond-shaped Egyptian eyes with their heavy lids, the delicate nose, the inscrutable mouth, or almost inscrutable except for the touch of resignation or sadness in the midst of her richness and understated elegance—were unmistakable. She had the dignified look of a monarch who regretted her destiny, but knew her duty in her bones. I admired her at once, even though I knew through some instinct that the old girl was, and always had been, impervious to any form of affection—her sacrifice to her position.

She didn't acknowledge me immediately, but instead bent her efforts to some elaborate maneuver with her motorized wheelchair, something like backing a car into a tight parking space. Finally, she faced me, her regal bearing restored, impressive on her portable throne.

She scrutinized me for a moment, and then, apparently satisfied that I posed no threat to her, nodded to her big friend, who nodded slowly in reply and withdrew quietly from the room, closing the door softly behind him.

"Miguel tells me that you represent Mr. Sultana's agency," she said. I nodded and tried to think of a way to explain my visit.

"Yes," I said. "My name is Hugo Demuth. I've been assigned to investigate a claim initiated on behalf of Mr. Victor Blessing, who, I believe, is your son." I paused for a moment, hoping that this would be enough—that Leona Blessing would take the cue—but she only sat there expressionless, waiting for me to continue. When I didn't do so for perhaps thirty seconds, she finally spoke.

"I see," she said. "Please do be seated, Mr. Demuth."

The moment I had been waiting for had arrived. My opportunity to try out that settle. It was just as hard as I imagined it would be, and very highly polished, so that it required a good deal of effort just to avoid sliding off the thing into a ridiculous heap right there on the floor. I was beginning to envy Mrs. Blessing the comfort of her wheelchair, despite whatever affliction confined her to it.

"Exactly what was it that you wanted to ask me?" she said. Since I really didn't know, I stalled by asking her a lot of routine questions about her son—his age (thirty-seven), how long he had worked for the company ("Oh, years," said Mrs. Blessing, dreamily), etc. Mrs. Blessing was extremely patient, answering most of my questions thoroughly—neither evading nor embellishing—although I'd really not broached anything of a sensitive nature.

"You must have an extraordinary memory, Mr. Demuth," she said to me during a pause in our conversation, as I thought of what question to ask her next. I could feel my earlobes tingle.

"I beg your pardon?" I said.

"I said you must have an extraordinary memory. You haven't written down any of my answers and I assume that you aren't recording this conversation without my knowledge." She blinked slowly and deliberately—infuriatingly—like a cat. "The other Mr. Hugo Demuth wrote down everything I said." The corners of her mouth broke into just the hint of an evil, triumphant smile.

Well, that was that. I expected Miguel to come walking through the door any second, to crush me into a ball, and drop kick me into a more modest neighborhood. Mrs. Blessing began to chuckle softly.

"Now, before you leave, why don't you tell my why you attempted this charade?"

I, in fact, was wondering why she had gone through a little charade of her own. Hugo had been to the house already. Even Miguel had probably known that I was an impostor when I had first identified myself as Hugo Demuth. So why even let me get in the door when the bum's rush was in order? Still, I was in no position to question the motives of Mrs. Blessing. Not with Miguel no more than twenty feet away.

So I explained everything—my curiosity about the nature of her son's claim, my intrigue over the circumstances of Florence Blessing's death, and finally my bewilderment over the cryptic attitude of Sultana's staff concerning the affair. Throughout my confession Mrs. Blessing listened attentively, with only an occasional cat-like blink and an infrequent nod. When I finished, she continued to look at me, although a certain vacancy in her expression suggested that she was considering the quality of my account rather than waiting for me to continue. Finally, she spoke.

"I am inclined to satisfy your curiosity to the extent that I am able," she said. She spoke very slowly, taking some time to choose her words with precision and to articulate them clearly, in complete sentences, as though intelligibility and coherence were the cardinal responsibilities of her caste, and, in fact, what she lacked in volume, she more than made up for in eloquence. It occurred to me that she had rehearsed this.

"I have suspected almost from the beginning of our relationship with the Sultana firm that they have not performed with the circumspection and thoroughness that I should have expected of a concern with its considerable reputation. It is, I suppose, partly my son's fault. He has always been too impetuous for his own good." Here she paused for a moment of introspection, as though she were mentally cataloging the innumerable instances of her son's impetuosity.

"My son's claims for damages are, of course, utterly without foundation," she continued. "He is incorrigibly irresponsible and always has been. Recognizing this, I disinherited him shortly after my husband's death. My husband's otherwise sound judgment was impaired by his overdeveloped sense of paternal loyalty. He was devoted to Victor, despite the fact that Victor was unworthy of such devotion. And believe me, Mr. Fargo, I do not make this charge lightly. Anyway, after I disinherited him, Victor, in desperation, married Florence, whose family was also of substantial means. Victor, after all, had a lifestyle to maintain. Years of self-indulgence had accustomed him to easy circumstance. Florence had few virtues, but she was at least shrewd enough to recognize Victor's opportunistic motives and to keep him away from her money through legal means. In fact, at this very moment, I believe that he is somewhere in Washington trying to contest Florence's will through *other* than legal means."

"Any chance he will succeed?" I asked.

"That is not what worries me," she replied impatiently. "Do you have any knowledge of the nature of this organization to which Florence bequeathed her fortune?"

I confessed that I had none, other than the brief reference to a religious organization in Florence Blessing's obituary.

"Religious organization," Mrs. Blessing said scornfully, and then followed this remark with another serene blink as though in an effort to dismiss the contempt from her voice, remembering, perhaps, that any emotional demonstration was beneath her. "That, of course, is how they would *prefer* to have the public perceive them. In fact, they represent the basest perversion of religious principles. They are, in reality, a horde of psychotics, committed to the extermination—the suicide—of the human species. It is only their laughable extremism that can account for the fact that they are tolerated at all, I suppose."

Again she halted, and again she made a visible attempt to suppress her agitation. I was fascinated watching her govern herself like this, and for a moment I entertained the notion that Mrs. Leona Blessing was slightly demented herself. It didn't seem to be an unreasonable suspicion, given her determined seclusion in this marble tomb of hers. I was about to ask her just how this organization intended to go about the eradication of the human race when she spoke again, having recovered her composure.

"But I have reason to believe that this organization presents a danger to my son. Therefore, I am prepared to offer you twenty-five thousand dollars plus expenses to locate and retrieve my son before harm can come to him."

I was dumbstruck, and apparently Mrs. Blessing took my hesitation for reluctance.

"Please, Mr. Fargo, do not deceive yourself into thinking that I make this offer out of senile generosity. I could have had you arrested the moment you set foot on my property. I am not in the habit of entertaining trespassers with the intimate concerns of my family. If you choose to refuse my offer, I shall protest your intrusion into my affairs to Mr. Sultana in such terms that he shall have no choice but to dismiss you. And as I do still exert some influence, it may be quite some time before you are able to secure worthwhile employment again in this city."

The formal detachment with which she delivered this ultimatum only served to reinforce the impression that she was equal to the threat, and, as though to emphasize it even further, Miguel opened the door and stepped softly into the room to reassume his ominous station at the door.

"It's not that I don't appreciate your offer," I said. "But I *have* misrepresented myself. I *work* at the Sultana agency, but honestly, I just push paper. I'm a rank amateur when in comes to this private investigation stuff. I—"

"I'm quite familiar with your background," said Mrs. Blessing, nodding repeatedly. "Until recently, you were an academic, a lecturer in Modern Literature, if I'm not mistaken." She paused for a second to allow me to challenge her remarks, as if that would even be conceivable with Miguel standing in the same room.

"That's true," I said. But I hardly think that that qualifies me to—"

"You don't understand, Mr. Fargo. I have asked this service of you precisely because you are *not* qualified. I have your welfare in mind as well as my son's, you see. This organization to which I have referred calls itself the Society of Trent. It is very sensitive about itself. It does not welcome investigations into its activities. On the other hand, it *does* seek to promote its superficial function as an evangelical organization. Therefore, I have devised a plan whereby you shall pose as a free-lance writer who has been assigned to do a story on this very topic for a national magazine. That, I think, is much less hazardous, since it is compatible with your background. They are certain to give you the standard public relations tour, which you are to accept without question. Of course, your *real* purpose will be to locate my son and deliver to him a message, the contents of which, I am sure, will encourage him to return before he embarrasses himself of his family, or, to be quite frank, before he gets himself killed. On the other hand, Mr. Fargo, as the size of the fee I am willing to pay you should suggest to you, your mission is hardly a boondoggle. Should you betray yourself—blow your cover is the parlance, I think—your peril will be considerable."

I was about to suggest to her that if the job was *that* dangerous, I'd be better off taking my chances on the unemployment line, but a better idea popped into my head.

"Why not send Miguel? He seems to be the perfect candidate for this sort of errand."

Mrs. Blessing gave me her slow-motion blink again and shook her head.

"That is not possible," she said. "Miguel is indispensable to me here. Besides, Miguel is nothing if not inconspicuous."

I was still trying to unravel all the negatives in that sentence when Mrs. Blessing suddenly exploded in a fit of surprisingly violent coughing, toward the end of which she switched on the motor of her wheelchair, executed a flawless U-turn, and whirred off in the direction of the door which Miguel held open for her. When she got to the door she stopped and spoke to me again hoarsely, over her shoulder, her episode of coughing having finally subsided.

"Miguel will supply your requirements. You can assume that anything he tells you has my approval. Please forgive me, but I am very tired now."

"Of course," I said, although I was slightly insulted by her presumption. But at that moment this entire bizarre performance seemed too incredible to dignify with objection. All I had to do was walk away from it, rationalize the entire experience as the expression of senile dementia. Mrs. Blessing zipped off into the labyrinthine recesses of her cavernous fortress, and, I hoped, summoning as much charity as I could, into some merciful oblivion.

But my sense of security was short-lived. Miguel accompanied me back to my car (I skipping alongside him like a child trying to keep stride with an adult), explaining in his improbable accent the details of my assignment.

"It is imperative," he said, "that you do not arouse suspicion. The ruthlessness of the people you shall be dealing with cannot be overestimated. You are to make no overt references to Mr. Blessing except as you are instructed. Your position is an extremely delicate one. You must pursue your assignment as a reporter earnestly enough to be credible. Yet, excess of zeal will put you in danger as well. Yes, a very delicate position," he said. "I hope you are equal to the subtlety of it all."

Well, he needn't worry, I thought. I had no intention of going through any of this James Bond stuff.

We stopped next to my car. Miguel withdrew an envelope from the back pocket of his fatigues and handed it to me.

"Your instructions are in here," he said. "You will also find five thousand dollars in advance payment, two thousand dollars in expense money, a photograph of Mr. Blessing along with his last known address in Washington, and a list of three names and addresses. The first name on the list will supply you with an automobile should you choose to drive to Washington. Mrs. Blessing refuses to fly and assumes that everyone else shares her fear. But how you get there is entirely up to you. The second name on the list will provide you with a firearm to be used in your own defense. Of course, you won't be able to take a firearm with you if you do choose to fly."

"Wait a minute, Miguel," I said. "This has been a fun morning and everything. Well, maybe not a *fun* morning, but it's had its moments, you know? But I don't like guns. I have been known to avoid social functions which I would otherwise have loved to attend, simply on the strength of a rumor, a *rumor* mind you, that an inoperative flintlock hung over the mantle. It's true. Furthermore (I was getting dizzy on my own wittiness), I don't know how this little scheme of your employer's strikes you, but it seems rather like an imposition as far as I'm concerned, don't you think?" This was putting it mildly. It was blatant extortion, is what it was. "You must be aware, an alert guy like you, that Mrs. Blessing, bless her imaginative little soul, is slightly less than intact, upstairs, if you get my drift. In short, I'd like to help, and I *do* apologize for the intrusion. Deplorable, really. It won't happen again. *Believe* me. Now, I've got to be running along."

Actually, Miguel was taking all this rather well. In fact, my entire speech seemed to constitute to him no more than the most trivial of distractions, like a fly buzzing frantically around his ear for a moment.

"The third name on the list," he continued, "is for emergencies only, should your situation become desperate in Washington. You should commit that name and phone number to memory and when you have accomplished the tasks involving the other two names on the list, it is to be destroyed. Do not neglect this."

"Now look here, Miguel—"

"By the end of the day I will supply your press credentials in your own name and a letter of introduction from the editor of the *Consumer Crusader*. Both the editor and the magazine are legitimate. We can't take the chance of your inadvertently giving yourself away in an unguarded moment. Therefore, it's best that you use your own name. Even that entails a certain risk, but it is extremely unlikely that they will have knowledge of your present occupation. After all, you're not technically an investigator."

It seemed unlikely that I would change Miguel's mind, so decided to humor him. All I wanted at that moment was to get the hell out of that decadent Shangri-La and back into the real world for some perspective.

"Okay, Miguel, I'll do it. But just this once. As a favor to Mrs. Blessing. But the next time she's gonna have to get herself another errand boy." I tried to sound indignant enough to convince him that I'd go through with it. I got into my car and tried to shut the door, to cap off the performance with an emphatic exit, but Miguel had a firm grip on the handle.

"One final word of caution, Mr. Fargo," he said. "Were I you, I should refrain from revealing the purpose of my departure to anyone. Especially Mr. Sultana or any of your fellow employees. I should think you could arrive at some plausible excuse for your absence. Admitting more people into your confidence at this time would only serve to increase the likelihood of your being exposed."

He smiled. At least his features relaxed for an instant. Miguel was probably congenitally incapable of a proper smile. He said something else, but I didn't hear it. Something about the fountain had caught my eye, and simultaneously and inexplicably, had thrown my pulse into erratic convulsions. All of a sudden my heart beat like a fish flopping around on a boat deck.

"What?" I said, turning my attention back to Miguel.

"Don't forget to actually write the article," he repeated. "You must act out the charade to its completion in order to ensure your safety."

I assured Miguel that I would write the story and that I wouldn't reveal to anyone that I was going to Washington. What did I care? I would have agreed to anything at that point. Miguel finally released my door and I drove away as slowly as I could in order to get a good look at the fountain. I glanced quickly to the rearview mirror to see Miguel, once again having struck his Senior Vice President of Bouncers pose, watching my departure. I was right beside the fountain now. In the months since, I have tried to explain away what I saw, or what I *thought* I saw as I was leaving the Blessing mansion that day. Maybe I had been overwrought by the extraordinary—even surreal—events of that day. Perhaps somebody had hosed down the statue, although the basin was as dry as when I had arrived. It had not rained, but as I looked at the figures of the statue, and I looked long and steadily, they seemed to glisten with moisture. Then I saw on the forehead of the female figure and running down the temple and the jaw line of the male figure something that looked like nothing so much as droplets of sweat.

CHAPTER 5

▼

VISITORS

Strangely enough (although my ex-wife wouldn't have thought it strange), all I could think about as I drove home was sardines. I wasn't even thinking about them; I was possessed by them. Only when I was back at my kitchen table halfway through a sardine sandwich and a can of beer did I remember the envelope that Miguel had given me. I opened it and found its contents to be everything Miguel had described to me. I guess I had expected to find nothing more than grocery store coupons or something—anything that would have justified my impression that the entire frantic, yet almost artificial, interlude of the morning had been nothing more than some malicious burlesque.

But now, the hard evidence before me brought back the sinister overtones of my treatment at the Blessing residence with renewed, and if anything more forceful, impact in light of the naiveté with which I had tried to dismiss the whole thing under the pretense of a craving for sardines. I lost my appetite and left the sardine sandwich half-eaten in front of me.

The first address on the list was that of a man named Arty Axtract. The address was out on Gratiot Avenue on a stretch of highway that I knew to be an endless succession of independent used car dealers. For years I had anticipated the demise of that strip of road. It had always seemed inconceivable to me that anyone would be desperate enough to buy a car from any of those scavengers. But apparently many people were just that desperate, because the strip thrived. And the customers always seemed to be the same—young, tentative married couples trailing behind the expansive, evangelistic salesman, pausing frequently for their private, meaningless conferences on the virtue of this or that car; young, excited teenagers, nearly ecstatic with the promise of vehicular freedom, their parents (who *should* know better), grim, distrustful, in tow...

The prospect of joining their sacrificial ranks did not make the assignment Mrs. Blessing had offered me any more attractive.

The second name on the list was one Quintus Tremble, Prop., Cutie's Gun Shop and Indoor-Outdoor Range. The address indicated that the shop was somewhere out in New Baltimore. As far as I was concerned, *Old* Baltimore wouldn't have been far enough away. There were enough errant bullets flying around the world without a few thousand drunken "sportsmen" blasting away and calling it practice.

The third name on the list—the one that Miguel had designated for emergencies only—was the most unlikely of all, a certain Haskell Stonestreet, who apparently was sensitive about his address, since only a phone number was supplied.

Also in the envelope was the photograph of Victor paper clipped to a smaller, sealed envelope, containing, presumably, Leona's irresistible letter to her son.

Last but not least (it's always so gratifying when a cliché redeems itself), there were 70 one-hundred-dollar bills wrapped up as tightly as a millionaire's bow tie.

I was thinking about whether or not it would be safe to just stick a half-dozen stamps on an envelope and mail the whole packet back to Leona—or better yet, to Miguel—when the doorbell rang. I pushed the buzzer that released the lock on the lobby door of the apartment building. A minute later there was a knock at the door. I opened it and Denise walked in.

She was flushed and out of breath and looked, as usual, as though she'd blacked out while buttoning her blouse. She sort of collapsed into the room, landing in the seat I'd just vacated to answer the door.

"My God," she said. "What a day!"

My first question was going to be what was she doing away from the office—especially at my apartment—in the middle of the day. But I decided I didn't want to sound imperious. I almost laughed. She thought *she'd* had an extraordinary day.

"A lot of work today?" I asked. Denise looked at me in awe.

"Are you kidding?" She asked. Then a moment later: "You don't know yet, do you?"

"Know what?"

"About Minerva."

"What about Minerva?"

"She's dead."

"What do you mean, dead?"

A brilliant question. Obviously, by dead, Denise meant what most people mean by dead. But she was too kindhearted to be sarcastic.

"I mean she's really dead. She didn't show up for work this morning and about ten o'clock, Mr. Sultana called somebody he knew at the police department and had him go over to Minerva's to check on her. I mean, you know how regular Minerva was in her habits. Well, the police found her at the foot of her stairs with a broken neck. I just left the office. Rudy told everybody to go home and closed up for the day. Look at me. I'm still shaking."

I looked at the hand she held above the table as though she were trying to levitate my sardine sandwich, but before I could detect any tremors, the index finger of the demonstrator hand pointed down to the table.

"Is that a sardine sandwich? God, I'm starved!"

I told her to help herself to the remnants of the sandwich and pressed her for more details of Minerva's death.

"What's to tell?" she said between bites. "I guess the police say she must have fallen down the stairs and landed the wrong way. They wanted to know where you were, by the way. Helen got all hysterical and started babbling about how you and Minerva were the deadliest of enemies—"

"*What?*"

"Don't worry," said Denise, trying to shoo away my anxiety with a wave of her hand. "I explained to them that you'd probably been at the hospital all night. By the way, how's the kid?"

"What kid?"

"You know, the kid with the snakebite."

The trouble with lying, as greater men than I have pointed out, is that the liar is forced to exercise rather rigorous vigilance over his memory in an effort to distinguish fact from fiction. I stared at Denise for a moment in private horror as my mind tried to retrieve this one from its voluminous store of falsehood.

"Oh, he's out of danger," I said at last, recalling my telephone conversation of the night before with Denise. "But what happened was that when my apartment manager went to the hospital last night, he collapsed under the strain of the whole thing and I had to go down there and fill out all the papers and everything, you know."

"Right," said Denise after polishing off the sardine sandwich and drinking a swig of beer. "I told them they could even check it out if they had any doubts."

I tried to imagine the police reaction when they discovered that not only had I not spent the night in the hospital out of concern for the manager of my apartment building and his snake bitten son, but that neither had the manager spent the night looking after the snake bitten son that he didn't have.

"Why do the police care where I was, anyway?" I asked. "Don't they think Minerva's death was an accident?"

Denise scanned the kitchen distractedly. I got the feeling that she was looking for something else to eat. Her eyes returned to the table and settled on the wad of hundreds only partially concealed in the envelope that Miguel had given me. Her eyebrows lifted just slightly in appreciation.

"You hit the lottery or something?" she asked.

"No, I uh, just got back from the bank. I'm buying a stereo system. I like to pay cash for everything." Denise glanced into the living room skeptically.

"You ever think of buying some furniture first?" she asked with a smile. "Maybe a couch or something?" The only piece of furniture in my living room was a relic of the previous tenant, an extremely worn (so worn that it was impossible to determine what color it had been), high-backed armchair. That wasn't counting the small table fan, which had long since refused to swivel and which sounded like an airplane propeller when it was running. That was sitting in the middle of the floor aimed directly at the armchair. It must have looked as though I had some real gala times around the house there by myself.

"I had a couch once," I said. "My ex-wife took it." That immediately sounded melodramatic to me. But the truth was, I really missed that couch. I'd sure grown plenty used to it.

"Well, myself, I can't listen to music unless I'm laid back," she said. "I like to have it surround me, you know, as though I was laying on a raft and floating on the music." I was going to ask her how laid back she had been the night before during that aural barrage in the Nauti-time, or wherever it was, but before I got to it the doorbell rang again. Again I reached for the buzzer. Denise twisted her head at me quizzically.

"Don't you ever find out who's down there before you let them in?" she asked. I didn't have an immediate answer for that one. The system included an intercom that allowed me to interrogate prospective visitors before unlocking the door for them. The truth was that the only other times my doorbell had rung had been mistakes, drunks punching the wrong button, that sort of thing, and even those occasions have been rare. I simply hadn't had the opportunity to get the hang of the entire procedure yet. In fact, I now looked forward to the novelty of three people occupying my dining room at the same time. Given my furnishings, I certainly couldn't have entertained them anywhere else. The only other time my apartment had been so crowded was when the building manager had showed me the place before I had agreed to rent it.

"It's out of order," I said. "You know how it is in these older buildings. They no sooner fix the damn thing, it goes on the blink again."

"On the what?"

There was a knock at the door. I opened it to a man dressed in a blue blazer and gray slacks and his wallet in his hand.

"Stephen Fargo?" he asked.

"Yes."

"I'm Detective Lazard, homicide." He flipped his wallet open just like on TV. I stared at the shiny gold badge affixed to the inside of the wallet. I'd never seen one up close before and was apparently giving it what he considered an inordinately thorough inspection. He flipped it shut.

"May I come in?" I stepped aside and closed the door after he had entered the room.

"Ah, Miss Raccette," he said, bowing slightly, as soon as he had entered the dining room. He pronounced her name as though she were a miniature racer. She did not correct him, but just said, "Hello, again, Detective."

Despite Lazard's impeccable manners, I could see that he'd analyzed the entire room almost immediately—Denise's presence, the envelope, the money. I had the distinct feeling that I was being caught in the act of something, although I couldn't say what.

"Were you expecting someone else?" he asked, turning to me with a tentative look on his face.

I shrugged. "I haven't expected anybody in months."

"I was just wondering why you didn't ask who I was downstairs," he said, gesturing towards the intercom. "You should exercise more caution. These places install security systems for a reason." Denise tilted her head and smiled at me, rather too triumphantly, I thought.

"It's out of order," I said. But now the explanation sounded hopelessly lame. I cursed myself for my inability to curb my mendacious tendencies, especially in such trivial matters.

"I see," said Lazard, turning his eyes back to the intercom. There was a long, decidedly awkward silence while he stared at it.

Denise finally broke it by standing up and announcing that she had to leave.

"Please don't rush off on my account," said Lazard pleasantly, but not too convincingly.

"Oh, no, really," Denise replied. "I really have to run. I haven't had a day off, I mean a *weekday* off in months. There's ten thousand things I can take care of. Thanks for the lunch, love," she said to me. I could feel myself reddening at this unexpected display of affection, despite the casualness of it. "I'll let myself out," she said.

When Denise had gone I gestured for Lazard to take a chair and we both sat down at the table. Lazard sat with his forearms on the table and his hands folded. He was a very malicious looking, unattractive man. His head was too small for his body, and, probably because of his posture, seemed to sink in between his shoulders like a vulture's. His hair was hard, black, and shiny, parted down the middle, and seemed all of a piece, like the hard shell of a beetle. His skin was leathery and deeply creased and hung loosely, especially from his throat, where a pouch like a pelican's ran straight down from his chin and waggled a lot when he talked. His eyes protruded and were set extremely wide apart, and more than once I got the feeling that his vision was somehow out of alignment. He also had a rather bad case of eczema. There were bright red and scaly patches of it around his nostrils, the outside corners of his eyes, and all along his hairline. The total grotesque impression he gave was of a man who had been assembled from various animal parts. I thought of *The Island of Dr. Moreau*, and all those animals turned into human beings by that book's demented do-gooder. The animals always reverted to their natural states at the most inconvenient of times. The tip-off was always the ears. They would start to get hairy and pointed, and you knew it was time to break out the wolfs bane.

Lazard's ears, at least, were reassuring. They were small, but exquisitely sculpted, feminine, almost translucent in their fineness. I decided that Lazard was still good for a while yet.

"You and Miss Raccette good friends?" he asked, inclining his head towards the door through which Denise had just departed.

"Uh, yes, we are," I said, just myself realizing that it was probably true, and feeling just the slightest trace of exhilaration about it. Lazard nodded slowly, staring at his clasped hands.

"I assume she has alerted you as to Miss Hewitt's demise," he said.

"Alerted me?" Lazard closed his eyes and squeezed the bridge of his nose between his thumb and middle finger. His fingers appeared at first to be abnormally stubby, but in fact his hands were slightly webbed. He opened his eyes and grimaced. He seemed to blush, but his skin was so red anyway that it was hard to tell.

"*Alert* isn't the right word, is it?" he said. "Forgive me. You see, believe it or not, whenever I find myself talking to an English teacher, for some crazy reason I go out of my way to make an impression. But all I do is get, whadyacall, pretentious. I've been that way since high school. I guess I get intimidated." He shrugged. "What I meant to say is I guess Miss Raccette already told you about Miss Hewitt."

"Well, not in any great detail," I said. I tried to be composed about it, but if he looked closely enough he probably could have *seen* my heart beating. But perhaps he was telling the truth. He had used the word "demise," too, which was also a bit off key, given the circumstances. I've encountered others like him. No sooner am I introduced to them as a Ph.D. student, then they start cramming their sentenced with every twenty-five dollar word they can manufacture.

"I understand she fell down the stairs or something," I added. Lazard grimaced again, as though he were unwilling to concede that.

"That's the working hypothesis at this point," he said.

"You have doubts?" I asked.

"I always have doubts," he answered. "Even when I'm absolutely sure. That's the crunch of this business." I kept silent, hoping that it would suggest my sympathy.

"I hope you understand, Mr. Fargo," Lazard continued, inspecting his hands again as if the webs had just started to form, "that this is not an official visit. I'm just a slave to detail." He really seemed to be suffering through this. "Everything about Miss Hewitt's death points to an accident. There's no evidence of foul play. No signs of forced entry or struggle. The neighbors reported no unusual noises and don't remember seeing anyone enter or leave Miss Hewitt's apartment near the time of her death. As far as we can tell, nothing was stolen or disturbed." He enumerated these facts in a sort of mechanical monotone, as if he somehow resented them.

"And she *was* found at the bottom of the stairs, having obviously fallen. And," he said, beginning to place more and more emphasis on the introductory "ands," "she was wearing a pair of ridiculously high heels. Honestly, I don't know women can move in those shoes. Imagine spending half of your life on stilts." He wagged his tiny head back and forth. He squinted and was silent for a moment.

"Would you like a beer?" I asked. "That's all I've got."

"Thank you," he said. "A beer would be fine." I got two cans of beer out of the refrigerator, opened them, and gave one to Lazard. He took a sip and began talking again, with much more vigor.

"But, you know, those stairs she is supposed to have fallen down..." He waved his hand in mild derision. "A matter of half a dozen steps. Hardly a staircase."

"No, I don't know, actually," I said. He smiled and played with the beer can, turning it slowly in his hands.

"You take me much too literally, Mr. Fargo. Simply a figure of speech, a verbal tic, you know. Miss Hewitt's stairway was the kind of thing you might turn an ankle or bang a knee falling down, but you'd have to try awful hard to kill yourself. And from everything I know of Miss Hewitt, she was prudent to a fault. She never drank, never took so much as an aspirin, didn't smoke, didn't drink coffee, and she's been living in the same apartment for seven years, so she was certainly familiar with it. She kept such regular hours that the neighbors could tell time by her." He paused here for a moment.

"Of course, none of this is conclusive," he continued. "The final verdict will probably be up to the medical examiner. It's just too much for me to believe that that woman broke her neck falling down those steps."

"Stranger things have happened," I offered. He nodded slowly as though he'd heard that one a thousand times before. He probably had.

"Mr. Fargo, one of the girls in the office, you know, Helen G.," (it seemed odd to me that he would refer to her like that) "mentioned that you weren't on the best of terms with Miss Hewitt." Somewhere in the back of my mind I had been preparing for this, but it still rattled me.

"We had a misunderstanding," I said. "But I neither liked nor disliked Minerva. I simply stayed clear of her." Lazard nodded quickly. He seemed to be a little embarrassed at having to ask the question, which encouraged me, since I felt unequal to dealing with its insinuation. I took a long drink of beer, and then wished I hadn't. Lazard hadn't touched his since the first sip.

"It's just that some people react strangely to rejection," said Lazard. "It's nothing personal, you understand." I guessed that I understood, but it was beginning to seem awful damn personal to me.

"I understand that you've just recently been divorced," he said. He pushed his beer can aside as though he had no further use for it and reclasped his hands.

"It's been eight months, actually," I said.

"Your wife still in the area?"

I shook my head. "No, she's in California, working for a movie studio."

"Oh, an actress?"

"No, she's a film editor."

"Sounds exciting," he said. "Must be very stimulating to deal in that kind of excitement every day. I envy her." I was convinced that he was baiting me. I kept my mouth shut for a moment, then decided I should say something.

"It's really a rather technical job," I explained. "I suppose it gets as boring as anything else sometimes." Lazard nodded in agreement. He got up from his chair and extended his hand. I shook it, wishing that my palms weren't so sweaty.

"Well, thank you for talking to me, Mr. Fargo. I'm sure you have more important things to do."

"No problem," I said.

"And thanks for the beer." That was funny. If I had known he was going to waste it, I would have let him drink from my can. I let Lazard out and sat down and drank from the rest of *my* beer in about three mighty swallows. The doorbell rang again. This time I pushed the intercom button and asked who it was, then wished I hadn't. It was Lazard.

"Ah, your intercom seems to have been repaired." He seemed real happy about that. "I just wanted to ask you to give me a call if anything at all occurs to you that you think might interest me. Even if it seems trivial. Although it's probably all academic anyway." I said that I would do so.

I sat down at the table and drank Lazard's beer. When that was gone, I dug out a bottle of Old Grand Dad that I had been saving for a special occasion.

CHAPTER 6

▼

MISCELLANEOUS ATAVISM

I woke up in the middle of the living room floor where I must have collapsed en route to the bedroom. Somebody was giving the doorbell a real workout. It seemed dark enough to be the middle of the night, but I couldn't be sure. I stood up and a headache introduced itself, as though it had been waiting for me to do just that. The headache came in and made itself at home, like an encyclopedia salesman or an obnoxious relative. That's the way bourbon headaches are—none too subtle.

I made my way to the dining room, using my arms as not very sensitive antennae and so burdened by the pain of the headache that I couldn't stand erect. I felt like the Hunchback of Notre Dame playing Blind Man's Bluff. When I finally found the light switch in the dining room, I turned it on and looked for the clock. A great migration of blood cells passed across the lenses of my eyes like a herd of germs under a microscope. It was nine-fifteen. I'd been out for about seven hours. The bottle of Old Grand Dad stood at attention in the middle of the table. I'd scarcely touched it.

My tolerance for hard liquor is almost nil, which is convenient considering my budget.

I pressed the button on the intercom and asked who it was in my best hangover voice.

"I have a package for Stephen Fargo," said an articulate, workaday voice. I let the messenger in and went to wait for him in the hallway.

*   *   *

I happen to be part Native American. One-sixteenth, I think. My great-grandfather on my father's side was a full-blooded Kiowa, or else a full-blooded Ottawa. His name was Christian Man. He married my great-grandmother, Helen Hyde, when she was forty-seven and he was thirty-four. It appears to have been a marriage of convenience, although how so I can't imagine. Great-grandmother Hyde had previously been married to a man named Michael Hyde, with whom she had fled the Great Famine in Ireland in 1848. They settled in Buffalo, where Michael worked as a laborer for the railroad until his death in 1859 at the age of thirty-seven. His widow went to work as a housekeeper in a rectory in Buffalo almost immediately following her husband's death. When one of the priests was transferred to Monroe, Michigan to assume the pastorate of a Catholic church there, he took Helen with him as part of his entourage. This pastor, a certain Jesuit named Father Branch, rose to a position of some social prominence in Monroe. There are references in the contemporary newspapers to George Armstrong Custer's entertaining guests in his home, among whom, on at least two occasions, was Father Branch. It's likely that my great-grandmother Hyde knew General Custer at least as well as a housekeeper and an infrequent distinguished guest could know each other.

According to church records, Great-grandmother Hyde became Mrs. Helen Man on July 23, 1875. Great-grandfather Man's occupation is listed as factotum. He had probably been converted to Catholicism, since it's unlikely that Father Branch would have performed the ceremony otherwise.

There is no way to tell from the marriage certificate that Great-grandfather Man was an Indian. For that, other sources are required. One is the records of the United States Census Bureau. Under the figures for 1880 appears the name of Christian Man, "Age 38 (?); birthplace, Oklahoma (?); ethnic origin, aboriginal American, Kiowa nation (?)." Except for name and age, all of this is at odds with the information in Great-grandfather Man's obituary in the *Monroe Democrat* of February 8, 1903. Apparently, the old boy had managed to build quite a reputation as a local curiosity in his years at Monroe, because his obit was rather longer and more detailed than most. In it, Great-grandfather Man is identified as a "longtime resident of Monroe," a native of Michigan, and a full-blooded Ottawa Indian descendant from Algonquin chieftains. I don't know how to resolve the discrepancy between the two accounts, but I'm inclined to believe the second. The census was probably based on an interview with Great-grandfather Man, and records being what they were at the time, it was probably impossible to verify his story, assuming that anyone even cared to. I imagine he tried to embellish his heritage a bit to impress this authoritative stranger who was flattering him with so many questions. After all, the Kiowa were famous as fierce, accomplished, proud warriors, while the Ottawa, who, historically, had been pushed around quite a bit by the Iroquois and Huron, contented themselves with the less bellicose occupation of trading beaver pelts. The obituary mentioned that Great-grandfather Man had often referred to himself as the product of the mating between an Ottawa squaw and a French trapper, one of the romantic *coureurs de bois* who still flourished in the early part of the nineteenth century, which would have made Great-grandfather Man half-white. This tale was generally discounted, though, as another embellishment by the old codger, especially as he only started to insist upon it after the birth of his only child, a daughter named Veronica, my grandmother.

This event seemed to have had a profound effect on everybody concerned, not least Great-grandmother Helen Hyde Man, who seems to have grown progressively obsessed by the whole thing, until she finally died in a Catholic sanitarium in Adrian, Michigan in 1894. I can see how all of this might have been too much for the old girl to handle. I can imagine the trauma of it—a pious, superstitious peasant of a woman giving birth to her first child, a half-breed, at the age of forty-seven, whose father probably paid lip service to Christianity, but who was undoubtedly compelled otherwise by countless generations of heathen consciousness behind him.

Veronica Man gave birth to an illegitimate son, my father, On March 15, 1908. He was adopted at the age of six weeks by a Detroit carriage manufacturer named Samuel Fargo. Fargo's business went bankrupt in 1913 and the family plunged into virtual poverty. Fargo died nearly destitute in 1921, but not before revealing my father's illegitimacy to him. My father embarked on an intermittent campaign to discover his heritage, although he kept his quest secret until shortly before his death. But, although he did manage to determine his mother's name and the fact of his illegitimacy, he failed, either through a lack of the proper temperament or facility for the rigor of the research, or, perhaps, through a sense of shame, to learn anything more. He died nearly ignorant of his lineage.

But I *do* have the temperament for this sort of thing. I have a *zeal* for it, in fact. In a matter of two weeks of intensive research, I had documented the genealogy just as I have presented it here.

The point is, I decided to go to Washington, decided even in the few brief seconds as I waited for the messenger to emerge from the ancient elevator across from my apartment door. I'm made that way. If there was a thing to be known, I meant to know it. If I could not know it, I would explain it somehow. I like a world full of answers—even bizarre, inappropriate answers. I like to think that that's the Indian in me.

*   *   *

There was a brief letter typed on plain white stationery and a check. The letter was, sure enough, addressed to me and was signed V. Blessing. It read as follows:

Dear Mr. Fargo:

No doubt you are perplexed. Please indulge my dear mother by accepting the courier assignment she has requested of you. Enclosed is a check representing partial payment for services. I have taken the liberty of booking you on the 10:00 a.m. American flight to Washington National tomorrow morning. My representative will meet you at the gate upon your arrival.

That was it. The check was for one thousand dollars. I'd made eight thousand dollars already and I hadn't done anything yet. But the nature of the assignment was becoming less sinister, if no less cryptic. Obviously, Mrs. Blessing, in her derangement, had exaggerated the peril of the job, and her more rational son had seen fit to reassure me. He had said *courier*. Nothing said about guns, or magazine articles, or dangerous secret organizations. I was simply to be a messenger. Well, not exactly that simple. It appeared that I was going to make a lot of money, more money than I had made in two years as a graduate assistant. I might also have the opportunity to clear up this mystery of the Blessing report. I thought again of the strange coincidence of Minerva's death. I shuddered and tried to dismiss it. After all, maybe Lazard was wrong. Most likely Minerva *had* died accidentally.

I called American Airlines. A woman who acted as though she had known me since childhood (it's amazing how they get women like that) cheerfully confirmed my reservation. I hung up the phone and it rang, which made perfect sense to me, the way things were going. It was Denise.

"Well," she said. "What did you think of the Lizard?"

"The what?"

"The Lizard. Detective Lazard. He looks like a lizard. God. Like trying to carry on a conversation with an iguana."

"He seemed reasonable enough, I guess, for a homicide detective." I lied. Actually, Lazard seemed menacing and insincere—even calculating—to me.

"My father used to say that ugly people were unreasonable by definition," said Denise. Her father must have been a charming fellow. I tried to imagine him. A cross between Josef Mengele and Oscar Wilde.

"Anyway," she said, "the reason I called was to see if you had talked to Rudy yet. He called me asking about you. Seems he'd been trying to reach you all afternoon. I told him I'd seen you around noon at your apartment. He seemed, I don't know, antsy, you know, with this Minerva thing. Then I started to get worried a little too."

"I was sleeping," I said. "I must not have heard the phone."

"Well, at least one of us is taking this thing calmly."

I had made a mistake. The last thing I wanted to do was give the impression that I was insensitive to Minerva's death.

"I guess I *am* preoccupied," I said. "The thing is, I've got this problem of my own with my ex-wife. As a matter of fact, I've got to fly out to California tomorrow to take care of it. I should be back in a day or so. Do you think you could explain to Mr. Sultana for me?"

"Oh, hey, sure," she said. "Look, I didn't mean to say that you were heartless or anything. What I meant to say was that at least you were keeping things in perspective."

This conversation, like every conversation I'd had for the past forty-eight hours, was beginning to take on a dissociative life of its own, like those snatches of sourceless, errant ventriloquism you tune into while lying in the bed in the middle of the night in a drunken stupor.

"Look, Denise," I said. "I've got a few things to take care of before I go, you know, packing and stuff. How about if I call you when I get back?"

"I'd like that," she said.

It was about nine-thirty. I was hungry, but I'd decided I'd had enough visits and phone calls for one day, so I decided to eat out. There was a small Italian restaurant about three blocks from my house. Inside this restaurant was the most underrated chef in America, a native Italian named Scotti. Scotti and I got along real well together. He was from Modena in the north of Italy. He always made a point of chatting me up during my aftermeal coffee.

The restaurant was named after him, anglicized, unfortunately, to Scotty's. There were red-and-white-checkered tablecloths and beyond that a refreshing lack of decor, except for an endearingly tacky and prominent painting of the Coliseum on the wall above the cash register. The dinners were served in authentic Italian style — antipasto, then pasta, then maybe some *pollo arrosto*, followed by cool crescents of sugar melon, plus big slices of warm Italian bread, all the ice-cold carbonated mineral water and room temperature Valpolicella you could drink, and finally, the best *café corretto* this side of the Atlantic, generously laced with grappa. I was running through this mental catalog on my way to Scotty's when I pulled up short about a block from the restaurant, possessed by the same hopeless sense of imminent catastrophe that had overwhelmed me upon my arrival at the Blessing mansion earlier that day. It was less intense this time, but the feeling was the same. I turned around. It was dark. There was nobody in sight, which made me feel even worse. I would have preferred being nose-to belly button with Miguel again to the desolation of that street. At the restaurant, I found that even Scotti had skipped out. He'd gone back to Modena for his first vacation in ten years.

When I got back to my apartment, I went through the contents of Miguel's envelope again. I took a good look at the photograph of Victor Blessing. Either it had been taken on a bad day, or else Victor was a major disappointment to his caste. He looked harmless enough, perhaps too harmless. There was a bourgeois complacency about the face that almost advertised a narrow intellect and a feeble imagination. His features had none of the regal distinction of those of Mrs. Blessing, nor did Victor's photo suggest any of his mother's alertness, the vigor of her elegance, and her serene dignity. This was the photograph of a man who had two hundred dollars in his savings account, who lost sleep over parking tickets, who stuttered and flushed while giving a speech before the father-and-son sports banquet. Maybe he **did** work in his father's factory, holding down some pathetic sinecure. I envisioned him prowling methodically up and down the line in his shirtsleeves and tie, ball point pens lining his pockets, a clipboard for a shield, humored and snickered at by blue collars and management alike, a sort of insubstantial supernumerary whose contribution to the company was a mystery to everybody. Yet, he served an indispensable function in the labyrinthine society of the assembly line, faintly ridiculous, but commanding enough respect by virtue of his name and white shirt to marshal the energy of the workers if only momentarily as he passed them on his way down the line, like a proctor at a final examination.

One of the most insidious things about the academic life is that it conditions you to be analytical, and despite the virtues of that habit, it's ultimately a very cynical operation. Who was I, after all to reduce Blessing to a salaried half-wit who couldn't lick a stamp if it weren't for his pedigree? Victor Blessing was probably a very capable young man.

CHAPTER 7

▼

MR. FARGO GOES TO WASHINGTON

Victor was certainly a lot more considerate than his mother or Miguel. *They* had expected me to buy a car from some sleazy used car dealer and drive it to Washington packing a handgun I had procured from some no doubt equally disreputable gun dealer.

The only trouble was that Leona Blessing's instincts about my preferred mode of transportation were right. I hated flying. I say hated rather than feared because, while it's true that I cringed at the thought of flying, I also resisted it intellectually. It still seems incredible, surrealistically incongruent that a huge jetliner can stay in the air, despite all the lucid lectures I've heard on the principles of aerodynamics and the statistical probabilities concerning my survival as compared with, say, sleeping on my left side.

That's why the next morning I was at the airport three hours before departure time, sitting in the lounge drinking martinis. They must hire a certain breed of bartender in airport lounges. This guy saw nothing at all irregular in my systematically drinking myself into oblivion at seven-thirty on a weekday morning. He was as jocular as if I'd simply stopped in for a beer after work.

By boarding time I had all I could do to stagger through the security system, sniggering like an idiot, congratulating myself that I hadn't visited Cutie's Indoor-Outdoor Range for a gun, past the gate, and down the aisle to my seat. But despite my physical incapacity, I possessed acute mental awareness that could only be attributed to intense anxiety. A stewardess passed by as I sat down and I asked her for a drink.

"I'm sorry, Mr. Fargo," she said, pouting in what seemed to be genuine alcoholic commiseration (where *do* they get these women?), "but you'll have to wait until we get airborne and start our beverage service." She continued forward and assumed her position at the front of the cabin from which, evidently, she intended to demonstrate the ritual sermon on emergency measures. As we were roaring down the runway, the businessman next to me said some damn stupid thing by way of being civil, but I explained to him very clearly that flying was *serious business* too me, and that I never socialize while airborne, that rollicking and all such boisterous behavior should be confined to terra firma. He shut up. I managed to drink four more martinis during the hour plus flight to Washington. When the plane screeched down at Washington National (after appearing almost for certain that it was going to ditch in the Potomac), two things happened almost simultaneously; 1. It occurred to me that the stewardess I had first asked for a drink had addressed my by my name, which I did not remember giving her; 2. I passed out.

Chapter 8

Nobody loves you when you're down and out

I woke up in what appeared to be a dingy hotel room, complete with pink neon pulsing weakly through diaphanous curtains and a sinister-looking figure standing, or I should say sitting, watch over me in an obscure corner of the room. Believe me, the scene is a lot more exotic when you read it in Raymond Chandler and Philip Marlowe seems a lot better prepared to handle it than I was. I could sense that the figure sitting across from me had anticipated my return to consciousness and was primed to nullify any sudden or violent reaction on my part. I lay still, trying frantically to recall how I had come to find myself in this predicament, but all I could recollect were fragmentary images of a ride in the backseat of an automobile. I couldn't remember if it was a matter of abduction, or even if I had been accompanied. I vaguely remembered a static face with all the charm of a fifth-rate embezzler's wanted poster in the post office lobby. Probably a cab driver's ID. Then I immediately realized that it wasn't a cabby's ID photo at all, but the photograph of Victor Blessing that Miguel had given me. I lay there wondering for a moment if I wasn't simply confusing images in the foggy aftermath of drunkenness.

Suddenly the lamp on the table next to where the figure was sitting snapped on and I was staring into a set of features about as animated as a trophy head on a den wall staring away forever into what might have been. It was Victor Blessing. He was one of those rare people whose photographs more than do them justice. The light did nothing for the room, though, except confirm my disappointment. I would not have believed that they still made rooms like that. It *was* dingy. Almost emphatically so. It was so earnestly authentic in its dinginess that it might have been a Hollywood sound stage done up for a remake of *Murder, My Sweet*. Blessing seemed to intuit my conclusion.

"I guess it ain't Buckingham Palace," he said, looking around the room. "But then you ain't the fucking Prince of Wales, either." I turned my attention once again to Victor and had all I could do not to embark on a terminal groan. He was pointing a gun at me, casually, to be sure, and perhaps not *directly* at me, but toward my half of the room, anyway.

I tried to think of something to say, but I'd only be talking to the gun. Blessing seemed to sense my apprehension, which didn't really mean he was very sensitive. I probably had an aura of terror around me that I could have stepped out of like Liberace stepping out of a feather boa.

"I don't have time to fuck around with you," he said, leaning forward in his chair and dangling the gun between his knees. "Where's the file?" He was referring, of course, to the Blessing file.

"What file?" I said, surprising even myself. Victor began to growl. It was a peculiar growl—not so much menacing as therapeutic, although decidedly feral. "Was it something I said?" I said. I was just getting gutsy as hell.

"Uh-huh," he grunted, appearing to have come to some momentous decision. "For a teacher, you ain't too smart, are you?" Considering I had allowed myself to get into this mess, I didn't feel too smart. A lot of people seemed to know more about me than I knew about them.

"Well, let me spell something out for you, Mr. Teacher. The way I figure it, you got the file from Minerva and whacked her in the process—"

"*Whacked* her? I didn't whack anybody."

Blessing shrugged.

"It's all the same to me. It's immaterial, which is all the more amazing when you understand that me and Minerva weren't only partners, we were in love." Jesus, this was touching. I was about to ask him for the loan of his handkerchief. "But you see," he continued, leaning forward and becoming uncomfortably more accurate in the waving of the gun, "the point is, I want those files so bad that I couldn't care if Minerva came back to life and somebody killed her again just because they missed the show the first time. So try to imagine, if you will," he said very slowly, "just how much grief your passing would cause me."

I felt an intense itch right in the middle of my forehead, which was also the spot, coincidentally, whereat Blessing's gun was now aimed.

"Look," I said, in a voice that surprised me by its steadiness, "as a matter of fact, I've been trying to get my hands on that file myself. Without success, I might add." He didn't redirect the muzzle of the gun.

"I have it on good authority that you were successful," said Blessing.

It was my turn again.

"Well, then, I suppose you'll have to kill me," I said, appalled, now, at the steadiness of my voice.

"Okay," he said. "Bye-bye." The man clearly had not seen enough movies to understand the protocol of this whole confrontation. According to the standard scenario, I was supposed to be immune from immediate extinction, based upon my alleged knowledge of the whereabouts of the Blessing file, the possession of which was crucial to Victor's plans. But he was having none of it. Or else he was bluffing. In either case, I had only one course of action, which was to fake unconsciousness, not too difficult since I was nearly unconscious already from a combination of fear, exhaustion, and alcohol. So I pretended to swoon off into never-never land as smoothly as a fresh nun at a black mass. I must have put on a convincing performance because Blessing said "son-of-a-bitch," with the sort of inflection that indicated he held me in somewhat the same regard as he would someone who had passed out at the sight of a needle.

I heard the gun clack down politely on the table. Then I heard the subtle crinkle of cellophane and then the scratch of a match. He was lighting a cigarette. He was going to wait for me to wake up. I had to do *something*. The trouble was I had no idea what that something might be. Suddenly, I felt a sharp pain on the back of my hand. I snatched my hand to my chest and heard Victor laughing robustly. He had burned my hand with his cigarette.

"Did you have a nice nap?" he asked when he had almost stopped laughing.

"Are you crazy?" I asked.

"No, Professor Fargo," he said, the insincere note of levity having vanished from his voice. "I'm in a hurry." He took up the gun again and pointed it at its favorite target. I could feel my forehead starting to itch again. No kidding. He had the cigarette tucked in the corner of his mouth and was squinting against the smoke that was creeping up along the side of his face. I was sure that at any moment I was going to hear John Huston shout, "Cut! Print it."

Instead, I heard a knock at the door, proving once again that life does imitate popular art. I would have signed over my admittedly meager fortune on the spot to that lovely person on the other side of the door at that instant. But in the next instant I would have taken it back and kicked him in the ass. Or her, I should say, because it was a woman's voice.

"Room service," is what she said.

Even I could see through that one. This place was lucky to have indoor plumbing, let alone room service. Now, Victor very nearly *smelled* like an intellectual flyweight, but only massive and irreversible brain damage could have prevented him from being skeptical.

"I ain't decent," he snarled. I had to agree with him there. "And I didn't call for no room service," he added, turning the gun toward the door and pulling back the hammer.

In the midst of the most critical situation of my life, something was beginning to bother me about Victor. All of this was just too much low-rent behavior for a member of the social elite. And Victor Blessing and Minerva Hewitt made no sense at all, although, in the sordid annals of illicit love, rational thought rarely figured in.

But my speculation concerning Victor came to an abrupt halt as there was another knock at the door. Victor snarled again, released the hammer on his pistol slowly and tucked it into his shoulder holster as tenderly as if it had been an orphaned kitten. He stood up and moved toward the door, and, certainly more out of a sense of desperation than courage, I leaped up, grabbed the lamp from the table, and hit him on the back of the head. I heard the nauseating sound that approximated that of a heavy mass being dropped on wet sand.

By the pulse of the neon sign I could see that Victor was on his knees with his face down on the carpet. I heard him groan, and, remembering that he was armed, I fell on him, turned him over and fumbled for the gun under his coat. I was, needless to say, anxious to relieve him of it, but he was putting up no resistance anyway. I finally got it out of the holster and stood up, wondering what to do next.

"Mr. Fargo?" said a tentative voice from the other side of the door.

I stood motionless. Clearly, I was indebted to the voice on the other side—a voice that was becoming more and more familiar as the tide of my drunkenness ebbed. On the other hand, I wasn't sure that I hadn't just inflicted a fatal injury upon Victor Blessing, not your run-of-the-mill extortionist, he, but the primogenital heir of one of the most legendary industrialist names in the country. He had treated me uncivilly, not to say shabbily, and had, in fact, threatened my life. But it might also be said (the Blessing fortune could no doubt influence a convention full of ambitious prosecuting attorneys) that he was doing so in the noble effort to preserve his family's dignity. I would certainly be looked upon as some scumbaggish blackmailer, some bottom-feeding opportunist who could be as nonchalant about besmirching the good name of a great American family as I might be about breaking wind in a cow pasture. All of this flashed through the soap opera of my mind in a matter of seconds—all in a coherent, even emotionally taxing vignette. All of which is to say that I was ambivalent about admitting my rescuer into the room. What if she were some sort of official person, some agent of authority? I have never yet made a figure of authority understand me.

Mr. Blessing, to make matters worse, was not doing well at all. He was incapacitated all right, but in an exasperatingly noisy sort of way. My blow to his head had rendered him a tasteless parody of the village idiot taking a siesta. He lay on his back sputtering and slobbering away in all his stentorian splendor, probably turning black with shock and just about ready to eject his eyeballs at high velocity in the apoplectic aftershock of my attack.

There was another knock at the door—more insistent this time— accompanied by a vigorous turn or two at the doorknob. Then there was silence for perhaps thirty seconds, during which time I didn't breathe, then I heard footsteps receding down the corridor.

I found the light switch near the door and flipped it on. A glare of astonishingly powerful wattage, especially for a hot sheet sweathouse like this one, flooded the room.

Quickly, I replaced to the table the lamp that I had bounced off Blessing's head, plugged it in, and killed the overhead light. Then I turned my attention to Blessing.

He was in less desperate condition than I had imagined. There was still something disturbingly strenuous and labored about his breathing—he breathed like someone who had just run a couple of miles—and a heavy white froth was bubbling out of his mouth and running down the side of his face. His eyes were half open, but he didn't appear to be able to see me. I lifted his head from the floor and noticed that while there was a slight seepage, there was nowhere near the voluminous flow that I had envisioned. More than anything, Blessing seemed to be experiencing a mild epileptic seizure.

He was wearing a gray, sharkskin suit that had been worn perhaps too many times even a year ago. He had on a rayon tie—one of those permanently knotted numbers—that had come unclipped from one wing of his shirt collar. The tie was pointing to an oversize and tastelessly elaborate monogram over his shirt pocket. The initials weren't VB. And either Blessing's shirts had gotten mixed up with someone else's, or I had been given some wrong information. The initials were HRD. The only person on my acquaintance, such as it was, whose initials even came close to that was Hugo Demuth.

CHAPTER 9

▼

AUDIENCE WITH A FUNCTIONAL EUNUCH

That's who it was, all right. His driver's license had his picture on it, as did another card that identified him as an employee, an *operative* to be exact (for some reason, I had thought that that term was obsolete—I had assumed that some euphemism, "investigative specialist" or something like that, would be *au courant*) of Sultana's company. Everything about him made a little more sense now. Everything, that is, except why Miguel had given me his picture telling me it was Victor Blessing and why Hugo was so anxious to get the Blessing file that he was ready to kill me in his impatience, as I was sure that he had been.

But at the moment I couldn't afford the leisure of satisfying my curiosity. I was going to get out of that hotel, hail the first cab I saw, get to the airport as quickly as possible, and catch the first flight back to Detroit. Or, hell, I might not even go back to Detroit right away, things being what they were. I might just fly out to L.A. and visit my ex-wife. Lay low, as it were. We might be incompatible, but at least she was civilized. Obviously, Victor, that is, Hugo, had never had much in the way of social training.

Besides, he was beginning to come around. He had blinked once or twice and had groaned a bit when I had turned him over on his side to get at his wallet. I doubted that he would be reasonable, even though I had his gun and could probably at least convince him to mind his manners a bit, you know, refrain from using people's hands as ashtrays, that sort of thing. But Hugo was going to be angry, that much was sure. Maybe Rudy would help smooth things over between Hugo and me when we got back to Detroit. Or perhaps I could feign amnesia.

But at the moment, I was doing absolutely nothing, with Hugo becoming clearer every moment. I had a strange urge to wait for him to be alert enough for me to apologize to him. But that cavalier notion was too unthinkable even for a sucker like me. I jumped up, opened the door, and found myself for the second time in my life, both within the space of an hour, staring into the muzzle of a handgun. This one was prettier than Hugo's functional blue steel. It was smaller, and shinier, being nickel-plated and pearl-handled, and, well, it just generally looked more elegant than Hugo's. The person pointing it at me was elegant too, and more familiar to me than Hugo. It was the omniscient stewardess whose voice was the last thing I heard before my little excursion to slumsville.

"Oh!" she said, looking past me to Hugo, who was now just about sitting up. He looked like someone who was trying to remember where he had misplaced his car keys. The stewardess seemed surprised that I had been able to subdue him. That made two of us. She surmised the situation very quickly.

"I suggest we leave before we're forced to deal with him again. He seems like a difficult man to deal with," she said. It *might* have been a suggestion, but she still had the gun pointed at me. I decided, however, not to get lost in any ambiguities for the moment. While accompanying armed civilians is not my idea of a fun date, she at least wasn't threatening me overtly. We walked quickly through a dingy hallway of peeling paint that had nourished who knows how many generations of ghetto children, down the most sinister, ill-lit stairway I had ever seen, out of the building into an alley full of overturned trash cans, just at that moment being drenched by a downpour of almost tropical proportions. I remembered the gun in my hand and threw it in the direction of one of the trashcans. Then we jumped into the relative heaven of her late-model Thunderbird.

The ride passed with remarkable casualness, especially in light of the clamorous events preceding it. The stewardess, who introduced herself as Joanna, unnerved me somewhat by driving with the gun still in her lap.

She explained that when I had passed out during the landing, she had gotten two of the other attendants to carry me out of the plane and deposit me on a couch in the lobby, but that by the time she had gotten there, I had disappeared. After questioning several bystanders as to my whereabouts, she had learned that a man had affected in a jocular fashion to be a friend of mine familiar with my weakness for liquor and had escorted me out of the lobby into a waiting car. But apparently the man had had some difficulty getting me into the car and had thus been delayed long enough for Joanna to locate him and follow the car to the hotel, from the lobby of which she had called Mr. Norrod for instructions.

"Mr. who?" I asked.

"Motherwell Norrod," she answered in a tone that suggested I should recognize the name.

"Who's he?" I persisted.

"Why, he's the Director," she answered. "The Director of The Society of Trent. I was supposed to escort you there. I'm afraid that he's going to be upset with me. But then I certainly couldn't have known somebody was going to kidnap you."

I thought about questioning her further. Specifically, I wanted to know what she could tell me about Victor Blessing. But I didn't want to draw suspicion to myself. Even though I no longer felt obligated to go through Mrs. Blessing's cloak-and-dagger charade, Miguel's ominous warning about the characters involved in The Society of Trent was still vivid in my mind. Besides, Joanna seemed more interested in playing tour guide. She pointed out all the sights as we passed through Washington's monument district, apologizing for the fact that they were much less impressive at night and especially on such a rainy night.

We crossed the Potomac and splashed our way through Arlington, Joanna providing a running commentary of history and architecture. I was only partially listening. Something was beginning to bother me. I had left Detroit at ten in the morning. The flight to Washington was about an hour and a half. That means we got in no later than noon. The green digital clock on the dashboard of Joanna's flashy T-bird read four-seventeen. That meant I had been in Hugo's custody for over four hours. If Joanna's narrative of the events following our arrival was accurate, then it had certainly taken her a long time to come to my rescue. Was she waiting for me to come to this realization? Is that why she still had the gun at the ready? I was almost beginning to wish that I was back with Hugo. At least with him I knew where I stood.

We passed through Arlington quickly. ("There's not much too it, really," said Joanna. "I think most of the population is in the cemetery." She delivered the line as though she had done it a hundred times before and still found it extremely funny.) And then we were in Alexandria.

We pulled into a modest-looking building set back about a quarter of a mile from the George Washington Memorial Parkway. The rain had subsided and if anything it had left the air more humid and hot. Just the short walk across the empty parking lot from the air-conditioned T-bird to the air-conditioned lobby of the building was miserable. While we waited for the elevator, Joanna stood with the gun still in her hand, even gesturing with it while she explained the absence of people around. Apparently, only Norrod was in the building. Apparently, he burned the midnight oil every night in the service of the Institute. Apparently, Motherwell Norrod was the epitome of devotion. Joanna spoke of him in low, reverential tones; she spoke, in fact, as though we were in a church. A church with elevators. Well, why not? The common man's ascension. Up, up, up, like a subtle thought through the mind of a beast. I was beginning to get giddy from the lack of food or else I was having a religious experience just listening to Joanna's testimony. At any rate, I was just about to pass out again when the elevator reached the top floor (the sixth) and the doors opened onto what was *my* idea, anyway, of a penthouse suite.

"Have a seat here," said Joanna, directing me to a huge couch. "I'll let Dr. Norrod know that we've arrived."

Doctor Norrod? I sat back into the couch and tried to figure out what was going on. Joanna put her gun away, the mission finally accomplished, and walked away noiselessly on the plush gray carpeting. I looked around at the room. The overall impression was one of immense silence, and, in fact, the entire surface of the walls was covered in cork and the ceiling appeared to be acoustical tiles. The room was sparsely, yet tastefully, furnished—a huge mahogany desk with nothing on it but an inkwell, pen, and a thick fresh pad of yellow legal paper. A high-backed, brass-studded leather chair behind it. An oil painting of some austere-looking Calvin Coolidge-type hung on the wall. That was it. Apparently this was some sort of reception room. Its whole purpose seemed to be to allow visitors to go through some sort of psychic decompression, to purge themselves of the din and distractions of the outside world. I was beginning to feel as ascetic as a monk.

"Jesus!" I said, stirring myself. "You're getting as flaky as your new friend, Joanna." The room swallowed the words, soaked them up like a sponge.

"Nothing serious, I hope, Mr. Fargo." The voice came from my left. I looked over my shoulder and saw a man standing in the doorway at the end of the hall. Joanna was nowhere to be seen.

"Please do come in," the man said. "We've been expecting you."

I wasn't surprised. It seemed like everyone had been expecting me. At the doorway he extended his hand.

"Motherwell Norrod."

"Stephen Fargo. Of the, uh, *Crusading Consumer*." That didn't have the right ring to it. I knew it as soon as the words were out of my mouth.

Norrod blew some skeptical air through his nostrils and turned to walk back to his desk. His office was much busier than the reception room, although the walls were lined in the same cork and this room, like the previous one, seemed to be as impervious to sound as a padded bank vault. The entire wall behind Norrod's back was taken up by bookshelves laden with books. He even had one of those ladders with rollers on it to allow access to the uppermost shelves. From what I could see of his library, he was either extremely well read, or he was trying to impress somebody. Along another wall was a bank of television monitors, all of which were operating. I recognized the picture on one of them as the lobby of the building. But the thing that really attracted my attention was a two-foot-high figurine standing on the corner of the desk, being used, it seemed, as a paperweight. It was a miniature of the statue I had seen gracing the fountain of the Blessing mansion.

"Giambologna," said Norrod.

"Excuse me?"

"It's called *Rape of the Sabine Women*, by Giovanni da Bologna, a vastly underrated Frenchman and a contemporary of Celline. The original stands in the *Loggia della Signoria* in Florence. But forgive an inveterate pedant. You are perhaps familiar with it already." He smiled and inclined his head slightly, half apologetic, half questioning.

"In a way," I said.

"Sometimes I forget that I'm not the only one to have ever been to Florence. It has that effect on one. One becomes proprietary about the repository of one's culture. Does Florence have that effect on you, Mr. Fargo?"

"I couldn't say," I answered. "I've never been to Florence. It just so happens that I saw the statue in Detroit. It was part of a fountain, to be exact."

"Ah, of course," said Norrod. "That dreadful replica of the Blessings'." Norrod paused and stared at the statue for a moment.

"Mr. Fargo, I think it's time, if you'll excuse the cliché, that we put our cards on the table. Coyness is not my style. Subtlety I can appreciate, but I find coyness vulgar and puerile."

I shrugged. Norrod withdrew a file folder from his desk drawer and pulled a pair of glasses from his vest pocket. He snapped the glasses open violently, like an adolescent with a new switchblade. He put the glasses on and began flipping through the pages of the folder. With longer hair and a change of costume, he would have been a dead ringer for Benjamin Franklin.

"In fact," he announced, "you spent the academic year of nineteen-seventy-four and seventy-five in Florence. On a Fulbright, I believe."

I shrugged by way of concession.

"You see, Mr. Fargo, I have the advantage of you." He fanned through the file before him. "In fact," he continued, " I have a complete dossier on you. But most important, I know that you are here as Leona Blessing's spy, that you are not a reporter for the *Consuming Crusader*, or whatever it is, but that you work for a private investigating organization. And I must tell you in good faith that you are out of your league."

He stopped to let me take that in, and, in truth, I was impressed and even a little bit flattered. Nobody had ever wanted to know that much about me and I told him so.

"That's because you never represented a threat to anyone before," said Norrod dryly.

"But I threaten you now?"

Norrod smiled patiently. "Not you personally, Mr. Fargo. Your species. At the risk of being melodramatic, I should explain to you that our organization has undergone a good deal of persecution from people who misunderstand our purpose. Foremost among those has been Leona Blessing, who still harbors a bitter resentment over her daughter-in-law's generosity to us at what she believes to be the expense of her unfortunate son. I suppose we can understand her attitude, but we refuse to succumb to it. You are but the latest in a long line of knights-errant that she has persuaded or coerced into her service. I presume you will not be the last. Leona is senile and very possibly deranged, but she has resources and influence that make her dangerous, or at the least continually bothersome. I presume that she will never realize the delusion of her vendetta. That

Mexican ward or whatever he is of hers encourages her in her delusions, I think. So you see, we have been required by circumstances to become extraordinarily vigilant, and to this end we have assembled our own security and intelligence group of the highest professional quality, whose sole purpose it is to intercept our enemies before they can discredit us. And believe me, Mr. Fargo, you are no match for this organization."

I started to protest that it wasn't my intention to discredit anyone, but Norrod put his hand up to stop me. He leafed through my dossier again, stopping at a page to read silently. Then he spoke.

"I see here that you enjoy Italian food, that you enjoy bourbon whiskey perhaps a little more than is good for you, and that you are at present in a spot of trouble with the police over the murder of one Miss Minerva Hewitt," said Norrod, looking up for me for my response. When I didn't give him one, he continued from the dossier. "I see also that you've recently paid a visit to Leona Blessing. You've been very busy these past forty-eight hours or so."

"So have you," I said.

"And more profitably so, it would seem, Mr. Fargo."

I almost started to tell him how much money I was making on this gig, but I checked myself. He probably wouldn't be impressed.

Norrod reached over to the panel in front of the television monitors and flipped on one of the screens. An overhead view of the lobby. The doors opened and in walked two people, Joanna and me. Norrod and I watched together as Joanna and I walked through the lobby to the elevators.

"Do you know *The Brothers Karamazov?*" asked Norrod. "Of course you do," he said before I could answer. "There was a minor character in the book, a Madame Hohlakov, a foolish old woman as I recall. I remember a scene wherein this woman tries to persuade Dmitri to abandon his self-destructive inclinations by trying to interest him in prospecting for gold. Do you remember the episode, Mr. Fargo?"

"Only vaguely," I said. Actually, I didn't remember it at all.

"Then you perhaps recall that this foolish old woman tried to convince Dmitri that she can tell from his stride that he is assured of success." Norrod laughed gently to himself. "It's one of those desultory episodes in one's education that always seems to stick with one for no very good reason. That scene, at any rate, has always stuck with me so that I always seem to arrive at my first impression of a man by observing the way he walks. It's shamefully unscientific, I'll admit, but I believe that there must be some validity to it, don't you?"

"I suppose so."

"Good!" said Norrod. He was looking at the monitor very intently now, and I, too, was paying a great deal of attention to the way I was walking. It's not something I'd had much opportunity to do.

"You see, Mr. Fargo, you have the stride of an academic, someone who has made so many trips to the principal's office, as it were, that he has come, in some perverse way, to make a career of it."

Norrod looked at me abruptly and turned the monitor off.

"I see you're not convinced," he said. "But then you have not the eye of the connoisseur in this matter. Or you are being defensive." Actually, I was thinking that Norrod was crazy.

"In either case, it doesn't matter," he continued, his voice taking on a harder edge. "Detective work is not your *metier*. It's not mine, either. But as you can see, I have people in my employ who are quite proficient at it—absolutely professional, state-of-the-art, you might say." He nodded toward his bank of monitors. Suddenly, something came to him and he pushed another button. The recorded voices of two men speaking Italian filled the room. Norrod smiled triumphantly at me as I listened. From what I could make out, the two speakers were going over the last minute arrangements for some sort of civic ceremony.

"Do you know who that is?" asked Norrod over the sound of the two voices.

I shook my head.

"That's the Pope in his private quarters in the Vatican having a private conversation with the Mayor of Rome."

"For all I know, it could be a couple of Mafiosi discussing anchovies," I said.

"Don't be tiresome," said Norrod as he snapped the tape off in mid conversation. "The point of this admittedly flamboyant demonstration is to make it clear that if I can bug the Pope's residence, I can, with infinitely less difficulty keep tabs on you. You are up against a much superior force in this matter. Under the circumstances, I think it would be prudent of you to abandon this foolhardy adventure of yours. I assure you that whatever Leona Blessing is paying you is small compensation."

"Is that a threat?"

"Mr. Fargo, a threatening posture is the highest form of exhibitionism. We are not in the business of exhibitionism."

"What business are you in?"

"We are not merchants, dear man. We are missionaries."

"To whom?"

"Why, to the world, of course."

I was beginning to think that he really meant it. Norrod seemed to be putting forth a remarkable effort at restraint. He seemed to have pent up in him the latent zeal and exuberance of the evangelist. It was nothing I could pinpoint, just this overall impression of a man ready to break into a revival spiel like any number of business-suited TV preachers. He had that same sort of slick, mass-media appeal, that video charisma that was indefinable, but nonetheless irrepressible. I felt that he was on the verge of holding forth on the virtues of his particular religious persuasion. A second later he launched into it.

"Did you know, Mr. Fargo, that young children, *children*, Mr. Fargo, not teenagers or young adults, mind you, but that *children* are becoming sexually active as young as ten years of age, some even younger? I don't know about you, Mr. Fargo, but at ten years of age, I was playing baseball.

Why, the term pre-marital hardly seems appropriate to a discussion of sex these days. Prepubescent is more like it."

"It's a wicked world," I said, as I tried, without success, to imagine Norrod playing baseball.

"More than that, Mr. Fargo, it is an unhealthy world. Despite the popular conception of Satan, he is not as theatrical or flamboyant as many people— many of my peers included—perceive him. He is subtle, Mr. Fargo. Blood is his medium. I have seen the face of Satan in its multifarious aspect in the diseased and anguished faces of hopeless patients in the hospital wards, hosts of the spirochete. In short, Mr. Fargo, the Devil is a microorganism."

"This has been done before, you know. Thomas Mann, *Doctor Faustus*."

Norrod stared at me with just the hint of a sneer.

"I'm not speaking of a metaphor, Mr. Fargo. I'm speaking about the very real presence of evil in the world and of the only possible way to deny evil its transmission.

"Your church worships condoms?"

"Virginity, to be exact. Universal virginity." Norrod was not putting me on. His expression was one of complete earnestness. I wondered what it was about him that Mrs. Blessing and Miguel could have found so threatening. As far as I could tell, he was probably unbalanced, but most likely harmless.

"I'm afraid I'm beyond conversion then," I said, for lack of anything else.

"Of course you are," said Norrod. "It's with the youth of the world that we must concern ourselves and therein lies the resistance to us. As you know, in the past decade or so, charismatic movements appealing to young people have fallen under suspicion, much of it justified. That's why *we* have no charismatic leader and why we maintain a low profile."

"Low profiles aren't compatible with evangelism."

"We have our methods."

"Militant methods?"

"Let's just say confidential methods."

I began to imagine all sorts of medieval practices like chastity belts and ritual castrations. Maybe Norrod was more dangerous than he looked.

"All the members of our organization are sworn to virginity," Norrod continued. "It's sort of a vestal society, but we have a corporate structure, no tax exemptions. We are funded solely by private endowments and donations and our own investments, which are a matter of public record. I am the Executive Director, and, yes, a virgin, or functional eunuch, as I prefer to think of myself."

Things were beginning to make a little more sense.

"And your chief patron was Florence Blessing," I said.

"Yes," said Norrod. "To the everlasting fury of her mother-in-law. Florence was a great woman—a woman of vision and compassion."

"And great generosity."

"Don't jump to conclusions. Her generosity went beyond mere philanthropy. You might call the Society of Trent her legacy. She, after all, founded it."

"Are you telling me that Florence Blessing was a virgin?"

"I am," said Norrod, with just a bit of truculence creeping into his voice.

I began to think about taking his advice and abandoning this wild goose chase. As far as I could see, both Norrod and Leona Blessing were certifiable and I could see no percentage in arbitrating a dispute between lunatics.

"You see, Leona Blessing believes that we swindled her daughter-in-law's money from her, despite Florence's protestations to the contrary."

"That's not all she believes," I said. "She said something to me about your organization being suicidal, and if you think of the logical extension of your program of universal virginity, you have—"

"Extinction?"

"Well, yes."

"That's a pessimistic evaluation. We prefer to think of it in terms of transformation, as part of God's plan."

"That sounds *optimistic*, to me. Any way you look at it, it's the annihilation of humanity, ultimately." I didn't know why I was bothering to get into a philosophical discussion of this question. Norrod had about as much chance of achieving worldwide virginity as I did of spitting out the sun.

"We are not simply an eccentric splinter group," said Norrod. "Our society is founded on the soundest canonical authority. Let me quote to you from the twenty-fourth session of the Council of Trent, November 1563, the tenth canon: 'If anyone says that the married state excels the state of virginity or celibacy, and that it is better and happier to be united in matrimony than to remain in virginity or celibacy, let him be anathema.'"

He delivered this line with a sort of pontifical solemnity that it seemed to me would be useless to argue against. His interpretation seemed a little narrow, to say the least, but I wasn't there to debate Counter Reformation dogma.

"Well, your mission doesn't concern me," I said. "I'm simply interested in contacting Victor Blessing."

Norrod looked at me for a moment in astonishment.

"*Contacting* him?"

"Yes. I'm just here to deliver a message. By the way, as sophisticated as your intelligence system is, I'm surprised that you weren't aware that Victor himself persuaded me to come. I had no more intended to pursue Leona Blessing's scheme than I have of subscribing to yours."

Norrod said nothing for a moment. Then he sighed and pushed himself back in his chair and laughed.

"Mr. Fargo, as sophisticated as our system is, it does have certain limits, and I'm afraid intercepting communications from the other side is beyond us."

"The other side?"

"Yes, Mr. Fargo, the other side. Victor Blessing has been dead for five years and as far as that goes, he was among the walking dead for fifteen years before that."

CHAPTER 10

▼

...AND CONFESSIONS OF
A NOMINAL VIRGIN

I couldn't sleep.

The *room* was comfortable enough. After apologizing for not being able to accommodate me there at the headquarters of the Society of Trent—I wasn't a functional eunuch, after all—Norrod had gotten me a room in a snazzy hotel back in Washington. I'd had room service send up a bottle of Jack Daniels, but it wasn't doing me any good. All I could think about was the end of my interview with Norrod and the revelations that it had provided.

He had explained that only after Florence Blessing had married Victor did she discover that he was in the first stages of STD deterioration. According to Norrod, Victor had been irredeemably profligate since adolescence, and even repeated venereal infections had not deterred him from his ways. Apparently, Florence had taken one look at him close up on their wedding night and had gotten religion. A virgin, she had decided to take a vow of chastity for the rest of her life, thus the origin of the organization.

And since Florence was born in Trenton, New Jersey, the organization was called the Society of Trent. All that stuff Norrod had told me about the Council of Trent was subsequent coincidence (or the hand of Providence, if you preferred Norrod's interpretation).

Florence's refusal to consummate the marriage drove Victor to further excesses. Florence tolerated her husband's conduct and maintained the marriage for the sake of form. At that time, Victor still confided sporadically in his mother (again, according to Norrod), and she, in turn, tried to pressure Florence into a more traditional marriage arrangement. But Florence was adamant, hence the enmity between the two women. They reached a partial truce when Florence agreed not to reveal Victor's condition publicly and Leona agreed to stay out of Victor's and Florence's affairs. Things stood like that for ten years, although Leona became increasingly irritated as Florence became more and more involved in the Society. Leona took this as an indirect attack, but refrained from retaliation. Only after Victor's death, which allegedly resulted from a combination of alcohol and barbiturates, and a presumed drowning from which Victor's body was never recovered, did Leona become more active in her attacks on Florence and the Society of Trent. She never believed that her son had died, or at least that he had died under the circumstances described in the official version of the incident. I was the fifth person Leona had hired to try to infiltrate the organization and learn the whereabouts of Victor. She had just recently enlisted the help of Sultana's agency, but they had only confirmed the official version, after which Leona had accused them of having been paid off by the Society.

I had asked Norrod how he could explain the note that I had received from Victor Blessing. He attributed it to Leona, who, he said, did it to ensure that I would take the assignment. The ploy, he said, was typical of her. She was old, he said, and certainly insane, but she was still very shrewd.

I had considered mentioning to Norrod the events that had taken place concerning Sultana's agency and the Blessing file *and* Minerva's murder (I, too, was beginning to think that's what it was) *and* my encounter with

Hugo Demuth, but I decided against it. Besides, if his intelligence system was what he said it was, he should be able to find out for himself.

About two o'clock in the morning the phone rang. It was Joanna, the stewardess. She explained that she had to be at the airport in two hours, but that she had some information that I might be interested in concerning my conversation with Motherwell Norrod. I finished off my drink and was just tucking in my shirt as she knocked. I opened the door for her. She walked past me and took off her coat.

"You've got it all backwards," she said as I shut the door. She walked up to me and began pulling my shirt out. She unbuttoned the first three buttons of my shirt, smiled, but her arms around my neck, drew me to her, and kissed me violently, her tongue pushing its way past my teeth and forcing its way around the inside of my mouth. Then she stepped back and was undressed in about fifteen seconds. She put her hands on her hips, cocked her head, and looked at me as though I were hopelessly stupid.

"It helps if you take your clothes off," she said. She knelt down in front of me and pulled down my pants. Then she had her hands on me, very lightly, as though she were inspecting me for venereal disease. Then I felt her mouth.

"At least part of you responds," she said a few seconds later. "Now, the first news flash I have for you is that not all of us in the Society of Trent are virgins."

* * *

While she dressed, Joanna talked about the organization.

"I couldn't help eavesdropping on your conversation with Dr. Norrod," she began.

"Is he a medical doctor?"

"God, no," said Joanna. "He got his Ph.D. through some mail order divinity school. He insists that we address him as Dr. Norrod because in his mind, it lends a certain legitimacy to the Society. He's very big on enhancing the legitimate image of the Society."

"That's understandable."

"Sure. But that's about the only thing an outsider would find understandable. I'm *inside* and I don't understand half of what goes on in there. Such as that building we were in just a little while ago. The North American Headquarters. Big fancy name. And it seemed like a pretty big place, didn't it?"

"I guess so."

"Oh, *fuck*," said Joanna. "I've run my panty hose." She sat for a moment, half inspecting the damage to her panty hose and half mourning over it.

"So what if it's big?" I said.

"What?"

"The building. What about the size bothers you?"

"Oh, yeah. Well, it's not just a matter of its size. The thing is, as far as I've ever been able to tell, the only person in that entire building is Norrod and his goddamn surveillance equipment."

I thought about this for a moment. Based upon my limited observation of the building, it seemed that there had been floor space enough to accommodate hundreds of people.

"What do you make of it?" I asked Joanna.

"You're the detective. What do you make of it?"

"What makes you think I'm a detective?"

"I heard Norrod say so."

"And it was Norrod who told you to accompany me to his office?"

"Right."

"Wasn't it awfully convenient that you were a flight attendant on the very flight I took?"

"Gee, I don't know. Dr. Norrod knew I was in Detroit—we're required to keep in regular contact with him, every twenty-four hours. He phoned me at my hotel and asked that I see what I could do about adjusting my schedule—you know, switch with another FA—so that I could escort you to the headquarters."

Something didn't sound right. Norrod had indicated that he'd had no knowledge of the note from Victor Blessing, and he had even seemed genuinely shocked when I told him about it. But if that were so, how could he have known that I would fly to Washington that very morning?

"How did Norrod know what flight I'd be on?" I asked.

"He didn't," she replied. "I found out. I just called down to my friend Sylvia who works at the reservation desk. She found out that you were on the American flight, and I work for American. It was easy."

"Yes," I said. "It sounds as though you were very lucky." I thought that the irony in my voice would provoke Joanna to explain further, but she just stood up and walked into the bathroom, where she began to reapply her makeup.

"Tell me something," I said. "How is it that you're so obedient in some things and not in others?"

"You mean sex?" She went on applying her makeup without a hitch.

"Yeah, sex. This delusion of universal virginity seems pretty important to Norrod."

"Really, Stephen, you didn't buy all that virginity crap, did you?"

"As a matter of fact, I did. As deluded as Norrod is, I had the feeling that he was sincere."

"Oh, he's sincere all right," said Joanna. "But he's also naïve. Boy, I remember when he and that Florence woman, you now, the one with all the money, used to get together and almost get off on each other talking about chastity and abstinence and purity and all that. It was like astral sex, you know? Like telepathic fucking. They were both serious as hell, and every once in a while some poor, misguided creature wanders into the fold—usually fat, ugly girls in their early twenties who have given up on finding a man—any man—and are prepared to make any kind of vow that Norrod can extract from them in exchange for a little self-respect."

"What about you?"

"What *about* me?"

"How did you get involved in the society?"

"Sweetheart, I used to be one of those fat ugly girls. And when I first joined the Society, I had every intention of living up to my vows. I was just like a nun. But the great thing about Dr. Norrod's organization is that he has vast resources, and, from what I can tell, not too many things to spend them on. The Society sent me to a plastic surgeon, to a therapist, who eventually seduced me, and finally to a special weight reduction spa therapy kind of thing in Italy, all to help me with my self esteem, so that I could better represent the Society."

"How many others are there in the organization?"

"Oh, I don't have any idea. Dr. Norrod's pretty tightlipped about those sorts of things."

"Don't you have meetings or something?"

"No. Dr. Norrod doesn't want the members to know each other. I've met maybe a handful of people in the Society, but only on a strictly business basis. We'll run into each other on an assignment now and then."

"Doesn't that bother you?"

"No. I don't ask questions. Dr. Norrod's organization provides me with a nice allowance, not to mention other things like loans and his influence when I've needed it. He got me this job, for example. All he asks is that I perform certain tasks for him now and then, and as far as I know, I haven't done anything illegal yet, although, as I say, I never ask questions."

"So Norrod has the whole building to himself, huh?"

"As far as I know." Joanna had finished dressing and was putting on her jacket. At the door, she paused a minute.

"Oh, I almost forgot the most important thing."

"What's that?" I asked.

"Well, I heard Dr. Norrod mention something about you being in trouble with the police, something involving the death of Minerva Hewitt."

"Yes," I said. "I was wondering about that myself. At least up until yesterday, I was only aware that she had died under uncertain circumstances.

A police detective told me that it was being officially described as an accident. I wonder why Norrod described it as murder."

"I don't know about that," said Joanna. "But I *can* tell you that Dr. Norrod knows more about Minerva Hewitt than he let on."

"What do you mean?"

"I *mean* she was a member of the Society."

I don't know why this came as such a shock, but it did. Then I thought about my relationship with Minerva, about her frigid, bitter attack on me and about what must have been her furtive affair with Hugo, and things began to fall into place.

"Are you sure? Do you guys have a secret handshake or something?"

Joanna rolled her eyes.

"Of course I'm sure. I've run into her once or twice before when I was on assignment for Dr. Norrod. I didn't know her well. She was pretty standoffish. But she was a member, there's no doubt about that." Joanna looked at me for a second. Then she gave me another hungry mauling on the mouth. I guess she was making up for all those years of virginity with every sexual encounter.

"Here's some advice," she said when she pulled away from me. "Dr. Norrod is probably wacko, but I wouldn't underestimate him. He's a powerful man and he has a great deal of influence. I'm not saying he's a murderer or anything, but people who give him trouble—except for Leona Blessing, of course—have a way of disappearing."

Then she was gone.

CHAPTER 11

▼

MUSEUM OF UNNATURAL HISTORY

The next morning, I was halfway through my second cup of complimentary hotel coffee when the phone rang. A tentative and barely audible voice on the other end of the line asked me if I was Stephen Fargo. I answered just as tentatively that I was.

"Kelly Stonestreet here," came the announcement from the other end. The caller's voice seemed to assume more confidence and volume as he identified himself. "Haskell Stonestreet, Jr." he said a few seconds later, as if he had been a bit too casual the first time.

"Well, how do you do, Mr. Stonestreet," I said after a few seconds of silence. I had the feeling he was waiting for me to initiate the conversation, which seemed already to be deteriorating.

"Fine, fine," he said with exaggerated animation. Then, again, there was an awkward silence.

"Look, Steve," Stonestreet said finally, "do you think we could talk for a few minutes?"

"Sure," I said.

"No, not over the phone. I was wondering if you would mind coming over to my home. I know it's a tremendous imposition—"

"Not at all," I assured him. Stonestreet gave me his address, thanked me (excessively, I thought) and then hung up abruptly.

I was still in a hurry to get out of Washington. The idea of Hugo lurking behind the Capitol monuments nursing a headache that would bring a grimace to the heads of Mt. Rushmore was not much of an inducement to stay. The way things were going, it was only a matter of time before he found out where I was. *Everybody* seemed to know where I was. Still, I was intrigued by Stonestreet's call. Miguel had given me Stonestreet's phone number with clear instructions to contact him only in an emergency. And now, here was this skittish invitation from the man himself. I called downstairs to the desk and notified the manager that I would be staying beyond checkout time. Then I called the airlines and changed my flight to an early evening one that same day. Then I called a cab. In half an hour I was getting out of the cab at the curb in front of the Georgetown townhouse of Haskell Stonestreet, Jr.

I rang the doorbell and waited. And waited. I began to get that familiar feeling that someone was scrutinizing me again. The threshold of a strange residence in daylight must be the most vulnerable of stations. The door finally opened slowly and I was standing face-to-face with a real live butler, complete with uniform, dignified formal expression, and an air of consummate discretion, with *serious* overtones of condescension.

"Mr. Fargo, I presume," he said, inclining his head slightly.

"Yes."

"Please come in," he said, extending his hand into the room and again bowing his head slightly. "Mr. Stonestreet is expecting you."

Well, of course he was expecting me. Protocol was one thing, but just by his demeanor, this butler seemed to be a born slave to convention. We walked into the middle of a room that was much larger than it would have been possible to imagine it to be from the outside. And it was a good thing, too, because mounted on its walls was what in my experience was the largest collection of game trophies assembled in one place. Wild boars snarled frozenly across the room at somnolent moose. Bats displayed their fangs. Huge swordfish with dorsal fins that looked like flattened out umbrellas parried each other. Pheasant and grouse and turkeys and even a vulture perched about the room. An eagle or hawk with a wing span as long as a pool cue was crucified against one wall. Tarantula spiders and coiled coral snakes sat frozen in Plexiglas cubes. Iguana and Gila monsters basked on some rocks near the fireplace, waiting, perhaps, to be thawed back into existence. The floor was covered in tiger and bear skins, the bears, their heads still affixed, looking like they'd been deflated by surprise

The butler cleared his throat. "Mr. Stonestreet is in the study, Mr. Fargo," he said. I turned to follow and ducked my head just in time to avoid hitting a dismembered branch sticking out of the wall, the posthumous perch of some fowl called a Laughing Kookaburra, according to the legend tacked to the branch.

I was ushered into another high-ceilinged room that complemented the previous one very nicely by being what appeared to be a museum of weaponry. The wall was covered with longbows and crossbows and sabers and scimitars and other ceremonial swords. There were also many different styles of daggers and bayonets and maces and lances and primitive-looking spears. A half-dozen gun racks were chockfull of flintlocks and blunderbusses, as well as their more modern counterparts like double-barrel and pump shotguns, high-powered rifles with scopes, and several semi-automatic rifles. At various posts around the room, hand-tooled pistol cases stood open on bookstands displaying ivory inlaid dueling pistols and service revolvers and little shiny pistols that looked more like cigarette lighters than death dealers. All told, there must have been about two hundred lethal weapons in that room. And that was all that I could plainly **see**. I began to wonder if the floor was mined.

Sitting beneath and in the midst of all this at a desk that faced an enormous tapestry of some medieval scene of carnage, sat a small, but compact man with his back to me. The butler, who must have graduated magna cum lauda from throat-clearing school, cleared his throat. The man in the chair swiveled in my direction.

"Mr. Fargo," said the butler.

"Ah, Steve," said Stonestreet. He catapulted from the chair and approached me eagerly, his hand extended. He shook my hand like someone who had learned early in life that a firm handshake was the highest virtue of a gentleman and the truest test of virility. I returned the pressure for a second or two, but when it became clear that at any moment we would descend into some ridiculous macho contest of grip strength, I eased off. I noticed the faintest hint of a smile on the butler's face. He had obviously witnessed many of these minor triumphs and took a good deal of satisfaction in his master's victories. Stonestreet must have noticed the exchange of glances between the butler and me.

"Thank you very much, Blakely. That will be all," said Stonestreet. Blakely nodded slightly and withdrew, that is if butlers ever do completely withdraw. They always seem to be lurking around on the periphery of things.

"Blakely's a bit too exaggerated in the performance of his duties sometimes," Stonestreet explained. "I rarely notice it except when other people are around. Then he gets ceremonious as all hell. I really just don't know what to do with him, to tell you the truth."

Stonestreet fell into contemplative silence as though the dilemma had only just occurred to him and that he had to make a decision on the spot.

"I guess butlers are pretty much a dying breed," I said in an effort to bridge the silence.

Stonestreet motioned me to a seat and resumed his chair at the desk.

"Well, the problem is, Blakely's more of a family institution around here than an employee. When my father died, I just inherited him, unofficially, of course."

"I can see how it might be difficult to dispose of a family institution," I said, being just diplomatic as hell.

"Christ, I can't seem to dispose of *anything*," said Stonestreet. "Just look at all this, this *shit*." He waved around the room. "Sure, there was a time in my life when all of this was extremely important—this and all those carcasses out there in the other room. But, sweet Jesus, I'm thirty-four-years-old."

I failed to see the correlation between collecting guns and trophy heads and the age of the collector, but I didn't feel like having Stonestreet try to clear it up for me. He lapsed into another silence, as though this new problem now occupied his mind to the exclusion of everything else. I tried to work him around to the purpose of his wanting to see me.

"I suppose Mrs. Blessing has been in touch with you," I said. "Or Miguel."

"Not fucking likely," he said. "I haven't talked to the old broad in ten years and I only talked to her when I had to before that. And Miguel's a pleasant enough guy, but his devotion to Leona precludes any amicable relationship between us. We just don't exchange social calls."

This led Stonestreet into a not too coherent narrative of his background, only partly as it concerned the Blessing family. He explained that he had been a former graduate student, former Peace Corps volunteer, former combat infantryman, former karate instructor, former white hunter, former taxidermist, former auto racing enthusiast, former political candidate, former prison inmate, and former divinity student. Everything about Stonestreet seemed to be former. But, no. Presently, he was a businessman.

"I own a few fast-food franchises and I've got controlling interest in two worm farms in Alabama. That's where the *real* money is. You wouldn't believe how much money there is in worms," he said.

He explained that his father was a relatively famous archeologist and a friend of Draper Blessing. Blessing had had an amateur interest in archeology and had helped finance several expeditions for his friend, occasionally accompanying him on digs.

"Hell," he said, "me and Victor just about grew up together all over the world—Italy, Mexico, Greece, Egypt. Miguel, too."

"You grew up with Miguel?"

"Well, in a way. We were on a dig in the Yucatan—I remember that I was about six years old—and one day Draper told my father that he was adopting an Indian kid—some orphan from a village nearby. That kid was Miguel. I found out later that that stuff about the adoption was only the official version. My father often hinted to me that Miguel was actually Blessing's illegitimate son. The whole thing was very hush-hush, but, apparently, the incident resulted in a severe strain between Draper and Leona, and, ever worse, between Victor and Miguel. I mean, shit, Blessing sent that Indian off to boarding school in England and then to college in France, while Victor struggled through public schools and dropped out of at least half a dozen colleges. And that wasn't the worst of it. When both the children began to become more conscious of the family fortune is when the real bitterness began to surface. Victor began to resent Miguel even more, and it became compounded when his parents began to demonstrate a clear preference for Miguel. The old man had these weird ideas, you see, about racial characteristics, you know, noble savages and all that. He thought that Miguel came from superior stock or some shit. He sort of viewed Miguel as an experiment. If you ask me, that's why Victor married Florence—as a sort of response to the rejection that he experienced at home. But of course even by then Victor was already pretty far down the road to ruin. Later, Draper began to feel some remorse, I guess, over having neglected Victor for all those years and he began to shower all kinds of affection on him. But it was too late to save Victor."

Stonestreet's posture and style of delivery had changed remarkably during his recounting of the history of the Blessing family. He had started out tensely, with his hands clasped so tightly that his knuckles were white—sitting forward, his forearms giving the impression of exerting great pressure against the desktop, as though to relax that pressure would result in the levitation of the desk. His tone of voice had been hesitant, or rather, deliberate, as though he were casting and rehearsing each sentence before speaking it. But, gradually, as though the reminiscence had a narcotic effect on him, he began to relax. He spoke more spontaneously and fluently. Finally, he was sitting back in his chair with his hands clasped behind the back of his head and his feet up on the desk, perfectly at ease.

He looked like a tourist lounging on the deck of a cruise ship. After he had finished his narrative, he lit a huge Havana cigar (I had refused his offer of one of these) with which he proceeded to further befoul the already pungent air of the room. I got the feeling that all those firearms discharged on the hour like alarm clocks, giving the room its distinctive aroma of gunpowder.

"Do you know for sure that Victor is dead?" I asked. The question seemed to take Stonestreet by surprise. He looked at me for a second, perhaps thinking that I was going to elaborate.

"Well, I haven't seen his rotting carcass, if that's what you mean," he said finally. "Is there any reason that I *shouldn't* think he's dead?"

I explained to him how it came about that I was in Washington, Mrs. Blessing's commission, Miguel's instructions, my conversation with Norrod (here Stonestreet snorted and said, "The well-financed ravings of a latent pederast.") and the mysterious letter from Victor, or his imposter.

"No kidding," he said when I had finished. "Old Miguel really gave you my telephone number, eh?"

"Yes, he did. That's why I assumed after your call this morning that he had contacted you."

"Christ, no" said Stonestreet. "It's completely out of the question."

"Then, if you don't mind my asking, how did you know I was in Washington?" What I really wanted to ask was what was Stonestreet's purpose in requesting this strange interview, but I thought I shouldn't be too direct about it.

"Oh, I don't mind your asking," answered Stonestreet. "I rather expected it. But I'm afraid the source of my information must remain confidential. It's for my informant's own protection, you understand."

"From whom?"

Stonestreet smiled. "Look, Steve, I know all this must seem all very cryptic to you, but it's not all that sinister, really. You must understand my position. Could I offer you a drink? I know it's a bit early in the day. When I was younger, I had a hard and fast rule—which I observed religiously—never to touch a drink before six o'clock in the evening. But over the years that kind of discipline has begun to seem, I don't know, excessive. Is bourbon okay?"

Before I could answer, the punctilious Blakely was standing just over my left shoulder with a glass of bourbon on the rocks. He had moved into the room as silently as a moon on its way to an eclipse.

"Here's my situation," said Stonestreet, after a preliminary taste of his drink, apparently in deference to Blakely, who, it seemed, never vanished until everything was to his master's complete satisfaction.

"I have over the years made a number of enemies, almost necessarily so, given the nature of some of my careers. As a result, I've become somewhat of a recluse. Too much exposure would almost certainly be fatal. Anyway, as long as I maintain this hermit-like existence, my enemies seem willing to tolerate the continuation of that existence. I'm sort of under house arrest, you might say."

I wouldn't have said that at all. It occurred to me that Stonestreet was just paranoid.

"Of course, while I don't take an active role, I still have access to information. To this end, I have over the years assembled a trusted group of friends, a kind of extended sensory network, who report faithfully to me. It's essential, after all, that I be able to anticipate any threat against me. So you see, then, that my informants must remain anonymous."

"And you perceive me as a threat?"

"Not necessarily. I perceive you as someone associated, for whatever motives, with those in my past who may, conceivably, threaten me."

"Such as the Blessings."

"Yes!" said Stonestreet, apparently pleased to have such an illustrious family for adversaries. "But that's only a coincidence. My more immediate concern is with Sultana."

"Rudy Sultana?"

"The very same," said Stonestreet. "Your present employer, I believe you said."

"I *did* say. But as I also told you, I'm not down here as an employee of Sultana. You might say I'm freelancing."

"And I might believe you. In fact, I'm inclined to do so."

"But why should Sultana be any danger to you?"

"I'd rather not get too specific about that. You might be tempted to become more interested. I can only tell you what's become a matter of public record, since I'm sure that you're enterprising enough to find that out anyway. You see, about eight years ago, Rudy and I were comrades-in-arms. We were in central Chile helping to suppress a labor dispute—"

"You were mercenaries," I said.

Stonestreet shrugged. "I make no apologies for my past, but I preferred at the time to call myself a soldier of fortune. I was young. The last thing I thought about was the moral consequences of my impetuosity, my adventurous impulses. I did eventually see the error of my ways, but that's another story. We were employed by an exiled Italian who had become a sheep rancher, and who had been less than scrupulous in his appropriation of land. It was a very local thing, almost insignificant. But somehow, in a way that was never clear to me, Sultana became involved in the assassination of Allende. There were some reprisals and an attempt on Sultana's life. I actually saved his life. A few years later, back in the States, when I had been convicted of smuggling cocaine into the country from Columbia, Rudy engineered my parole from prison by way of repaying the favor."

"It doesn't sound like Sultana's the kind of guy you should be worried about."

"I'm not worried. Just cautious. Rudy's still a mercenary at heart. Believe me, the private investigation stuff is just a cover. What do you know about Sultana? How often do you see him?"

I had to admit that I caught only rare glimpses of the man.

"I thought so."

"But he doesn't seem to be hiding. The guy leads the life of a heavy-weight champ."

"Sure," said Stonestreet. "He wants to maintain a high profile. He knows people are watching him. He wants everything he does to be obvious—even exaggerated. Anything covert would be an invitation to disaster. Hell, he's got more enemies than I do. But his present occupation is very convenient. It allows him to collect information, to observe. He's got his early warning system just like I do. Only he has more sophisticated resources."

I thought of Norrod's elaborate surveillance and security systems. It seemed that I *was* way out of my league with these guys. It began to be clear to me why Minerva had always been so testy about access to the files. I could only imagine their contents. I had assumed that the information therein had only been potentially scandalous and embarrassing. But it was probably even more explosive than that. The Blessing file and all the strange events surrounding it began to assume new significance.

Blakely was somewhere behind me again, clearing his throat. I thought I detected a different tonal quality to this throat-clearing, a note of urgency. Hell, give me a week with Blakely and we probably wouldn't have to articulate to each other, just grunt back and forth all day like a pair of peccaries.

"Yes, Blakely?" said Stonestreet.

"Mr. Crofts is here, sir."

"Thank you. Tell him I'll be right with him."

"Very good, sir," and Blakely was gone like a vagrant thought.

"Crofts is my accountant, a very highly scheduled man. I'm afraid you'll have to excuse me. I've enjoyed our little talk very much." He extended his hand and I prepared myself for another test of strength. But either his first triumph was sufficient, or else he needed an audience, for this handshake was something less than bone-pulverizing. "Unfortunately, I don't think we shall meet again."

I preceded him out of the room and into the foyer where I encountered a very little man impeccably dressed in a three-piece suit, and carrying an oversized briefcase. Stonestreet did not introduce us, and Crofts stared at me defiantly as I walked past him towards the door. It was apparently a facial expression he had practiced a good deal to perfect in order to compensate for his diminutive size. I think he could have packed himself comfortably in his own briefcase. I wondered if this was one of Stonestreet's many informants. Undoubtedly, it was.

At the door, Stonestreet stopped me for a word of warning. These, too, were becoming obligatory, it seemed, with anyone I met.

"I realize all of this intrigue with the Blessings and Sultana seems fascinating, but believe me, pursuing it will only bring you to harm." I gave Stonestreet the benefit of the doubt by assuming that he wasn't threatening me personally. I had enough to worry about. I thanked him and left.

CHAPTER 12

▼

EMERGENCIES

I decided to walk the nine or ten blocks to my hotel. The burgeoning activity and vitality of Georgetown on this Saturday morning seemed to be the very antidote I needed to recover for the moribund atmosphere of Stonestreet's residence. I could sort things out amidst the variegated pedestrians, sidewalk sales, and bustle of naïve commerce.

I had proceeded two blocks in terms of distance and not at all in terms of mental clarity when a silver Mercedes pulled up to the curb next to me. Its horn sounded once, very shortly, as if the driver had just jabbed at it with a finger. In the driver's seat a crisp and venomous-looking chauffeur motioned with his head to the rear seat of the car. The rear window, tinted darkly enough to be nearly opaque, slid down to reveal the smooth, pink features of Motherwell Norrod.

"Been out sampling the local curiosities, I see," he said. A tone of reprimand lined his voice, as if I were an errant child who had wandered off. "May I offer you a ride?"

"Actually, I'd prefer to walk. I thought I might stop at a few shops," I said, innocent as a tourist.

"Well, that's up to you," said Norrod. "But the next offer you get might be a bit more insistent and your reception at your hotel might be something less than warm. It seems the police have found a dead man in your room. A Mr. Demuth. And since he's not being too cooperative, they're looking for the room's more lively occupant."

I'd like to report that I said something clever here, but I've never said anything clever under highly stressful conditions. I *have* learned, however, in light of this deficiency, to keep my mouth shut. Norrod opened his door and slid over. Georgetown lost all of its charm. I got into the back seat and the Mercedes drove off like an excursion boat to a dream.

The back seat of the Mercedes looked like a miniature version of Norrod's office. There were two telephones, three small television screens, and several other incomprehensible devices. There was even something that looked like a radar screen. A heavy plate of glass sealed us off from the chauffeur, with whom Norrod communicated by one of the phones.

"The airport, Giacinto. National. *E fa attenzione*." The chauffeur nodded slightly. I suddenly wished that I hadn't agreed to this escort.

Norrod pulled an airline ticket from his coat pocket and handed it to me. The voucher had my name on it. I was booked on a one-way flight to Rome, via New York.

"I've heard of being taken for a ride," I said. "But isn't this a little extravagant?"

"I would call this more of a rescue than an abduction," said Norrod.

"I guess that would depend upon your motivation," I said, mindful of the ambiguity of my recent adventures. I was already contemplating an escape, but the car was moving at a pretty good clip. I began to hope for traffic signals in my favor.

Norrod pulled out his glasses, gave them his patented aggressive snap, and put them on.

"This may interest you, then," he said. He reached to a panel of buttons on the console in front of him and depressed one of the buttons. One of the monitors blinked to life. The scene was of the front exterior of my hotel building, where, around the entrance, a cordon of police restrained a small, but avid accumulation of onlookers. After several seconds, two emergency medical technicians emerged from the building rolling a stretcher between them. On the stretcher was what appeared to be a body, completely covered by a sheet. The medical technicians wheeled the stretcher to the rear doors of an ambulance, and, in one smooth, efficient movement, hoisted it and slid it into the ambulance just like a huge loaf of bread being slipped into an oven. The ambulance drove away and Norrod reached forward and switched off the picture.

"Your guys just happened to be on the scene with all their equipment when this took place, right?"

"I'd like to think that we enjoyed such powers of anticipation, or luck, if you prefer," said Norrod. "It would save us a lot of money on surveillance. I don't believe in luck, myself. No, in fact, in this case we were alerted."

"By anybody I know? Maybe the same people that told you I was coming to Washington?" It only just then dawned on me that I had been set up. Probably by Stonestreet. That CPA-type Crofts had been, in reality, Stonestreet's hired assassin returning to report the success of his mission. Norrod ignored my question.

"By the way," he said. "You should know that they found a gun. And you can probably guess who's fingerprints are on it. Mr. Fargo, it seems you've stumbled onto something here that places you in serious danger."

"Is there any other kind?"

"Really, Mr. Fargo, this bravado of yours is quite unbecoming, quite beneath you. I have been instructed to offer you assistance in this matter, and I assure you that the source of my instructions has only your welfare in mind."

"Yeah," I said. "Whoever it is wants to turn me into an international fugitive. That would really ice the thing, wouldn't it? I *do* have an alibi, by the way."

"You're welcome to pursue that course if you wish. I have no intention of forcing you into anything." I said nothing and Norrod seemed to take my silence for assent. "Now, from Rome you are to take the train north to Trento," he said, scribbling away at the back of a business card. "Your contact there is a man named Claudio Niccolo. Here is his address."

I read the card. The uneven scrawl on the back indicated an address somewhere on a street called Via Calepina in Trento.

"Not *the* Trento," I said. "They got another council in session or something? An emergency convocation to consider the prohibition of amorous glances, perhaps?"

"Your sarcasm is wasted on me, Mr. Fargo. I am not so easily provoked. Do you have any cash?"

We had crossed the river. Out of the window on my side of the car, I could see above me the headstones of the Arlington National Cemetery like so many rows of teeth pushing up through the ground. In a few minutes we would be at the airport.

"No," I said. "I left everything in my hotel room." Norrod took some bills from his wallet and passed them to me. A thick sheaf of hundreds.

"Now, Mr. Fargo, there's something you must know," said Norrod.

But I'd heard enough. We had slowed down to about fifteen miles per hour. A lane of the parkway was obstructed by a disabled semi in the right-hand lane about two hundred yards ahead. I stuffed the money into the pocket of my Levi's, opened the car door, and jumped.

The next time you're trapped in a sluggish stream of morning rush hour drivers and you think that you won't be able to tolerate it for another second, try stepping out of your moving vehicle and strolling to work. I was hoping to hit the ground running, as they say, but instead, the ground hit me, real hard, scraping sizable patches of skin from my knees and elbows and forehead, and tearing up my clothes. I struggled to my feet, partially dazed, and ran up the embankment, expecting at any moment to hear the report of small arms fire. Norrod probably wouldn't stoop to such levels, but his chauffeur looked like the kind who carried an Uzi just to impress the ladies.

I reached the top of the embankment, hunkered down behind an abutment, and peeked back down at the highway. The silver Mercedes had continued about a hundred yards down the road, its rear door still open. There was an exit about a quarter of a mile down the road and I assumed that, no doubt, Norrod was on the horn to his chauffeur ordering him to circle back and pick up my trail. *"And this time, no more Mr. Nice Guy, Giacinto,"* Norrod was probably telling him. *"This time we're gonna take him out."*

I started running back toward Washington.

*   *   *

I was sitting in a coffee shop catty-corner from my hotel, working on my third cup of coffee and trying to get up the nerve to sashay into the lobby of my hotel and ask the desk clerk if there'd been any messages for me. Just play the thing with as much sangfroid as I could muster. But things didn't look good for me. If Norrod was telling the truth, I was in a lot of trouble. I decided I needed some outside help.

I paid for my coffee with one of the hundred dollar bills that Norrod had given me or that I had *stolen* from Norrod, depending on your point-of-view (everything I did just seemed to drag me in deeper), which did not endear me to the cashier, who made it very clear to me through the lugubrious manner with which she counted out my change, that I had just about cleaned her out. Imagine her cooperative spirit, then, when I asked her if she could give me a couple of dollars worth of change for the phone. You'd have thought I had asked for her lungs. She would be sure to remember me.

"Oh, yes, officer. He came in about one o'clock this afternoon. I knew there was something wrong with him immediately. He was all bloodied and torn up

and out of breath like he'd just finished raping a few infants, flashing around these new, very large bills, and staring real nervous out the window over there. Yes, officer, he did seem to be real interested in the hotel. He just sat there staring at it for about an hour. Of course I'd be able to identify him..."

I left the coffee shop and walked to a phone booth. Inside, I called Denise's extension at the office, but there was no answer. Then I called Helen G's extension with the same result. Things were not working out.

I decided to call a sportswriter friend of mine at the *Detroit Free Press* named Bill Midwiff. I hadn't spoken with him for months, but when he answered the phone it was as though we talked to each other every day or so. The problem was, he only wanted to talk football.

"Fargo," he said. "You're just the man I wanted to talk to."

The last time I'd talked to him was just before the Super Bowl when he'd given me one of his typically unreliable tips and I had dropped a hundred dollars on the game. Before I could even start to say anything, he was halfway through an explanation of some new betting theory of his.

"...so, you *see*, you forget this home field advantage bullshit. *Especially* on artificial turf. *Especially* the underdog at home. The homedog advantage is a fable, maintained, most likely invented by, oddsmakers and bookies to appeal to sentimental suckers like me and you. If anything, the home team relaxes at home. Relaxes too much, and there's nothing the visiting team likes better than demolishing the local team in front of its own fans."

"Bill," I said, cutting in before the call cost me more than I would be able to afford, in more ways than one, "the goddamn football season doesn't start for two months yet."

"Hey," he said, "that's another thing. The other part of my system is to go through the entire schedule, up to the playoffs, of course, and determine how I'm going to bet *before* the season even starts. And I'm not going to change my mind, no matter who gets hurt, no matter who gets fired, no matter what the point spread. And then, I'm not gonna bet those postseason games at all. Those are for the real suckers. It wouldn't surprise me if every one of those postseason games was fixed, like they had a scenario to follow or something—"

"Bill—"

"But that homedog advantage myth is the real breakthrough—"

"Bill, I need some help and I don't have much time to talk."

"Oh, yeah, sure. Shoot."

I explained that I was doing some research for my job and that I needed some information on the Blessing family.

"I need whatever you can get me in terms of documented history, but I'm particularly interested in any persistent rumors or legends about the family. Maybe you could talk to that gossip columnist you're dating—"

"*Was* dating," said Midwiff. "She hasn't spoken to me since the Derby. I convinced her to put a grand on Bold Ego."

"They named a horse after the national bird?"

"No *Bold Ego*. Rhymes with 'gold.' Shit, I don't know *what* ego rhymes with. You know, Freud, the three divisions of—"

"It's not important. Just see what you can find out for me, will you? I'm calling from out-of-town, uh, New York, and I don't have access to this stuff."

"Okay," said Midwiff. "I'll see what I can dig up. Give me your number and I'll—"

"No, I'll call you," I said. "I mean, I don't know where I'll be for sure."

"It's your money," said Midwiff. "I got about one-twenty. Call me back about three."

Leaving the phone booth, I caught a glimpse of myself in the reflection of the tinted window of an office front. I looked bad. Ripped up and bleeding. This was no way to promenade around the Capitol, mere *yards* from the White House. I'd have police and various other security types dropping down on me within minutes. Besides, Norrod was out there somewhere, looking for me, and I was leaving a trail like a rogue elephant gamboling through a cornfield.

I passed a couple of bars, but they were too public. Clean, well-lighted places full of well dressed businessmen and women lingering over after-lunch martinis and cigarettes, discussing how to eviscerate the competition. I'd stick out in one of those places like a vulture in a hospital nursery.

About three blocks from the coffee shop I came across a topless bar. I peeked in. It looked about right. Dark, all the attention focused on the stage and a meager and anonymous clientele.

I entered the bar and sat at a padded banquette as far as possible from the lights of the stage. I ordered a beer from a staggeringly well-built wait-ress who looked like a slightly anemic Sophia Loren. She wore a modified Victorian maid's costume, the modification providing the opportunity for her breasts to express themselves without restraint. The only thing that spoiled my impression of her was a rather large rent in her black, fishnet stockings, which sort of cheapened the whole effect. But then, what did I want anyway? The place was a dive. Up on stage, one of the Silicone Sisters was going through an unimaginative dance step to some song called "Thirty Days in the Hole," the sort of double entendre that causes spontaneous lesions on the brain.

After the waitress brought me my beer, I went to the restroom to clean up. I was pleasantly surprised to find the men's room almost antiseptically clean. I had anticipated scummy floors, the urinals all stopped up with cigarette butts, toilets stuffed with paper and even worse. But this place looked like an executive washroom, which it probably was.

I cleaned up the blood, dirt, and tiny, embedded pebbles from my wounds and wished that I had a change of clothes. It occurred to me to go buy some, but I didn't want to waste the money, especially since I didn't know when or if I'd be getting any more. I'd brought a thousand dollars with me, but most of that was back in my room, hidden (at least I *hoped* it was still hidden) inside the battery compartment of an inoperable flash-light in my suitcase.

Back in the bar, I finished my beer and ordered another. I watched the entire review of five dancers until the girl that was on stage when I came in climbed back up. Most of the customers had gradually slipped out, so that there were only about six of us diehards left in the bar, and I was feeling more and more conspicuous. I didn't want to call Midwiff from the bar, so I paid the tab and was just about to walk out the door when I spotted an all too familiar silver Mercedes and an even more familiar Latin chauffeur leaning against its fender. He seemed to be looking in my direction, but it was hard to tell.

I did a casual about-face and walked over to the bar. The bartender, a surly looking devil who didn't seem to be the type to tolerate shenanigans, stood behind the bar washing glasses.

"Excuse me," I said. "This is rather embarrassing, but could you tell me if there's another way out of here? You see, I just started to walk out and I saw my wife heading this way—"

"The only way out is through the front door," said the bartender without looking at me. A real sadist.

"There must be an emergency exit or something. I mean, that's code, right?"

"Look, Sweetheart," he said, putting down his glass and leaning forward. His hands were still under the bar, dangerously close, no doubt, to his blackjack or baseball bat, or even worse, his .357 Magnum. "The emergency door is for just that—emergencies. Your problem with your wife don't qualify. So why don't you just leave by the front door and take your lumps like a big boy."

"You don't know my wife," I said. "She's a judge."

Mr. Bartender just stared at me.

"A federal judge," I said.

Nothing.

"A federal judge who would think nothing of padlocking every titty bar in the country just to punish me."

A couple of guys at the bar were taking an interest in our conversation. The bartender hesitated. Obviously, he'd heard about a thousand excuses from as many customers wanting to slither out the back door. But I had raised the ugly specter of official and potent respectability, and, although I couldn't have looked like what any self-respecting member of the judiciary would marry—not even on a perverse impulse—my story was plausible enough to work.

"Go ahead," he snarled. "Just don't take any detours. And don't show your fucking face in here again."

A corridor led to the rear exit. On the way I passed the dressing room of the dancers, the door of which was open. The girls were sitting around smoking. When they saw me an almost imperceptible change came over them. An instant before, they had been relaxed, unselfconscious. Now they were alert, their postures and expressions signaling a combination of eagerness and tension, as though they had a reflex for displaying themselves. Clearly, the real performances took place backstage.

Once out, I walked quickly down the alley until it emptied into the street. I went into the first drugstore I came to and called Midwiff.

"Where do you want to start?" he asked. "If that family doesn't get into the newspaper once a week, they try just that much harder the next week."

"Just give me what you've got."

"Well, Draper Blessing was a German immigrant and a late bloomer. His real name is Arnold, by the way. Draper's his mother's maiden name and his middle name. I guess he didn't like Arnold. He was basically anonymous until the age of fifty-one, when he patented some part for automobile transmissions. It made him a gazillionaire. He built his own manufacturing company from scratch. It's listed on the New York Stock Exchange. He married when he was fifty-six, a Leona Calvin, a would-be hoofer from New York. They had two children. One kid, Benjamin, died accidentally on a skiing trip to Squaw Valley in 1961. The younger son, Victor, died about four or five years ago—a drowning. He fell asleep in a swimming pool. Drugs and alcohol were apparently involved."

"Are you sure about that?"

"That's what I got. I haven't verified any of this."

"Then the body must have been recovered."

"Sooner or later. I mean, did you ever see what happens when something that big gets caught in your filter?"

"Okay, okay."

"There's also an adopted kid—a Mexican. Draper died about two years ago at the age of ninety-six. From all accounts, he was still lucid, not to say cunning, right up to the end, and there was a good deal of controversy and litigation over the will, which is still pending. His widow is still alive, but she's reportedly suffering from an advanced case of lung cancer. The heir apparent is the adopted Mexican. His name is Miguel." Midwiff paused.

"Is that all?"

"That's the public record," said Midwiff. "But Elaine tells me the family's riddled with scandal. There were persistent rumors, as you call them, about Miguel's parentage, first of all. I guess the old man couldn't keep it in his pants, even in his old age. Legend has it that his progeny are scattered all over the country and a few other countries as well. Of course, that happens when a rich man dies, but there's supposedly some truth to this. Then there was some irregularity in the death of Benjamin. I didn't have time to find out exactly what it was, but there was some grab-ass involved with his brother and some friend of the family named Stonestreet. And then there's the case of Claude Nickle."

"Who's Claude Nickle?"

"That's a good question. Back in the late sixties, he was writing an informal history of the great families of Detroit. So the story goes, he came upon something while doing some unauthorized research on the Blessing family. It seems that one way or the other he was paid off. Nobody's heard from him since 1968. He just dropped off the face of the earth."

"Any family or friends?"

"None that are talking. The Phantom Biographer. Oo-oo-oo-oo-oo."

I was getting impatient. Norrod and his chauffeur were probably even now prowling the streets. Midwiff's feeble attempts at humor came off as distinctly juvenile. It wasn't his fault, of course, but it irritated me that he wasn't treating this whole affair with the gravity that it required.

"Can you tell me anything else? ?

He told me a few more things that I already knew about Victor and Florence.

"Oh, I almost forgot again," he said. "I got a call from Valerie yesterday." Valerie was my ex-wife. She and Midwiff had been friends in college when I'd met both of them. "She was trying to get in touch with you. It sounded urgent. Nobody seemed to know where you were except for one of the secretaries where you work. But she said that you'd gone to visit your ex-wife. Obviously, she was misinformed. Where the hell did you say you were? New York?"

"Uh, yeah. Val have anything else to say?"

"Yeah. She's gonna be in town tomorrow. I'm picking her up at the airport. You gonna be back by then?"

"I'll try," I said. "Look, I gotta go. I'll call you tomorrow at home. What time is Val getting in?"

"Ten-thirty. We should be back by noon."

"I'll be talking to you," I said. Then I hung up. I asked the clerk at the counter how to get to the bus station. Then I just about crept out the door of the drugstore. The silver Mercedes was nowhere in sight.

CHAPTER 13

▼

HOMEDOG

The bus ride to Detroit was about as exciting as you could imagine an overnight, thirteen-hour tour of the industrial heartland of America to be. I had to transfer three times—in Pittsburgh, Cleveland, and Toledo of all places. On the first two stops, I bought identical vending machine sandwiches, cellophane-skinned numbers with roast beef slices as filmy as onionskin, and three cups of coffee that tasted like it had been flushed through several radiators. I decided to pass on the food while waiting to transfer in Toledo.

Throughout the ride I was tired and cramped up. All my organs seemed to have shut down except for my brain, and that was functioning erratically, like a light bulb *in extremis.*

I passed the entire ride seated next to a pharmaceutical salesman from Windsor who'd been to a convention in Washington. He seemed to be a lonely and bitter little man. He looked like a man who suffered from a fierce and chronic case of heartburn. He wasn't at all gregarious, but he did engage me in low-key conversation during the first part of our journey,

probably because I was the only one of the fifteen or so passengers in our
train that looked more miserable than he did.

We got into a discussion of the merits of riding the bus as opposed to
other means of transportation. I explained to him that I couldn't endure
flying unless it was absolutely necessary—and that I could only do it then
under the influence of sedatives and alcohol, often in near lethal combina-
tions. He explained that he enjoyed riding the bus—especially the longer
trips—because of the extended, enforced confinement, which allowed him
the opportunity to pursue his avocation. He was, he explained, compiling a
dictionary. He told me that he had been working on it sporadically for ten
years. He was working alphabetically and very selectively. That is, it was a
very idiosyncratic document, at least as far as it went, which was up to the
letter M. He showed me his latest entry, which he had written in an incon-
gruously round and florid script in a small spiral notebook. The entry read:
"Marriage: the moral equivalent of _____."

"I haven't decided what it's the moral equivalent of yet," he said. "But I'm
sure it's the moral equivalent of something. It'll come to me." He opened his
attaché case, extracted a sheaf of yellowing manuscript, and offered it to me.
I leafed through the pages. Most of the entries were standard words, even if
the definitions weren't.

Under "Eat," for example, he had written the following definition: "To
introduce substances into the oral cavity in order to prevent their appropriation by others." Following "Enthusiasm," he had written: "The
process of cooling the body by exposing it to ridicule."

But sprinkled throughout the manuscript were coinages of the author's
(whose name, according to the title page, was Ambrose Jensen). One of
these coinages nearly paralyzed me. The word was "Homedog," which
Jensen had defined simply as "A masochist."

"Did you know that this is also a gambling term?" I asked, pointing to
the word.

"What?"

"Homedog. It's sort of a portmanteau word. It refers to the phenomenon, in football at least, whereby the underdog playing on his home field is supposed to be a good bet, other things being equal. I was just discussing this very thing with a friend of mine earlier today."

"My definition of the term derives from an experience of my childhood," he said, staring off into his past. "When I was seven years old, my father bought me a dog. It wasn't home with us more than two days before my father began to mistreat it savagely. I've often thought since that he bought it as a surrogate for me. My mother always forbade him to strike me. I soon found this abuse of the dog so despicable that I would take it for long walks and abandon it. As cruel as it sounds, it was much better than my father's brutality. But no matter how far away I deposited that dog, it would always somehow manage to find its way home. And the first person it would run to, or cringe to, I should say, was my father, who would promptly beat it for running away. My father eventually killed the dog one night with a sickle. He was drunk. He nearly decapitated the wretched animal. Then my father cried like a baby and vowed to get another dog the next day. But by then my mother had had enough. She threatened to turn him over to the police if he got another dog. It didn't make any difference anyway, since my father died himself about six months after that. So that's how I came up with the term 'homedog.'"

Jensen had related these events in the dispassionate style of a trained observer who had been investigating reports of cruelty to animals for forty years. A moment later I sneaked a look at his definition for "Father." It consisted of one word: "Fertilizer."

The bus rolled into the cavernous Greyhound terminal at about eight-thirty in the morning. It was Decision Time. My options, however, were limited. First, although it took me a few seconds to realize it, it was Sunday. The streets were nearly deserted. That meant I wouldn't be able to downshift into anonymity by blending in with the crowd. If I hung around the desolate landscape of the city, I'd be forced to suffer the high-voltage anxiety of conspicuousness, and there was no telling how many APBs were out on me—official and otherwise—no telling how many lenses I was being magnified through, no telling how many high-velocity projectiles were waiting for me to get open, even now as I moved east along Jefferson Avenue. I had already decided to go it on foot; Hollywood had taught me what marvelous sources of information cab drivers were and, in any event, the possibility of even spotting a taxi just out cruising in Detroit on a Sunday morning was nonexistent. It's not a taxi city even on weekdays.

I walked swiftly through the warehouse district, parallel to the Detroit River. And, in fact, in the direction of the Blessing homestead. I realized this with a start, but I didn't even break stride.

Something was happening to me. During my years as an academic, I had cultivated prudence; I had disciplined myself to observe caution. But now (and indeed since the beginning of the whole confusing Blessing affair) I was relying more and more on impulse, surrendering myself almost gratefully to instinct. It was perhaps not the wisest course of action for a man in my perilous situation, such as I perceived it, but it had the advantage of unpredictability. I comforted myself with the notion that if I didn't know what I was going to do next, it wasn't likely that anyone else did.

There were few people out and about. Occasionally I would see some derelict staggering hyperbolically through an alleyway or supine on some stoop. Almost every bum that I saw seemed to be dressed for a blizzard, even though it was a mild mid-July morning, so mild in fact that I could already feel drops of perspiration sliding down my back. And although my pace was steady, it certainly wasn't strenuous. It was just going to be hot.

Besides the bums, the only people I encountered, at least for the first half-hour or so of my hike, were occasional pairs or trios of young black men who never looked at each other directly even when their conversations were animated. Instead, they gave their ear to their interlocutors and their eyes to the horizon, alert to potential menace. They reminded me of the first furtive residents to emerge from their homes after an overnight occupation of the city, like during the Detroit riots in 1967. Years of mistrust of authority had conditioned *them* to their vigilant social posture. I had been exposed to that pressure for only about two days and already I was comporting myself about as subtly as a drum major with Saint Vitus' Dance. I began to understand, a bit, the importance of "cool."

It was a long walk from the barren heart of downtown to the pseudo-bucolic splendor of Grosse Pointe Shores and the Blessing residence—a good eight or nine miles and a couple of cultural light-years—and it took me the better part of two hours to cover it. When I finally got to the wrought iron gate of the house, the omens of hospitality that had lured me into the house on my only other visit were gone. The gate was chained and padlocked, and a sign bolted to the gate warned potential trespassers that they would be prosecuted, assuming, of course, that they survived the blitz of the "Vicious Attack Dogs" that were allegedly patrolling the grounds. I couldn't see the house or garage, both of which were obscured by the hedge and fountain. I *could* see that the fountain still wasn't working.

I walked along the fence that enclosed the north side of the property. This side of the house had denser foliage so that the eight-foot-high fence was nearly hidden from the street. They don't take too kindly to nosy loiterers in Grosse Pointe Shores, Michigan. This side of the house also had the advantage of being hedgeless. At various points along the route, I peeked in looking for dogs, but all I saw were squirrels. And since I had never yet seen a dog of even playful disposition let a squirrel go about its business unharassed, I concluded (albeit lacking the sort of conviction that instills confidence) that the warning sign was probably a bluff.

There were no breaches in the fence, but at one point a maple tree grew close enough to the fence to allow me to climb it and drop from a branch to the fairways of the Blessing estate. I was on the side of the house where the sandblasters had been working three days earlier when I had visited Leona. To my left I could see a trellis leading from a rose garden to a greenhouse that seemed to adjoin the rear of the house. The trellis was covered with vines and looked like a much safer route than a hundred-yard sprint to the house across open terrain—especially if there *were* dogs.

I crept along the fence, all the time looking for dog droppings and listening for the telltale tinkle of choke collars and dog tags until I reached the grapeleaf-canopied trellis. Once in the tunnel I felt relatively secure, camouflaged as I was by the fabric of leaves. I had proceeded about halfway down the tunnel when I stopped dead in my tracks. There it was. A definite tinkle. Some noiseless Doberman had no doubt gotten wind of me. I could already imagine my jugular splashing its contents all over the bright green lawn. Well, as I say, I was motionless, but I was nearly lurching forward rhythmically with the force of my heart beating. I mean to say I was scared.

But my heartbeat wasn't the only rhythm within my awareness. I could hear a soft moaning—a decidedly erotic moaning—not the moan of a dog-bite victim. The sound came from my left, from the rear of the property. I couldn't see anything through the grape leaves, so with enough caution and deliberation to put an angry cobra to sleep, I moved my arm to the wall and pushed aside a leaf or two so that I could see.

An empty tennis court occupied the northeast quarter of the back yard. The entire rear area of the grounds was enclosed by the hedge. Except for the tennis court, the landscape was commendably free of ornamentation. No treacherous Japanese gardens, no plastic shrines of the Madonna posted in the middle of the yard like a miniature scarecrow in drag, no potbellied Bacchine, no fin-de-siecle mazes. I saw only one of those tiny oriental trees—apparently in late bloom, since it was covered in pale, pink, fleshy petals—and a birdbath. The only immediate sign of life in the backyard was a few boisterous sparrows at the bath, chirping and splashing around, as happy as a reunion of aunts at a bridal shower. This was my second indication that bloodthirsty hounds weren't on the prowl. My third indication came when I realized where all the tinkling and moaning was coming from. In the obscure angle of the hedge opposite the tennis court, a young couple lay on a blanket—that is, a young lady was lying on the blanket—a young man was lying energetically on the young lady.

The tinkle came from a collection of chains and trinkets that dangled from the neck of the young man. The moans issued from his partner. They were a couple of remarkable specimens. Blonde, bronzed, and well developed (from what I could see of them), they seemed to have been airlifted in from Malibu for the pornographic diversion of the upper class…like life-size, animated knickknacks. Besides his jewelry, the young man wore only his white sweatsocks and tennis shoes. The girl seemed to have undressed (or to have *been* undressed) with a bit more deliberation, since she was completely nude. Nevertheless, the unceremonious scattering of her tennis apparel about the yard, including a bra hanging like a limp parachute from the side of the hedge, testified to the urgency of their passion.

I watched while the young man's buttocks contracted a few more times. Then the girl locked her legs around his waist and he shivered through his climax and rolled off her with all the class of a drunk falling off a park bench. They lay on their backs, their chests heaving. They seemed generally nonthreatening.

I walked back down the tunnel and emerged from it, strolling in the direction of the lovers as casually as You-Know-Who stepping among the flora and fauna of his prelapsarian demesne.

The girl noticed me first, but she didn't react much. She simple lifted her head from the blanket and shaded her eyes to get a better look at me.

"We're not alone," she said to her friend, who made up in alacrity what he lacked in poise. He was on his feet and into his tennis shorts so fast that it seemed he'd anticipated such an intrusion. The girl noticed this, too, and didn't appear to appreciate his lack of gallantry. She showed her disapproval by unhurriedly getting to her feet and going through a very sensuous process of shaking fresh grass clippings from her hair and brushing them from her body. She was stunningly beautiful and I found myself only partially aware that the guy was talking to me.

"…but we never made it, to the tennis court I mean," he was saying. "We were just so overwhelmed by how awesome the morning was that we just couldn't help but take advantage of it. Right, Hon?"

I didn't look to see if Hon confirmed this. If I was going to keep a clear head, I was going to have to wait until she got some clothes on. Besides, if further testimony was necessary, I was there to say that they certainly had made the most of it.

"I don't see why you're being so apologetic about it, Randy," said Hon. "He's the one who's trespassing."

I looked at her *now*, and she looked right back at me, defiant. Randy was just looking at me now. His girlfriend had sown a seed of doubt in his mind—I could see suspicion creeping slowly across his features—but his was not a fertile mind, and the doubt was slow in taking root. I saw my opportunity.

"My name's Hugo Demuth," I said, trying to sound like Robert Stack. I wondered how many times I was going to try to get away with impersonating poor Hugo, and I immediately began to panic just a bit. I had only tried once before, with little success. "I'm an investigator with Sultana Investigations. The Blessings are clients of the agency."

"Oh, hey, sure," said Randy. "I heard Miguel mention the name. Sultana, I mean." He turned to his girlfriend, smiling and nodding, but she didn't look convinced. And I had to admit that anyone with more than coffee grounds for brains wouldn't be. I looked more like someone who was one jump ahead of the bloodhounds than an investigator.

Randy stepped forward to introduce himself.

"The name's Randy Atlas," he said, shaking my hand. I thought about what his hands had been doing only moments before. "And this," he said, gesturing toward his mate, "is my main lady, Randi."

He flashed me an impish smile, just begging me to say something precious about the coincidence of their names. But I was in no mood to humor him. Christ, he'd probably been through this hundreds of times and thoroughly enjoyed each episode, whereas anyone with the least amount of sense would have never embarked on a relationship based on such an absurdity. Finally, he could contain himself no longer.

"It's the same name, get it? Randy and Randi. Only hers is with an i." He was absolutely beaming. To her credit, Randi didn't share his enormous satisfaction. She had the good sense to be just a little embarrassed by the whole thing.

"Randy," she said, "could I talk to you for a second?" They huddled for a moment or two. I could tell that Randi with the i was doing most of the talking.

The conference over, Randy shuffled towards me. He was clearly troubled.

"Look, mister," he said, "I'm kinda keeping an eye on the place while Miguel's taking care of the arrangements. I mean, you gotta understand that I've got a responsibility here." He glanced back at Randi to get her approval for his remarks. She just stared back at him without changing her expression. "So you can understand," Randy continued, "if I gotta ask you for some I.D., right?"

"I suppose so," I said. "But I could ask the same of you. Perhaps we should ask Mrs. Blessing. I'm prepared to let her vouch for my credentials. On the other hand, the way you keep watch over the place suggests that you may be a bit too, uh, easily distracted."

"Hey, really, we got permission."

"Randy, if he works for Mrs. Blessing, ask him why he doesn't know she's dead," said Randi.

Well, now I was on the spot. This was clearly no bluff. Midwiff had told me that Leona had lung cancer and I remembered her wracking cough. I also remembered that I was in some pretty messy trouble because I had accepted Leona's errand partly, of course, for the generous fee, but also partly out of my compassion for and awe of the woman. Now Miguel was the only person who knew about it that could clear me if anything got sticky. And the way people seemed to be dying off, I hoped that Miguel, as formidable as he was, was taking care of himself.

"I just saw Mrs. Blessing Thursday," I said.

"Well, unless your gaze confers immortality," said Randi, "I don't see how that makes any difference."

"Look," I said. "I think we can clear this up. I was hired by Mrs. Blessing on a private matter. Miguel knows all about it. Just ask him. I just got in from Washington about two hours ago. I was traveling incommunicado. I had no way of knowing Mrs. Blessing had died."

"Oh, you're *Fargo*," said Randy.

"Right! Stephen Fargo. Sorry about that little masquerade. I wasn't sure who I was dealing with and Mrs. Blessing and Miguel had charged me with absolute confidentiality in this matter. Miguel must have told you about me then, huh?"

"Yeah," said Randy. Then a look of concern clouded his face. He turned to look at Randi again. She gave him no help this time. I had apparently come clean enough to satisfy her. She sat down on the lawn and began lacing up her tennis shoes. Randy turned his attention to me once again.

"I know how to get in touch with Miguel," he said. "He's taking care of the funeral arrangements and everything, but he told me to contact him if you showed up." Randy looked at me for a moment. The look of consternation hadn't entirely left his face. He was clearly troubled. I was beginning to feel uneasy myself.

"Why don't you ask Mr. Fargo in?" said Randi, after a sigh that nearly stirred her boyfriend's locks. She was exasperated with him, but she was doing her best to control it. Identifying myself had resulted in a marked change in their behavior toward me—especially Randi's. They were being transparently cordial. "Maybe he'd like to clean up," she said when Randy failed to take the cue on her first suggestion.

For the first time, Randy seemed to ascertain my condition, as though he hadn't been aware of how I looked prior to Randi pointing it out. I must have looked a sight, too. Ripped up and scabbed over from my floor exercise on the George Washington Parkway, rumpled and unkempt from my overnight bus trip, cadaverous from lack of sleep and my eight-mile hike on an empty stomach, not to mention my psychological strain.

"Yeah," said Randy, really taken with the idea now. "Yeah, why don't you come in and shower off and have a cup of herbal tea, or, hey, we got some great papaya juice. And while you're doing that I'll call Miguel."

Well, if he was really going to call Miguel, his invitation was acceptable. I needed a shower at least, and I didn't know how safe it would be to return to my apartment. On the other hand, I still didn't trust him. Really, I didn't trust *her*. She might convince him to call the police. And I didn't want to talk to *them* until I'd had a chance to talk to Miguel. I had to sort a few things out, and with Leona dead, Miguel was the only one who could help me. Nevertheless, since Barbie and Ken here seemed to be my only safe lead to Miguel, I had little choice.

"Sure," I said. "Lead the way."

I accepted the offer of the shower, the fresh towel, even the loan of a pair of khaki slacks and shirt from both genders of Randy with as much graciousness as I could. But it wasn't easy. The whole scenario was pre-posterous. They had no reason to invite me, a total stranger, into a house that not only wasn't theirs, but over which they were supposed to be alert to just such an intrusion. But was it an intrusion? Randy had said that he was watching the place for Miguel. But, Jesus, they were the unlikeliest security one could imagine.

Of course, once inside the house, I could see that there wasn't much risk in offering me this hospitality, because, even if I had been a thief, I'd find slim pickings here. Everything had been removed, assuming that there had been anything in the first place. I remembered the sparseness and austerity of the furnishings that I had noticed during my first visit a few days earlier and my speculation at the time that the mansion was being vacated. Now I could see only the kitchen and part of a larger room that appeared to be the den as I passed through on my way to the bath-room following Randy's lead. Except for the larger appliances such as the stove and refrigerator and a few pieces of Shaker furniture, I saw nothing that would indicate that the home was being occupied on a permanent basis. In fact, the only indications of any occupation at all were cans of diet soda stacked in the corner of the kitchen and the remnants of a twelve-hour-old Burger King entrée. No doubt the beauty secret of the Randies—Whoppers and herbal tea.

The bathroom Randy led me to wasn't lavish, but it had the advantage of being at ground level and of having one of those frosted glass windows that latched from the inside. I took off my clothes and put on Randy's khakis, which were about a size too big, but otherwise very comfortable indeed. I even felt kind of guerilla chic. Then I turned on the shower at full volume, locked the bathroom door, and, after struggling for a moment with the window latch, which apparently hadn't been used for decades, hoisted myself through the window and dropped to the lawn. Upon hitting the ground, I wished that I had remembered to take a leak.

Windows weren't a dominant feature of the Blessing Mansion. They seemed to have been allowed for only grudgingly. The one I finally found myself peering through to get a look into the house was a composite of triangular lenses crosshatched with lead fittings, so that I had a sort of fly's eye perspective on the activity taking place in the house. I was looking into the den or study that I had passed by on my way to the bathroom. Randy and Randi were sitting opposite each other at a desk. Randy was seated at the desk proper and was talking on the telephone. Randy's end of the discussion was animated, full of shrugs, heavy nodding, and other extravagant gestures. Randi was watching him with a look of disdain. When Randy hung up the phone, Randi started in on him. They argued heatedly for two or three minutes, the last minute of which was taken up by a stern lecture from Randi. After that they sat in silence for another couple of minutes. Then Randi said something to her boyfriend and he got up with a petulant flourish and left the room. Another minute or so passed. Suddenly, Randi, obviously responding to a call from her mate, jumped up and also left the room in a big rush. My disappearance had been discovered.

It was only a matter of time before they determined my means of egress. Even Randy wouldn't take more than an hour or so to figure that out. My cue to relocate.

This time stealth was out of the question. Some voice of reason in me urged me to flight. But my curiosity had been aroused by that strange expression of perplexity on Randy's face out in the backyard and by the pantomime I had observed in the den. Something told me there was an opportunity to learn something here. And, besides, where was I going to go?

Well, I had to go somewhere—fast. Preferably someplace on the grounds where I could watch what was going on around the house unobserved. I looked around for a likely hiding place and began to regret the lack of ornamentation. I crept along the wall toward the front of the house just in time to see Randy burst through the front door and sprint past the fountain and down the driveway toward the gate. Maybe his huge leap to a conclusion was my opportunity. Maybe he and Randi had assumed that I had intended to make a complete escape. Maybe I should have. Maybe they knew more than I did. Maybe they thought I knew more than I did, too. Maybe I could crouch there petrified with speculation until I was as vulnerable as one of those statues of black footmen at the entrance of the grounds.

I retraced my steps to the window and peeked in again. This time it was Randi's turn to use the phone. Her style was less demonstrative than her boyfriend's, but there seemed to be something tense in her conversation, too. She was standing—and doing a lot of nodding. With the twisted logic of the chaotic mind, I decided I'd like to hear some of her conversation. And the only way to do that was to get back into the house.

I slid back to the bathroom window and pushed it ever so slightly, hoping that in his haste, or stupidity, Randy had neglected to latch it. He had. I had to pull myself through the window, the bottom of which was about at eye level, and at a critical point about halfway through I had some difficulty, but I managed to get in without too much clamor. I don't think I could have roused more than a roomful of corpses with the entire maneuver.

Randy had at least thought to turn the water off. But the room was still steamy, even though the door was half-open. In that foggy atmosphere, like a Hollywood version of heaven, the sound of Randi's voice came through as pure mumble. I might as well have been trying to pick up a ghost rehearsing a conspiracy. I finally heard the receiver rattle back into its cradle and then the receding squeak of tennis shoes.

I stuck about a millimeter of my nose into the hallway and held my breath. When nothing happened, I stuck my head out, hoping nobody would attack it. But nobody was around. I tiptoed through the den to the huge room where I had had my interview with Leona Blessing. Beyond that, through the wide-open front entrance, I could see Randi walking past the fountain in lukewarm pursuit of Golden Boy.

I did the express tour of the main areas of the house. I even jogged upstairs through the bedrooms. Except for an occasional isolated piece of furniture, the place was about as homey as a deserted gymnasium. On my way back to the staircase, I noticed from the window that the Randies had stationed themselves at the entrance of the driveway. They were apparently waiting for someone, most likely the folks at the other end of the phone calls.

I decided that right where I was was as good a place as any to stay for the moment. I had a commanding view of the front of the house, and would have the advantage of any hostile raiding parties approaching. And they weren't likely to search upstairs if they thought I'd already escaped.

I watched Randy use the side of the kiosk for a footrest while he tied his shoe. There was something very wrong about his occupying the Blessing mansion and it went beyond the obvious facts of his incompetence and vacuity. It had more to do with a sense of style, perhaps giving rise to an even more fundamental incongruity. Randy was physically capable of discouraging intruders, but he and his girlfriend exuded your basic California tradition-is-as-old-as-the-latest-trend mentality. The whole setup was too casual for Grosse Pointe, especially for the House of Blessing. It disregarded too much protocol.

As I stood observing the agents of this impropriety, a car pulled up to the gate, which Randy promptly opened. The car rolled just inside the gate and stopped. Randy walked around to the passenger side of the car and leaned in to talk to one of the occupants. A few seconds later, the car started to move again towards the house, with Randy following along behind it. The other Randi seemed reluctant to accompany the group. She hung back at the gate, as though she were still waiting for someone. The riders in the car seemed to notice this, because the car stopped and Randy hustled over to the passenger window again. A second later, he gestured to Randi, who took another quick look up the road, then turned to follow the car.

I stood by the window long enough to get a glimpse of the two men emerging from the car after they had parked it. One of them was a smallish man with a bald dome and a heavy black beard. The other man was much taller, with reddish brown hair in tight ringlets and very pale skin. They were both dressed in bulky sweat suits, which seemed a little odd, given the heat. I couldn't remember seeing either of them before. I left the window and returned to the head of the stairs where I crouched and waited for the party to start.

It was a short and very grim party.

I heard about a minute's worth of low conversation, none of which I could make out. Then I heard a sharp popping sound, followed by a quick scream from Randi, which was cut short by another pop. Then there was a pause and two more sharp cracks resounded through the desolate house in quick succession.

I was too stunned to move a muscle. I could hear activity downstairs. Some more muffled conversation, the sound of something being dragged across the floor. Then I heard the sound of someone going in and out of the house. Then there was silence for a moment or two. Suddenly, I heard the sound of car doors slamming shut and an engine starting up. I crept to the window, sticking my right eye in the corner of it just in time to see the car drive down the driveway, past the gate and turn left into the street. There didn't seem to be anyone in the backseat of the car.

I waited for a couple of minutes, then cautiously walked downstairs.

The house was deserted. I looked around for signs of the atrocity that I had overheard, but there were none. No bodies, no blood—nothing to indicate that anything out of the ordinary had taken place, let alone a brutal double murder.

Then the shakes came, and the lightheadedness and nausea. I felt no emotion at all, so that it was just like a bad physical reaction, a simple nervous response. I ran to the bathroom heaving, but there was nothing in my stomach to vomit up. After a while, I staggered back into the main room, only to find myself standing once again in the line of fire of a handgun. It was nickel-plated. I'd met it before. And its handler.

"My God, Stephen," said Joanna. "What happened?"

CHAPTER 14

▼

REUNIONS

"Where's Randi?" she asked without waiting for me to answer her first question.

"What are you doing here?" I asked.

"I got a call..."

"From Randi?"

"Yes."

"Why did Randi call *you*? Where do you know her from?"

"Stephen, where *is* she?"

We weren't communicating well, but then again, that gun was still between us. She hadn't learned anything about handgun etiquette since I'd last seen her. And just what was the deal with her and that gun? Had she ever fired it? Did she brandish it everywhere she went, like a fashion accessory? Did she actually take it on flights with her? Was that even legal? Nevertheless, notwithstanding the irritation that the gun caused, it was somehow comforting to learn that she had talked to Randi, who, at the time of the arrival of the assassins, had not seemed overjoyed about it.

"Do you have a car?" I asked.

"Yes," she said. She looked around the room, perhaps hoping that Randi would suddenly materialize out of one of the back rooms.

"Randi's gone," I said. I didn't want to express my worst fears while she still had the business end of that piece pointed at my center of mass. Who knew? Maybe she responded to tragic news with spontaneous twitching of the fingers.

"Come on. I'll explain in the car."

Joanna took the news about Randi badly. Badly enough that she had to pull over to the side of Lakeshore Drive to compose herself. But even with the car stopped, its nose pointed in the direction of the tranquil blue basin of Lake St.Clair, her hands never left the wheel—in fact, they gripped it more tightly—and she continued to stare straight ahead, as though she were waiting for some phantom traffic light to change so she could plunge the car into the lake.

She kept asking me if I was sure about things. About the gunfire, about the screams, about the sound of bodies being dragged across the floor. And I kept saying, no, I wasn't *sure*. But I think we were both sure.

"I wish you had *seen* something," she said after a long pause. I knew what she meant. It was not a matter of perversity, but of needing confirmation. It just sounded strange, as though having witnessed the massacre, I would have been able to provide a more gruesome account of it. I didn't have the heart to tell her what she was probably already aware of anyway—that if I had seen anything, I probably wouldn't be around to tell her about it.

"Do you know what Randi was working on for the Society?" I asked Joanna. It wasn't much of a guess, really. Something in Randi's demeanor—even her promiscuity—had reminded me of Joanna, although I hadn't noticed it until I had seen Joanna again. I wondered if all the Daughters of Trent had this nearly indefinable attribute—something to do with the paradoxical impulses toward loyalty and defiance, devotion and irreverence. Maybe that same contradiction had something to do with Minerva Hewitt's death.

Joanna wasn't quite ready to commit herself, even though it was clear to me from her reaction that I had hit the mark. "I think I told you that none of us knows the other members of the Society," she said coldly.

"Yes, but you also said that you'd run into some of the other members on occasion."

Joanna finally looked at me. "I can do without the interrogation right now, Stephen," she said. "Randi was a friend. Whether or not she was a member of the Society, or a member of the Girl Scouts for that matter, hardly has a bearing on anything."

I looked out across the lake. A few sailboats sat on the horizon like crisp moths. A young couple all done up in designer jogging gear and mono-grammed sweat bands trotted by, accompanied, in the desultory fashion of all dogs, by their Irish Setter, stopping every ten feet or so to piss against a tree or to sniff at something invisible—a lover of distraction—then charging off at full speed to catch up with and outstrip his plodding masters, a streak of pure exuberance. People should learn how to exercise from their pets, I thought. Or from children. I remembered how my father used to take my brother and me to the beach when we were kids, and how he used to shout *Go!* to us so that we could race in our bathing suits and bare feet over the soft pavement of wet sand. I suddenly wished that my brother and my father were there right now so we could do it again. But they were both dead. Christ, everybody was dying.

"I suppose we'll have to go to the police," I said. I had no intention of doing so, but I wanted to see how Joanna would react. After all, Randi was *her* friend.

"I suppose," she said without enthusiasm. But she made no move to start the car.

"What was Randi doing here—in the Blessing house?"

"I don't know."

"Why was she hanging around with a moron like Atlas?"

"I don't *know*," she said with a bit more of an edge.

"Then you did know her boyfriend?"

"I'd met him. And boyfriend is hardly the appropriate word."

"Lover?"

Joanna shot me a withering glare, as though I had just suggested barbe-cued kindergartners for brunch.

"Whatever Randi was doing 'hanging around with Atlas' as you call it, I'm sure she had her reasons," Joanna said. It hit me then. Randi and Joanna were lovers.

"Or Norrod's reasons," I suggested. "Did Norrod give you any instruc-tions concerning me?"

"Of course not. I haven't spoken to him since I last saw you."

"Did you know that he personally tried to deport me the day after you left?"

"No."

"Did you ever hear of a man named Hugo Demuth?"

"No."

"Haskell Stonestreet?"

"No!"

"Have you ever met any of the Blessings—other than Florence?"

"No. Stephen, I've already told you everything I know. Randi called me because she wanted not to be alone if certain friends of Randy's showed up. That's all she told me."

"How did she know you were in town?"

"I live here" she said.

"You never told me that."

"You never asked."

"Did she say she was afraid of these visitors she was expecting? I mean, did you get the impression that she thought her life was in danger?"

"No," said Joanna slowly. The effort to recollect her conversation with Randi, to detect significant nuances or subtleties that had escaped her at the time, showed on her face. "It seemed more like a nuisance," she finally concluded. "I got the impression that I was rescuing her from a tedious bout of entertaining Randy's boring friends."

Anything but boring, I thought. Or friendly. I described to Joanna the two men I had seen entering the house with Randy, but, as I expected, she claimed not to know them. This whole Gestapo routine had exhausted me. I lay back against the seat and thought about how hungry I was. Joanna started the car, jerked the gearshift lever into reverse, and backed the car out onto Lakeshore Drive. In another moment, we were cruising past the Grosse Pointe Yacht Club.

"Do you want me to drop you at the police station?" Joanna asked.

Something pertinent about the yacht club had just about crystallized in my mind when Joanna's question shattered the conception.

"Don't you want to come with me?"

"I don't see why," said Joanna. "I'm not a witness to anything." Her irony was not lost on me. Technically, I wasn't a witness to anything either.

"She was *your* friend," I protested.

"There are other ways of dealing with these matters," she said. "I've never yet met a cop with any real intelligence or sympathy." The way she said it suggested that she'd had some experience with the police. I wondered if she was talking about Norrod when she spoke of 'other ways,' but I decided I had interrogated her enough.

"In that case," I said, "can you give me a ride to my apartment?"

"No problem," she said.

With one index finger, she swung the car into a U-turn and we were headed back towards downtown Detroit. Within fifteen minutes we were pulling up to the curb in front of my apartment building. Joanna didn't bother to park and when I didn't get out of the car, she raised an eyebrow at me.

"Uh, if you're not in too much of a hurry," I said, "would you mind parking it up the street for a few minutes?"

Joanna shrugged, drove about a half block up the street and expertly tucked the car up against the curb between a metalflake van and a Volkswagen Beetle painted to look like a Kool cigarette ad. I twisted around in my seat to keep an eye on the entrance to my apartment building.

The building had been converted from a hotel, and although there were several exits, only the front door officially allowed entrance into the building. There was a fold-up fire escape on the north side of the building, but it was inaccessible to anyone at ground level. The only other possible means of entrance was a service elevator at the end of a small loading dock at the rear of the building. It was used infrequently now, usually when moving furniture into and out of the building, and opening it from the outside required a key. Once inside the building, however, one could operate it with the mere touch of a button. In fact, since my apartment was near the back of the building, I made frequent use of this elevator, which was sturdier and less temperamental than the regular elevator, the old-fashioned bird cage type, which I had always thought allowed a bit too much exposure for a proper elevator.

I could feel Joanna's eyes on me.

"I suppose you think I'm being melodramatic," I said, not taking my eyes off the building.

"I think you have a flair for intrigue," said Joanna. She sounded almost amused.

"And I suppose you now doubt my account of what happened to your friend."

"I didn't at first. You shocked me into accepting it. And I don't *doubt* you, even now. I just wonder if you might not have misinterpreted the whole thing."

"Do me a favor," I said, trying to ignore her. "Drive around to the back of the building, would you?" Since I had a key to the service elevator, I decided to use it. The manager, who had given me the key, was very big on building security and had asked me not to abuse the privilege of the rear entrance. But, hell, this was an emergency.

It became even more of an emergency once we got around the back of the building. There was the car, backed up to the loading dock.

"Pull it over there behind the fence," I said, pointing to the boundary of the building's parking lot and the alley. Joanna obeyed with a monumental sigh. No sooner had she parked the car than the elevator doors parted and the two men emerged walking abreast. They had changed their clothes. In the place of sweats, each now wore a suit.

"That's them."

"Who?"

"The men who did whatever they did to your friend. They must have thought I'd go straight home. They probably think I'm driving."

"I suppose they're after you, too," said Joanna. "That's the reason for all the cloak-and-dagger, right?" Her tone was unmistakably ironic. I didn't bother to answer her.

The tall redhead got behind the wheel and waited while his buddy threw a bag of some sort into the trunk. He then climbed into the passenger side and the car moved off.

I noted the license number: RWC 776.

"Now what?" asked Joanna when they were out of sight.

I didn't know what. I got out of the car and leaned my head back into the window.

"Wait for me," I said. "If that car comes back...well, do *something*." I started toward the loading dock.

"Do *what*?" Joanna screamed from the car. I ignored her.

I turned the key in the lock next to the elevator doors and they slid open as smooth as silk curtains. But once inside, they squeezed me off from the real world with the solidity of a bank vault. I felt like one of Edgar Allan Poe's premature burial victims. I had never been claustrophobic, but now I experienced a sudden rush of it and began to wish that I hadn't taken this course of action so impulsively.

The elevator was slow; you could almost *wish* yourself upstairs faster, and I distracted myself by reading the graffiti. The usual banalities, mainly. Some of it was as much as twenty years old and after all my night flights on this lurching contraption, most of it was as familiar as my ex-wife's signature on our cancelled checks. And then I caught something even more familiar—my own name, and an inscription to accompany it:

7/21/81
Count your Blessings, Fargo.

Bigger than shit, in fire-engine red magic marker.

My heart became sluggish with doom, like a boxing glove trying to open and close itself. The elevator caught me by surprise, stopping at my floor with the suddenness and violence of a respectable automobile collision. The door, at which I still gaped in awe due to the message I had just read, opened to reveal the empty hallway. For a second, I considered just taking the elevator back down, but just as the doors began to close, I stepped through them.

The hallway was silent, dark, and as slick as the inside of a square gun barrel. I walked softly to my apartment door, put my ear against it for about thirty seconds, and, when I convinced myself that there was no one inside, I gingerly unlocked the door and let myself in. My first priority was to hit the john. My bladder was now exerting enough pressure to override caution.

In the midst of relieving it is when I detected the odor. I suppose it was the odor of death.

Not anything as pronounced as the rotting of flesh; this was more subtle, but no less insistent. I had once had a full complement of wisdom teeth extracted at one sitting and I remembered spending the entire day in my bedroom, propped up on pillows, holding ice packs to both sides of my jaw and not really feeling too much discomfort except that I couldn't stop the bleeding for several hours. The room had reeked of the drainage of life. This was the same smell.

I zipped up and stood still, wondering what to do. Suddenly it seemed important to flush the toilet. I did so and the sudden deafening rush of water made me regret my action immediately. Somebody, I thought, would remember that the toilet had flushed. I saw the prosecuting attorney questioning my neighbor, the building manager.

"*Yes, Sir. I heard the toilet flush.*"

"*About what time was that?*" asks the slick prosecutor, leaning on the rail of the jury box and smiling triumphantly at the jurors.

"*It was eleven-oh-three exactly,*" says the building manager with nauseating precision. "*See, I got one of these digital clock radios on my nightstand—I tend bar part time, see, and the exact time is real important in my profession—so anyway, I looks up 'cause the toilets in our building is real noisy, ya know, and I work late hours and everything being a bartender, so I like to sleep late as possible* (here he shoots me a dirty look over at the defendant's table where my attorney is sitting next to me shaking his head sadly back and forth), *and besides, this Fargo is a weirdo. Hell, once he told the police that he'd taken me to the hospital to see my son, which I don't have, who'd been bitten by a snake, and that I'd even had a heart attack there. Hell, do I look like I've had a heart attack? Fuck, no, I ain't had no heart attack!*"

"*No further questions, Your Honor,*" says the prosecutor...

I shook my head, possibly hoping that this fantasy would roll out of it like the ashy residue of a consumed mind. Jesus Christ! Was I going crazy? Yes, I think I was. There were too many rhetorical questions floating around unanswered.

I walked carefully back into the living room. It seemed to be just as I had left it, which wasn't too unexpected, since there wasn't much in it to be re-arranged. Then I screamed—involuntarily—even though I was anticipating trauma like an S&M freak touring a slaughterhouse. They were sitting at my kitchen table, chins on their chests, their arms dangling at their sides, just as though they'd fallen asleep waiting for the soup to cool. Randy and Randi. Almost absurdly dead.

I crept up to them slowly, almost thinking that a sudden noise might spark a flinch of life back into their dangling hands. Beneath Randy's chair I could see a small disk of blood—a footnote to the grisly text above—but that was all. A large bloodstain covered the front of Randi's shirt, and on the left side of her head her hair was matted with blood. The left side of her face was badly discolored and her left eye seemed nearly black. Randy's back was to me, but I could see that the side of his head was in much the same condition as his girlfriend's—the results of the coup de grace—and that was all I needed to see.

It took me a few seconds to realize that a car was blowing its horn somewhere outside. It took me about another second to realize that it was probably Joanna's horn, and that she was probably blowing it for a reason.

I made a dash for the door, let myself out and walked quietly to the elevator. I pushed the button, but the door didn't open. The car had been summoned back downstairs. I ran back towards the front of the building and ran down the stairs to the lobby. Luckily, it was empty. In another second, I was out the front door and running around the block to the back. Only when I was sitting in Joanna's car and we were already three or four blocks from my apartment building did I realize what a spectacle I had made of myself. Hell, I looked a *lot* guiltier than the murderers.

And, apparently, it was all for nothing.

"Where did they leave their car?" I asked Joanna when I had caught my breath.

"Who?"

"The two guys in the elevator. The ones I told you to watch out for. Isn't that why you blew the horn?"

"I didn't blow the horn," she said. "Oh, *that* horn. That was some other car. I heard it too."

"Who got in the elevator?" I asked.

"Nobody. I mean, I didn't *see* anybody. I was looking for the car."

I strained to remember if I had always waited for that elevator—whether it returned to ground level automatically—or whether that was the other elevator, but it was hopeless.

"My God, Stephen. What's wrong with you? You're trembling. It must be ninety degrees already and you're *trembling*."

"Take me to a phone booth," I said.

* * *

Somehow, the world had tilted; the physical laws of the universe had magically altered. A new system of proportion had been imposed. I lay cool and supine in an oversize chaise longue situated on the lofty balcony of Denise Raccette's apartment building amid her rampantly efflorescent houseplants. She stood about two yards in front of me in a skinny halter-top and a pair of cut-off Levi's—cut off high enough to be just barely wearable—tending to her plants with all the earnest solicitude of a nun in a field hospital. An hour ago, I'd been playing hysterical host to the two most attractive execution victims in Detroit in my own squalid apartment. Now I basked in the aftereffects of my half-hour shower—compliments of Denise—clad in only a towel, a gin-and-tonic complete with lime wedge at my elbow, and the most unconsciously sensual woman in my experience within thermal wave range. Maybe the shower had been a sort of baptism. Maybe my cleansing had triggered paradise.

When Joanna had driven me to the phone booth, I had called Midwiff, only to be forced to endure a strenuously clever, mechanical version of his voice on a recording telling me that while he was unable to come to the phone at the moment, he'd be delighted to return my call if I'd leave my name and number at the sound of the tone. I hung up at the sound of the tone, looked up Denise Raccette's phone number, and called her, trying to sound as nonchalant as possible about inviting myself over, using the paltry excuse that I had left my keys to my apartment in my luggage, which had somehow parted itineraries with me between Washington and Detroit. But, after all, my subterfuge had been unnecessary. She had been overjoyed to hear from me and had insisted that I come over for lunch.

And try as I might, I had been unable to detect the slightest hitch of dissimulation in her voice. I had then called Midwiff back and left a message for him to call me at Denise's.

I had not told Joanna of my hideous discovery. She made it easy for me by not questioning me further, probably because she didn't want to encourage what she considered my diseased imagination. She told me that she had to get back home to get ready to work a two o'clock flight that afternoon. When she dropped me off at Denise's spectacular high-rise, I promised to get in touch with her either in Washington or in Detroit. She gave me numbers for both bases.

Denise had completed her rounds with the watering can. She now stood erect, facing me, and surveying her plants to make sure that she hadn't missed any. Her flawless waistline was at my eye level. God, even her navel was exciting.

"You have to be careful," she said.

"What?"

"The plants. You have to be careful not to give them too much water. God, I killed off whole *jungles* of them before I learned that. It's just that they're so *helpless*, you know? I mean, they can't *tell* you they're thirsty, so the temptation is to give them water every time you look at the poor things. They're tougher than we give them credit for." She sat down in a lawn chair opposite me, picked up a marijuana cigarette from the ledge of the balcony, and lit it, taking a tremendous drag that pulled the skin taut over her ribcage. She offered the joint to me.

"No thanks," I said. I'd long since soured on drugs. I was a hopeless, not to say slavish, devotee of alcohol. My refusal didn't seem to bother her though.

"It helps to stimulate my appetite," she explained. "I have to remind myself to eat half the time. If I didn't smoke grass, I'd waste away to nothing."

Never, I thought. The world wasn't *that* cruel.

I started to feel ashamed of myself for lying my way into the sanctuary of her apartment and I was on the giddy verge of a complete confession when she jumped right into the conversation with both of her exquisite bare feet.

"I really didn't expect to hear from you," she said. I waited a second for her to explain that remark, but since she was in the middle of the breath-holding stage of the marijuana smoking ritual, the explanation was in abeyance.

"Why not?" I asked.

"Oh, I don't know," she said finally behind a voluminous issue of smoke. "You've just always been so withdrawn, I guess."

"Dangerously," I said.

"And the fact is," she continued, "people have a way of just vanishing from the agency. The turnover is terrific. One day you just get to know somebody and the next day they're out of you life."

"Like Minerva?"

"Oh, no. Nothing like *that*. I mean, as far as I know, nobody has died, other than Minerva. People just disappear." She offered me the joint again.

"No thanks," I said.

"*Jesus*, that's right. You just told me you don't smoke. Shit, I'm losing it already. This stuff'll take your head off. Hey, I've got a little coke left if you'd rather do that."

"No thanks," I said again. I wanted to have an intelligent conversation with her before she lost it completely. "Anything new on Minerva's death?" I asked.

"Not that I know of," she replied. She was busy now with the intricate process of affixing the nearly-consumed marijuana cigarette to a roach clip, a feat that had always seemed to me to be the pinnacle of achievement, for those equipped with the prehensile appendage, especially stoned.

"Heard anything from Rudy or Helen?" I asked.

"No, but as far as I know it's business as usual tomorrow morning."

"What about Lazard? Heard from him?"

She looked at me quizzically. "Why should I hear from him?" she asked. The tone of her voice suggested that I had cut through the marijuana fog.

"Oh, I don't know. You shouldn't have, I guess. It's just that in my conversation with him, he seemed to have some lingering doubts about Minerva's death. As a matter of fact, he led me to believe that he wasn't satisfied that her death was accidental."

Denise stared at me for a moment and then broke into a paroxysm of laughter, exaggerated, no doubt to a great extent, by the effect of the marijuana. This reaction perplexed me at first, but her laughter was so spontaneous and genuine that I couldn't help being infected by it.

"What?" I kept asking between episodes of my own slightly less exuberant chuckling. "What's so funny?" And of course each repetition of my question sent Denise on a new and even more alarming display of hilarity, so that I nearly began to doubt her sanity. But I remembered having reacted in just the same manner myself while under the influence of marijuana—laughing myself silly over the most innocuous remarks. Somebody would say "Pass the salt," and I would be reduced to a hopeless mass of spasmodic tissue for ten minutes. Denise, understandably, was a veteran of this sort of thing, so that her episode lasted only two or three minutes. But even after her laughter abated, she was still sobbing and her chest heaved from the rigor of her laughter.

"I'm sorry," she said when she was finally able to articulate again. "This weed is just too much. It's just that when you mentioned Minerva and Lazard in the same breath, I couldn't help myself."

"Why's that?"

"Well, about a year ago, Lazard had the hots for Minerva. He used to hang around the office quite a bit before then—I guess he's some sort of buddy of Rudy's—and, well, I guess you should know as well as anybody how Minerva acts—or used to act—when men propositioned her. And, God, in Lazard's case I almost couldn't blame her. He's so repulsive. And *nobody* trusts him. Even Rudy kept a close eye on him. Besides, he's such a slime and he's got such a sneaky style. So one day he squirms his way over to Minerva's desk and I guess he must have asked her out or something. We really couldn't hear what he'd said. But we could sure hear what

Minerva said." Here Denise broke into another fit of laughter. When it subsided, she seemed to have forgotten the conversation. I had to ask her to tell me what Minerva had said.

"Oh, she asked him why he didn't just hop back onto his lily pad. I know it doesn't seem too funny now. You had to be there, you know, to see Lazard's face. I guess it had been a long time since anyone had called public attention to his physical features, if you know what I mean."

I began to understand Lazard's preoccupation with rejection during his conversation with me.

"From then on, Lazard steered clear of the office," Denise continued. "That is, until Friday morning." She paused to frown. "I suppose he'll be a more frequent visitor again now that Minerva's gone."

The marijuana had apparently had the desired effect on Denise's appetite because she was famished, or "vamished" as she pronounced it, and she asked if I were ready to eat. "Ready to eat" didn't begin to describe my hunger. I was "vamished" too.

While Denise prepared lunch, I went through the Sunday paper looking for news about Minerva's death. There was a death notice, but nothing else. That meant that the medical examiner had probably ruled that there was no foul play involved in her death. Or else, the whole thing wasn't newsworthy enough to pay attention to.

Leona Blessing *was* newsworthy, however. Her obituary took up about a quarter of a page and included a photograph taken in 1960 when Leona was still a stunning beauty. Actually, the entire obituary dwelt on Leona's life only up to about the same time. It discussed her fleeting Broadway career, her marriage to Draper, her brief tour of duty as a Grosse Pointe socialite, and ended by saying that she had become a recluse after the accidental death of her son Benjamin in 1961. The article also mentioned Victor's death, calling it an accidental drowning that, oddly enough, had occurred on July 4, 1976, smack in the middle of the Bicentennial celebration.

The obituary mentioned two surviving relatives—an adopted son, Miguel, and a sister, a Mrs. Arthur Niccolo, currently residing in New York.

What was conspicuously absent was a rundown of Mrs. Blessing's philanthropic gestures over the years and her résumé of community services. These sorts of references were obligatory in the obits of most socially prominent Grosse Pointers. Indeed, many of these elite throughout their lives seemed to compete with each other in a continual effort to demonstrate the potency of their charitable instincts. What else did they have to do?

But either Leona had felt no obligation to finance a gallery acquisition or stock a library or build a hospital wing, or else she had gone about it anonymously, or at least with the stipulation that her gifts not be publicized. I wondered which was the case. It was impossible for me to decide simply on the basis of my one interview with her.

"I haven't told you quite everything about what's been happening to me lately," I said to Denise as I helped her clear the dishes from the table after lunch. I had almost blurted it out, surprising myself with the unexpectedness of my candor. But if I expected Denise to be surprised by my revelation, I was the one who was about to be disappointed.

"I know," she said, flipping on the garbage disposal, which roared loud enough to give me the opportunity to react to her words. I felt an instant's panic as it occurred to me that I might be in the company of another of the Daughters of Trent. Christ, why not? They were everywhere else. The garbage disposal gargled its throat clear and Denise shut it off, but she didn't turn around. "I know you didn't go to Los Angeles. In fact, you gave that away yourself just this morning when you called me. You told me you lost your luggage between here and Washington." Well, *that* didn't sound right at all. We didn't know each other well enough for her to allow herself the privilege of being petulant. She turned around.

"So how do you know I didn't stop off in Washington on my way back from L.A.?" I asked. Our relationship was turning bitter even as I sat there.

"Oh, I *don't* know," said Denise, slapping her arms against the sides of her legs in frustration. "But there are other things. Lazard, for example. I wasn't being absolutely honest about not talking to him. He called me Friday afternoon to tell me that he had checked out your story about your landlord's son or whatever it was, and that it had been just that—a story. And I guess he had also checked with the airlines and found that you hadn't gone to Los Angeles, but to Washington. And he's talked to your wife."

"My wife?"

"Yes. I think he said her name was Valerie."

I didn't bother to correct her. I didn't like the feeling I was starting to get. All of this was coming too fast. In my head, I was hearing doors slamming and locking one after another. And Denise wasn't finished.

"So, anyway, Lazard seems to think you're in some danger."

"I'll just bet he does," I said. "He thinks I'm in danger of escaping before he gets his amphibious little hands on me, right? And I suppose he told you that if I got in touch with you that you should try to detain me until he got here, right?"

"Stephen, you're taking this all wrong."

"I'm surprised you haven't slipped off to call him," I said, a horrible notion dawning on me. "Or have you?"

Denise's head was lowered and she was fidgeting with the saltshaker. "While you were in the shower," she said softly.

Baptism, my ass. More like a ritual cleansing before the sacrifice. I was just too goddamn trusting for this business. And if I couldn't trust Denise, who *could* I trust? Even now, she seemed incapable of this duplicity, this *treachery*. And now she was starting to cry. Hell, I was the one who should have been crying and I told her so.

"I can't help it," she said. "I'm afraid."

"Well, don't worry. Despite the fact that I seem to leave dead bodies in my wake, I'm not going to hurt you." I was feeling bitter and noble at the same time like any dutiful martyr. "I've never had the stamina for revenge. I don't seem to be able to concentrate long enough for it."

"What are you talking about?" asked Denise with rising indignation. "I'm not afraid *of* you. I'm afraid *for* you, you jerk."

How endearing. She could still make it seem as though "you jerk" was the most potent epithet she was capable of.

"Well, that makes two of us," I said, for lack of anything more clever. "It's just that you have a funny way of demonstrating your concern. I mean, delivering me up to Lazard—"

"*Delivering you up?*"

"Of course. Don't you realize that Lazard suspects me of having murdered Minerva?"

"Stephen, you're wrong," said Denise, relinquishing the saltshaker and clasping my hand in hers. "Lazard doesn't suspect you of murdering Minerva. Minerva's death was an accident. This goes far beyond Minerva."

"You got *that* right. It's gone way beyond Minerva, and as far as Lazard is concerned, I'm looking better and better for all of them."

"All of who?"

"It's a long story," I said. "Maybe Lazard will tell you all about it when he gets here. I really can't stay. Thanks for the lunch." I started to stand, but Denise's grip on my hands became a desperate clench.

"Stephen," she screamed. "You don't understand." You *can't* leave."

I panicked and disengaged my hand from her grip rather more forcefully than necessary, nearly pulling her across the table, which overturned and sent Denise sprawling to the kitchen floor among the shards of cups and saucers. I felt a pang of regret, but this was no time for chivalry. I heard Denise struggling to get to her feet as I dashed over the plush lime carpeting of the living room, leaping a knee-high philodendron with the ease of an antelope taking flight over the veldt. But like all metaphors, this one too was doomed to exhaustion. I opened the door and collided with the two people obstructing the passageway.

"Stephen, *wait!*" screamed Denise from somewhere behind me.

"Yes, Mr. Fargo. Please do," said Lazard, smiling and extending his arm either to restrain me or to cushion the impact. Jesus, even his reflexes were ambiguous. His other hand held the suitcase that I had abandoned in the hotel in Washington.

"Hello, Stephen," said Valerie.

*   *   *

"I believe this is yours," said Lazard, sliding the suitcase over to me. Things had calmed down a bit. All of us—Lazard, Valerie, Denise, and I—sat in the living room sipping gin-and-tonics. (I was surprised to see that Valerie was drinking gin with no apparent distaste or ill effects. She had always scrupulously avoided clear alcoholic beverage, preferring bourbon to all other spirits. She always used to say that anything you could see through was a waste of money, time, or attention, a remark she also applied to people, art, and every brilliant idea I'd ever thought I'd conceived. She had always been ready with a pithy remark. It was one of the two or three crucial elements of her personality that had originally attracted and ultimately repelled me, perhaps because she could so easily see through *me*.)

The kitchen table had been restored, the havoc of its upending had been redressed, stiff introductions had been made, drinks poured, cigarettes lit, and preliminary sighs and throat-clearings accomplished. Now it was time for Lazard to get on with it. Slap on the cuffs, read me my rights, and generally humiliate me in front of my former love and, at least up until fifteen minutes previous, my potential one. The suitcase was the most obvious giveaway. His possession of it was proof that he knew about Hugo Demuth, knew that I was a fugitive—perhaps even knew about Randy and Randi. Hell, it was a good thing that Leona had died of natural causes, or I might even have been hauled in for that.

"I suppose you've been through it," I said to Lazard as I accepted the suitcase.

"Mr. Fargo, I have no cause to examine your belongings," he said, looking as though I had accused him of sodomizing my ex-wife in the elevator on the way up. "So far as I know, you have not forfeited your right to privacy." He raised and opened his hands, like a priest preparing to give the benediction. "And you don't appear to be the victim of foul play," he added, glancing at Denise with the faintest suggestion of a leer. "Not *yet* anyway." I guess that was an effort at humor, and under less tense circumstances, I might have argued the point with him. But at the moment, Lazard was the one person I didn't want to hold up my end of the conversation with. My end was heavier than his.

Lazard occupied one corner of the couch and Valerie the other, like bookends. Valerie looked, well, she looked California-ized. Tan, slightly more creased around the eyes, thinner, more tired. She was dressed in one of those flowing white poplin numbers—baggy, lightweight slacks with elbow-deep pockets and matching white tunic—the uniform of leisure. But she also looked older, and her face expressed a tenseness that belied her apparel.

Occasionally, Valerie let her glance slide over to Denise, who sat uneasily in a wicker chair off to one side, absently curling the leaf of one of her plants between her thumb and index finger—a reluctant spectator. There was no rancor in Valerie's eyes; she was too sophisticated for that. She was curious, like a parent might be about her child's new playmate.

"So, how are you, Valerie?" I asked. If this was just another of Lazard's unofficial visits, I was determined to be sociable, even to the point of banality. Let them make the first move.

"Wonderful," she answered, with conviction that went about skin deep. Then after a pause to dab at her nostrils with a handkerchief, she said: "Gore Kemp has hired me as an assistant film editor for his next film." She announced this with exaggerated enthusiasm, as though she were trying to spark the proceedings into conviviality. She seemed to have been coached for this performance.

"Well, that's a step up," I said. "Or a step in some direction."

Valerie had gone to Los Angeles soon after our divorce and had immediately landed a job as a post production assistant, or some damn thing that she never clearly explained to me, with a company that filmed everything from used car commercials to government training films. She had moved up steadily and quickly. She was good at editing. She had edited *me* right out of her life. And hiring on with Gore Kemp was really breaking into the big time. He produced about a half dozen low-budget films a year—mainly slasher fare. They weren't artistic triumphs, but they made money. And Kemp was the kind of producer who probably made a film editor's job easy.

"How long are you going to be in town?" I asked. "I have to be back in L. A. tonight," Valerie said. She looked at Lazard.

"I'm afraid that I unintentionally alarmed Miss Cadieux," he explained. Cadieux was Valerie's maiden name, a very old Detroit name and one she had always at least tacitly resented having to relinquish when we had married. She had re-assumed it about ten seconds after our divorce was final. I didn't blame her. Fargo wasn't such a great name and since it was only a couple of generations deep anyway, I had never felt any irresistible obligation to it. Maybe if I had become Stephen Cadieux the marriage would have endured.

"But I *wanted* to come," said Valerie, clearly distressed.

"I feel like I have a terminal disease nobody's telling me about," I said, looking from Valerie to Lazard.

"In a way, you just may have," said Lazard.

"I was trying to make a joke," I said.

"I'm not," said Lazard. "I asked Miss Raccette to call me if you should contact her. I'm afraid I rather insisted that she do so. So you shouldn't go too hard on her. You see, after our last conversation, I made some inquiries. Five minutes with your landlord was enough to confirm my suspicion that you were not telling the truth about your whereabouts the previous evening. If you'll pardon me, Mr. Fargo, I must tell you that you are a terrible liar, practically speaking. And that's unusual, since your wife tells me that you've done a good deal of it—are somewhat addicted to it as a matter of fact."

"My *ex*-wife," I corrected him, with probably infantile satisfaction.

"I never said that," Valerie protested. Then, after a raised eyebrow from Lazard and further thought about her disavowal, she said: "I didn't mean it that way." The blush beneath her tan gave her a burnt sienna hue. It was very becoming against all that white.

"What I meant was that the more Stephen lied, the less effective he was at it. That's all. I didn't mean to imply that his lying was destructive or malicious. He never lied about anything *important*. Just a lot of little things."

"Please," said Lazard, holding his hand high, palms front to fend off further objections. "I didn't mean to make a moral judgment. I'm talking from a professional standpoint. Some people are very nearly congenital liars. Some are better at it than others." I noticed that he was directing these remarks almost exclusively to Valerie, being very obvious about it. "I'm giving an expert opinion here," he continued. "I'm not imputing any wrongdoing. A cop doesn't take a lie personally." He turned to me. "In fact, our conversation in your apartment convinced me that you weren't responsible for Miss Hewitt's death."

"Are you saying that somebody other than Miss Hewitt was?"

"You're getting ahead of me," he said with some irritation. His urbane veneer was easily scratched. He wanted this scene to run according to his direction.

"Miss Cadieux's time is limited. Everyone's time is limited."

Well, I could certainly agree with that.

After his brief display of temper, nobody seemed anxious to impede Lazard's progress along the Yellow Brick Road of Explanation that led to the Emerald City of Understanding. He continued with the journey, and a captivating tour it was, too, full of all sorts of magical highlights, thus:

After learning of my departure before he had been able to confront me with my deflated alibi, Lazard had telephoned Valerie to verify my arrival in Los Angeles, which, of course, she could not do. But Valerie had been happy that he had called because, almost coincidentally, earlier in the day, two men had come to her office to question her about her ex-husband. They had identified themselves as government agents, but it was only after the interrogation had finished and the men had left and only their invisible sinister residue floated around the room, detectable at only a few parts per billion, so subtle was their menace, that Valerie had realized that the two men had never specified what government they were agents of.

"You remember that Kent State rally fiasco in 1970?" Valerie interrupted at this point with the indulgence of Detective Lazard. She was talking to me through her handkerchief. She seemed to be having some trouble with her nose. She didn't sound as though she had a cold, but her nose was running almost continually.

"You remember," she insisted, "that whole Dustin Hoffman mess when we spent the night under house arrest, or whatever it was."

Well, it would be hard to forget, since it was the only time that I had been arrested, the only time I had assaulted an officer of the law (a slight exaggeration), the only time I had ever impersonated a movie star, and the first time I had sex with Valerie, who, ten months later, became my wife. Lazard, citadel of efficiency that he was, knew about the arrest, technically for trespassing during a rally to protest the Kent State shootings in May of 1970. But he hadn't been aware of my impersonation of Dustin Hoffman, and that interested him.

"I was a dead ringer for him," I explained. "So when the cops arrested me and Valerie, I told them I was Dustin Hoffman and that I wanted to call my lawyer—Melvin Belli or F. Lee Bailey—I forget who I said. Anyway, it was just an impulsive thing, but I really had them going there for a while. The last thing they appeared to want was some hot shot celebrity lawyer coming down on them. So they contacted some federal agents or maybe they were secret service. I never did get it straight. They kept us under a sort of house arrest—detention, they called it—in a federal office building. They found out real quick that I wasn't Dustin Hoffman, but they were *real* nice about it, right Val?"

She reddened again at this veiled reference to our amorous adventures in the federal building that night.

"You see, they asked us to spend the night in this building we were in— fed us an incredible dinner, champagne, the works. Then the next morning they let us go with their apologies and best wishes and the charges dropped."

"Didn't that whole procedure seem a little irregular to you?" asked Lazard.

"I wasn't in a position to question their hospitality," I said.

Well, the journey continued after my short digression (and after Lazard recruited Denise to agree with him that I didn't look much like Dustin Hoffman at all, especially with my beard. "More like Al Pacino as Serpico," said Denise, bless her heart). Lazard had explained my sudden disappearance and the circumstances of Minerva's death to Valerie, who expressed her concern and almost immediately announced her intention to fly to Detroit as soon as possible. Lazard had insisted that there was no immediate reason for her to do so, but Valerie had been adamant.

"And so here we are," said Lazard, bringing his narrative to a screeching halt. "Everybody safe and sound."

"What about my suitcase?" I asked. Lazard looked from me to the suit- case and said nothing for a full ten seconds. "Oh, your suitcase," he said finally. "That arrived at the precinct late last night. Flown in by special courier, no less." He fished in his vest pocket and withdrew a slip of paper. "It was apparently sent up by the Marriott in Washington. No explanation as to why they chose to send it to us."

"I forgot it," I said lamely.

"Well they certainly went to extraordinary lengths to return it to you. It even got here before you did."

I couldn't be sure whether Lazard was letting me know that he was aware of my movements or not, nor was I prepared to pursue the matter. Maybe by "here" he simply meant Denise's apartment. At any rate, run- ning down every fugitive gesture, remark, or action that I seemed to scare up like so many startled hares in a field was becoming as exhausting as it was unproductive. Such distractions were the curse of a subtle mind. And an overabundance of subtlety was the prelude to paranoia. I didn't want to be subtle anymore. I didn't have the intellectual fortitude for it. I determined then and there to practice obtuseness with the devotion of a monk. People were going to have to start spelling things out for me.

"Look, Lazard, I really did forget it. I was encouraged to forget it by some people in Washington who were trying to frame me for murder and/or smuggle me out of the country for some purpose that I'm not aware of." This information didn't shock Lazard in the least.

"I told you that you aren't under suspicion for Minerva's death. In any event, the medical examiner has ruled that her death was accidental, so that it wouldn't make any difference what I thought."

"Yeah, but you don't believe that any more than I do," I said. "Anyway, it's not Minerva's death that I'm talking about. I'm talking about Hugo Demuth."

"Hugo?" said Denise. Her I *had* surprised.

"Yes," I said. "Ask Detective Lazard. I'm sure he knows all about it. I'm sure he's been talking to the Washington police."

"You're wrong," he said. "Why don't you tell me about it?"

So I did. I told him not only about Hugo, but about everything since the day I had first seen Draper Blessing's name in Hugo's report. (Well, not everything. For example, I left out the juicy stuff about my anti-romantic tryst with Joanna in the hotel.) And what an audience I had! Everybody looked as if, by special invitation, they were witnessing their first public execution. Except for Lazard, of course, who looked like he was witnessing his ten thousandth. I spoke nonstop for fifteen minutes, and when I had finished, nobody said a word for another minute.

"So these two bodies are still in your apartment?" said Lazard in a voice just dripping with condescension.

"They were there an hour ago," I said. "I mean, Jesus Christ, we're not talking about somebody forgetting their gloves on my dining room table or something. These are dead bodies. Do you know how obvious a dead body can be around the house? And how much of a nuisance? They never pass the mashed potatoes and you're always moving them around so that you can sweep under their chairs. They don't even get up to answer the phone? That phone'll ring ten, fifteen times a day and they're sitting there five feet away from it. But do you think they'll get up to answer the god-damn thing?"

This was a bit excessive, admittedly. But Lazard's attitude had irritated me. Everybody's attitude was irritating me. Valerie and Denise were taking my account most strangely—a lot of averting of the eyes and minute nervous activity of the hands. Valerie was paying more attention to brushing a stray flake of cigarette ash out of her white slacks than to Lazard or me. Denise got up and walked over to a highboy and took a stack of coasters out of one of the drawers. Then she made the rounds of the living room, depositing a coaster under each of our sweating glasses. It was all theatrics. Valerie could have extracted one of her teeth with less energy than she was now expending, and Denise's coasters—a gift from some doting aunt, no doubt—had probably sat in that highboy for five years. For all the reaction my story had gotten, you'd have thought I had just recited verbatim several hundred pages of the phone book. A conspiracy of some sort was being played out here, and it suddenly occurred to me what the motivation for it was. They all thought I had gone crazy.

Lazard looked at his watch. "May I use your phone?" he asked Denise.

"Of course," she said. "It's in the bedroom. I'll show you. Could I get anyone another drink?"

"Please," said Valerie.

"Easy on the tonic," I said, handing Denise my glass—not a routine maneuver given the way her hand was shaking.

When Lazard and Denise left the room, Valerie lit another cigarette and looked around the apartment. Then she stood up and began pacing around the room. When she got to the archway leading to the kitchen and dinette, she asked:

"What kind of view is there from the balcony?"

"The river," I said. "Canada. The west end of Belle Isle. Have a look for yourself."

"No. Show it to me, won't you, Stephen?"

There was a time in our turbulent relationship when I wouldn't have shared a balcony with Valerie that was any higher than three feet off the ground for fear that one of us would have left it by the wrong way. But while Valerie looked a bit jittery, and I *felt* a little tense (a *little* tense—I felt like I was trying to breathe through the soles of my feet), our animosity for each other had diminished over the past few months. I judged it was safe enough, so I got up and escorted Valerie to the balcony.

When we got there, she swung the French doors closed behind us, leaned her elbows on the railing, and looked out over the river. A freighter slid downriver toward Lake Erie, its four-story-high bow pushing a white curl of spray against the river's astonishing blue. Pleasure boats bounced along on either side of the freighter like exuberant pilot fish.

I looked back to Valerie. In the sunlight, the skin of her face took on an even more leathery texture, and the lines radiating from the corners of her eyes seemed to deepen and lengthen. A breeze stirred her hair, revealing her ear. Pinned to her earlobe was a silver trinket inlaid with turquoise and in the shape of an ankh.

"I need money, Stephen," she said, still surveying the view.

She had never been big on preliminaries. That is, while she had always been admirably discreet, when compelled to a decision, she had never much agonized over options. "Dilemma" was not part of her vocabulary.

"You wound me," I said, laying my hand over my heart. "Here I thought your visit was out of simple compassion. I mean Detective Lazard—"

"Lazard is an asshole."

"The trouble with you is that you always underestimate people," I said. "A perilous habit."

"Spare me the lecture, Stephen," she said. "I don't care if Lazard is a fucking genius. I doubt it, but I just don't care. I needed to see you as soon as possible and this little crisis of yours seemed to be as good a way as any to approach you."

"I'm flattered," I said.

"I need fifty thousand dollars," she said, ignoring my sarcasm.

Now, Valerie could be many things. She was narcissistic, cynical, misanthropic, indifferent to the suffering of others—all in a passive sort of way, of course. But she had never been unrealistic, so that her request came as a double shock to me—first, to think that she would even make such a request, and second, to realize that she believed I was in a position to grant it. Nothing less would have brought her three thousand miles to see me. She actually assumed that I would pull a money clip from the pocket of my borrowed khakis and peel off fifty thousand-dollar-bills. I knew she believed it by the tone of her voice.

"I need it to buy a share in Gore's next film," she explained. "See, he's having trouble getting financing from the studio on this one and he's looking for backers. And—"

"Gore Kemp can't get the studio to finance one of his films? His films are like money in the bank."

"Well, he wants to do something important this time and he's having artistic differences with the cretins that run the studio. He's hoping that this next film will make enough money to allow him the artistic freedom to branch out."

"You *believe* that? You believe that Gore Kemp is going to make an important film, whatever *that* is? You must be kidding! Gore Kemp thinks a chain saw is a surgical instrument."

"Stephen, I don't have time to argue with you," said Valerie, tossing her cigarette away and turning to me. "I guarantee that I'll have the fifty thousand back to you within six months. I'll even sign a promissory note. I'll pay you interest. But I *need* the money. Today."

"What about your father?"

"There's nobody else I can ask. Don't start running through names. I didn't come here for financial counseling."

"Well, okay, I'll play. What makes you think I have fifty thousand dollars to lend you? For that matter, what makes you think I have *fifty* dollars to lend you? I bring home fifteen hundred a month. Christ, I'm still paying the lawyer—*your* lawyer—for our divorce. I don't have a car or a TV. I live in a goddamn rookery—"

"I should never let you get started," said Valerie, wagging her head. "You never fail to stir yourself up into indignation. It starts out as histrionics and ends up as oratory every time. It's like you talk yourself into your own righteousness. Now, look—I can understand that you might not want to help me. I don't agree. I never will accept that I am responsible for your emotional well-being, or lack of it, simply because of my decision not to let you run my life."

"I never ran—"

"Stephen, let's not get into this again."

"Valerie, think back. *You* left *me*, remember? If you do, you'll probably remember your reasons why. I was a perpetual graduate student making forty-one hundred dollars a year. That's so far below poverty level that I nearly suffered the bends when Sultana offered me thirty thousand a year. Don't you remember why you left? I had a 'romantic delusion about the virtues of poverty,' don't you remember?"

"Stephen, please. Keep your voice down. They'll hear us."

"So what? Are you so embarrassed to be in need of money? It's very nearly a universal affliction, you know. You'll pardon my indignation, as you call it, but even if I *did* have fifty thousand dollars, I wouldn't give it to you. Not because I'm bitter or because you don't deserve it, which you don't, but because I would consider it a bad investment. You see how far I've come?"

"Stephen, at least have the courtesy not to lie to me if you're going to refuse me. I know all about your windfall."

"What windfall?"

Valerie gave me an ironic smile and shook her head slowly. During my story to Lazard I had mentioned that Leona had hired me to find her son in Washington—but she hadn't hired me fifty thousand dollars worth.

"What would you say if I told you that I had $200 on me and I *stole* that?" I said.

Valerie continued to shake her head slowly. "Don't you know when someone's doing you a favor?" she asked.

"Just how are you doing me a favor by borrowing—and I use the term loosely—fifty thousand dollars, which, I repeat, I don't have?"

"I've already spoken with my lawyer," she replied. "He's pretty sure that I can sue you for the money that you didn't report during the community property settlement. That includes any inheritance money. But, you see, I need the fifty thousand right now," here she withdrew an envelope from the pocket of her slacks and opened it, " so I'm willing to sign this letter of agreement that my lawyer drew up by which I relinquish all further claims to your estate."

"My estate?"

"We have witnesses right here. Detective Lazard and Miss Raccette. She's a charming creature, by the way, but so *young* and undernourished."

"I'll show you my goddamn estate," I screamed at her. "It's about five miles from here. It's real picturesque. Full of pimps, topless dancers, and whores. Out in front, little black girls skip rope chanting lyrics about heroin. The other day I picked up a wine bottle on the stoop in front of my apartment building and some wino jumped me from behind and started wrestling me for it. There had to be almost a whole teaspoon left in the bottle and he was willing to kill for it. Now, do you really think that I would continue my residence there if I had fifty thousand dollars? Who do I look like, Mother Theresa?"

Valerie was looking past my shoulder, upriver. "My Lord!" she said. "Look at that smoke."

I turned around. A few miles off, a tremendous billow of smoke drifted slowly across the river.

"Looks like a fire," said Valerie.

"It looks like a hell of a fire," I said. "But don't change the subject. And don't act like I'm boring you. I know I'm not. Not when it comes to money. As far as your document goes, you can sign it or not. I don't care. I don't have fifty thousand dollars, and despite this fairy tale you've been getting from someone, I have no prospects of *getting* fifty thousand dollars. Kemp's going to have to make this wonderful transition from sexploitation to great art without my help."

"Stephen," said Valerie, an expression of displeasure just beginning to invade her features, "you needn't get so hostile about this. I'll let you think it over. I'm really not trying to make this sound like an ultimatum."

"Valerie, you have no way of knowing what's been happening to me over the last forty-eight hours."

"Of course I do," she said. "You just told us. By the way, you didn't happen to leave anything out, did you? Perhaps something about meeting a Mr. Millar Crofts?"

"No," I said. It was true. If she was talking about Stonestreet's account-ant or goon or whatever he was, we had never really been introduced.

"Well, he seems to know you. And he assures me that you're due to come into some money."

"Just who the hell is this Crofts, anyway?"

"He's an investment counselor,' said Valerie after a pause. "He has a few clients in Los Angeles, but his office is in Washington. Part of his interest is in locating investors for independent filmmakers."

"Why doesn't *he* finance Kemp's film then, instead of telling stories about me? Just where the hell is all the money I'm supposed to have? Or should I say, where's it supposed to come from?"

"He didn't say."

"I'm sure he didn't," I said. "It sounds like he's trying to get you to swindle me so that he can swindle you."

There was a tap at the French doors behind us. I turned around to see Denise holding up two frosty glasses.

Valerie pulled open the doors. "Oh, my dear, we've been terribly rude," she said, raising her voice a bit and slipping into her socialite persona. She accepted her drink from Denise.

"I didn't mean to interrupt," said Denise, "but Detective Lazard has to leave and he wanted me to ask you if you were driving back downtown with him or making other arrangements." It wasn't clear to me who Denise was addressing with these remarks, but Valerie spoke right up.

"I'm afraid I must go back with him," she said. "Let's go back into the living room, shall we? Perhaps we can prevail upon the detective to allow us to finish our drinks."

Christ, you'd have thought *she* was the hostess here.

Lazard was standing in the middle of the living room looking like a man who had just spent twenty minutes or so in a washing machine. With all the commotion, I hadn't noticed his suit before. It was gray and horribly wrinkled. The pants were too long and the sleeves of the coat were too short. The wings of his collar curled upward. One would think that a man of Lazard's hideous appearance would attempt to compensate for nature by dressing with more fastidiousness. But not Lazard. I began to think that it was all part of the design—that he wanted to stress his ugliness to disarm people, like Columbo was his inspiration. Immediately after that thought, I decided that I was wasting too much time analyzing Lazard.

"I checked on that license plate number that you mentioned," he said, as though he had waited for me to complete my mental appraisal of him before speaking. The man really did have an uncanny sense of timing. "The car's registered to an Arthur Axtract of Detroit. It's a dealer's plate, so he probably uses it on different cars."

I considered telling Lazard that this was the name of the used car dealer Miguel had given me. That was another detail that I'd left out of my narrative in the heat of telling the story. But I decided to keep that information to myself for just a while longer. I had a pretty good idea that Axtract and his buddy Quintus Tremble, the other name Miguel had given me, had executed Randy and Randi.

"What about the bodies in my dining room?" I asked him.

"Yes, well, I took the liberty of calling the resident manager of your building and asked him to take a look," Lazard said. Then he shrugged, a gesture that retracted his shiny head even deeper into the well of his shoulders.

"No bodies," he said. "No blood. No sign of anything unusual. Those were the manager's very words."

"What the hell would *he* know?" I said. "He doesn't even know what 'usual' is. He's been looking at the world through an alcoholic haze for so long that he's got his own personal reality. And believe me, it doesn't square with yours or mine. Half the time when he sees me he calls me Mr. Yolanda. Yolanda is an exotic dancer that lives down the hall from me and turns tricks three times a week between eleven and two in the afternoon to support her crack habit." One of Lazard's eyes seemed to slide over to Valerie. Maybe it was some kind of signal to her that she should humor me. I didn't bother to look at her.

"Is that normal police procedure?" I asked. "I mean do you normally recruit civilians who make it a point to be shit-faced by ten a.m. for official investigations of serious crimes?"

"Let's just say that demographic is not an insignificant source of information in our investigations," he said. "But, of course, you are right. That's why I thought I'd accompany you back to your apartment. We can have a look for ourselves. Miss Cadieux—"

"Oh, don't bother about me," said Valerie. "I can get a taxi. I'm sure I've been the cause of enough disruption already." God, she was polite. It was enough to make you pee in your pants to see how accommodating she could be to people she hardly knew. Only a minute ago she had said that she had to return with Lazard.

"Hey, what about Bill?" I asked.

"A good question," said Valerie. "He was supposed to pick me up at the airport, but he never showed. He was never the dependable type, though. He probably stopped at the racetrack on the way to the airport to bet the first race and, knowing Bill, his horse in the first is probably *still* running." Valerie had always thought she possessed a great sense of humor, but, in reality, this was as good as it got.

"I don't know," I said. "It's not like him to forget something like that."

"Who said he forgot?" said Valerie.

I could have pursued this argument. I could have insisted that lately a lot of people I've been in contact with were behaving strangely, that is if they were lucky enough to be behaving at all. But I was beginning to resent heavily the way I was being humored, like a child charged with an overactive imagination. It was time for the show half of show-and-tell.

"Are you sure we can't give you a lift somewhere?" Lazard asked Valerie.

"No, please," said Valerie. "I've kept you from your other duties long enough, I'm sure."

"Not at all," said Lazard.

"Nevertheless, I can't tell you how I appreciate your help," said Valerie.

"I've done nothing," said Lazard almost sadly, certainly apologetically.

Well, things were getting so cordial in there that it was getting hard to breathe and the leaves of all the houseplants were beginning to wilt. Not a moment too soon, Lazard glanced at me with an expression in his eyes that said, "You ready to go?" and I gave him a tilt of my head in the direction of the door which said, "Jesus, Mary and Joseph, could we possibly leave this place before my ears start to hemorrhage?"

We were just at the door when Valerie spoke up again:

"Stephen, you've forgotten your suitcase." Then she glanced at Denise. "Or have you?"

Well, I had, but the thought that my money might still be in it while it was subject to Valerie's inspection was reason enough to take it with me.

*   *   *

Denise's apartment had been air-conditioned and even the balcony, exposed as it was to the steady offshore breezes from Lake St. Clair, had been downright cool. But at street level, it was hot—nearly hot enough to liquefy asphalt. It was also humid, as only Detroit in the middle of summer could be—the kind of day that if you hung your clothes out to dry, you were wasting your time. And the farther Lazard drove north toward my apartment and away from the river, the hotter and more humid it got. My apartment by now would be *real* pleasant. On days like this, you could scrape spontaneous bacteria cultures from the linoleum every other hour or so. And, to top things off, I now had two corpses slumped in my dining room, well past the stage of cellular death.

Lazard, under his sixty-nine dollar wash-and-wear suit was sweating copiously. He used a handkerchief frequently to mop his forehead and upper lip. The red blotches on his face seemed to be even more inflamed that they had been in Denise's apartment. He probably really suffered on days like this.

Occasionally, the radio in his car squawked into articulation, but Lazard ignored it as though it were some parrot that he tolerated because his wife liked parrots or something, but which he wasn't about to honor with conversation. After we had been rolling for several minutes, however, he did honor *me* with conversation, although that is undoubtedly the wrong term to describe it.

"I know you haven't seen your wife for some time," he began. "Excuse me, your ex-wife." Lazard, by the way, had a great voice—smooth, mellow, the voice of refinement. Not at all the voice of a cop. It was more like the voice of a priest. Unfortunately, and I was sure of this, he had the mentality of an inquisitor, which made carrying on a conversation with him something like playing "Mother May I?" in a minefield.

"But—and please tell me if I'm being too personal—do you know if she ever had any problems with drugs?"

This came as something of a shock, but I didn't want Lazard to know that.

"Do you mean was she allergic to penicillin or something?"

"I'm talking controlled substances here," he said. "Illegal narcotics and their abuse."

"She occasionally got a little tipsy at a cocktail party, but never so bad that she couldn't drive *me* home," I said. "Are you trying to tell me that Valerie is a drug addict?"

"I'm telling you that we have information from the L. A. P. D. Narcotics Division that she's a heavy consumer. She buys a lot of cocaine and she doesn't sell any. So she's either real generous—which most coke users sooner or later aren't—or else she's got a real expensive habit."

Things were beginning to make a little more sense to me. Valerie's chronically drippy nose, her desperate need for money.

"So, if you know all this, why are you asking me?"

"Her supplier is apparently a man named Millar Crofts. His business is smuggling, and cocaine is only one of the many types of contraband he specializes in. Another is illegal aliens. And guns, especially to Central and South America. His legitimate cover is as an importer and investment counselor and he's very clever—or very lucky. In any event, half the law enforcement people in the country, from the Justice Department on down to crossing guards, have him under surveillance almost every minute of his life."

Lazard paused here and took a look at the neighborhood we were passing through.

"You know," he said, "every summer I drive through here and wonder how long it's going to be before these people go bananas again." This was a reference to the '67 riots. We were passing through a particularly blighted area of Detroit's near east side—a neighborhood of abandoned and fire-gutted incomes packed so many per street that it would be difficult to walk between two houses without turning sideways. Where buildings had been demolished, the empty lots were buried under a rubble of bricks and litter or else were reclaimed by waist-high prairie grass. And now I lived on the fringes of just such a neighborhood. Nothing had changed. The firestorm of the riots had passed over, the rhetoric of politicians had blown through, and now the permafrost of neglect had taken hold, Coleman Young notwithstanding. It bespoke an existence that was grim beyond tolerance, desperate beyond reason. Like Lazard, although perhaps from a different perspective, I, too, wondered about the flashpoint of such areas. Grosse Pointe in all its opulence was less than ten minutes away by car.

"I'm going to be candid with you, Mr. Fargo," said Lazard, "because I truly believe that you've been swept up into something that you don't know the magnitude of. We got an anonymous report yesterday and a couple of photos over the telex. The photos show Crofts entering a residence in Georgetown and you exiting the same residence. Then I get this information concerning your ex-wife, who my sources contend is into Crofts for a rather large sum of money. Then I get your suitcase dropped into my lap. The coincidence is too much for a man of my professional persuasion to dismiss, especially coming as it does on the heels of this Hewitt affair, your visit to Mrs. Blessing, and your sudden disappearance. Now, putting the most charitable construction on this that I possibly can, I can only assume that your rendezvous with Crofts was for the purpose of, at least to some extent, settling your ex-wife's account with Crofts with funds that you somehow managed to obtain from Mrs. Blessing, a woman on death's doorstep who was possibly having delusions about her dead son's resurrection. How am I doing so far?"

"Very imaginative," I said. "In fact, it's very good. Maybe *you* should think of moving to Hollywood, too. If Gore Kemp is going to become the next Ingmar Bergman, he's going to need plenty of help if his past efforts are any indication."

"I hope you're not going to tell me that it was all coincidence," said Lazard.

"That's exactly what it was," I said. "At least as far as it concerns any intent on my part. The closest I've come to meeting this Crofts is walking past him in the hallway. I told you about my visit to Stonestreet. Well, that's where I saw Crofts. Stonestreet indicated that the guy was his accountant. Believe me, we never even said one word to each other. I didn't mention him before because I had no way of knowing he was such a celebrity."

We stopped at a light and heat waves overtook us. About fifteen feet away on the front lawn of a corner house, a few black kids—all drooping, waterlogged cut-offs and protruding bellybuttons—were dashing around erratically and screaming while one of their playmates squirted them with a garden hose. The hose had one of those lever-type nozzles that regulated the concentration of the spray. Suddenly, the kid with the hose caught sight of Lazard's car, turned, assumed the kind of combat stance one would use with a handgun, and let loose with a stream of water in our direction. The water hit the side of the car with surprising impact. The kid simulated the sound of a machine gun and ran the stream of water along the length of the car. Some of the water splashed in the window of the driver's side. Without comment, Lazard slowly rolled up the window, much to the delirium of the kids.

The light changed and Lazard pulled away and rolled the window back down. Once again, hot air swirled throughout the front seat.

Either Lazard was satisfied with my explanation concerning my knowledge of Millar Crofts, or else he was simply willing to let it drop for the moment. At any rate, he changed the subject.

"I checked with Washington while we were at Miss Raccette's apartment," he said. "They were surprised to learn that there had been a murder at the Marriott. Apparently no one had informed them of it."

"What are you being so cute for, Lazard?" I asked. "I told you all I know about it. I told you what Norrod told me about the film he showed me of a body being wheeled out of the hotel lobby. That's all I know. Maybe he staged the whole thing to spook me. Maybe it was file footage. I mean, you should *see* the facilities this guy's got—the *equipment*. All I know is that I had reason to believe him. It *looked* authentic. And he had me over a barrel. He knew about my little altercation with Hugo the night before. He knew I would be a prime suspect should Hugo turn up dead."

"I think you underestimate us," said Lazard. "That kind of frame is pure Alfred Hitchcock. Ah, here we are." He pulled up at the curb in front of my apartment building.

"Pull around back and we'll take the freight elevator," I said. "I want to show you something." Lazard obliged, and two or three minutes later we were both enclosed in that slothful elevator as it made its interminable way up to my floor.

"You say they used this elevator?" asked Lazard.

"Yes. And look here." I pointed to the graffiti that had rattled me several hours earlier. Lazard shrugged.

"Doesn't appear particularly menacing," was all he could say. "It's a common adage, after all. Rather inspiring, actually."

"That depends on your interpretation," I countered. "First of all, it's addressed to me. Second, 'Blessing' is capitalized. I'll spare you the lecture on conventional English usage. Third, it's like Ten Little Indians, you know? The way people have been dying lately and the strange circumstances surrounding the deaths of those two Blessing kids and now the matriarch herself—"

"Mrs. Blessing died of asphyxiation, a complication of her lung cancer," said Lazard. "There's no indication of foul play."

"What happened to your suspicious nature?" I asked. "The newspaper didn't actually say she died of lung cancer. It said she had suffered from the disease for some time, whatever that means. And quite frankly, although she didn't exactly look in the pink when I saw her Thursday, she didn't look like she was at death's doorstep, either. But that's not what's really bothering me now." I pointed to the inscription. "I think it's a warning. I think that it was written by one of those gorillas who dumped the bodies in my room. I think they were probably here to kill me, but found me not at home."

"Yes," said Lazard, wallowing in meditation. "Those bodies."

The elevator came to its patented whiplash halt and its door sprang open for us. The hallway was empty, but Yolanda's door was open and I could hear her talking loudly. It sounded as though she were talking to someone on the phone. As we passed her doorway, I looked in and saw her standing next to her television in her robe and slippers, smoking a cigarette that was stuck in her ridiculously long cigarette holder, which she waved to me like the burlesque version of the Tooth Fairy.

Yolanda and I were pretty good friends. I had made it clear to her that I disapproved of her friends, habits, and occupation, and she had *still* insisted that any time I wanted to watch her spiffy new color TV with remote control (compliments of her brother, who was one of the neighborhood's leading burglars), I should feel free. She had even given me a key to her apartment for that reason. I took her up on it now and then, but I really thought that, since she was never home evenings, she wanted someone around to ward off burglars, from whom she wasn't immune by virtue of her blood relationship. No doubt she had cash and drugs squirreled away all over the place.

As soon as I opened the door to my apartment, I knew I was ushering Lazard into a heavy dose of anti-climax. The odor was gone. The general ambience of impropriety that had assaulted me so powerfully on my last visit home even before I had discovered the bodies of the Randies had vanished, as though someone had ventilated the place in my absence. But, like a hospital attendant on his way to empty a wardfull of bedpans, I pressed ahead. Sure enough, the dining room, wherein no more than a couple of hours previous the Randies had slumped over my dining room chairs like exhausted finalists of a pinochle marathon, was now free of cadavers.

"Of *course*," I said to Lazard. "The bodies are gone." I didn't look at him directly. I didn't want to see him go through the effort of rendering his features compassionate—a considerable task for him. Besides, I didn't want his pity.

"We could search the rest of the apartment," he offered. *What a strange suggestion*, I thought. I mean, what kind of cop says something like that?

"It wouldn't be very productive," I said. "There aren't many places to stash two adult corpses in this place." Lazard looked around the room as though he were gauging its dimensions, then he returned his gaze to me. We looked at each other stupidly for about ten seconds.

"Hey, Fargo, you in there?" It was Yolanda, calling from the hallway.

"Yeah," I said. "I'm here." I walked back across the living room to the door. Lazard followed, but not, it seemed to me, enthusiastically. Yolanda was leaning against the doorjamb with a newspaper under one arm and her foot-long cigarette holder in the other.

"Brought your paper back," she said. I subscribed to the Sunday *Free Press* and every now and then Yolanda would borrow it from me. "And I didn't even mix up the sports pages," she added, winking. She looked over my shoulder and caught sight of Lazard walking into the room.

"My, Fargo," she said, raising her voice and affecting a Southern mammy's indignation. "You sho is associatin' wif a questionable class o' folks deese here days."

"Nice to see you, Yoyo," said Lazard.

"Wal, I sho 'nuff doesn't know 'bout dat," said Yolanda, frowning a bit. Her effort at dialect was becoming less authentic and more transparent with every word she uttered. I had never heard her talk like this. I wondered if she was stoned. "No suh," she continued. "Seem lack ebby times I sees y'all, I be's in a world o' trouble rat quick."

"I take it you know each other," I said, as always, master of the obvious.

"*Shee*-it, yes," said Yolanda. "Me and the Lizard go *way* back, don't we?"

"I wouldn't put it that way," said Lazard. He was much less animated about this encounter than Yolanda was. "We've run into each other a few times. Under somewhat less innocuous circumstances." Yolanda, who was taking a pull at that cigarette holder of hers, let her eyes widen at this remark of Lazard's.

"Jes lissen at doze twenty-fie dollah words," said Yolanda in mock awe of Lazard. "Dey teaches 'em thangs lack dat overt poh-leese 'cademy," she said to me confidentially, as though Lazard were a trained bear putting on a performance for us.

Suddenly, Yolanda's performance struck her as hilarious and she began laughing and slapping her thigh with her free hand while still doing a marvelous balancing act with the ever-lengthening ash of her cigarette.

"I'd like to stay and chitchat with you, Sugar," she said to me in her normal accent when she had recovered from her fit of laughter, "but I gotta hot date to get ready for. And this one's the real thing, Lazard," she said to him over my shoulder

"Did you notice any noise in Mr. Fargo's room this morning, Yoyo?" asked Lazard. "Or perhaps any particularly heavy traffic in the hallway?"

"Lazard, you *ought* to know by now that I don't notice *nothing*. It ain't healthy to be going around noticing things all the time. The only thing I notice," Yolanda continued, pointing at Lazard, her eyes flashing now and real venom bleeding into her voice, "is that you're getting too personal for *this* nigger."

"Actually, Yolanda, it would kind of help me out if you *did* hear something," I said.

"I don't know nothing about hearing nothing," said Yolanda, still glaring at Lazard. "But you had a visitor this morning. A big white dude with a pot belly and glasses."

"Midwiff," I said. "What did he say?"

"Hell, he didn't say nothing. He was standing at your door when I came around the corner. He took one look at me and he was gone."

"What time was that?" Lazard asked.

"About nine," Yolanda said to me. "And that's *all* the time I can spare on small talk. Ciao, Baby." She wiggled her cigarette holder at me and strolled down the hall toward her own room.

I turned back to Lazard, who had the kind of expression on his face that looked as though he was trying to track a flea through the carpet.

"Why didn't you say you knew Yolanda?" I asked.

"Huh?" he said, looking up. I had distracted him from some Herculean deductive effort, no doubt.

"Yolanda," I said, nodding in the direction of her departure. "I mentioned her at Denise's. Why didn't you tell me that you knew her?"

"I didn't *know* I knew her," he said. "After all, there must be any number of Yolandas in this city."

"Any number of Yolandas? Are you kidding?"

Lazard shrugged. "Anyway, I knew her as Yoyo. She was kind of well known around the precinct. They called her Yoyo because that's the way she went back and forth from the lockup to the streets. At least I thought that was why. Hell, all these whores have nicknames. None of them use their real names. I didn't know it was short for Yolanda. After the coincidences you've been expecting me to swallow, I should be allowed this one, right?"

I guess that sounded reasonable enough.

"This Midwiff," said Lazard. "He's the one who was supposed to pick up your wife—your ex-wife—at the airport?"

"Yeah."

"Do you often use the freight elevator rather than the normal one?"

"That or the stairs."

"These men that you saw getting off the elevator—how do you suppose they gained access to it without a key?" Lazard asked. He was getting very urgent about things all of a sudden. These questions were coming with only a second or two pause between them.

"You only need a key from the outside," I said. "On the inside, you simply push a button just like with any other elevator. All they had to do was get in the front door and the elevator was theirs. Theoretically, only residents can get in through the lobby, but, after all, we aren't exactly on Park Avenue here. The security system being what it is, if someone wants to get in badly enough, they can."

"What about Midwiff?" said Lazard. "Was he familiar with your habit of using the freight elevator?"

"I don't remember," I said. "It's not the kind of thing I've devoted much thought to. I haven't seen too much of Bill since my divorce. He *may* have known, I guess."

Lazard squeezed his eyes shut and massaged his temples as though he were stunned by the exasperation this affair was causing him.

"Mr. Fargo, I'd like to help you," he said after his short self-administered therapy session. "But I have nothing material, nothing *physical* here to work with. All I've got is some graffiti on the elevator door. I don't *dis*-believe you, you understand. I think that what it might be is that someone is making you the butt of a rather elaborate joke. Any of your friends capable of this? Midwiff, perhaps?"

"Not in a thousand years," I said. "What would anybody go to this much trouble for?"

"Possibly it's a campaign of terror," said Lazard.

"But why?"

"I don't know," Lazard conceded. "But this connection with Millar Crofts worries me. He's dangerous and subtle at the same time. A lethal combination. People that he wants out of the way eventually *do* get out of the way in one fashion or another. He's, uh, reputed to be a possessor of the evil eye."

"*What?* Come on, Lazard."

He shrugged. "I don't buy that kind of crap either," he said. "I'm just telling you what I know."

"Well, what you know is just a little bit less than worthless," I said. I couldn't help feeling that he was trying to humiliate me in his own ingratiating way.

"I've wasted enough of your Sunday," I said. "Thanks for the return of my suitcase and the ride home. But if you don't mind, I've been up for about thirty straight hours, and I'd really like to get some sleep. In fact, you know, maybe you're right. I just could be hallucinating all this out of fatigue. A nap is exactly what I need."

Lazard studied my face for half a minute and then nodded. "You misinterpret my intentions," he announced after his inspection. "It's just like second grade, remember? The policeman is your friend." He smiled as much as any iguana could be said to have smiled and walked to the door.

"Keep in touch. And especially let me know if you are contacted by Crofts or anybody else you don't know or don't trust. I'm really here to help," he said, pulling the door shut behind him.

It seemed as though I had been sleeping for about five minutes when the phone woke me. But the room was dim and the clock read nine-thirty-eight, which meant that I had erased about seven hours of the day with my nap; nevertheless, when I answered the phone, I was still too groggy for my brain to register what the caller was saying. The voice sounded as if it were being carried through a drainpipe. But just by the tenor of the voice I knew that the news wasn't good. I had picked up three words clearly enough: *dead on arrival.*

"*Who's* dead?" I asked. *Now* who's dead, I thought.

"Midwiff. William B.," said Lazard. "There was a fire late this morning aboard a boat at the Grosse Pointe Yacht Club. Midwiff had apparently spent the night on board, uh, perhaps entertaining a young lady—at least, a witness saw a young lady leave the area about seven this morning."

"Wait, wait," I said. Lazard was zipping through this report as if the call was costing him by the second. "How could Midwiff have been on this boat all morning if Yolanda saw him here at my apartment?"

"There are any number of explanations," said Lazard. I could almost feel him shrugging over the phone. "Midwiff could have made a quick trip over to your apartment. Or Yolanda could have seen someone other than Midwiff. Or Yolanda may have seen no one at all."

"Why would she lie?"

"I don't know," said Lazard. "The one unalterable fact we have is that Midwiff is dead. He was badly burned, but we did manage to get a couple of prints. It's a positive I.D."

Now, Midwiff and I had never been the greatest of friends, but we had always gotten along. We were at least close enough so that news of his death began to stir within me feelings of guilt. I began to think that, by enlisting his help, I had exposed him to the contagion of death that seemed to swirl around me.

"There are a couple of other details," said Lazard. "First, the boat that Midwiff was found on was owned by the Blessing family. Or, at least the Blessing family had once owned it. Leona sold it about a month ago to somebody named Oliver Malvern. We're talking about a pretty sizeable purchase here. I guess you could call this boat a yacht."

You could call it that, all right. I remembered the boat vividly. The memory of it had been what was scratching at the back of my mind when Joanna and I had driven past the yacht club earlier that morning. When I was a kid, I used to have a friend whose father was the harbormaster at the Grosse Pointe Yacht Club. We used to hang around there quite a bit during summer vacations. And always, the most fascinating thing about the club was the Blessing yacht. No one ever seemed to use it. It just sat there alongside the seawall, fat, white, and majestic, almost like a floating version of the Blessing mansion. My friend had told me that the owners never used the boat in the summer, but that in the winter they would take it on long cruises to Florida and the Caribbean.

"The other thing," said Lazard, "is that your friend didn't die as a result of the fire. He had suffered one gunshot would to the head. A .38 caliber revolver was found at his side."

My pulse snapped like ropes within the shaft of my throat.

"Can you recall anything of your conversation with Mr. Midwiff that might throw some light on this?" asked Lazard.

"I told you what our conversation consisted of." I was lying just a bit—a sin of omission. I had not told Lazard *everything*. Only that I had asked Bill to get me some information on Victor Blessing. I had not, for example, mentioned Claude Nickle.

"Well, Mr. Fargo, just between you and me, I believe everything you've told me about this entire affair is the truth. I wasn't sure before, but I am now. The only problem is, I'm afraid there is nothing I can do about it officially except to caution you as emphatically as I can to avoid exposing yourself to danger."

"What do you mean there's nothing you can do? You just said that Midwiff was murdered. You're not going to investigate that?"

"I didn't say that the death was being considered a homicide," said Lazard. "I said that he died of a bullet wound to the head. Suicide hasn't been ruled out. Or accidental death."

"Accidental, my ass," I screamed. "People don't blow their brains out on strange yachts. What kind of shit are you trying to hand me, Lazard? Somebody killed Midwiff and left him to fry on the Blessing yacht. And you're trying to tell me you're just going to let it go at that? What are you covering up?"

"Not me," said Lazard patiently. "All I know is that the investigation into Midwiff's death is officially closed."

"They didn't waste much time on it," I said. "I'll bet the *Free Press* would be interested in my story and how Midwiff is involved."

"Mr. Fargo, I understand your feelings about this. You've been through an extraordinary series of events, not the least of which is the loss of your friend. Coming on the heels of the disclosures about your wife, it must be doubly traumatic for you. But believe me, I am powerless in this. There is something irregular going on, but I haven't the slightest idea who's behind it. I can't overrule the coroner, and my superiors have ordered me, on pain of suspension, to abandon any further inquiries into this case—"

"Hey, are you reading from a script or what? People are dying some very unnatural deaths just like clockwork and you're telling me you can't get involved? You're *in* on this, aren't you? You're tied in through Minerva somehow, or maybe through Sultana."

"Don't be a fool," said Lazard. "I'm not a party to this. You've got more than me to worry about. I'm trying to warn you that, although you've somehow managed to avoid harm so far, I think your life is in danger."

"Well, that's all right," I said. "I've got Detroit's finest to protect me." I slammed the receiver down. The phone rang again a few seconds later, and I unplugged the phone wire from the jack.

My father went to a funeral home once in his life and refused to go ever again. He would always say that you could judge the level of a society's civilization not by the lengths it went to deny death, but by the steps it took to explain it. So, for him, the highest honor we could bestow upon the deceased was not to sew up all their orifices and embalm them, so that they weren't much more than life-size wine skins, and then put them on display for a couple of days before burying him (this showcase segment of the ritual was what had so appalled my father), but to make death somehow accountable. The autopsy, although it too could be abused by the incompetent or manipulated by the unscrupulous, was the height of religious observance. For what else was art or religion, my father would say, but a challenge to death?

He got quite a few arguments about this, as might be expected. But he never wavered in his conviction, and it was probably the strength of his resolve that helped to impress me so thoroughly with the virtue of his philosophy. I, too, had been to a corpse display only once, and that was because I had been forced into it. The pastor of the Catholic church where I attended grade school had dropped dead of a stroke one day while castigating some poor bastard in the confessional. Father Collins was his name—a Nazi who had taken refuge in the Church. Anyway, he was stuffed and starched and laid out in front of the altar of the church and the entire student body was lined up and marched past his casket. Every student in the school hated Father Collins, but we were all paraded dutifully by, under the intense vigilance of a squad of nuns stationed around the bier, undoubtedly there to ensure that nobody defiled the body. But despite their precautions, one of the older students, an eighth grader, had managed to silently bring up a tremendous mass of phlegm, which he launched right into the serene and waxy face of Father Collins. The fury of the student's attack and the violence he demonstrated while being dragged away kicking and screaming the sort of obscenities that I had always assumed would bring instant death to the utterer under such circumstances suggested that the motivation for his act went beyond adolescent mischief, and it occurred to me only years later (I was never a precocious child when it came to matters of sex) that Father Collins had probably sodomized half of the enrollment of the school.

I sat thinking about this and occasionally taking a hit from my bottle of Old Grand Dad. Nostalgia always seems to follow on the heels of personal loss. I noticed my suitcase at the foot of my bed and opened it. I dug out my flashlight, unscrewed it, and found my roll of hundred-dollar bills lining the tube. While I'm at it, I thought, I might as well see what Leona had to say to her dead son. After all, they were both dead now, and I couldn't see how I would be betraying anybody's confidence. The dead were beyond embarrassment. I tore open the envelope and found only a picture post-card—a very old one, if the faded colors of the picture were any indication. The photo offered an aerial view of the Grosse Pointe Yacht Club. The other side of the card contained a short, handwritten verse:

> *The key to the traitor (That's traitor, not freighter)*
> *Opens nary a door, nor a gate e'en.*
> *Yet the script by the man you*
> *Call Arnie (How can you?!)*
> *Under both lock and key lies awaiting.*

This was what I had risked my life for? What Leona had been willing to pay me twenty-five thousand dollars to deliver? Six lines of doggerel? This is what people were willing to live and die for?

Then, almost without thinking about it, I found myself going through the pockets of my borrowed khakis in search of the airline ticket that Norrod had given me. It wasn't there. I had left it in my clothes in the bathroom of the Blessing house.

But I still had plenty of money and I also had a plan. I was going to practice what my father had preached. I was going to make death answer for the havoc that it had wrought around me. The source was in Italy, probably in Trento. I could almost feel myself being compelled there. It was either my dad's legacy or Old Grand Dad's influence, but, whatever it was, I was going into my heroic mode.

CHAPTER 15

▼

AERIAL AGONIES

Gentle Reader, can you stomach another digression? A short one? And perhaps not so digressive? Perhaps an intermezzo—yes, that's it, an intermezzo.

I sat in the window seat as our 747 passed over the Atlantic like the eyes of a holy man over sacred text. I don't necessarily like to look out the window (I don't mind it either), but since the flight didn't even leave New York until midnight and half of our trip would be under cover of darkness, not to say clandestine, it didn't make much difference whether I looked out the window or not. I say clandestine, for certainly in my case, if anyone was aware of my present activity, it wasn't through any announcements I had made. I hadn't even told Denise. But, as I was saying, I like to sit next to the window, well, I guess because it reduces by fifty percent the chances that someone will try to engage me in conversation.

But, unfortunately, not on this particular trip. I found myself amid the usual distribution of summer tourists on their way to Italy: entire Italian families (including infants and displeased grandmothers in perpetual mourning); a choral group on a European tour; a group of college students on an archeological expedition (near Trento, coincidentally); nuns, priests, and various other pilgrims; a stunningly beautiful, but petulant, princess being fussed over endlessly by a matronly companion—your basic *Airport* cast.

By two-thirty in the morning, most of the passengers were asleep. Those who weren't were reading or talking quietly. I sat sipping steadily on my fifth beer since takeoff and playing audience of one to the nearly non-stop bitching of the guy sitting next to me. His name was Clifford Dowagiac. He had not taken the hint when I had failed to offer my name in return for hearing his. He was one of those jerks that held your hand hostage while he peered expectantly at you and said "And you are?" Tact is lost on these people.

He was accompanied by his quiet (and, I suspect, long suffering) wife, to whom he would turn frequently for confirmation at various points along his monologue ("Am I right, Sweetheart?"), the gist of which was that the world had fucked him over continually since birth. I learned later that he was also accompanied by his twenty-year-old son who was sitting across the aisle trying to get past the massive obstacle of the princess' companion. But success was unlikely. The son looked like a resurrection of Sid Vicious.

There's a joke about a second grader who fails at the end of the school year to be promoted to the third grade. When asked by his parents to explain his failure, he simply says, "Politics." I imagine Clifford Dowagiac to have been that child. He explained that he had been an assistant professor of art history at USC, where he had been denied tenure, due to what he considered the treachery and envy of his colleagues. He had then become the assistant curator of European Painting at the Indianapolis Museum of Art, where "ultraconservative factions" within the board of trustees caused him to be passed over when the senior curator died and another one had to be appointed. He resigned and along with two partners he opened a gallery in downtown Indianapolis only to close it again three months later. This failure, according to Dowagiac, was due to a combination of his partners' mismanagement and the "philistine inhabitants of that fucking outpost." I imagined Dowagiac trying to sell a Duchamp urinal to the owner of an International Harvester dealership.

"But I'm really on to something now," he said, winding up his personal history. "I'm going to Trento to accept the presidency of the Anamorphosis League."

I didn't want to hear about this. Really, I didn't. The coincidence of our destinations was almost depressingly ominous. But Dowagiac told me about it anyway. He was just that kind of guy.

He explained that *anamorphosis* was a term used, in the artistic sense, to describe a style of painting much in vogue in the seventeenth and eighteenth centuries, which expressed extreme perspective for effect. Dowagiac pulled a book out of his briefcase to illustrate. It was full of strange drawings that appeared to depict one thing when looked at head on, but when the book was turned and you looked at the drawing lengthwise, a previously distorted image revealed itself. There were also some circular paintings that made little sense to me no matter how I looked at them.

"Those, my friend, are cylindrical anamorphoses," said Dowagiac. "For those you need one of these." He took from his briefcase a stainless steel or chrome cylinder about five inches long and about the diameter of a tailpipe.

"You position it so," he said, standing the cylinder in the middle of one of those unintelligible color splotches in the book. "And voila." The cylinder reflected the undistorted image; in this case it appeared to be an eighteenth century squire copulating rear-entry style with a scullery maid who was bent over a table.

"Spicy, no?" said Dowagiac. "Quite a few of them are like that. Pornographic or scatological. A lot of women squatting over chamber pots and that sort of thing. These things were really popular in the eighteenth century in France. Looking at anamorphic drawings, especially cylindrical anamorphoses, was parlor entertainment, respectable titillation, if you know what I mean. That, I think, is one of the reasons why the phenomenon isn't taken too seriously in academic circles. And, of course, the artistic quality of many of these things is marginal at best." This seemed to be a painful concession on Dowagiac's part, so I couldn't help retaliating for his intrusion on my privacy by throwing in a disparaging comment.

"Maybe they're right," I said. But that was the kind of challenge that Dowagiac lived for. I should have expected no less from the president-elect of the Anamorphosis League.

"What would you say if I told you that one of the first examples of anamorphosis perspective occurs in the Codes Atlanticus of Leonardo daVinci?" said Dowagiac. Maybe he expected me to go into spasms of contrition at this disclosure, but I wasn't going to give him the satisfaction.

"So, the League's mission is to rectify this neglect?" I asked.

Dowagiac squinted with the effort of his response. "Actually, the League is a fraternal order," he said finally. "We specialize in political consultation. We believe that political orientation is largely a matter of perspective and to that extent we are inspired by the example of anamorphic artists. Mainstream politics, either of the right left, or center is moribund. We believe that extreme measures are necessary if we are to achieve true world government."

Dowagiac was really turning up the zeal now. His wife was dozing next to him. Obviously she had long since become immune to his enthusiasm. But for all his fervor, Dowagiac wasn't being very specific—he was just spewing vague rhetoric. Normally this would offend me, but what I didn't need at that moment were the details of another crusade for the hearts and minds of the world's population. I'd had enough of that lunacy from Norrod. But the thought of Norrod did bring to mind another question.

"So you say this Anamorphosis League is headquartered in Trento?"

"Not at all," Dowagiac replied emphatically. "Hell, I wouldn't open a *shoe shine* stand in Italy. I've *been* to Italy. Did you ever see the way those people conduct business? Did you ever try to cash a traveler's check at an Italian bank? Mussolini may have gotten the trains to run on time, but I'll bet even he couldn't have gotten a guinea bank teller off his lazy ass." Dowagiac, with all the diplomacy of the xenophobe, was virtually shouting. I was about to remind him that he had just insulted three-quarters of the passengers when Mrs. Dowagiac beat me to it.

"Clifford," she said without opening her eyes. "Remember your blood pressure." This gentle reminder seemed to strike instant terror in Dowagiac's eyes. He became more subdued almost immediately.

"It's in Duluth," he said.

"What is?"

"The headquarters of the Anamorphosis League. You see, our principal benefactor, whose name, unfortunately, I am not at liberty to reveal, resides in Trento. And a condition of his generous endowment is that the president of the League be installed under the supervision of his representatives in that city. Of course, one must concede to the philanthropist his eccentricities."

"Yeah, it's a real blessing to have the support of influential people," I said. I felt like James Bond trying to feel out a potential contact. But despite my amateurish emphasis on the word *blessing*, Dowagiac did not react as though I'd uttered a shibboleth. Either he was much shrewder than I gave him credit for, or the name of Blessing meant nothing to him. He simply gave me a solemn nod of agreement and began to hold forth again.

"In this case," he said, "we're doubly blessed. An Italian recording company has taken an interest in my son's musical group and has offered him a recording contract complete with a European promotional tour."

Apparently, Dowagiac's disdain for the efficiency of the Italian economy didn't apply where opportunities for his immediate family were concerned.

"How nice," I said. Now that the coincidence I had imagined hadn't panned out, I was quickly losing interest in Dowagiac. I flagged down a passing stewardess and asked for another beer. Dowagiac took the opportunity to order another scotch and soda. I could see that at any moment, I was going to have to explain to him my philosophy about rollicking at thirty thousand feet.

"Yes, isn't it," said Dowagiac.

"Isn't what?"

"Isn't it nice about my son's good fortune," said Dowagiac. "It hasn't always been so easy for him. His music has been persistently misunderstood. That's him over there." He pointed to the juvenile delinquent who was still harassing the princess in a muted and puerile fashion.

"That's your son?"

"Yes, that's Dingo." Dowagiac was simply glowing with parental pride.

"You named your son after a wild dog?"

"No. We named him Clifford Dowagiac, Jr. He chose Dingo himself, as a stage name at first, but now that's his legal name. He just changed it recently. Before that it was P. T. Enroot. I'll bet you don't know where that name comes from."

I admitted that I didn't.

"Well, Dingo was in the Army for about six months following high school. He was totally unsuited for a military career, of course, and he was discharged after six months, as I say. But he tells me that during basic training, the drill instructors would try to fit in the recruits' physical training, or PT, while they were marching them back and forth from rifle ranges and other ludicrous activities. It was called PT en route—a euphemism for double-time. Get it? P. T. Enroot."

"Oh, hey, I get it," I said. "P. T. Enroot. Dang, that's clever." Where, I wondered in agony, *where* was that stewardess with my beer? I decided that she made her rounds all too infrequently and that I was going to have to order another beer as soon as she returned with the one I had ordered eons ago.

"But then he got into this punk music and formed a new group," said Dowagiac. "They called themselves the Doormats, so my son acquired his new name and they became Dingo and the Doormats."

"So now he's Dingo Dowagiac," I said. "It has a sort of ring to it." At last I could see the stewardess approaching with our drinks. I was tempted to hurdle Dowagiac and meet her halfway down the aisle.

"Nope," said Dowagiac.

"Nope what?"

"It's just plain Dingo," he said. "You know, like Halston or Liberace—just the one name. A stroke of genius, really."

I looked across the aisle at the genius whose arm was half concealed beneath the skirt of the princess, who sat frozen and wide-eyed with terror while her portly chaperone snored away indelicately.

The stewardess arrived with my beer and when she leaned over to hand it to me, I grabbed her by the wrist. It was the thinnest wrist imaginable, no bigger around than the shinbone of a dog, but certainly a higher class of dog than a dingo.

"Miss," I said, "silly me, but I have this medical condition. It's myoendocarditis actually. Its flare-ups can be extremely painful and I'm afraid that I've packed my medication with the rest of my luggage. Do you have anything for pain?"

"We have aspirin," she said.

"No. No aspirin. Aspirin is absolutely contraindicated. I also suffer from pernicious anemia and just one aspirin could result in spontaneous hemorrhaging. I'd bleed dry before you could say Amelia Earhart." The stewardess was getting alarmed.

"If it's an emergency, perhaps I should alert Captain Prusinowski," she said.

"Excuse me," said Dowagiac, "but did you say Captain Prusinowski?"

"Yes. He's the senior officer on board."

"Is he of Polish extraction?" said Dowagiac. This was great. Dowagiac was actually turning pale before my eyes.

"I don't know," said the stewardess. "I suppose he is."

"I was thinking more along the lines of something like Percodan or Demerol," I said to the stewardess.

"I'm sorry," she said. "We only have aspirin."

"Well, in that case, bring me two more of these," I said, hoisting my can of beer.

Dowagiac didn't say anything for a long time after the stewardess left. The idea of putting his life in the hands of a Polish pilot had really shaken him. After a while he spoke.

"Myoendocarditis. That's some kind of a heartache, isn't it?"

"It sure is," I said.

"Goddamn, you look awful young for heart trouble."

"I am," I said.

CHAPTER 16

▼

TRENTO BY NIGHT

We landed at Ciampino outside Rome in the cool, slick aftermath of a cloudburst at about nine o'clock on Tuesday morning. I managed to avoid much of the monumental confusion of the siege at customs and baggage claim and was heading for the bus while the Dowagiacs were still bickering with porters and searching for Dingo, who had apparently wandered off in pursuit of the young woman on the plane.

In Rome, I went directly to the train station and bought my ticket for Trento, after making it clear to the pruritic clerk that I *didn't* want to go to Taranto, which lay about two hundred miles in the opposite direction. Whatever affliction caused the clerk to scratch incessantly at his chest, face, neck and arms must also have impaired his cognitive faculties.

After a short wait, I was on my way to Trento. For most of the trip I slept, although I was repeatedly awakened by passengers entering and leaving my compartment. One stretch of the trip was especially disruptive. An entire family clamored into my compartment at the stop in Florence and didn't get off again until Bologna. To Italians, traveling by train is somewhat akin to installing wheels on their homes. The eat, play cards, drink wine, fondle each other, argue politics, grab ass, fart, and generally do whatever else Italian families do in the privacy of their living rooms. So, for a couple of hours, I slept precariously, like a seagull on a piling, ruffled and battered by domestic turbulence.

I woke up reasonably refreshed as the train was chugging its way out of the Rovereto station. The sun was sitting fat and orange over the fields and vineyards. The view was suitably magnificent and I enjoyed it in merciful solitude for the last leg of the trip. Within half an hour I was hopping off the train at Trento.

Trento nestles in a valley alongside the Adige River. From there, you're just about within yodeling distance of Austria—at the foot of the Dolomites, to be precise, and the scenery is spectacular, just like a postcard come to life. In the distance, the mountains dominate the modest, yet picturesque skyline of the city. After years in the flatlands of southeastern Michigan, it was invigorating to find myself in the middle of terrain with some muscle to it.

In the train station I got a map of the city, a tourist guide printed in Italian and German, and a list of hotels. One fourth-class place called the Accademia seemed ironically appropriate and was located near the center of the city within easy walking distance of the train station.

At the Accademia I paid eight thousand lire in advance for a small room without bath, telephone, or air conditioning. I did *not* feel deprived. In a place such as this, I reasoned, I was surely unlikely to be sharing the bathroom down the hall with any Dowagiacs, who, from what I had been able to learn of them, wouldn't survive a week without access to a swimming pool and minibar.

I ate dinner at a small restaurant down the street from my hotel and walked around the city for a while. I made a point of locating the address that Norrod had given me prior to my taking abrupt and unceremonious leave of him in Washington. It was next door to the *Museo di Scienze Naturali*. I considered dropping in to pay my respects—my curiosity, intensified by the long journey, almost overwhelmed me at this point—but I contented myself with looking near the door for the names of the occupants. There were none. Finally, I wandered back toward the center of the city. There I got a look at *Il Duomo*, that famous site of the Council of Trent, took an obligatory stroll around the inevitable Fountain of Neptune in the middle of the piazza, and then sat at one of the outdoor tables at a place called the Café Bristol, whose façade gave onto the entire piazza.

I ordered a carafe of wine and contemplated my agenda for the next day. Subterfuge was out of the question. That tactic had gotten me nothing but trouble. I decided that I was going to play this scene straight—just knock at the door of that address on Via Calepina and introduce myself to whomever answered. Explain the purpose of my visit and its urgency. Demand (civilly, of course) some answers. And trust to the goodwill and reasonable disposition of my audience.

Several of the archeological students who had been on my flight to Rome walked by and waved to me.

"Yoo-hoo," one of the girls said. "Remember us?" I smiled and waved back. Suddenly, I realized that I was in the worst possible location if I wanted to avoid certain people—namely, the Dowagiac clan. I finished off my wine and was just about to leave when a disturbance broke out behind me. A group of soldiers complete with bright red epaulets and cute little Tyrolean hats with feathers in them were arguing loudly among themselves. How anyone could take these guys seriously as warriors was beyond me, but they were obviously capable of rowdiness. Two of the soldiers seemed about to come to blows and the other three were boisterously trying to restrain them. A bartender hastened up to them and in lavish and magnanimous Italian managed to defuse the situation. In a moment, the soldiers were seated again, laughing and slapping each other on the back.

I turned my attention from this squabble and looked back out over the piazza again, just in time to see a car turn slowly into a parking space just off to my left in front of the café. A prescient twitch of my hand almost caused me to drop my wineglass. This car wasn't a silver Mercedes—it looked like an Alfa Romeo—but even before they emerged, I could tell that the occupants were old friends of mine. The driver got out of the car and opened the rear door for his passengers, one of whom was a marsh-mallowy, pink man in a light-blue three-piece suit. Norrod and his tense little commando-chauffeur. The other passenger was a muscular, bearded man in Levi's and a CUNY sweatshirt.

The chauffeur assumed his familiar leaning attitude against the fender of the Alfa Romeo, shook a cigarette loose for a pack and lit it. He watched as his boss and the bearded man entered the café and sidled past a few tables until they found one to their liking near the back where there were fewer people. A waiter approached their table, but Norrod shook his head and waved him away. A vigorous but subdued conversation between the two men ensued.

I sensed a disagreement between them, but there was really no overt indication of one. Neither man varied his expression, nor did either make any telltale gestures. After about two minutes of conversation, Norrod pushed himself away from the table and started to leave the café. Just then, the table full of soldiers or boy scouts or whatever they were erupted into another vociferous disagreement. Norrod glanced over to get a look at the cause of the commotion. And, of course, I found myself almost directly in his line of vision. He looked right at me and I saw his eyes widen in recognition. That's all I had to see. I got up and began weaving my way out of the café. I heard my name being called, and I broke into a sprint. At the curb, I bowled over a photographer who was hunched over, peering into the viewfinder of his camera, which was perched on a tripod. He cursed me in some language that sounded Germanic, and I apologized in short-winded Italian.

I looked back over my shoulder and saw that Norrod was making urgent, spasmodic gestures to Giacinto, who was apparently having trouble interpreting these signs. By the time he grasped the significance of this flurry of activity, I was already ducking around the corner. I ran for a couple of blocks, then took another left and jumped into a taxi parked against the curb.

The driver had been dozing, but he woke up when I slammed the door shut. At first, he just turned around and looked at me as though he'd never before had a fare jump into the back seat of his car. But he'd probably just never had one sit down on the floor in the back seat and cover his head before. Then he lifted himself in the seat, tapped the rearview mirror a couple of times (which didn't seem to adjust it one bit) and asked me where I wanted to go in a voice that sounded as though he gargled with grout.

Well, I'd certainly had enough of a tour for one night, even though it was abbreviated. Any further nocturnal excursions, especially with Norrod and Giacinto around the city—and it wasn't that big of a city, nor did it offer any titty bars that I could dive into for sanctuary—would be perilous. I told the driver to take me to the train station. I remembered seeing a *negozio* in the neighborhood. I reasoned that it might still be open, given its proximity to the train station. I didn't know what system of logic made me think that the *negozio* might stock Jack Daniels by the fifth, but I did.

The cabby dropped me off in front of the shuttered-down *negozio*. I tell you what, you gotta shop early in Italy. The only place in the area that seemed to be open for business was the bar adjacent to the train station. I managed to talk the bartender into selling me a bottle of wine, which he agreed to do after I bought each of us a shot of grappa, although I suspect he would have sold me the bottle anyway.

What the hell was Norrod doing in Trento? Had he known I would be in the city? If so, how? I had plenty of things to learn. Yes, to learn. The infinitive becomes imperative. So, like the diligent student that I was, I returned to the Accademia, a two-liter bottle of wine under my arm and an inquisitive itch erupting throughout my soul to beat the hell out of anything that *impiegato* at the train station in Rome had suffered with. Back in my room, my attempts at ratiocination lasted as long as the bottle of wine. In the morning, all I had to show for my efforts was a headache.

CHAPTER 17

▼

DIGGING

Two heavy thuds sounded at the door to which the blood sloshing around in my brain responded with thuds of its own.

"*Signor Fargo.*" The thick voice of the *albergatore* seeped through the door like wisdom through the skull of an idiot—myself, for example. "*Ci son' otto.*" This was followed by two more thuds, as though he were kicking the door rather than knocking on it. A graduate of the SS School of Hotel Administration.

I felt around the nightstand for my watch. I had closed the shutters the night before and the room was still quite dark. I finally found the lamp switch and turned it on. My watch read eight-twenty. Close enough. I had asked the hotel clerk to wake me at eight. But, hey, no problem. You learn to deal with inefficiency like this. I would eventually think of something equivalently petty to harass him with. What this world needed was a little more justifying of things.

"*Grazie,*" I said.

"*Prego,*" said the heavy voice, lethargic with insincerity.

I put aside my irritation and walked down the hall for a quick shower, possibly made quicker by the fact that the hot water ran out about two minutes after I stepped under it. I added this to my mental catalog of slights.

I got a shot of espresso down in the hotel lobby and at about ten minutes to nine I was standing at the entrance of the house next to the *Museo di Scienze Naturali* waiting for someone to answer the doorbell, which I had just rung for the third time. A man walked out of the museum. I didn't know him, but his face was familiar. I had seen him the night before with Norrod in the Café Bristol. He caught sight of me and yelled something in Italian.

"*Per la scava?*" he repeated after I didn't answer him. Now, I consider Italian *la piu bella lingua del mondo*, but I was, after all, rusty.

"Are you here for the dig?" he said, finally descending into English.

"Not exactly," I said, not exactly sure what he was talking about.

"Well, Professor Stonestreet isn't home. He's at the excavation site. He won't be back until a little after one."

"Where's the excavation site?" I asked. We were standing about one hundred and fifty feet apart and this conversation was beginning to seem a little absurd in its hyperbolic conduct.

"I'm on my way there now," he said, starting to walk towards a van parked in front of the museum. "I can give you a lift if you want."

"Thank you," I said, following him towards the van. He was wearing Levi's, heavy work boots and a T-shirt. He was tanned and sinewy and about forty-five years old, with curly black hair and a beard full of tight ringlets. He looked like a middleweight Hercules.

"I had to come back for film," he said, showing me a roll of 35-millimeter film. He said it as if it was supposed to mean something to me. When I got within distance appropriate to civilized conversation, he announced his name with noticeable emphasis and formality—almost aggressively.

"Claudio Niccolo," he said, thrusting his hand forward in a fashion that looked more like a fencing maneuver than a greeting.

"Claude Nickle!" I exclaimed in spite of myself. The way he withdrew his hand, you would have thought I had just yelled out that I had leprosy.

"Okay, pal. Just who the hell are you?" he said, hands on his hips now, ready for action.

"Stephen Fargo."

"Well, I'll be a son-of-a-bitch," he said, relaxing somewhat. He peered intently at my face as if by doing so he could confirm my identity. "Well I'll be a god*damn* son-of-a-bitch. I guess you *do* want to talk to the professor."

The excavation site was about twenty minutes west of the city. On the way, Claudio explained casually that he had been living in Trento for about twelve years, working as an assistant to Professor Stonestreet. Beyond that, he volunteered no information about himself. He was very tentative. I sensed that he wanted to confide in me, but prudence or suspicion held him back. I wanted to ask him why he had disappeared in the middle of his research on the Blessing family, but I thought it better not to be too pushy. Besides, he was the one who was doing most of the questioning. He wanted to know the details of Leona's death, the whereabouts of Miguel and Haskell, Jr., and how I had gotten Professor Stonestreet's address.

I answered him truthfully, but only in the most cursory fashion, and I could tell that he didn't consider my answers completely satisfactory. I was relieved when Claudio pulled the van up to the site and parked it.

The dig was located on a small plateau at the base of one of those mountains I had seen from Trento. A one-hundred-foot-square hole about ten feet deep had been gouged out of the plateau. Half of the floor of the hole was marked off with strings and stakes in a grid, each section measuring about a meter. Each square was being meticulously scraped and probed by the workers with small trowels. I recognized many of the people in the hole as the students I had flown over with. Occasionally someone would run up the ramp with a wheelbarrow or a bucket of dirt, which would be taken to an area off to the side where two more students processed the dirt through filters, washing it through with the water stream from a hose. In another area covered by an awning, several students were sorting and marking material that had apparently been recovered from the hole.

I stayed up on top while Claudio descended the ramp. He moved carefully to the far corner of the hole where he knelt down next to an elderly man who seemed to be giving advice about troweling technique to one of the female students. Claudio spoke into the man's ear and gestured towards me. The older man (it could only be Stonestreet) turned to look at me. We stared at each other for about fifteen seconds before he returned the girl's trowel to her with a few more words of encouragement, got to his feet and started up the ramp toward me—his stride suggesting agility and yet resignation.

I studied him as he approached. He was probably in his late sixties with a full head of white hair and a deep tan. He wasn't tall—perhaps several inches shorter than I was—but his body was trim and his bearing was imposing. As he got closer, I could see his eyes, which were a rich blue, but almost opaque—like star sapphires. He had a narrow hawklike nose and a sturdy mustache. Something about his expression reminded me of Leona Blessing. It had that same stoicism about it—not like a martyr, exactly, but like one committed to survival and at the same time convinced of the futility of it. What he *didn't* remind me of was his son; I could see no resemblance. Nor did he look like any professor I had ever seen.

"Stephen," he said, shaking my hand and grasping my forearm in his left hand. It was just like we were old friends who hadn't seen each other in years. "I'd like to tell you what a pleasant surprise this is, but I must admit that I'm not much surprised."

"Nobody seems to be much surprised to see me," I said. "Perfect strangers seem to find my sudden presence absolutely natural."

"Maybe they're not such perfect strangers as you think," said Stonestreet. Claudio was still hanging close by and his presence seemed to inhibit Stonestreet for some reason, although that reason didn't seem to be a matter of distrust.

"Nickie," he said to Claudio, "keep an eye on those kids, will you? I want them to take it down to a uniform ten centimeters."

"*Si, dotore*," said Claudio, who, perhaps as an example to me, seemed determined to assert the formality of their professional relationship. He turned and headed back down the ramp. If he resented this obviously contrived dismissal, he didn't show it.

Using both arms, Stonestreet escorted me towards the sorting tables like a soldier helping a wounded comrade off the battlefield.

"These students are enthusiastic and tireless, but they are also inexperienced," he said. "In just a moment of impatience and zeal, they can disrupt hundreds of years of a culture's history."

"What are you looking for?" I asked, nodding towards the hole.

"Dear boy," said Stonestreet in mock horror. "You make it sound as if we're prospecting for gold. Any archeologist worth his salt doesn't look for *anything*. There's no room in our profession for arrogance or presumption. Certainly not in the field. In the classroom we can afford to be pontifical, but here we must be humble. We must take what the earth yields up. Ours is an interpretive science, not a speculative one."

We had arrived at the table where the students were busy labeling and cataloging the artifacts, which to my untrained eye looked unremarkable; flint fragments and pottery shards looking more or less like the products of human craftsmanship.

"You know," said Stonestreet, "I used to do quite a bit of work in Central and South America. But about halfway through my career it occurred to me that the pre-Colombian cultures were too seductively glamorous for a middle-age scholar to immerse himself in. So I came here." He picked up a ceramic fragment that one of the students had just labeled with impossibly tiny numbers and had set down to dry. It was a small section of the rim of a very crude, orange clay pot—no more than three inches long.

"Look at this," he said. He pointed to a wavy line that the prehistoric potter had engraved just below the rim for the purposes of ornamentation, I guessed. "We might pull a hundred reasonable well-preserved pot shards out of that hole in a week and perhaps only one or two will evidence even this much elaboration. You understand that existence was grim for these people by our standards. Jesus, by almost *any* standards. If you'll pardon the cliché, it was an incessant struggle for survival. And here you have someone compelled by the artist in him to distinguish a mundane clay pot with a single undulant line. I tell you, Stephen, it says more to me about the irrepressibility and continuity of the human imagination than all the Mayan ruins in the Yucatan."

He paused abruptly, as though he had suddenly become conscious of rhetorical excess.

"Excuse me," he said. "An old man can afford to indulge his romanticism. Were I a young buck," he said, winking at me, "I'd have to pretend to disdain such histrionics in the name of professional objectivity. Besides, I'm sure you didn't make this journey just to listen to me prattle on about the virtues of Neolithic craftsmanship."

A note of cynicism had crept into his voice and the friendliness went out of his eyes briefly. He replaced the shard as carefully as if it had been a religious relic.

"I'm not exactly sure why I came," I admitted.

"There. You see? You have the soul of an archeologist," he said with renewed animation. "Take things as they come."

"Well, lately, things have been coming pretty hot and heavy."

"I dare say they have," he said softly. He very nearly seemed to be commiserating with me. "Come on," he said with sudden energy and determination. He maintained his grip on my arm and began leading me away from the table. "Let's take your mind off your troubles for a moment. We had a spot of luck yesterday."

He led me to another large hole about two hundred yards away. On the way, he explained that the day before, construction workers preparing the foundation for what was to be an apartment complex had unearthed an ancient burial site.

"It's a marvelous country like that," he told me. "You can stumble on your human heritage all over the place."

Great, I thought. He'd going to cheer me up by showing me somebody's grave.

The difference between the two holes made me appreciate the systematic approach of the archeological method. The first hole was clearly the site of a scientific exploration. This one was simply a hole. But in one end of it a small cave had been scooped out. Three men were clustered around this cave. One was taking photographs, one was writing or sketching in a large spiral notebook, and the third was squatting with half his body inside the cave. Above them, on ground level, a group of workmen sat around their earthmoving equipment talking and smoking. At our approach, one of the workers saluted Stonestreet, who acknowledged him with a nod.

"*Buon' giorno, dottore,*" said the man, bowing with a flourish. That brought a round of snickering from his companions. The sense of hostility between Stonestreet and the man who had addressed him very nearly crackled across the distance between them.

"I'm afraid I'm holding them up," Stonestreet explained to me. "There's a quaint, but nonetheless healthy respect for scholarship over here that amounts to virtually an official sanction of our priority here. For the moment, I'm a more powerful *padrone* than he is. Of course, I can't suspend his operation indefinitely and he knows it. So he's hanging around being mildly derisive to assert his authority."

By now, we had descended the ramp and were almost to the cave cut into the sidewall of the hole. I could see now that the man crouching half inside the cave was doing some close work on the floor of the cave with a brush. I hung back for a moment while Stonestreet walked up to the three men and began conversing with them in Italian. These men were obviously not the novices at work in the other hole. Stonestreet treated them more like colleagues, listening carefully to what they were saying. After the explanation was complete, Stonestreet called me over. As I approached, the three Italians withdrew to smoke cigarettes. This encouraged the foreman above to strut back and forth across the front of the hole going through a series of gestures apparently mimicking the activity of the archeologists.

"Look at him," said Stonestreet in amazement. "Just like some jealous minor deity, temporarily deranged by impotence." Stonestreet shook his head and guided me gently to the cave. "Here's what he wants me to shovel out of here like it was so much coal, so he can get back to his bloody apartment building."

Stonestreet directed the beam of the flashlight into the cave. I saw a remarkably intact, brown skeleton, much of it still partly imbedded in the earth. The arrangement of the bones suggested that the corpse had been buried in a sort of fetal position, its legs drawn up and its head bowed down. One arm extended downward and the other lay across it in what seemed to be a very casual arrangement—almost like a sleeping position. The exposed parts of the skeleton had been brushed clean. The rib cage had collapsed, but the skull seemed to be in almost perfect shape, although the jawbone had become detached from it. The skeleton seemed small, and I asked if it was that of a child.

"Probably a young woman," said Stonestreet, "judging from the accoutrements of the gravesite. The skeleton is perhaps six thousand years old, and yet you can see by the way the body was deposited how much respect and tenderness they afforded their dead. Of course, that's not to say that she wasn't strangled to death in a squabble over who was supposed to milk the goat that morning."

Stonestreet cut the beam of the flashlight.

"We'd better let these boys get back to work before that tyrant up there loses his patience completely and decides to speed things up with his back hoe."

We retreated from the entrance to the cave and the three Italians moved in to resume their work.

"So Motherwell Norrod directed you to me," said Stonestreet when we were out of the cool dampness of the hole and walking through the bright sunshine back towards the first excavation site.

"That's what he *tried* to do, to put it mildly. But I came on my own." I didn't bother to tell Stonestreet that it was Claudio whom Norrod had sent me to see, and not him. "Did you know that Norrod's in town, by the way?"

"Oh, yes," said Stonestreet, nodding emphatically. "They should all be swooping in here about now." When he didn't elaborate, I asked who he was talking about.

"Why, all of Draper's beneficiaries, of course. Leona's death was the signal. The race is on."

"What's the prize?"

"The legacy of Draper Blessing," said Stonestreet. His words brought to mind Valerie's vague reference to my impending inheritance, but I said nothing of this to Stonestreet.

"Why Trento?" I asked instead.

"Because this is where Draper is."

"You mean he's buried here?"

"In a manner of speaking. You might say he reposes here."

"I thought he was buried in Detroit," I argued.

"Ah, there was a memorial erected to him there. But *he's* not there. I'm not trying to be cryptic, if you'll excuse the pun. But we can't talk about it here. I think we can leave things here in Nickie's hands for a couple of hours, anyway. We can go back to my apartment and discuss this in private." I got the feeling that Stonestreet's reluctance to confide in Claudio was the reason behind this remark. I took a chance on the hunch.

"You know, I saw Claudio, or Claude Nickle, as he used to call himself stateside, last night with Norrod—" Stonestreet dismissed the rest of my sentence with a wave of his hand.

"Amateur political maneuvering," he said. "I suspect they were trying to strike some inconsequential bargain or other."

When we were back at the first excavation site, Stonestreet galloped down the ramp and over to Claudio. He said a few words, to which Claudio seemed to assent reluctantly. Then Stonestreet turned and climbed back up the ramp.

"Come on," he said when he had rejoined me on top. "We'll take my car."

Claudio had not moved since receiving his instructions from Stonestreet. He stared up towards us with a malevolent squint. The knuckles of his right hand were white with the intensity of his grip on the trowel, which he held point down in rather predatory fashion, for an archeologist.

CHAPTER 18

▼

THE KEY TO DIVINE STATUS

Stonestreet's apartment was a small, clean, even Spartan affair. It looked as though someone had taken a saw to all of the furniture; all of it was very low to the ground, giving the apartment an Oriental flavor. Stonestreet busied himself preparing lunch in the kitchen. I sat just outside the kitchen in the adjoining courtyard at a white wrought iron table in the shade of a huge umbrella, sipping at the Amaretto that Stonestreet had ceremoniously poured for me. At his insistence, I was explaining the events of the past week, although in doing so I felt like an insurance man trying to explain a policy to a maitre d'. Stonestreet kept excusing himself to answer the telephone or the door, or to retrieve some ingredient from the attic, which apparently doubled as a food cellar. At least I saw him descend from it once with a huge salami cradled in his arms.

He apologized repeatedly for the interruptions and urged me to continue, but really, he didn't seem to be paying much attention to what I was saying. He finally joined me at the courtyard table with a huge plate of antipasto and a bottle of wine.

"I hope you don't mind," he said when he had deposited his burden in the center of the table. "I've never gotten used to eating those heavy midday meals like the natives. And, as you can see, I never seem to be able to wait for midday for it."

"It looks great," I said.

"Please, help yourself." The phone range again. "Damn," he said, although his inflection didn't suggest that he was all that irritated. "Excuse me once again."

"You ought to hire someone," I suggested when he had returned from his telephone conversation. He looked at me quizzically.

"Oh, you mean domestic help or something like that?" he said. "Nah," he said, brushing the idea away from his head with his fork. "Somebody always underfoot. I've been cursed all my life with an independent streak. Actually, I usually manage very nicely, but with this dig things are a little hectic. Nobody seems to be able to make decisions."

"What about Claudio?"

"Well, Claudio's competent enough, but he's not really an archeologist."

"What is he?"

"I'm not really sure," said Stonestreet, frowning a bit over something he had tasted in his salad. "Do you think it's a bit heavy on the oil?" he asked.

"No. Just fine. Doesn't he have an occupation of some sort? Claudio, I mean."

"Oh, he fancied himself as a writer at one time, I believe. But I suppose he had nothing to write about. That's no occupation for a man, anyway. The tools of the trade are too meager, too common. My father was a carpenter, just like the Savior." He affected a palsied bow of the head in mock reverence. "He used to say that a man's worth could be determined by his ability with tools. The farmer with his plow, the potter with his wheel, the athlete with his ball, the soldier with his weapon, the surgeon with his knife. Claudio's father was a surgeon, by the way, although a rather unlucky one, I've heard. In fact, one of his own colleagues once confided to me that the old boy couldn't cut mold off cheese. I understand that a rash of malpractice suits drove him into a career as a sales manager for a company that manufactures prosthetic devices. Irony can be gruesome, don't you think?"

"But since Claudio's mother was Leona Blessing's sister, I don't suppose the family could realistically fall too far from social grace," I said, hazarding a guess.

Stonestreet lifted his glass to me in salute. "I see you're not completely in the dark," he said.

"Not as much as some people," I said. "Your son, for example. You ought to get in touch with him and clear a few things up. He thinks his father's dead." If I had expected this announcement to rattle Stonestreet, I was mistaken. He continued slicing his prosciutto with great care, as if he were tenderly performing vivisection on a favorite pet.

"Kelly has every reason to think his father's dead," Stonestreet said. "After all, he is."

Jesus! Of course! The realization dropped into my consciousness like a hanging victim through the trapdoor of a gallows. Draper Blessing was Kelly Stonestreet's father! He had said that he had inherited his butler Blakely when his *father* had died. It was easy to see that Stonestreet Senior wasn't the type to have butlers fawning over him. And even if he *was* the type, archeology professors just didn't make that kind of money. Kelly Stonestreet had made a gross slip of the tongue and I had not even registered it. It was as though a tank had plowed through my living room and I had responded by getting up and closing the window.

Stonestreet chuckled. "I hope you're not going to go into shock," he said. "It's really not so astonishing as all that. Especially if you knew Draper Blessing. Save your astonishment. You're going to need it. If you intend to lapse into a stupor every time you stumble across one of Draper's offspring, you'll find yourself dribbling oatmeal down your chin and a lot of people in white coats scolding you for pissing your pants. Who can tell about paternity? Women have the advantage of us there. Only they know for sure that a child is their own. Even poor Joseph had his moment of crisis."

Stonestreet poured me another glass of Amaretto.

"Here," he said. "Brace yourself."

"You see," he continued after I had taken his advice, "Draper Blessing was rich, powerful, and famous, not necessarily in that order. And as with many men upon whom fortune has smiled, his success only served to amplify his weaknesses and increase his appetites. He considered himself above morality, almost as a duty of his position. In fact, he considered himself his own version of God. Hell, he just about outlived the traditional version. And, really, it was only just a slight delusion. Do you know how he made his money?"

"An invention of some sort," I said. Stonestreet made a derisive gesture.

"Draper never invented anything in his life. The one you're thinking of was the result of industrial espionage and blackmail, the two occupations, by the way, at which Draper excelled. The imaginative effort was the product of a talented designer who loved to gamble but who didn't like to win and who borrowed money from the wrong people. To make a long and sordid story short, Draper convinced this designer to relinquish his rights to his invention. It gave Draper his legitimate foothold in the industrial world and consigned the designer to everlasting obscurity as an archeologist."

"That's quite a leap," I said. "From automotive engineer to archeologist."

Stonestreet speared a wedge of tomato from the huge salad plate.

"That was Draper's idea," he said. "He was generous like that to people he had a sort of captivating influence over. He financed my education, saw to it that I landed the right jobs, and made sure that I got sent to the places he wanted me to be sent to."

"Why?"

"You have to understand—you will understand shortly—that Blessing considered people extensions of his own personality. He had an interest in archeology and so he used me as a surrogate. I didn't mind. In fact, as you can probably tell, I grew to like it. In any event, to get back to Kelly's parentage, Draper's proprietary sense over his acquaintances also included the spouses of his acquaintances. Are things clarifying for you?"

"So Blessing seduced your wife?"

"No, Draper *raped* my wife," said Stonestreet, emphasizing the word as if it was going to be on some Great Final Exam some ultimate day. "In my presence. I made the mistake of trying to intervene and he had two bodyguards hold me so that I was forced to watch the whole thing. After Kelly was born, my wife divorced me."

I said nothing for a moment, waiting for some display of outrage on Stonestreet's part. But if the events he was relating were appalling, his lack of rancor was even more so.

"That's despicable," I said, trying to be as level-headed about this thing as he was. After all, it was his house, his story. "Yet you talk about it with such equanimity."

Stonestreet shrugged.

"It was a lifetime ago," he said. "Besides, I haven't finished. Blessing never acknowledged paternity, but he did provide for most of Kelly's support for years, including some rather bizarre adventures that Kelly managed to involve himself in—everything from African safaris to the formation of a mercenary army."

"Yeah," I said. "He filled me in."

"Self-aggrandizement," said Stonestreet with a sneer that made him seem suddenly less forgiving. "His story is not completely reliable."

"And yours is?"

"I suppose that's for you to judge," he said, apparently without taking offense at my remark. "Would you like some coffee?"

I said that I would, and Stonestreet excused himself to prepare it in the kitchen.

Damn! Stonestreet had the manner of a Bavarian count and the fastidiousness of an aging priest. Even this little courtyard of his looked like something out of *Portrait of a Lady*. Right next to my elbow stood a majestic bush of vermilion peonies the size of grapefruit, the petals of the flowers as full and as lush as the lower lip of a starlet. Bursts of hyacinth, crocus and lily erupted throughout the courtyard. My father used to hate flowers. "Nobody's better with flowers than a gangster," he would say.

Stonestreet returned with a tray bearing a small espresso coffee maker and two demitasse cups. He poured the heavy black liquid into each of the cups, sweetened his with an alarming dose of sugar, and resumed his seat. He slurped away at his coffee in typical Italian style, taking a fifty-fifty mixture of air and liquid.

"Leona, needless to say, never forgave Draper," said Stonestreet, abruptly resuming his story. "She could tolerate his fornicating with strangers, but the rape off an associate's wife was outside her moral perimeter, as, I suppose, it's outside of most people's."

"Why didn't she divorce him?"

"I don't know," said Stonestreet. "Probably because Draper wouldn't let her. Possibly because divorce was *also* morally unacceptable to her. Leona was as straight-laced as they go. My personal feeling is that she stayed married to him in order to be a living admonishment to him, not that he would notice. That was her style. It was right after this incident that Leona had that ridiculous fountain built in front of the house. Jesus! As though a libertine like Draper would reform at the sight of a statue. I think Leona was already a bit unbalanced at that point. And then when Ben died in '60 or '61 she lost it completely. Just sat in that fortress of hers and let her imagination run wild."

"Where was Blessing all this time?"

"*Nobody* ever knew for sure where Draper was. I only saw him once or twice after Kelly was born. But I'm sure he knew of my activities. What he wanted to know, he knew." He said it as though Blessing's omniscience was as natural as gravity. "Let me give you an example. The last time I spoke to Draper was in the summer of 1972. He called me here in Trento from some godforsaken desert someplace where he was taking instruction from some Indian medicine man. It was a couple of days after the Watergate break-in. He was cackling away like a prospector who had just found the motherlode. He told me who was involved in the break-in, how extensive the political implications were, and that I could expect not to see Nixon finish out his second term, a prospect that caused Draper no little joy. It was all a huge global game to him at this point. In his own way, I guess he was just as crazy as Leona was.

"He had this theory that each person, no matter who he was, had at least one thing about himself that he was so ashamed of that he would suffer pain, deprivation, humiliation, slavery, extortion, manipulation—almost anything, rather than have his secret exposed. He believed, for example, that the *only* motivation for suicide was shame—one would choose to destroy oneself rather than reveal one's inadequacies—his failure at love, his financial ineptitude, his inability to find the world interesting."

Stonestreet paused to finish his cup of coffee and to pour himself another.

"Sounds to me like he just set psychology back about five hundred years," I said, accepting another cup of coffee from my host and watching him administer another lethal helping of sugar to his drink.

"Draper wasn't practicing medicine," said Stonestreet with a slight edge of reproval. "He was manipulating people. And it worked. He held people hostages to their own fears of exposure. Some very important people. He also managed to develop an information network that's the closest thing to total knowledge this side of divinity. He began funding a wide assortment of agencies and foundations—virtually underwriting their operations. He placed no restrictions on the use of the money, so that you'll find any number of opposing political, social, and religious—even academic—viewpoints supported by Blessing money. Of course, not many of the recipients of this largess are aware of the source. The only stipulation that Blessing made was that he have complete access to the files and computer systems of any organization he funded—ostensibly to insure that his money was not being utilized for purposes which ran counter to the Blessing philosophy—which is a joke, of course. Draper was about as ethical as a hyena. His only real ethic was that information was power, to slightly distort an old aphorism, especially information that people were sensitive about."

Stonestreet paused again. He was getting a bit hoarse, so he poured himself a glass of wine and drank three-quarters of it in two swallows. While he had his nose pointed towards the sky, I noticed for the first time a lengthy scar running across throat. It seemed to be in about the right position for a tracheotomy, but it was perhaps six inches long and very narrow.

"That's all very interesting," I said, resisting the urge to ask Stonestreet how he got the scar. "But it doesn't explain why total strangers seem to know how many fillings I have, why some other people are throwing money at me like rice at a wedding, and why people around me—including friends and fellow employees—are dying…well, goddamn it, I wish I could say something clever about the way they were dying, but in any event it's at a rate above the national average statistically. Christ, I feel like Horatio sharing the stage with a bunch of stiffs in the last act of *Hamlet*. Now my ex-wife is mixed up with some wall-eyed gun runner who specializes in cocaine and double whammies."

The last part of this I tried to emphasize by bringing my open hand down sharply on the tabletop. But wrought iron, unfortunately, just doesn't have the resonance of wood and my gesture came off as ridiculously tinny. Nevertheless, my mild outburst seemed to remind Stonestreet that I was there for a reason.

"I know this all sounds damnably incidental," he said, clearing the dishes from the table, perhaps in anticipation of another violent display on my part. "But it is all vitally important." He balanced the tray on the kitchen window ledge behind him and returned to the conversation in earnest.

"You're referring, I take it, to Millar Crofts, *il malocchio fortissimo*." He added a swirling flourish with his hand here, as though to underscore the sarcasm of his words. "Mercenary, black marketer, general unsavory type who, nevertheless, commands a certain amount of respect. Seems he's absolutely fearless under fire. He's also reputed to be an ambitious tactician who occasionally flirts with recklessness.'

"Do you buy that shit about the evil eye?" I asked.

"No," Stonestreet responded immediately. "I just think Crofts is ugly. But what I believe makes no difference. He has some sort of reputation as a *jettature*. Superstitious folk keep their pregnant woman and livestock away from him and wear amulets as protective measures when he's around. I've met him twice and I've never heard him speak. I suspect he has a lilting soprano that would entirely destroy his image. I think *he* believes all this garbage about the evil eye, and you'll see him do a lot of squinting and rolling his eyes. Who knows, maybe it keeps the Honduran peasants in line."

"So Haskell Junior and Crofts were comrades-in-arms then?"

"Yes. Along with Miguel Blessing and Rudy Sultana. They got into some trouble in Chile, which sent them all into other lines of work."

"Yeah," I said. "Worm farms and extortion, to name just a couple."

But Stonestreet wasn't listening. His eyes were trained on something above and to the right of my head. Then I noticed the sound—the dull, percussive throbbing of a helicopter rotor. I had been hearing it all along as it approached, but I simply hadn't allowed it to distract me from the conversation. But when I turned to look at it, I could see how it would qualify as a distraction. It was a blue and white executive helicopter with pontoons. It hovered about a hundred yards off and a couple of hundred feet in the air. It was close enough that I could almost make out the features of the two occupants. As much as I hated to think about it, we seemed to be the objects of their attention.

The color seemed to go out of Stonestreet's face for a moment, but he recovered quickly.

"I don't believe I've seen too many helicopters around this town," said Stonestreet, frowning. "I *know* I've never had one pay a house call." Almost as soon as he had spoken the helicopter tipped sideways and began to slide off to the left, the sunlight flashing off its windshield. A moment later it was out of sight, although I could still hear it in the distance for another moment or so.

"I believe the mobilization is underway," said Stonestreet with just a hint of weariness in his voice. I wondered if I should expect a horde of Austrian Irredentists to come flopping down into the courtyard.

"I don't understand," I said. Hell, too bad I wasn't a bandleader. That could be my theme song.

"You've been followed, don't you see?"

"What's that, a joke?"

"No," said Stonestreet. "I mean you've been followed to Trento."

That didn't surprise me. I was beginning to think I could never be surprised again—that my life from here on was going to be no more than a leisurely backstroke to that Great Eternal Deep End in the sky. But I had underestimated Stonestreet's talent for startling revelation.

"Has it occurred to you," he asked, "that there might be a very good reason for all this attention being paid to you?"

"It occurred to me that there must be a reason. How good it is I couldn't say, since I don't know what it is."

"Let me give you a scenario," said Stonestreet, sounding more like a cabinet member than an academic. "A great man—an amasser and custodian of a tremendous store of information to which he alone has total access—approaches death. This man is the nerve center for a network of information gathering facilities that he has endowed and that he sanctions still. To this point, he has been able to keep these other facilities in line— through the force of his personality and the threat of withdrawing funds. And in the two years since his death, this huge network has remained intact *and* in line through the rumored existence of a document prepared by this great man that would make it possible for a successor to continue to exert control over these various agencies.

"Now, the problem for the man is to select a worthy successor, not a simple task when you consider how extraordinary the bequest is. That is, it's not unlikely that, in addition to the personal information available to the custodian of this source, there is also a good deal of highly confidential data of military and political importance. I may not overstate the case when I say that the data contained in this document could be pivotal to the course of human history."

I could feel a yawn sealing off escape hatches throughout my sinuses. Stonestreet stopped his narrative long enough to heft a cantaloupe. He set it on the table in front of him and halved it cleanly with a large chef's knife, releasing the pleasant, sweet odor of the fruitmeat into the air. He then cut two sections out of one half of the melon and offered one to me. I declined the offer.

"You're not hungry?" he said with an ominous inflection. Christ! I hoped he wasn't going to get metaphorical on me. What I didn't feel like doing at that point was deciphering any analogues. The story was taking long enough as it was. He carved a crescent chunk of orange melon away from the rind, sliced it crosswise, speared a section with the point of the knife, and then fed himself with the knife, just like a proper *cacciatore*. He resumed his story.

"The man is in somewhat of a quandary about the ultimate disposition of this alleged file, shall we call it. He realizes that, should it fall into imprudent or malicious hands, the balance of power and, in fact, world stability—or what there is of it—could be seriously threatened. Nuclear war and the extinction of the species in not an impossible consequence of the irresponsible use of this file. To complicate matters, the old boy has a naïve faith in primitive man, based, no doubt, on an early and indelible infatuation with Rousseau, which has led him, impetuous fellow that he is, to father an illegitimate child by a woman who he fancies is of Mayan extraction. He subsequently adopts the child and bestows upon him all the advantages his fortune can offer, much to the chagrin of his legitimate offspring. But the selectively doting father has miscalculated. His adopted son begins to express his racial consciousness in ways that the father had not anticipated. The son becomes embroiled in revolutionary activities all over Central and South America. Hence, the father reacts by paying belated attention to his only remaining legitimate son, who is, however, already so dissolute that he is beyond redemption. The legitimate son, perhaps overwhelmed by this tardy affection, is found shortly after its onslaught face down in a swimming pool.

"Now the old man—stunned by a combination of disillusionment and remorse to the point that he is probably not as rational as he should be, perhaps becomes susceptible to delusion. In a chance conversation with his brother-in-law, who used to be a doctor, but who has become a marketing representative for a prosthetic limb firm, the old man learns of a female amputee—perhaps senile and certainly addled by the ravages of diabetes—who is living on welfare and doesn't have the money to pay for an artificial leg. The woman first claims that she should be provided with the limb because she is half Native American. When that fails to produce results, she begins ranting about how, as a young girl, she had been involved in a brief affair with a young man, which had produced a child, of whom the woman had kept the father ignorant, probably thinking him no more than indigent. Unable to care for the child herself, she had to put it up for adoption.

"Years later she sees the photograph of a wealthy manufacturer in the newspaper and detects a resemblance to her old paramour. But she had relinquished the child with the stipulation that the new parents would not disclose their identities. So, little does she know that her child is now a middle-aged machinist in the factory of the millionaire manufacturer. She probably never knew it."

Stonestreet reached across the table slowly and splashed some Amaretto into my glass. I must have looked like I needed it. I drank it down in a hurry. The air seemed thin and nothing moved. Even the heavy peonies, pendant on the gooseneck stalks, seemed inauthentic. I felt like a mere feature—perhaps no more than a splotch of fleshtone—in a Van Gogh landscape.

But some of the color must have come back into my face, because Stonestreet sat back in his chair and resumed his story.

"All of this must have been no more than a diverting anecdote to the limb salesman, who, after all, had learned to become adept at this sort of thing in his new line of work. But the old man is profoundly affected. He recalls a similar ancient liaison—no more than a one-night stand among a voluminous catalog of one-night stands—and determines to locate this adoptee. And who's better equipped for such a project? But he's too late. He finds that the object of his search has died. But the fact that the man whom he had sought had been an employee of his confirms in his mind, which is already inclined to confirmation, the veracity of his brother-in-law's tale. He learns that his son, as he now believes him to be, has lost a wife to cancer and his eldest son to war. Vietnam, I believe."

"Da Nang," I said.

Stonestreet scooped out another chunk of cantaloupe, but he didn't eat it.

"It was probably the shortest tour of combat duty on record," I said. "They were shelling the airstrip when his plane landed. He was running from the plane trying to get to cover when a piece of shrapnel caught him in the temple. By the time they dragged him off the runway he was dead."

Stonestreet spread his hands in a gesture of helplessness.

"Anyway," he said after a moment, "Blessing began to interest himself in the career of the surviving son. *You.* When you applied to graduate school, he saw to it that your application was approved, in spite of some question as to your academic performance as an undergraduate. He saw to it that you were given a teaching assistantship, that you won scholarships, writing contests. When you applied for a Fulbright to this fair country, he expedited your application, shall we say. Had you not decided to chuck it all, I can assure you that your dissertation would have been published, that you would immediately have been offered tenure at wherever you had chosen to teach. Your articles would have been published in the most prestigious journals in your discipline. Undoubtedly, you would have become the chair of your department—perhaps even dean or university president eventually. I know," he said softly. "I've been around the same track."

He probably expected a reaction from me here. He probably expected me to protest or to wither or to melt or to weep or to tremble or to vomit or to drop dead. And I thought about doing each of them. I did nothing.

"You see, Draper finally believed—he wanted to believe very badly—that he had another refined Native American for an heir. Don't question the logic of it. It's what he believed. And he was quietly grooming you for succession. My guess is that he announced his intentions to Leona, who, since she had never accepted the fact of Victor's death, considered you a pretender, albeit an ignorant, and therefore, an innocent one. In such a frame of mind, and probably desperately aware of her own impending death, she was probably only too ready to concoct or listen to any scheme to get you out of the way. She probably figured that by associating you with Norrod, her bitterest enemy and a man who loathed everything that Draper stood for, she could somehow discredit you.

"Maybe she even thought you would meet with an unfortunate accident, although that sounds a lot more like Miguel, who was being a bit more thorough, I suspect. He was obviously setting you up for a confrontation with this Demuth. He probably assumed that, lacking Demuth's experience, you would not survive. It goes without saying that any weapon he would have provided for you would have malfunctioned."

"But he couldn't be sure of that," I said. "It seems like a very risky enterprise."

"You forget that he has Blessing blood in him. That's the way Draper operated—observing behavior, choreographing events, and predicting results. Yes. He was taking a chance. But he would have been taking a bigger chance by disposing of you himself. In all likelihood, he's behind the murder of this Hewitt girl, although it could have been Sultana. Both of them are experts at assassination. Making it look like an accident would be child's play for either of them. But to dispose of you in a similar fashion would arouse suspicion so soon after the girl's death. I think you're right in assuming that she was working for Norrod. Somehow, probably through access to Sultana's correspondence or by eavesdropping on his conversation, she became aware of your status. It's certainly no accident that Sultana hired you. He wanted you close by, where he could keep his eye on you. And you were undoubtedly a hot topic of conversation among the quadumvirate of

Sultana, Miguel, Crofts, and my son. They are cautious men, but they were running out of time and they may have been getting careless. Somehow, they discovered Minerva's treachery and they did away with her.

"But before doing so, they had to find out if she was working alone. So they baited the hook with that phony insurance claim in the name of Victor Blessing. They certainly didn't want to put it in *your* name. They didn't want to alert anyone who wasn't already privy to the knowledge of your connection to Blessing. Including you. But they *did* want to spook any spies into reckless action. So they identified Victor as an employee of Blessing Industries, the company your Father worked for—thus subtly signaling their knowledge of your Father's relationship, perhaps I should say *alleged* relationship—to Draper. Well, Demuth took the bait and swam with it all the way back to Washington to consult with Norrod. While he was gone, Sultana or Miguel murdered Minerva. My guess is that Demuth probably gave Sultana some excuse for going to Washington. And when he called back to check in with the boss, Sultana told him of Minerva's death, implicated you, and told him that you were on your way to Washington. Then he had Kelly send you that note and the promise of a big paycheck in order to convince you to come."

"And then when Hugo and I failed to blow each other's brains out, Kelly invited me over for a little chat so that they could stash Hugo's body in my room and try to frame me for the murder," I said.

"That's a reasonable assumption," said Stonestreet.

"But why?"

"Why what?"

"Why am I such a threat? If this document or file exists, I certainly haven't seen it. And, okay, that story about my father being Blessing's bastard son is fascinating—I mean you really had me going there for a moment—and maybe it's even plausible, but I doubt that I could make any claim stick. Hell, if I could, that would mean that your son is in for a bundle, too."

"I'm sure the possibility has occurred to him," said Stonestreet. "But any inheritance money is incidental when compared to the power that the Blessing file would confer. I'm really not exaggerating when I say that world domination would not be out of the question for its possessor."

"Jesus, you're talking about a human being here. World domination went out with Ming the Merciless—it's just too incredible."

"That's why it's possible," said Stonestreet almost gleefully. "It's the destiny of humankind. I mean, I hate to sound mystical—I've got my professional integrity to think about. But it's all a matter of King of the Hill, isn't it? I mean, in theory we have this exponential dungheap of information. Anyone with the interpretive key can achieve some threshold of ultimate knowledge. It's insinuated in the long tradition of western thought. I believe that Blessing had the key. His whole life testifies to it. But he was in awe of his own secret. And the world won't submit to a humble god. Hell, it won't even submit to an arrogant one."

CHAPTER 19

▼

YEAH, BUT

"Yeah," I said, "but I don't have this document."

"A mere formality," said Stonestreet. "The document is secured in a bank vault here in Trento. Incidentally, it's insured for a cool billion. Once your identity has been verified, you can claim possession."

"Sounds simple," I said. "Especially for such an earthshaking prize."

"Well, it's not that simple. Your driver's license and social security card won't quite do it. Your passport won't even do it."

"Okay, so what do I have to do? Try on a glass slipper or something?"

"Or something," said Stonestreet. "You just have to submit to a fingerprint test."

"How's that going to prove anything?" I asked. "What are they going to compare them to? I've never..." Stonestreet smiled and nodded.

"May, 1970," he said.

"You mean Blessing somehow got my fingerprints from the FBI when I was arrested during that rally?"

"Well, of course, you were never really arrested," said Stonestreet, over-doing it a bit, I thought, with the impishness of his smile. "Draper simply thought that you might be in danger. So he had you detained. While he was about it, he took the liberty of obtaining your fingerprints for future reference, you might say. You must admit the ingenuity of his plan. He couldn't risk an imposter's succeeding at acquiring the file."

"Presumably," I said. The file had piqued my interest, but only briefly. Now I felt disappointment settling in. And weariness. And, yes, okay, resentment. I had always thought back on my arrest at the Kent State rally with fondness and pride. It had been the one time in my non-committal existence when I had actually stood for something. It had been only months after my brother's death and I had thought of the arrest as at least a partial atonement. Now, to find that the whole thing was a private farce—that my one courageous gesture was no more efficacious than turn-ing over in my sleep—was disheartening.

"Yes," said Stonestreet, his arms folded across his chest now, his head inclined to one side. "Everything hinges on the significance of the Blessing document. If it's only some inconsequential memorandum, a lot of people have gone to a tremendous amount of trouble and expense for nothing. But, you see, in your case it makes no difference. You are the only one who has to know the contents of the document. The mere fact that you possess the knowledge of those contents—no matter *how* meaningless they may prove to be (this he added energetically, as thought to forestall the skepti-cism that was probably altering my features even as he spoke) gives you the power over your adversaries."

"Suppose I don't play the role here?" I said. "Just jump back on that ole 747 back to the States. Forget I ever heard of Draper Blessing."

Stonestreet thought that over for a moment and then grimaced and shook his head very quickly as though he had smelled something unpleasant.

"I dare say your life—that is, as much of it as remained to you—would be miserable," he said. "The power vacuum would be intolerable. I wouldn't give a nickel for your continued existence. In fact, your dilemma is most urgent. If you don't accept this legacy, the threat that you pose—the constant possibility that you may *change* your mind and accept—makes you increasingly more vulnerable. And if you *do* claim the Blessing document, you assume an awesome responsibility, although in that case you're probably immune to attack." He was beginning to sound like a chess commentator.

"I could go to the authorities," I suggested.

"You've already tried that, haven't you? I'm telling you that Draper *was* the authority. Mere officialdom existed at his pleasure. You're not so naïve, I hope, to believe that the legal system can arbitrate this affair for you."

I thought of Lazard's ineffectiveness in the case and conceded Stonestreet's point.

"If it hadn't been for someone's intervention—Norrod's, probably, or perhaps Draper still has some loyal agents lurking about—I have no doubt that, at best, you'd have been locked up a long time ago."

And, at worst, I thought to myself, I could be sitting quietly at my dining room table with Randi and Randy, or frying to a crisp with Bill Midwiff.

"Why should Norrod be such a guardian angel?"

"He wants to ensure a benign continuity, you might say. The man's a lunatic, but he's not a monster."

"Well, he certainly doesn't seem to be in need of Blessing money," I said. "Victor's widow left him millions when she died. And, from what I could see of his operation, he didn't look like he was hurting for cash even without her donation."

Stonestreet laughed. I think he was beginning to have doubts about my worthiness as Draper's successor. I must have seemed woefully ignorant to him. And, I was in for another revelation.

"It all boils down to Blessing money," said Stonestreet. "Although, I have repeatedly tried to impress upon you the crucial fact that the money isn't the important consideration here."

I had been at Stonestreet's apartment now for almost two hours. I was saturated with Amaretto and overloaded with my host's narrative. I

wanted to sleep. I wanted to be back in my apartment in Detroit, or, better yet, back in Denise's apartment.

"But why Trento?" I asked wearily.

"It's middle-class heaven," Stonestreet, who had an answer for everything, said. "Hell, did you ever notice the obligatory Italian graffiti around
here? You'll usually find it discreetly displayed in the *sottopassaggi* so as not
to affront the bourgeoisie. And even there it's neatly spray-painted in block
letters and very nonspecific. *Boia* or *figlio di troia*. That sort of thing."

"What's the moral of this story?" I asked.

"I'm trying to tell you that this place doesn't attract attention to itself.
There aren't many tourists. It's not on the itinerary of heads of state. The
Red Brigade doesn't have a garrison here. The Mafia can't be bothered to
corrupt the place. When was the last time you heard a story about Trento
on the evening news? Yet, it's anything but provincial. Draper always
found it refreshingly noncontroversial and safe."

Deep in the apartment, the phone rang indistinctly, as thought somewhere off in the motionless, serene early afternoon someone was sounding
one of those bells you see on children's tricycles. The phone had been rev-
erently silent for over an hour. Stonestreet excused himself to answer it.

Deep in my own mind, nothing sounded but a tiny voice, my rational
counterpart, no doubt, intoning a cappella against the Wailing Wall of
Ardent Testimony, "Bullshit!" Nobody had told me the truth, not the
complete truth, in at least a week. Perhaps longer. This whole adventure of
mine had started out as a solitary boat ride in some two-bit carnival
Tunnel of Love, which had spilled into larger and larger tributaries and
had eventually emptied into the sea. But not the Sea of Love.

I could almost feel myself getting seasick (Christ, this whole mess was
probably nothing more than my acute sensibility to auto suggestion)
when Stonestreet returned to the courtyard. He was clearly preoccupied,
but steadfastly cordial.

"Stephen, I have to get back to the dig," he said, as though he regretted it as much as the inevitability of death itself. "Why don't you come back with me? I'll make an archeologist of you."

"Thanks anyway," I said. "But I'm just about out on my feet. Jet lag, I guess. I think I'll just go back to my hotel for a snooze."

"Rest here," Stonestreet said eagerly. I'm pathologically slow on the uptake regarding these kinds of things, but it flashed through my mind that Stonestreet might be gay.

"I give you my solemn assurance that you won't be disturbed for at least five hours," he said

"No, really. I couldn't impose. Besides, all my stuff is back at the hotel."

Stonestreet nodded, but my refusal didn't seem to set too well with him. He hesitated for a moment, pinching his chin between his thumb and forefinger, his other hand supporting the elbow of the pinching hand.

"By the way," I said. "Where do I go to see about claiming this alleged document?"

"Call me this evening," said Stonestreet. "About seven. I'll see what I can do about arranging it. Most of the banks are only open in the morning. And for God's sake, be careful."

"If there's one thing I do carefully," I said, "it's sleep."

CHAPTER 20

▼

PHALLICIES...

But I didn't have a chance to sleep, at least not right away. As I walked along the shadeside of one of Trento's narrow, medieval, shuttered-down and deserted streets, a car pulled up just behind me at curbside and shadowed me at my walking pace.

"Hey, Fargo."

I bent at the waist without breaking stride and peered into the passenger-side window.

"Hello, Dowagiac," I said. He sat behind the wheel, looking like a traveling salesman in mourning. Dark suit and tie, white boutonniere in his lapel, pallor over his unhappy face.

"Need a lift?" He was so abjectly plaintive about the offer that I couldn't refuse him. I climbed in next to him and he pulled away from the curb, his car, a lumpy Renault, fumy and flatulent in acceleration.

"Nice suit," I said. "But a tad severe in terms of standard tourist wear, don't you think? Especially in this climate." Jesus, it had to be close to ninety degrees.

"I wish I found that funny," said Dowagiac. "It would be the first light-hearted moment I've had since I arrived in this fucking burg."

"Sorry," I said, really meaning it. "The enervated brain produces tired humor. Where'd you get the car?"

"I rented it from a Fiat dealership near the train station," he said "I can't stand to be without a car. Even a heap of shit like this." Dowagiac struck me, in fact, as *just* the sort of person who couldn't stand to be without a car.

"I'm staying at the *Accademia*, I said. "Do you know where the *Santa Maria Maggiore* is?"

Dowagiac lifted his lip in contempt. "I'm not here to see the sights," he said. "And I'm not here for the amusement of sex perverts."

"I don't suppose *many* people are here for that," I said.

"You'd be surprised," said Dowagiac, who suddenly pulled over to the side of the road and gave a ferocious yank at the emergency brake, nearly sending me through the windshield.

"Goddamn, Clifford," I said. "I'm not here to be a traffic statistic, either."

"Look, Fargo," he said, ignoring my outburst. "What's this Stonestreet's game?"

"He's an archeologist," I said, a bit disconcerted to learn that Dowagiac knew anything at all about Stonestreet. "He's got a bunch of college kids up at an excavation site about five miles out of town. He's got them emptying a big hole by the bucketful."

Dowagiac snorted. "That may be his public façade," he said. "But believe me, the guy's got some heavy deviant tendencies."

"What makes you say that?"

"Before we get into that, why don't you tell me just what your connection is to Stonestreet?"

Clearly, Dowagiac was suffering the effects of some trauma that made it impossible for him to trust me. The chronic whiner had finally found the objective correlative for his paranoia. I decided that if I was going to get anything at all from Dowagiac, I was going to have to cooperate—to gain his confidence somehow. Not an easy task. Dowagiac was a classic case. So I gave him the insurance investigator routine. I explained that my company had sent me over to interview Stonestreet concerning a claim that was too confidential for me to discuss. Dowagiac seemed to buy it.

"If ever a guy needed investigating," he said, "Stonestreet's it."

"I'm not investigating him," I insisted. "I'm simply here to interview him."

"Well, he *should* be investigated," said Dowagiac.

"Why?"

"Hell, I don't know." Dowagiac loosened his tie, perhaps to facilitate response, get that blood flowing freely to the mushroom cloud of the brain.

"Fraud. Yeah, that's it. Fraud. Or breach of promise."

"What did he promise you?"

"I thought I told you all that on the plane," said Dowagiac, beginning to cave in to suspicion again.

"Oh, yeah, the Presidency of the Anamorphosis League," I said. "So Stonestreet's the one who's supposed to approve you?"

"Hell, *no*," said Dowagiac fiercely. "The elected choice of the membership isn't subject to his approval. It's just that the installation must take place here. But I get here and what do I find? First, nobody knows anything about the Anamorphosis League. Second, I get invited to a cocktail hour and reception last evening, right? I think it's all part of the festivities. So I show up at the hotel ballroom with my wife and they have the fucking *balls* to refuse to let my wife enter the reception area. So I ask to see someone in charge and some cross-eyed pygmy named Craft comes out and tries to stare me down for a couple of minutes or so—Christ, it was the *weirdest* goddamn thing—and when he finally sees that I'm not about to turn into a frog or something, he tells me that there's been a mix-up and that I should get in touch with this Stonestreet character who's supposed to be coordinating these social events all over Trento or something. So, I finally get in touch with Stonestreet this morning and he keeps putting me off, telling me that he has important meetings all morning. So I rented this car and sat in front of his place for a couple of hours. I was going to wait until his company left so that I could get some answers from him. But who should walk out of his apartment but you? So I figure, since I *know* you, I'll talk to you first."

Dowagiac was assuming a lot in terms of the intimacy of our relationship, but I let it pass.

"Can't you get in touch with the former president?" I asked him. "Ask him how this ceremony is supposed to be conducted?"

Dowagiac's face reddened. "As a matter of fact," he said almost inaudibly, "I'm the first. Our organization is quite new, you see, and the membership is quite small—quite select, I should say. We were really a rather informal group until we started getting those anonymous contributions I told you about. That led us to believe that we should impose some structure on ourselves in order to give us more credibility. We wanted to be worthy of our benefactor's generosity."

Dowagiac sounded almost apologetic. He must have realized it, because his next outburst was full of vehement indignation.

"But that doesn't give that son-of-a-bitch Stonestreet the right to humiliate my wife and keep me cooling my heels like I was some kind of door-to-door salesman."

"No, it doesn't," I said, and in fact, I did feel a little sorry for him. He was the kind of person who was going to feel exploited and abused for the rest of his life, but now he had a legitimate gripe. He had come expecting a coronation, and he had experienced nothing but frustration and exclusion. "The secret to a tolerable existence," my father always used to say, "is low expectations."

Dowagiac suddenly belched loudly. He dug into his pocket, pulled out a roll of antacids, and ate several of them.

"*Hasenpfeffer*," he said with disgust, smiling grimly. "Christ, I thought we were in Italy. Spaghetti. Pizza. The wife and I go to the hotel restaurant last night and half the goddamn menu is German. Wiener schnitzel. God, you should have seen everybody wolfing down Wiener schnitzel. So the wife thinks we ought to get adventurous and order hasenpfeffer. So now I got a *malignant* case of heartburn."

"I guess there's a strong German influence in this part of the country," I said.

Dowagiac looked at me askance. "I don't give a *fuck* about the fucking demographics around here. What I want is to see this Mister Stonestreet hanging by his balls."

"I don't know," I said. "Stonestreet didn't seem like the obnoxious type to me. He was decidedly refined—civilized. What gave you this notion about perverts and deviants?"

"Okay, last night, when the wife and I were waiting to get into this reception I told you about, we were standing at the door. Well, when the first guy I had talked to went to get Craft, I pushed the door open to see what was going on. I see that the lights are all turned down and there's a spotlight turned on this huge obelisk. It looked like a replica of the Washington Monument, as a matter of fact, but I mean it was *big*, about ten feet tall, anyway. Then I hear this drum roll and people start doing a lot of hooting and whistling and clapping and this obelisk starts rising off the floor and I can see that it's covering something. And as it's going up the crowd's getting more and more vocal and the obelisk is finally lifted completely off this thing and I see that it's a big dildo. No shit. A huge Plaster of Paris dick.

"Well, I guess I don't have to tell you that I wouldn't have taken June in there now with me, even if they had offered to carry us in on a curtained litter. I mean, if they're going to have male-only entertainment, I should be forewarned. I'm just glad June didn't see that thing. She might have keeled right over."

My, my…phallic worship? Rightcheer in Stonestreet's fair bourgeois exemplar of Western Europe? Whatever it was, it didn't appear that Dowagiac was fabricating this story. He had neither the imagination nor the motive, as far as I could tell. He was too scandalized by the incident to have invented it. But what the hell was Crofts doing as sergeant-at-arms of a stag party in Trento?

"Did you happen to see a big guy—almost seven feet tall—dark, Mexican or Indian features, British accent?" Christ, even the description sounded absurd.

"I didn't see anybody but some twerp at the door and this Craft character with the Peter Lorre eyes. It was too dark in the conference room." I could see the recollection of the incident beginning to work on Dowagiac's sense of decency. His eyes had lost their focus with the distraction of his thoughts.

"I wouldn't mess with these jokers," I cautioned him. "We're a long way from home."

"Oh, I'm not going to mess with them," said Dowagiac. "I'm even going to pass on their little party tonight. I won't even call the vice squad. Do the Italian police have a vice squad? No, Stonestreet's the one I want to talk to." Dowagiac was looking straight ahead, nodding his head rhythmically and rapping his knuckles against the steering wheel, almost as if he were falling into some trance of vengeance.

"What party?" I asked.

"Hell, I don't know. They got some big shebang planned for tonight at some place called Molveno. Some drunk told me about it at the bar. I guess he assumed I was a fellow conventioneer or whatever. Course, I'm not likely to be invited now, anyway. Not that I want to be. All I want to do is have a little discussion with Stonestreet."

"Look, Clifford, why don't you let me see if I can set up a meeting with Stonestreet for you? This may all be a misunderstanding. No sense in going off after him half-cocked."

"Hey," said Dowagiac, opening his hands—the very soul of restraint— "I'm a reasonable man. I'm just performing my duties as I was elected to do. But I got rights."

"Of course you do," I told him. "And I'm gonna help you. Now, can you tell me anything about this party?"

"Not really," he said. "The guy said something about a lodge near the lake. I wasn't much interested in the drunken ramblings of a pervert."

"Can't blame you, Cliff." I wondered why he found his pornographic works of art so appealing. "Look, why don't I just get out here. I'm staying just a few blocks from here and I like walking in the city, to tell you the truth. Where are you staying, by the way?"

"The Grand Hotel Trento," Dowagiac said. "Home of hasenpfeffer, heartburn, and intercontinental ballistic dildoes."

I got out of the car. "Don't do anything about this until you hear from me," I said. "Take in the sights and forget about this mix-up for a few hours. It'll go easier on your stomach."

"Okay, Fargo."

I started to walk away, but Dowagiac grabbed my forearm. "Like I said," he cautioned me, "I'm a reasonable man. But if this Stonestreet doesn't come through, I'm gonna twist his fucking head off."

Only then did I realize the investment that Dowagiac had in the League presidency. He had probably staked what was left of his reputation, dignity, fortune, sense of worth, and in fact, his life on it. I thought he was going to twist *my* arm off right there just for the practice. He was trembling, and there were tears in his eyes—tears of desperation and rage. I worked my forearm free and slapped him on the shoulder.

"Come on, Cliff," I said. "Lighten up." The poor son-of-bitch had worked himself into paroxysms of near-despair. "'Humiliation is the beginning of sanctification,'" I said. "John Donne."

Dowagiac smirked at me. "Sainthood is for suckers," he retorted, even looking for a moment like an overdressed Mickey Spillane. He sped off— such as his Renault could be said to speed off—behind a screen of blue exhaust. Sometimes the stupidest people say the cleverest things.

On the way to my apartment I stopped at the SIP to make a couple of transatlantic calls. It cost me almost twenty bucks for the calls, but all things considered, the price was about right.

CHAPTER 21

▼

…AND PHONEES

Back in my room, I lay on my concave bed and rotated with the Earth for a while. But my mind was as active as a cage full of gerbils, making sleep impossible. My first phone conversation at the SIP had been with a couple of Detroit police. I had called Lazard's precinct, forgetting that I was seven or eight hours ahead of him. Some sympathetic desk sergeant, carefree with the impending termination of his shift, had given me Lazard's home number after a minimum of coaxing and a maximum of impersonation, coated with a heavy Italian accent that wouldn't have fooled the audience at a high school play. I pretended to be Stefono Tonto, *Capo di Polizia*, Trento, with important news for Lazard concerning that international fugitive and spurious bon vivant, Stephen Fargo.

But what the desk sergeant had neglected to tell me was that Lazard was out of town. I found that out when I dialed the number that the sergeant had given me, which turned out not to be Lazard's home number at all, but rather the number of someone calling himself Pauling, and claiming to be Chief of Detectives and Lazard's superior.

"Where are you, Fargo?" asked Pauling, once we had gotten our identities straightened out.

"I'm in Trento," I said, immediately wishing I hadn't, for some reason. "Where's Lazard?" There was a long pause on the other end. "You're really going to have to speak a bit louder," I said, irritated by Pauling's reticence. "Unless you want me to hang up and call you back collect."

"You're a real smartass, aren't you, Fargo," said Pauling. "Well, Lazard's whereabouts are none of your business, so go ahead and hang up."

"Whoa!" I said. "You don't have to get so sensitive about it." That was funny. A sensitive Detroit cop. I would rather have talked to Lazard, but Pauling was going to have to do.

So I told him of my conversation with Stonestreet, Senior (Pauling had already explained to me that he was fully knowledgeable about the Hewitt case) and suggested that he do something about getting Miguel and Stonestreet, Jr. behind bars. Then I told him he should start to work on extraditing Crofts, who had probably murdered Hugo Demuth and who was up to no good here in Trento. As I say, he listened as patiently as a man could who was being told how to do his job by someone he probably considered prone to psychotic episodes and who seemed to do his best work in fugue states.

Then he told me that my efforts at deduction were ingenious, but misdirected. Didn't I think that his department had considered these men as suspects? Wouldn't I imagine that he had done his job, so far as he was able, and had established what their participation in Minerva's death might have been? He knew, he said, as much about these men as I did, and he could assure me that my theory (more precisely, Stonestreet's theory) was dead wrong. They all had impeccable alibis; he himself could and would vouch for them.

Well, imagine my stupefaction at this bombshell. Its aftermath allowed hiatus enough for Pauling to deliver a thorough scolding. I should keep my nose out of police work. I had as much claim to the Blessing fortune as a Burmese untouchable. I should not pay attention to the strident slander of a disgruntled opportunist masquerading as a family friend. I should get my ass home and see to the rehabilitation of my ex-wife, who was flirting with perdition through her dalliance with cocaine. I should, in short, butt the fuck out. Click.

My second call, at least somewhat motivated by Pauling's admonishment, was to Valerie in Hollywood. Unfortunately, Valerie wasn't in Hollywood, according to Valerie's lisping and huffy (I had awakened him at the "inhuman" hour of five a.m.) live-in lover, who identified himself only as Monte.

"She's in Italy working on some fascist cinematic project with Gore Kemp," Monte had said. "The location is hush-hush and the crew is incommunicado. Now observe: I could have lied to you and said she had moved or something. I hope you'll repay my honesty by not disturbing me again. Goodbye."

As I lay there reliving these conversations, a knock sounded at the door, followed by the slothful enunciation of the desk clerk.

"*Signor Fargo, telefono.*"

I rolled out of bed and followed the desk clerk down to the lobby. By the time I got there, he was already seated behind the front desk, smoking a cigarette and flipping through an *Epoca* magazine whose cover depicted a bikinied Princess Caroline in the casual embrace of some jetsetter type in shades, 18-karat gold chains, Riviera tan and jock-strap-type swimsuit.

It was Norrod on the phone.

"So you took my advice—part of it at least—after all," he said. "You gave us rather a fright, you know, leaping form the car like that."

"Well, you gave me rather a fright yourself. And little reason to trust you. At the time, your advice sounded more like coercion."

"In any event, you are here," he said, sounding very satisfied about it. "And I assume Stonestreet has briefed you on the Blessing cipher."

"The what?"

"Then he didn't tell you?"

"Well, he didn't use that precise term. He said there was a document or something, and that by some sequence of events too labyrinthine and incredible to rehash, I may be the heir to it. But if you believe that, well, you probably *would* believe that."

"Have arrangements been made for you to claim the material?" said Norrod, ignoring or oblivious to the insult.

"Hey, Norrod, you know, I don't feel the slightest obligation to satisfy your curiosity." The desk clerk looked up at my exclamation, and I began to wonder if he understood English, or perhaps recognized Norrod's name. Or maybe I was beginning to sound a bit too clamorous for his genteel establishment. "Just what's your interest in this document, besides the fear that your funds are going to be cut off and you'll have to send your virgins out panhandling in airport terminals?"

Norrod chuckled. "Your belligerence towards me is really quite unwarranted," he said. "I can think of nothing I've done to deserve it."

"Well, how about playing me for a sucker, for starters."

There was no response for a moment. Then, in a tone of voice that must have passed for contrition in Norrod's tonal repertoire, he said:

"Granted, Fargo, I haven't been perfectly candid with you at all times. On the other hand, it was never my purpose to deceive you."

"Oh, really? Well as a gesture of your goodwill, suppose you fill me in now on what you left out before. I promise to be captivated."

"Yes," said Norrod with determination. "But not now. Not over the phone. I have business to attend to at the moment. Meet me at the *Sardagna Funivia* Station in an hour. Do you know where that is?"

"The *Sardagna Funivia* Station," I said. "I'll find it."

After hanging up, I leafed through the telephone directory until I found the listing for the Grand Hotel Trento. I dialed it and when the tremulous soprano on the other end answered by confirming that I had, indeed, reached the Grand Hotel Trento, I asked her if I could speak to Valerie Cadieux, who was with the Gore Kemp entourage. It was a longshot. They might not even be in Trento; they probably weren't. And if they were in Trento, they might be in any of several hotels, although Valerie wouldn't tolerate anything even half as humble as the *Accademia*. If they were incommunicado, as Monte had said, they probably wouldn't be registered under their own names anyway.

After a few seconds, the switchboard operator informed me in her most apologetic Italian that there was no one registered in the hotel under those names. I then asked to speak to Clifford Dowagiac. While I was waiting for her to find the right circuit for that one, I noticed the desk clerk peering at me over his magazine. He was probably tallying up my phone calls to add to my bill. Somehow, that was more comforting that the thought that he might be eavesdropping.

"Hello," said Dowagiac in a voice bristling with antagonism.

"Hey, Cliff," I said, trying to sound cheery. "It's Fargo."

"Oh, Fargo," he said, his voice losing its edge. "I was hoping it was Stonestreet."

"Sorry to disappoint you."

"Have you talked to him?"

"No, but I'm working on it."

"Well, I don't have a lot of time. Dingo's gotten himself in a bit of trouble here. Apparently, some broad he met on the plane sunk her claws into him. They won't leave him alone, you know. It's that rock star thing. The girl's aunt was just here giving me hell. She says if I don't find them, she's going to the police. Imagine the *nerve* of the bitch. Her nymphomaniac niece seduces *my* boy, and *she's* going to the police."

"They'll turn up," I said. I didn't have the heart to tell him that his son was about as innocent in this affair as a child molester on a school playground. "You know how these young kids are. They're probably right here in town."

"Is this a consolation call, or what?" said Dowagiac, getting testy again.

"Actually, no. I was wondering if you've run into any of your friends from last night there at the hotel. Of maybe that big guy I asked you about."

"Sorry," he said. "I've been busy minding my own business."

"By chance, have you seen a film crew checking in at the hotel? Or a guy with a Fu Manchu mustache and an earring?" I was describing Gore Kemp. At least that's what he had looked like in the last photo I had seen.

"Come on, Fargo," said Dowagiac. "What do you take me for, a bellhop?"

Suddenly, the operator broke in on us, announcing, in English this time, an emergency call for "Meestair Dowojock." I was put on hold and probably would have remained there forever if I hadn't hung up and dialed the Grand Hotel Trento again. But by the time I had re-identified myself to the operator, Dowagiac, she explained, had left. Could she tell me the nature of the emergency? I was, after all, a close friend of Mr. Dowagiac. *Si*, she supposed she could tell me. *Eet was soamsing consairning heese soan.*

Well, in that case, I guess I had to forgive him his lapse of etiquette. I asked the operator if she knew where Dowagiac was headed, but she professed not to know, only saying that Dowagiac had asked her how to get to someplace called Lavis. I thanked her and hung up. A lot of telephone conversation for a very few answers. I looked up to see the desk clerk eyeing me again over the top of his magazine. I walked over to him, scratching at the side of my head as if under the spell of some knotty problem.

"I hear your mother blows dead donkeys back to life," I said. He stared at me with what *appeared* to be the vacancy of incomprehension.

"*Solo italiano*," he said, sounding like rolling thunder. So I asked him in Italian how much for the phone calls. He told me that they'd be added to the bill; I shouldn't worry myself about them. A gesture with the hands and a distinctive, Elvis Presley sort of expression around the lip indicated that the cost of the calls was so trivial as to be beneath my notice.

I walked back up to my room, promising myself that I wouldn't yield to surprise should I discover that the desk clerk had a Masters Degree in Hotel Management from Princeton.

CHAPTER 22

▼

FARGO TAKES THE HIGH ROAD

An hour or so later I was walking along the river towards the *Trento-Sardagna* cable lift station. In fact, I was about a half-hour late for my meeting with Norrod. I had taken the time to do a little geographical research in my room with the help of my handy-dandy travel guide and map. Sardagna sat perched on a lower shelf of the mountains just to the southwest of Trento. According to the travel guide, the village had little to recommend it other than the panoramic view of Trento that it offered, the cheap thrill of the cable lift across the river and up the cliff about two thousand feet or so (a bit hairy for acrophobics like myself, but much less time-consuming and troublesome than hiking four hundred vertical meters up the shimmering, anfractuous asphalt road), and perhaps a dash of local color.

Strangely enough, Lavis, to which Dowagiac had run off in search of Dingo, was also remarkable, at least as far as most tourists were concerned, for its cable lift, which offered a shortcut to some mountain vantage point called Paganella, which was at the center of the scenic and recreational attractions of the area. Lavis was about three or four miles up the road from Trento—a northern suburb, actually.

The other reason for my tardiness was that I decided, on impulse, to shave my beard. I'm not sure that simple disguise was the whole motive (even though I also bought a tube of haircream, which I had not applied since a short-term emulation of Frankie Avalon in my fourteenth year, and a pair of sunglasses, an accessory I had found superfluous even in the most pitiless of sunlit days, since early adolescence); maybe I felt some climax at hand for which naked cheek and jowl were *de rigueur* (ceremonial decoration by an Italian magistrate?). Whatever the reason, I had to find an open *negozio* (no easy task at that midday hour), then go through the actual quasi-religious ritual of de-bearding myself (a very slow process, since you can only travel at the speed of one inch-long stroke per minute because the safety razor quickly becomes clogged with hair), and then grieve over the results of my mad impetuosity for longer than some people mourn dead family members.

Kee-rist! What a transformation! In the years since I had last exposed facial skin to open air, my chin and jaw had undergone some horrible process of recession and atrophy. I looked like a chipmunk with a mustache, and although the mustache I had retained was of sufficiently debonair dimensions to qualify as dashing—very narrow and tidy, like something out of a Valentino movie—I could tell straight off that I wasn't going to strike fear in the hearts of these jackals that I was dealing with.

But at least it was a dramatic enough change to give me the advantage of momentary surprise with thugs looking for a full-bearded professor with uncombed hair. In order to further befuddle prospective assailants or abductors (my experience with Norrod in Washington was still very fresh in my mind and I *still* didn't trust the sumbitch), I used about half of the tube of haircream to slick down my hair, which I parted precisely down the middle. All I needed was a white coat and a towel over my arm, and I would have looked like one of those waiters in the Café Bristol. Not dangerous, but somehow more sophisticated. And also more uncomfortable. My skin under my beard was chafed, and now red blotches began to appear all over my face. They itched, as did my scalp, unused to the greasy glazing I had given it, all of which was exacerbated by the heat, which measured no less than ninety degrees in my room and had to be pushing ninety-five out in the sun. Finally, I donned my sunglasses. They were those chrome, no-see-through, reflector-types that chain gang bosses and Highway Patrol cops wear. The face looking back at me from the mirror made me shudder to think how insubstantial, how superficial was this cosmetic of identity that we either nurtured so fastidiously or accepted willy-nilly. I almost began to feel more, well, more Mediterranean, I guess, although I couldn't exactly say how. But there was no doubt that my "disguise" had bolstered my confidence, despite my disappointment in the bone structure of my face. Almost immediately, I lost the self-consciousness that had nagged me since my visit to Leona Blessing. This new confidence lasted at least until I passed through the lobby and stopped in front of the figure of the desk clerk, who was still reading and smoking. He might have been reading the same sentence and smoking the same cigarette for all he had changed position in the interim. I slid my key across the counter and watched his eyes for some sort of reaction— shock, amusement, perplexity—*anything*. But he simple nodded and tossed my key into its cubicle, unimpressed. I felt a strange twinge in my chest. I was going to feel awfully bad if I had sacrificed my beard for nothing. On the other hand, this clerk was an obtuse specimen, if ever there was one. I would delay my dejection for the time being.

I would also, it seemed, delay my meeting with Norrod longer than I already had. As I approached the riverside cable lift station, I noticed a crowd of excited people around the entrance, pointing and gesturing to the opposite end of the cable up at Sardagna. The lift was not operating. I pushed my way through the crowd, entered the station, and listened as the operator tried to mollify ticket holders waiting to be hauled up to the village. From what I could make of his fevered explanation, there had been an accident at the other end of the lift—nothing involving the lift itself, he assured everybody repeatedly—but the accident was serious enough to shut down the lift temporarily as a precaution. I was a rank behind the people questioning the operator, and by the time I got to the front with my question (How long did he think the lift would be out of order?), he was announcing that the lift was ready to go again.

I bought my ticket and packed in with twenty or so other passengers still chattering about the delay. We slid over the river, then began to ascend smoothly and nearly vertically along the cliffs. In a few minutes, the cable car was docking in the Sardagna station about twelve hundred feet above Trento.

The station hung precariously over the rim of the steep declivity. The view of Trento was, indeed, impressive, certainly worth every bit of the fifteen hundred lira *andate e ritorno* ticket. Beneath me, the entire city—a pleasing cluster of orange tile rooftops and sun-bleached stucco—radiated eastward from the banks of the Adige. Hills and smaller clusters of buildings stood in the intermediate distance, while even farther off, world-class, bluish-gray, snow-peaked mountains dominated the picture postcard scene.

As my eye traveled back to the cable lift station across the river, the cars began their simultaneous journey across the expanse of rock and water. I watched the approaching car until its run was almost complete, when I caught sight of some activity on a shelf of rocks below me. A squad of men in fluorescent orange jackets and matching hard hats was retrieving a line with one of those contraptions attached to the end, which are used to strap in disabled mountain climbers. I wondered if the *incidente* that had temporarily shut down the cable lift might have been due to some unlucky climber's mishap.

I had about five seconds to speculate on that. Then someone tapped me on the shoulder—firmly enough so that I involuntarily grasped the railing more tightly.

"Meestair Fargo." It was clearly a salutation; not a hint of the interrogative. Boy, what a clever disguise, huh? I turned to find myself staring into the nearly inexpressive features of Giacinto, Norrod's chauffeur.

"You please will follow me," he said.

"Where's Norrod?"

"He waits for you in a secure location." Giacinto didn't have his chauffeur's uniform on today. He was dressed like a local—everything tight, and very few buttons buttoned. He could scarcely conceal his anatomy, let alone any weapons.

"Look, Giacinto, I'm starting to lose my patience with Motherwell Norrod."

"Please follow," Giacinto insisted. "My inglese ees no good to esplain you. Come."

Well, he didn't have that signature Uzi hanging from his shoulder and judging from his accent and lack of fluency, he probably *wasn't* competent to "esplain" me, so I followed him, promising myself not to climb into the back seat of any cars with Norrod.

We walked a couple of hundred yards up the road to a combination bar-café, a small place with half a dozen tables, a top-heavy barmaid with overwrought mascara, and a Foosball game off to one side, at which two muscular Italians were slapping away at a frantic game. Norrod sat at one of the tables, all shiny and pink in his powder-blue seersucker suit.

"Ah, the elusive Mr. Fargo," he said, greeting me expansively. So much for my disguise. I sat down at Norrod's invitation and ordered a beer when he asked what I was drinking.

"I'm glad to see that you arrived safely," he said.

"Didn't you expect me to?"

"Not when I heard about the American's accident. You were late, and I must admit that I jumped, well, not jumped, perhaps hopped to the conclusion that you were the American that had met with the misadventure at the cable lift station."

"What American?" I asked.

"You must have missed all the excitement," said Norrod. "Just about a half an hour ago, an American somehow managed to fall over the barrier and halfway back to Trento. A tree broke his fall and he survived, miraculously, or so it's been reported to me. All the same, I imagine he's in a very bad way."

"Fell over the barrier? That would seem difficult without help," I said.

"I am of the same opinion," said Norrod, seeming very satisfied with the corroboration. "I intend to be direct with you. It's possible that the fall was actually a push, and that the victim was mistaken for another American who was due at the station at about the same time."

"Goddamn it, Norrod. Enough of this cloak-and-dagger shit. What's going on?"

I hadn't raised my voice, but the intonation was enough to attract the attention of Giacinto and the two gorillas playing Foosball.

"Friends of your?" I asked, inclining my head towards the two men, who seemed ready to pounce on me at a word from Norrod.

"Bodyguards," he said.

"Oh yeah? They functional eunuchs, too?"

"Oh, I expect they're fully equipped, although I haven't bothered to ask them," said Norrod, chuckling.

"Well, call them off. I'm harmless."

"I wonder if you are," said Norrod. He gave his goons a short wave of his hand, and they returned to their game with no apparent decline in vigor. Giacinto, too, turned in his barstool and resumed his conversation with the barmaid.

Norrod took a sip of his anisette and dabbed at the corners of his mouth with his napkin.

"First," he said, "may I offer my condolences on the death of your friend Mr. Midwiff?"

"What do you know about it?" I asked quickly.

"I suspect he was a civilian casualty, collateral damage," said Norrod. "In the wrong place at the wrong time."

"Just like that, huh?"

"Mr. Fargo, I don't wish to sound insensitive, but you aren't the only one who has suffered losses around here," he said, trying to be patient.

"You make it sound as though there's a war going on."

"That's precisely what it is. A campaign of terror conducted by a group of self-styled guerillas, most of whom are descendants of the Blessing line."

"Yeah, I know all about it," I said.

"Survivalists, they call themselves," Norrod said with disdain. "They await the apocalypse—indeed, they provoke it—unrest and rebellion in the Third World and in our own urban areas—"

"Jump down from the pulpit, will you Norrod? You're talking about a handful of psychotic soldiers of fortune. They probably don't think much of you either."

"Hardly so few," said Norrod. "We've managed to identify over sixty thousand of their membership, among them some alarmingly influential people, including no less than one former presidential candidate. Theirs is a secret society and there's no telling how extensive the membership truly is. Their delegation alone is five hundred strong and all of them are here in Trento."

"It wouldn't have anything to do with this Blessing document, would it?"

"It would. Presumably, the knowledge acquired through the Blessing cipher would make them invincible."

"I've heard this horror story before," I said. "And my response is still the same. I don't believe that any one man could have possessed that much potential power, if you'll forgive the marginal redundancy."

"I'm inclined to agree with you," said Norrod. "But we can't take the chance that we're wrong. And the presence of the other side here in Trento and their demonstrated willingness to commit serious crimes to reduce competition for the cipher suggest that they are not willing that anyone else should possess this information if they are unable to."

"Well, from what Stonestreet tells me, they sure won't get this document by killing me. They need my fingerprints."

"Assuming that you are the chosen one."

"Do you think I am?"

"There are strong indications that you are. But I'm sure Stonestreet has briefed you on those, no?"

"Yes. But it all sounded rather contrived to me."

"It could very well be contrived. Nevertheless, you may be heir to a document that may or may not have tremendous implications."

"So. Like I said, why would they want me dead? Without me, nobody gets the document, right?"

"Don't be too sure," said Norrod. "Once you have the document you may become too powerful for them to dislodge it from you. You may be ideologically opposed to them and in a position to destroy their organization."

"Or yours."

Norrod smiled, but I don't think he was amused.

"Unless I have radically misjudged you," he said, "I don't think that you subscribe to a credo of unbridled venery, a political system that repudiates social justice and equality, a social realignment that reverts to savagery, a—"

"Okay, okay. Jesus, Norrod, this isn't "The Oral Roberts Hour." My use of the word *hour* seemed to recall him to a sense of urgency. He checked the time on a pocketwatch that he pulled from his vest.

"They call themselves Ultimi," said Norrod, in a more sober tone of voice.

"Sounds like a woman's perfume," I said.

"You couldn't be more wrong," said Norrod. "They stink of machismo. And their obsession with male supremacy has led them to rapaciousness of every imaginable form. But time is short. We anticipate action of some kind from them within twenty-four hours, perhaps even tonight following their convocation."

"Whose?"

"Ultimi's, of course. You are the pivotal person here; we've been able to determine that much. So any action that they take will likely involve you."

"Nothing violent, I hope."

"Possibly."

"Then what the fuck did you try to bully me into coming here for?"

Once again, the Foosball players interrupted their game and came to the ready position. Norrod ignored them. It was *easy* for *him* to ignore them.

"You are the catalyst," he said in a voice that was almost soothing. "If it hadn't happened here, it would have happened in Washington or Detroit.

Leona's death seems to have been the signal. It became open season on anyone found meddling with the so-called Blessing cipher—Minerva Hewitt, Hugo Demuth, Randi, your friend Midwiff, and the unfortunate Mr. Dowagiac."

"What?"

"Dowagiac," Norrod repeated. "He's the American who fell over the barrier. Of course, I don't believe for a moment that he fell."

"But Dowagiac's as harmless as they come," I protested. "Why would they try to kill him?"

"There could be a couple of reasons," said Norrod. "First, his assailants may have believed that you and he were confederates. You arrived on the same plane, have similar backgrounds, come to the same city, and are seen meeting under rather suspicious circumstances."

"I see *you've* been busy, too."

"Or," said Norrod, sailing right through my remark, "it may be his son's meddlesome involvement with a certain young woman who happens to be a member of the Society."

"The blond on the plane?" I said. "Jesus Christ, Norrod, when was the last time you didn't know what I was up to?"

"Well, we lost you for fifteen hours or so after you jumped from my car. I assume you didn't fly back to Detroit. We've usually got the airports pretty well covered. And then we lost you again for several hours when you were en route from Rome to Trento. In fact, it was only after I caught sight of you last night in the café that we were absolutely sure you had come to Trento. But forget about that for now. The third reason, and I'd like to think that I'm wrong about this, is that Dowagiac was attacked because he was mistaken for you."

"So you're trying to tell me that I should leave?"

"Not at all. I don't believe you could if you wanted to. And I really don't think you want to, do you? No, what I'm offering you is protection."

"What's your price?"

"We only ask that you exercise prudent judgment when you do acquire the Blessing cipher."

"Seems fair enough," I said. Then I stood up. "So why don't we go over to the bank and get it all over with? The suspense is killing me—not to mention lots of other people. And the sooner I get my hands on this document, the better off everyone's going to be. From what everyone tells me, I'll be just about invulnerable, so you won't *have* to protect me. And Ultimi, or whoever that gang of good old boys is, will have lost its chance at the document *and* me."

"I would very much like to do that," said Norrod. "Believe me. But, unfortunately, I don't know where the document is being held."

"I *told* you. It's in a bank. How many banks can there be in Trento, for Chrissake? Finding out which bank holds the document should be a cinch for an operation with your resources."

Norrod looked uncomfortable. The dome of his head was glistening with perspiration, and the collar of his shirt seemed to be choking him.

"Be that as it may," he said, "we have been unable to determine its whereabouts. By the way, we're not sure that Stonestreet's information is reliable. Did he say what bank it was in?"

"Didn't I just make it clear that I don't know?"

"There you go," said Norrod.

"But if nobody knows where the thing is kept, how am I supposed to get my hands on it?"

"I didn't say that nobody knows where it is. Somebody does. Leona almost certainly did. She may have told Miguel before she died. Or the answer may be contained in the file that Sultana kept on the Blessings, which disappeared after Minerva was killed. But somebody knows it location. Perhaps Stonestreet does know. I, unfortunately, do not. If I did, I wouldn't needlessly endanger your life by postponing your acquisition of it. Others may have different thoughts about this. And different agendas." A reference, no doubt, to Stonestreet. "That's why I plan to infiltrate this Ultimi convocation tonight. Something important may be revealed."

I didn't tell Norrod so, but I doubted it. If Dowagiac had been inadvertently invited and if drunks were blabbering away about this party, security had to be rather lax.

"So, what did you have in mind for me to do?" I asked.

"We're headquartered at a chalet in Andalo, not for from here," said Norrod. "It's completely secure. We'd like to offer you our hospitality—at least for the night. Perhaps before the evening is over, we can have some good news for you."

"And you."

Norrod smiled. "Have you had a better offer? If I'm correct, and whoever tossed Dowagiac over the barrier was sent after you, how do you suppose they knew that you would be at the funivia station?"

"The desk clerk?" I said. Norrod shrugged. Once again, he withdrew his timepiece.

"It's getting on towards five o'clock, and I have preparations to make. I would remind you that sooner or later those responsible for trying to dispose of Mr. Dowagiac are going to realize their error—if they haven't already. I really don't think it's safe for you to be wandering about alone."

"I've managed so far," I said.

"You have at that," said Norrod. "But then you haven't been entirely alone, either. Shall I review your activities for the day, or would that be too tedious of me?"

"Save it," I said.

A few minutes later we were climbing into the blue helicopter that I had seen earlier in the day at Stonestreet's apartment. We buckled up—Norrod, Giacinto, and me—and the pilot fired up the rotor and the helicopter lifted off.

"I wouldn't advise any spontaneous evacuations this trip," said Norrod. The quip seemed to please him. He chuckled well beyond the joke's humorous value. I looked down at the village slipping away beneath me. It was the best advice I'd had all day.

CHAPTER 23

▼

DINGO DOES HIS DUTY

The horses began to snort (a recondite expression of my father's which meant that a chain reaction of significant events had been irrevocably set into motion) about nine-thirty that evening. I was engaged in an interminable, one-thousand-lira game of snooker with Giacinto on an absurd, Italian joke of a table whose pockets were only just able to accommodate the diameter of the billiard balls. Norrod had left us together in this game room and had gone off to make his "preparations" for the evening. I would have preferred to play table tennis, but we had been unable to find a net, so we had agreed to the game of pool. Neither of us was very good at snooker, especially on such an unforgiving table, and the game was just then breaking into its second hour. Giacinto, however, was just a little better than I was. While he was no more proficient at pocketing balls, he was very adept at snookering me, which almost invariably led me to scratch, which, in turn, cost me points. After an hour of play, I was down forty-four points; neither of us had sunk a ball yet.

This was part of the reason for an incipient orneriness that was beginning to bleed into my soul. The other part of the reason was that I was beginning to sense an uneasy ambiguity about my status there at the chalet. It wavered between guest and detainee. The doors didn't seem to be locked, but Giacinto had been very attentive, to put it mildly.

"Bullshit, Hyacinth, you cur of a swindler, you," I exploded after missing yet another shot. "Minnesota Fats himself couldn't sink a ball on this table. Christ! It's like being constipated."

Giacinto responded by promptly sinking the first ball of the game, after which he showed no emotion whatsoever, as though there was never any doubt that he was going to make it. I felt like spearing him with my pool cue, but since we had arrived at the chalet, he had strapped on a shoulder holster, complete with a nifty, short-barreled nine millimeter.

He was lining up a shot on the seven ball when a commotion reached our ears from elsewhere in the chalet. At first it was difficult to make out the nature of the disturbance. Giacinto set his cue on the table, slid the nine millemeter from its holster, and motioned me to get down behind the pool table, all in one smooth, continuous move. He was composed as a corpse and very professional. He had obviously not spent all of his idle hours waxing the Mercedes.

I could now hear someone yelling—an American by the sound of him—and very much agitated, not to say infuriated. He wanted to see somebody. The gist of his request was, "Get your stinking hands off me, you guinea swine. Where's that bastard Fargo?"

"I'm not in," I whispered to Giacinto.

"*Zitto!*" he hissed at me. He crouched alongside the table and rested the pistol—which he held in both hands—along the ledge. The gun was pointed at the door. Suddenly, the voice on the other side of the door subsided. A moment later, a knock—which Giacinto apparently recognized as friendly—sounded at the door. Giacinto glided over to answer it, motioning for me to stay put. He opened the door a crack and had a few second's worth of conversation with whoever was on the other side. I saw him holster his pistol, so I stood up and relaxed a bit. Giacinto shut the door and came back towards the table. He picked up his cue and set his sights once again on the seven ball. He stroked the cue, but the ball rattled in the corner and hung up there. He laid the cue on the table.

"What gives, Giacinto?" I asked.

"*Finito*," he said.

"Hey, what do you mean? It's my shot."

"*Finito*," he said calmly. "Please to follow."

"Well, I'll be damned if I'm going to pay you," I said to his back as he turned away from the table. I followed him through the door and into the main room of the chalet. Dingo sat on a couch in the middle of the room. It was his voice I had heard, and it only occurred to me then that I hadn't recognized it because I had never heard him speak before. He hadn't seemed like the oratorical type. He was wearing the same punk leather outfit that he had worn on the plane. He sat hunched over, his head in his hands. Norrod's two bodyguards stood on either side of him.

"Fargo!" he snarled when he looked up to see who was entering the room. He tried to stand, but the bodyguards pushed him back down into the couch.

"Dingo. What's going on?" I said.

"As if you didn't know," he said through his teeth. He sounded a little bit overdramatic and strained, as though he were trying to impersonate an angry Kirk Douglas. "Tell me you didn't set the old man up." Such filial solicitude from a punk rocker was absolutely touching.

"What do you mean, set him up? He went looking for *you*."

"Yeah, and he didn't find me. *You* saw to that."

"What the hell are you talking about? I didn't even know he was going after you until after he had gone. Why should I set him up? I hardly even know him."

Dingo didn't answer. He let out a roar and charged off the couch with surprising fury for a jejune lead guitarist. He got about as far as one of the bodyguard's fists, which caught him square in the solar plexus and sent him back to the couch, where he slumped over and struggled for breath. I made a mental note to avoid antagonizing the bodyguards. They thus joined an ever-growing list that had begun with Minerva Hewitt, ran through Miguel, Hugo and Giacinto, and was threatening to turn me into a wretchedly submissive hombre.

The thought of my personality diminishing so ignobly, whatever valor that constituted it draining so meekly from a million valve-like pores, roused me to decisive action. I pulled Giacinto to one side—gently—after all, I had not quite jacked myself into foolhardiness. He stared at my hand on his shoulder as if someone had just draped a slab of liver over it as a joke. But Norrod had apparently insisted that he be indulgent with me, and he allowed himself to be dragged off a discreet distance from the other three men in the room.

I began to reason with him, as well as I could reason in Italian. I explained who Dingo was, the reason for his violent behavior, and suggested that if I could talk to him alone for a few minutes, I could quiet him down. To a man in Giacinto's position, reason was irrelevant. He entertained suggestions only insofar as they fell within the purview of his responsibility. He countered my suggestion by proposing that we gag and confine Dingo until Norrod returned and decided what to do with him. Even in this, I had the feeling that Giacinto was going out of his way to be lenient. He probably would just as soon have garroted Dingo on the spot and rolled him back down Paganella towards Trento.

But mercy prevailed. I hinted strongly that, since Dingo was indirectly a victim of injustice, his reaction was not altogether unprovoked or unwarranted, and Norrod might disapprove of Giacinto's harsh treatment of him. Finally, I explained that I would not take kindly to any abuse of the young man, and might consider any refusal of my request grounds for defection. Giacinto relented, explaining that his only interest was my safety. I acknowledged this, but insisted that, as it concerned my safety, I was best able to deal with Dingo. Giacinto agreed to withdraw, but warned me that at the first sign of aggressive behavior from Dingo, he would intercede to prevent any injury to me. We were getting so cordial with each other that we almost needed a career diplomat to interpret.

We returned to the couch and Giacinto growled an order to the two bodyguards. Then all three men left the room, leaving Dingo still coiled in anguish on the couch. I sat down next to him and said nothing for a few minutes. The bodyguard's blow had taken all the fight out of him, and I had a momentary evil wish that all the punk rock fans in the world could see one of their heroes now. Dingo grunted some obscenity or other, but he was still too disabled to accompany it with anything physical.

"Yeah, well you just sit there and recover for a minute and let me explain a few things to you. The first thing you should know is that the very instant you get pushy, Darth Vader and his buddy there are going to be all over you again like stink on shit." You have to know how to talk to these antisocial types.

Dingo groaned something unintelligible, but he was growing more manageable by the second.

"The second thing is, I had nothing to do with your father's accident," I said. "The way I figure it, somebody told him to take the cable lift at Lavis and he either got the directions wrong, or else in his anxiety to find you, he simply got careless and got on the wrong lift. At any rate, there's a good chance that somebody mistook him for me, although I can't imagine how, and pushed him over the edge thinking they were doing away with me."

Dingo sat up straighter and rested his head on the back of the couch. "All I know," he said, "is that the old man kept saying your name—over and over. They got him punchy on Demerol in the hospital so he couldn't say much, but he told me where you were staying. I called your hotel and somebody told me you were hiding out here."

"Hiding out?"

"His exact words," said Dingo. "So I put two and two together."

Well, in a way, Dingo had it right. I *was* hiding out in a manner of speaking, but not because I feared Dingo's wrath. I decided it was time to straighten this kid out, at least as far as you could straighten out a professional juvenile delinquent. I once again fell back upon my insurance investigator impersonation and explained to him as much as I thought necessary to vindicate myself in his eyes. He immediately grew interested, but I found out very quickly that his interest had nothing to do with bringing his father's attackers to justice. Dingo wanted to know if I could do anything about getting some girl back in the States to drop a paternity suit she had brought against him. He protested his innocence vigorously and within minutes he seemed to have forgotten about his father's problems.

"One thing at a time," I told him. "Right now, I'm wrapped up in this murder case. I'll see what I can do for you after I've cleared this mess up. Now, this guy who told you I was hiding out here at the chalet; did he speak with an accent?"

"Not that I noticed," said Dingo.

"Did he give his name?" That, of course, should have been my first question, but Dingo didn't seem to notice the sequential lapse. Dingo was the type who didn't notice much of anything, unless it was of childbearing years.

"No," he said.

"How did you get here?"

"I drove the car the old man rented. A real piece a shit. The goddamn thing won't do over forty."

"Here's what I want you to do," I said, sounding as much like Robert Stack as I could. Dingo was really getting into it. He had forgotten about his pain, his father's mangled body, and the girl he'd left behind. He was leaning forward on the couch, peering intently at me through the smoke of his cigarette. I could probably have talked him into taking Holy Orders.

"I want you to leave me the car and take a bus back to Trento. When you get there, go to this address." I gave him the card Norrod had given me back in Washington. "See a man named Stonestreet. Tell him what's happened. Tell him I'm going to the party in Molveno tonight. He'll know what I'm talking about. Then get back to the hospital and keep an eye on your father. I'll be there as soon as I can. You got the keys?"

Dingo handed over the keys to the Renault. "Wait here a minute," I said. I walked through the archway under which Giacinto and the two bodyguards had passed when they had left the room. They were standing there just inside the next room, doing what bodyguards do about as well as anybody—hanging out. I explained to Giacinto that I had convinced the boy to give up his one-man crusade and to return to the hospital where he could take care of his father. Giacinto still preferred to keep Dingo there at the chalet where he could keep an eye on him, but I convinced him that he had mistaken the young man's grief and outrage for malicious intent— that it was all an unfortunate misunderstanding brought about by the distress of his father's accident. Giacinto thought about it for a moment, then agreed to let the kid go back, but only if one of the bodyguards drove him. Well, that was *va bene* with me; I had been wondering how I was going to get rid of those stooges.

I returned to the couch and told Dingo. He said it was all right with him, so long as the guy who hit him wasn't the one who drove him back. We finally got everything straightened out, and I told Giacinto that I was going to walk Dingo out to the car. The chauffeur didn't like that idea very much either, but I reminded him that I was a guest there at the chalet, not a prisoner. It was as much for my own peace of mind as for Giacinto's edification that I had clarified the point. Giacinto grudgingly assented, but told me to be quick about it. Then I mentioned to him that Dingo had told me he had seen someone snooping around the back of the chalet when he had approached the front door. Giacinto nodded and dispatched the remaining bodyguard to check it out. That left Giacinto standing alone in the doorway of the chalet as Dingo, the other bodyguard, and I walked towards the car.

We had to walk about twenty-five yards to the Alfa Romeo. On the way there, I told Dingo that the driver was going to drop him off at the hospital, but that he should get over to Stonestreet's as soon as possible after the bodyguard left. It was just about completely dark outside. The last orange glow of the sunset silhouetted the rugged mountains off to the north.

"Where's your car?" I asked Dingo as he climbed into the Alfa Romeo next to the bodyguard. He pointed down the hill and I could just make out the outline of the car about a hundred feet off beneath some pine trees that lined the driveway. I shut the car door behind him and the car pulled away. I waited until it had traveled down the driveway and had turned onto the road.

"Fargo." It was Giacinto, standing back in the doorway. I didn't look back, but broke into a sprint in the direction of the Renault.

"*Fargo!*" I heard his feet hit the gravel driveway. Now it was a footrace, to use the football announcer's cliché, but I had a good fifty yards on Giacinto and I comforted myself with the thought that he certainly wasn't going to shoot me. Things still seemed to be working out rather well.

Rather well, indeed! I pulled on the door handle and it refused to open. Dingo—delirious with grief, desperate for revenge—had had the presence of mind to lock the car, damn his bourgeois instincts. There under the pine trees, even the light of the moon was blocked out and I scratched in vain across the surface of the car door with the key, trying to find the key-hole. Giacinto's cry had alerted the other bodyguard, and now the sound of his footsteps crunching quickly along the driveway joined Giacinto's. By some miracle, I found the keyhole and jerked the door open. The engine started just as a couple of fists banged against the trunk. I turned to see the white smear of Giacinto's disembodied face between the palms of his hands, which were flattened against the passenger-side window. I jammed the gearshift into first, doing irreparable damage to the transmission, judging from the sound of the maneuver, and lurched out of the paltry grasp of my pursuers.

CHAPTER 24

▼

FIVE HUNDRED BRIDES FOR FIVE HUNDRED BROTHERS

The road was one of the darkest I could ever remember traveling, and I probably would have driven right into Lake Molveno if I hadn't realized about halfway there that I had forgotten to turn the headlights on. They helped a bit, but I still had no idea where I was going and the road was still very dark. I kept glancing in my rearview mirror for an ominous set of headlights indicating that Giacinto and the remaining bodyguard had scared up a Ferrari someplace and were closing the gap. But that never happened, and I continued down the road *festina lente*, like a passed pawn. Within a very few minutes, I was rolling through the resort town of Molveno, which seemed, pretty much, to have shut down for the night.

I expected to have some trouble finding out where the Ultimi were holding their convocation, as Norrod had called it. It seemed to me that the police were out of the question. Any organization as outré and secret as Norrod and Stonestreet had led me to believe that Ultimi was, had to be very tightlipped about its activities, right? I mean, *loose*-lipped drunks notwithstanding, Ultimi wasn't about to notify the local chamber of commerce to be on the lookout for errant delegates.

I pulled to the curb in front of a sidewalk café where half a dozen teenagers stood at the curb huddled around a motor scooter. When they approached my car at my gentle summons, I realized why it still seemed so damn dark; I had my sunglasses on. I told the kids that I was from California and that I was here with a movie studio shooting on location. I was in the area for a production meeting with the cast and crew at some lodge but had gotten lost. Had they heard of any such event taking place around here?

I didn't bother to explain why a movie exec would be driving around in a dilapidated Renault that was one stoplight away from the boneyard, but they were impressed enough to consult avidly among themselves for a minute or so on the possibilities of my destination. Finally, they returned to my window and their spokesman, a lanky gigolo with a bass voice who obviously wanted to show off his ability in English told me with solemn certainty that the lodge was about half a mile down the road on the north shore of the lake. I couldn't miss it. Yeah, I thought, as long as I had my headlights on and my sunglasses off.

"*Naturalmente!*" I said, whacking myself sharply in the forehead with the palm of my hand. They offered to guide me there (I tried to imagine all of them climbing aboard the motor scooter like some circus act), but I declined, thanking them, and sputtered off.

I pulled the car off to the side of the road about a hundred yards short of the lodge, which was right there where the kids said it would be. The lodge looked blatantly unsinister, and I wondered for a moment if I had the right place. It was well lit and quiet and it seemed an unlikely place for rabidly subversive activity. I put on my sunglasses (I was still hoping that my disguise would stand me in good stead, but, shit, even Dingo, who had hardly noticed me on the plane, had had no difficulty recognizing me) and walked up to the entrance.

The veranda was the length of the building and was strewn with obscure obstacles like umbrella tables, lounge chairs, and potted plants. I bumped into several of these on my way to one of the large windows, but since no floodlights went on and no sirens started to wail, I had apparently so far avoided detection in spite of my clumsiness. I finally got to the window and peeked in.

Well, I was prepared for any sort of bizarre ritual that might meet my eyes—sexual perversion, human sacrifice, outlandish initiation rituals—but what I saw looked more like a sorority tea. About ten young women sat around talking and laughing quietly. I could detect no evidence of duress. Each of the young ladies wore a long white dress. Forget the sorority tea; this looked like a brides conference. Off to one side, I noticed another woman. She was older than the others and dressed much more casually in a pair of designer jeans and a velour pullover. She sat smoking a cigarette in a familiar attitude—legs crossed, elbow of smoking hand supported by the palm of the other hand. A clipboard lay at her feet. It was Valerie.

There was one other familiar face among the group. One of the women in white was the young girl on the plane, the one who had been involved in the quasi-elopement with Dingo, and who, according to Norrod, was a member in good standing of the Society of Trent.

I felt a wave of futility sweep over me. The words of Bob Dylan's "All Along the Watchtower" jumped into my head in all their ill-remembered trenchancy—something about there being too much confusion and the inability to find relief. I sat down carefully on some nearby pool furniture and tried to figure out what to do next.

A pair of headlights swung up the driveway, accompanied by the sound of a much classier ride than mine. I thought at first that it was probably Giacinto and The Hulk, who had talked to the same group of teenagers that I had ("Did you see a funny-looking guy with greasy hair and sunglasses looking for a party?") and had followed me to the lodge. I jumped behind one of the potted plants and held my breath.

The car pulled up to the entrance, where its doors opened to disgorge three men. They were all decked out in tuxedos, and one of them had had a hard time finding one to fit, I'd bet. It was Miguel. Haskell Stonestreet, Jr. and Millar Crofts walked along on either side of him. They rang the doorbell and somebody on the inside whom I couldn't make out opened the door for them. They went inside, and I jumped back to the window.

Apparently, the room full of brides was an anteroom that did not connect to the main entrance of the lodge. I saw none of the men pass through it, nor did any of the young women give any indication that they had seen anyone enter. While I was looking into the room, I saw Valerie pick up the phone. She listened for a couple of seconds, spoke a few words, then hung up. She consulted her clipboard, then said something to one of the girls, who stood up, smoothed down her dress over her legs, patted her hair gently, accepted a warm farewell that included a clasping of hands with one of the other girls (all smiles), and then followed Valerie's lead out of the room, or at least out of my view. Valerie returned in a minute or so and resumed her former station. It was beginning to look as though this was some sort of audition.

But for what? If Gore Kemp was here shooting a movie, what did it have to do with Ultimi? I was going to look awfully stupid if I went crashing the set of a movie under the pretense of saving a bevy of damsels in distress, especially if their *particular* distress was that they hadn't landed a part in the last six months. I decided to hold off on the rescue until I could figure out exactly what was going on.

I tiptoed off the porch and circled around the building to the lakeside. I could hear the waves slapping quietly against the rocks somewhere not too far in the distance.

Somehow, the rhythmic sound of the waves instilled in me a sense of regret over my own fatuity. All of this was just too preposterous. I could not rid myself of the feeling that I was unwittingly doing someone's bidding every step of the way. Even now, skulking around this lodge. There *had* to be some pattern to the events of the past two weeks.

I tripped over a sprinkler head and fell into a flowering shrub of some sort. So much for introspection, I introspected, extricating myself from the bush. And so much for those stupid fucking sunglasses. *Jesus!* What was I doing sneaking around an unfamiliar area at night with sunglasses on? I got around to the lakeside of the lodge where things were at least a bit more illuminated. Some of the light came from multi-colored lamps submerged just below the water line of a swimming pool that comprised a good part of the deck extending from the lodge towards the lake. A few gaslight fixtures were also on. These were stationed at the corners of the deck and suffused the area in a thin yellow glow.

I climbed over the short basket-weave fence that enclosed the deck and crawled towards the nearest window. I looked in on what appeared to be an amphitheater. The rear of the room, which was closest to me, was dark, but I could make out that all the seats were taken. There had to be several hundred of them anyway, and each seat was occupied by a man wearing a tuxedo. At the front of the room was a small stage, well-lit but with the curtain down. Above the stage hung a huge banner "*Fatti maschii, parole femine.*" Masculine deeds, feminine words? What? To the left of the stage, about a dozen men sat at a long dais. Three of those men were Miguel, Stonestreet, Jr., and Millar Crofts. Two of the seats, right in the middle of the dais, were empty. Off to the right, a film crew stood around waiting for whatever was going to happen to happen. Each man in the crew also wore a tuxedo. One of them was Gore Kemp. Under the influence of the banner's admonishment, no doubt, nobody was talking.

A moment later, the curtain rose revealing a large, four-poster bed in the middle of the stage. Lying spread eagle on the bed, each of her extremities tied to one of the posts, was the girl who had followed Valerie out of the anteroom. She still had her dress on. Some bright lights off to the left flashed on and one of the film crew hoisted a movie camera to his shoulder.

A pornographic movie? But why under these conditions? Why such a large, austere, and well-dressed audience? Why at a lodge in northern Italy and not in some sleazy motel in southern California? Was this Gore

Kemp's quantum leap to the big time—pornographic extravaganzas? But budget smut? Was this the dire conspiracy that so obsessed Norrod and worried Stonestreet?

At a nod from Millar Crofts, one of the men sitting at the end of the dais stood up and walked up the steps to the stage. He walked across the front of the stage and over to the head of the bed and turned to face the young girl fastened to the bed. For a moment, he stood at attention, head bowed, eyes closed. Either he was going through some private invocation, or he was psyching himself up for something. I began to get very uncomfortable about these proceedings and considered going to find the police. What I would tell them, I wasn't quite sure.

While I was debating with myself over whether my civic duty extended beyond the boundaries of the United States, the man on stage came out of his reverie and began to undress. He did so very deliberately, very ceremoniously, and when he was naked, he once again stood before the girl. Her expression didn't change, although her eyes seemed to have widened a bit. She seemed alert and calm. The man again closed his eyes and became very still.

Very slowly, he began to get an erection. It took about a minute, and the strain of the effort seemed to show on his face, but finally will prevailed and he was standing there with serious wood. The assemblage broke out in a polite applause and appreciative nods to one another.

When the various expressions of approval (short of vocal displays, of course) subsided, the fiercely aroused stud up on the stage took himself in hand and approached the girl on the bed. He crouched down and began to caress her face with his glans penis. The girl, for her part, was giving a remarkably restrained performance. She was the very picture of passivity, even as her partner zeroed in on her mouth and pushed past her lips. With his hands on the back of her blond head, he began sliding her back and forth along the shaft of his dick, steadily increasing the tempo until the maneuver assumed a frighteningly brutal and frenzied pace.

Suddenly, the man withdrew. He walked around to the foot of the bed, still mightily aroused, and knelt down on the bed between her spread legs.

Another man in a tuxedo entered from stage right bearing a sliver tray upon which stood a jar. He offered this to the naked man, who took it and applied some of the contents to his erection, and then between the legs of the girl. He then carefully positioned himself above the girl, took aim, found the mark, and thrust forward. Again, his tempo increased steadily so that at the peak of its intensity, the woman looked as through rhythmic jolts of electricity were coursing through her body at half-second intervals.

Now there was no steady increase in tempo, but only a wanton and furious ramming. After only a very few seconds this time, the man froze at the height of the front leaning rest position, held it for about ten seconds, then collapsed on top of the young woman. After a few more spasmodic seconds, the man dismounted, walked around to center stage and bowed to the audience, who were on their feet, clapping whistling, and yelling "Bravo!" (Accolades apparently not prohibited by the banner) in a tumult thunderous enough to rattle the window pane that stood between me and all this pandemonium. After a few minutes, the curtain descended on the two performers.

I ducked away from the window and sat on the deck with my back against the fence. My first thought was to spirit Valerie away so that I could perhaps learn from her just what was going on. But how to do that without attracting the attention of this entire fashionable fraternity was a big problem. I made my way back to the roadside entrance of the lodge, where I once again took my position at the window. Things had not changed much on this side. Valerie still sat there smoking cigarettes and the brides still chatted amiably among themselves. My teeth chattered even though it was a hot, humid evening. And it occurred to me that that was because my body knew what I was going to do even before I was conscious of my intentions. What the hell? Why *not* be just thoroughly obvious and go knock on the bloody door? The audacity of the move thrilled me; only a coward can truly appreciate a courageous act.

I gave a jaunty, musical, even lighthearted knock at the door and suffered a barrage of misgivings in the eternity between my knock and the opening of the door. The doorperson was none other than Valerie.

I could tell immediately from the expression on her face that she didn't recognize me, although there was perhaps something familiar about the face that stared at her from out of the darkness.

"Yes," she said tentatively. "What is it?" Like all impetuous acts, mine now encountered the inevitable obstacle of the blank mind. What was it, indeed? I was taking too long to answer.

"Uh, Valerie," I said.

"Stephen? Stephen! What are you—"

Her voice was gathering in shrillness. I pulled the screen door open towards me, grabbed her by the hand that she had neglected to remove from the door handle, pulled her out onto the veranda with me, and, rather histrionically, I suppose, fit my palm over her mouth. Her obedient lips moved softly against my hand, but she made no sound, nor did she offer any other resistance to my petty abduction. I guided her off the veranda and around to the side of the building.

"Now, don't scream," I said, slowly removing my hand from her mouth.

"Don't flatter yourself," she said in normal conversational tones. "What are you doing here? What the hell have you done to yourself?"

"Never mind that now. Do you know what the hell's going on in there?"

"I know perfectly well what's going on," she said. "Gore is getting some documentary footage."

"He's participating in a polite orgy, is what he's doing," I said.

"Now, now," she said. "We mustn't be judgmental."

"Those girls that you're tending to are being systematically and variously raped before an audience of all-male opera-goers."

"Don't be ridiculous, Stephen. Always the righteous bumbler." She began to laugh. "These are consenting adults." She tilted toward me and lowered her voice. "Although I'll grant you, a couple of these prom queens only qualify by a matter of hours." She raised her voice again. "For once, the legal term is so descriptive, yet so clear and succinct. So much legal jargon seems aimed at obfuscation."

Obfuscation? I never heard her use that word in all the years of our meaningful relationship. Was obfuscation the newest trendy word in California?

"If you intend to kidnap me, or whatever," said Valerie, "let's get on with it. If not, I gotta get back inside. They've got this shindig choreographed like a quadrille."

"Hey, if you're worried about criminal behavior, you'd better start thinking about your employer. Not me. Come on back around here, and I'll show you just what you're setting these girls up for."

"Oh, you're hopelessly squeamish, Stephen. If we must continue this conversation, you're going to have to come inside. I've already been gone too long."

"I'm not dressed for it," I said.

"Miss Cadieux?" It was one of Valerie's assemblyline brides leaning her veiled head out of the screen door.

"Coming," Valerie answered sweetly. I still held on to her arm and I could feel her pulling away from me.

"Look," I said. "You don't know the half of what these people are involved in. You're not safe here. They murdered Bill, you know."

Valeria wrenched her hand free of my grip.

"What are you talking about?" she said. "You're hysterical. *Who* murdered Bill?"

"This secret society that you're acting as social director for. Blessing and Stonestreet. And your pusher friend Crofts. And Gore Kemp, for all I know."

"What do you mean, my pusher friend?"

"I know all about the cocaine. I know that's why you wanted the money that you imagined I had stashed away. Or that somebody told you I had. You see, they all think that I'm the heir to the Blessing fortune. It's a long and complicated story. Right now, the important thing is for you to come with me. We'll go to the police, that is if this tourist trap has any police in it."

"Stephen, you've got it all wrong," said Valerie as though she were trying to pacify an escaped lunatic. "Gore is filming a documentary here. This is only part of it. It's like an updated *Mondo Cane*."

"Yeah, well Hitler had his own private film makers, too. You mean to tell me you condone the behavior going on in that auditorium? You condone rape?"

"Oh, it's hardly rape, Steve." It was Stonestreet, Jr.'s voice behind me. I turned around to find myself facing him and Miguel.

"Get away from me or I'll strangle you with your own cummerbund," I said. Amazing the words that'll slip out of your mouth when you perceive that you are in a desperate situation. But my impulse belied my bravado. What I really felt was the irresistible and unchivalrous urge to shield myself with Valerie's body.

"Now that *would* be criminal, don't you think?" said Kelly Stonestreet, amused by my threat.

"Absolutely barbaric," said Miguel.

"Yeah, and I suppose what you guys got going back there is a bridge tournament. Since when is rape a parlor game?"

"Your impertinence is tedious," said Miguel, noticeably irritated.

"Actually, we've been expecting you," said Stonestreet. "We have a seat reserved for you. A place of honor."

"I appreciate the offer," I said. "But I really must beg off."

"Ah, but we insist," insisted Stonestreet. "If you don't accompany us, I'll have to ask Miguel to escort you."

"There's no reason to get nasty," said Valerie, who was beginning to have doubts about the way Miguel and Stonestreet were behaving. "Stephen didn't mean anything."

She was sure wrong about that. I meant to get out of the immediate vicinity as soon as possible. But Miguel, especially, presented an imposing obstacle to my escape.

"Miss Cadieux," said Stonestreet, "please return to your duties. We have no intention of harming Mr. Fargo." A moment of silent confrontation followed between the two, and then Valerie turned abruptly and strode back to the veranda without looking back. So much for the allegiance of ex-spouses.

"Now," said Stonestreet, turning his attention to me. "Won't you join us?" By way of augmenting the invitation, Miguel grabbed my arm, around which his hand fit like mine did around a broom handle.

*   *   *

They made me an offer. I guess that's what you could call it. And from their point of view it was probably a very generous one.

They had conducted me to a small office at the head of a spiral staircase on the second floor of the lodge. On the way there, I heard some more wild applause from the auditorium below us, signaling that another "marriage" had been, er, consummated.

"Your appearance here in Trento hasn't been exactly unanticipated," said Stonestreet *fils* after we had all sat down, sipped at our glasses of bourbon, and, no doubt, mentally rehearsed the approaching scene.

"So I have already discovered," I said. Stonestreet was sitting across from me at the desk, assuming much the same attitude that he had taken during our interview in Georgetown a few days earlier. Miguel and Crofts were seated on either side and somewhat behind me—just on the periphery of my vision.

"Well, then I won't waste time with lengthy explanations," said Stonestreet. The chair on my right—Miguel's—scooted a bit on the floor. "We propose," said Stonestreet, "to invite you to be a member of our organization, and, of course, to enjoy the rights and privileges attendant upon that membership." He made this pronouncement as though there were no possibility of my declining it.

"Oh," I said. "Rights and privileges, huh? Like subversion, murder, and minor percs like public *violenza carnale*? Hey, I could be just like a dismounted Hell's Angel."

"Your talent for misinterpretation is appalling," said Stonestreet laconically.

"My source seemed to be authoritative," I said.

"Norrod is not an authority on anything," said Stonestreet. "Least of all the real world. The realpolitik world."

"I was referring to your father."

"My father is dead," said Stonestreet coldly. He took one of his huge cigars from the inside pocket of his jacket and began to fiddle with it. "I should say *our father*," he added, nodding towards Miguel and Crofts. "Our father who art in heaven." On my left, Crofts sniggered suddenly, sounding like a grouse flushed from a copse.

"This offer of yours," I said. "It wouldn't have anything to do with rumors that I might be in line for a windfall, would it?"

Stonestreet lit his cigar, a process that took about a minute and partially concealed him behind a vast cloud of smoke. He waved himself clear of it, put the cigar down in a cut glass ashtray that was far too small for it, and leaned forward on his elbows.

"I don't have a lot of time for these negotiations," he said. "So you'll forgive me if I sort of cruise through this. First of all, I don't like you. I think you're a smartass and a pussy, like all professors. But my brothers here have convinced me that you may be a relation of ours and that you may, indeed, have a claim to our father's estate. Knowing my father, I wouldn't doubt that a hundred such as yourself exist. But you are the one who seems to have introduced himself into this affair and so you're the one we have to deal with."

"Introduced myself? Maybe you better ask Miguel about that. He's the one who sent me on that expedition to Washington, thinking, no doubt, that I wouldn't return from it. Boy, did you guys botch that one."

Stonestreet disregarded my interruption and continued.

"But laying my prejudices aside, I'll appeal to whatever manhood you have left. Day-by-day, hour-by-hour, the world is becoming feminized. You see it in the enervation of our national policy, the passivity of our industry and commerce, even in the waywardness of our daily domestic lives. I assure you, it is a global affliction and one which threatens our species with extinction."

"Isn't Ronald Reagan supposed to take care of all this?" I said to Stonestreet. "Is this the standard indoctrination speech?" I said, turning next to Miguel. "If it is, you can tell him to save it."

Miguel said nothing. I turned to Crofts, who immediately sent his face into contortions, especially around the eyes. If this was one of his legendary attempts at fascination, it looked pretty ridiculous, and I answered him, maturely, I thought, by crossing my eyes and letting my jaw go slack enough for drool to start trickling out of the corner of my mouth. Crofts relaxed his features a bit, but his eyes narrowed in anger.

"Round one to me," I said, winking at him.

"It comes down to a very simple truth," said Stonestreet, raising his voice almost to a shout in order to regain my attention. "Woman is death, man is life. Life can exist side-by-side with death, but life must predominate—it must prevail. The whole history of civilization, the whole of *natural* history testifies to the righteousness of masculinity."

"That's pretty simple, all right," I said.

"What you have witnessed here tonight," continued Stonestreet, again ignoring my sarcasm, "is not an exercise in lust, not a lecherous performance, but a reaffirmation of the universal and historical preeminence of the masculine duty. It is, in fact, a mass, and the performers are our celebrants. Nobody is forced to do anything against their will. Every one of our participants has made ethical and spiritual commitment to—"

Stonestreet was interrupted by a prolonged and intense scream issuing from somewhere in the lodge.

"Please excuse me," he said, rising from his chair and walking to the door. Crofts and Miguel got up and followed him, but at the door, Stonestreet said something to Miguel and he returned to his seat.

"Sounds like someone just made another ethical and spiritual commitment," I said loudly to Stonestreet's back as he closed the door.

"Hey, Miguel," I said. "Old buddies like us, why don't we cut through the crap. Is this guy serious or what?"

Miguel motioned me to keep silent and went to the door. He opened it a crack and closed it again after satisfying himself that nobody was standing on the other side.

"I assure you he is very serious," said Miguel. "I would say that he is deadly serious, but I abhor melodrama." Boy, that English accent issuing from that gargantuan Indian frame was a real kick. "This diversion is fortuitous," he said. He walked over to where I was sitting and picked up my glass of bourbon, which I had neglected since my first sip.

"Please," he said, "do finish your drink. It's the devil's own task getting good bourbon in this part of the world. It'd be a shame to see it go to waste."

I drank the bourbon down as ordered and replaced the glass on the desk.

"Now then," said Miguel. "I'll try to make this as painless as possible."

It flashed through my mind that he was going to hug me, but he quickly slipped a forearm under my chin and began exerting the sort of paralytic pressure against my neck and throat that I felt certain was the prelude to death. My whole life did not pass before my eyes in an accelerated cavalcade. Instead, the image of Dowagiac's anamorphic paintings jumped into my head. Or else that was the distorted look that I was getting of my immediate surroundings. Then there was nothing.

CHAPTER 25

▼

EXCUSE ME, IS THIS PLOT TAKEN?

I was still suffocating, and it was still dark, but this was different. The tremendous pressure was gone and I was awake, or at least partially awake. I was damp and cold, and from somewhere I could hear the muffled sound of machinery. It seemed to be approaching, and then, when it was very near, I could feel a distant concussion, as if someone on the floor above me had dropped a sandbag. But I wasn't in a building. I was in a hole of some sort and it suddenly occurred to me in an instant of panic, that someone was bulldozing dirt over me. I was being buried alive.

The darkness was so profound that it was impossible for me to orient myself. I had some room to move around in the cavity—which was apparently cut into the sidewall of a deeper hole, just like the one I had seen earlier in the day when I visited the burial site with old man Stonestreet. But the space around me was limited—only a foot or two on the sides and overhead. I started clawing frantically at the walls, but although the dirt crumbled away easily enough, I was quickly becoming exhausted and I slumped back down to the floor. There wasn't enough room to extend my legs completely. I had to curl them up and bow my head towards my knees. The fetal position! I was in Stonestreet's Neolithic burial site. A just barely living anachronism, about to become part of the foundation of a low-cost housing project.

I got to my knees again and resumed my clawing at the walls, accompanying my efforts with screams for help that only sounded like I was bawling with a very bad cold. It was useless anyway. I could no longer hear the sound of the machinery, which meant that whoever had been operating it had completed the task. And whoever it was wasn't about to come to my aid anyway.

I slumped against the wall of the cave and probably would have started weeping in fear if I hadn't felt so faint. I remembered from innumerable mine cave-in movie scenes that the last thing you were supposed to do when oxygen was scarce in a confined space was to exert a lot of energy. There was no telling how many cubic yards of air I had used up in my thirty seconds or so of frenzy.

I reclined in resignation along the floor of the cave for what seemed like hours, but was probably only ten minutes or so, speculating on what a shock I was going to be to some future archeologist, listening to the sound...Yes! There was a sound now. Very faint and almost rhythmic, a sound that I could almost feel rather than hear, like someone beating a rug clean in the distance. And as the sound became steadily more distinct (you wouldn't believe how sensitive your hearing becomes and how completely you can concentrate under such circumstances), I could hear the occasional scrape of metal against stone, and finally, miraculously, a fissure appeared, revealing the moonlight, and some of the earth began to crumble in on me and sweet air filled my lungs once again.

The excavation stopped for a moment and I took up the task from the inside and screamed and pleaded at the top of my lungs in terms that I don't even remember. The digging on the other side resumed at a more rapid pace so that there finally appeared a hole large enough for me to squirm through. I tumbled at the feet of my rescuer, who grabbed me by the shoulders and supported me until my respiration was somewhat back to normal.

"Hullo," he said. "Back from the dead, are we?"

It was Claude Nickle, or Claudio Niccolo, I suppose, depending on which side of the Atlantic you happened to find yourself.

"What happened?" I asked.

"A reasonable question," he said. "Come on. I'll explain what I can on the way."

"On the way where?"

"I should think you'd like to tell Professor Stonestreet in person that he was a bit premature in burying you."

"Stonestreet did this?"

Claude laughed, a high-pitched, gleeful sound.

"Come on," he said, lifting me to my feet. "I've got a bottle of grappa in the van. Dreadful stuff, but it will restore you fully to the realm of the living."

*   *   *

The grappa was, indeed, awful, but every bit as restorative as Claude had promised it would be.

"It was a good thing that you had that boy come over to the house with your message," said Claude when we were underway. I realized that I had been right about our location. Even in the dark, I could tell that we were driving toward Trento from the excavation site that I had visited that morning. "And it's an even *better* thing that I was there to receive that message or you'd be running out of air by now, I would think."

"How did you know Stonestreet would take me there?"

"Oh, that was predictable enough," said Claude, somewhat jauntily it seemed to me. He seemed to be enjoying this whole episode. "My theory is that this isn't the first time he's used this modus operandi."

"You're kidding!"

"No," said Claude. "Notwithstanding your obvious distress, I can't tell you how thrilled I was when I saw Stonestreet and Miguel deposit you in the burial site. You know, the workmen were scheduled to resume construction on the apartment building at dawn tomorrow. Professor Stonestreet had given his approval. That was irregular enough. We haven't *nearly* done a thorough job of excavating that site. Christ, there are still artifacts strewn about the floor. Yes, quite irregular."

"So you assumed from this deviation from standard operating procedure that Stonestreet was going to dump me there?"

"Well, I didn't know whose body it would be, but I knew he was due for stunt like this. What I didn't expect to find, actually, was that whoever he put in there would still be alive. I'd just about convinced myself to wait for a half-hour to be sure that he wasn't coming back. But he got out of there in quite a hurry. He probably realized that what he was doing was real risky, using the backhoe and everything at that time of night. This place isn't so secluded that he might not be detected. Why he didn't kill you beforehand is beyond me though. It certainly wasn't a matter of his squeamishness. The fucker's as ruthless as they come." Probably too many witnesses, I thought.

"How do you know all this?"

"Oh, I've been on to the good professor for a few years now," said Claude. "In fact, you might say that he's the one who told me what he was up to. Not directly, of course. He doesn't do *anything* directly."

Once again, Dowagiac's anamorphic art obsession crept into my thoughts. The limited, eccentric, even severe perspective.

"In fact," Claude continued, "I've often felt like a sort of tacit conspirator in some of Stonestreet's little intrigues. He seems to have this perverse need for someone to appreciate his efforts, even if his efforts are criminal. Not that I ever approved. But he's very clever. For all my suspicions, I've never been able to catch him at anything overtly illegal. Up to now, that is."

"What sort of suspicions?"

For the rest of the ride back to Trento, Claude related the events of the past dozen or so years. He had been working as a staff writer for a New York-based tabloid, a frustrating niche for a Columbia journalism graduate with talent and ambition. All his life, his mother had told him fascinating stories about her sister, who had married a mysterious Midwestern industrialist and manufacturing genius. Soon after the marriage, the sister, Leona Blessing, had suffered a nervous breakdown, from which she apparently recovered, only to become a virtual recluse thereafter. She no longer corresponded with her relatives or former friends. In fact, she refused to have any contact with them.

Claude, sensitive to the fascination of American society for the private lives of its most successful and mysterious members, recognized immediately the possibilities of the story and his opportunity as a quasi-insider. He embarked on an enterprise to research the story and turn it into a book. He had even managed to make contact with the millionaire industrialist, who, more and more, seemed to be the crucial protagonist in the history of the family whose story Claude intended to chronicle. At first, his subject had been uncooperative, to say the least. He threatened lawsuits and other reprisals of a non-litigious nature if Claude did not abandon the project.

Then, there had been an abrupt change in Blessing's attitude. His letters became more cordial, and a little bit coy, too. He would consider cooperating—even authorizing—the biography under certain murky conditions. He would not meet with Claude personally and he insisted that he be allowed to choose those sources of information that Claude should pursue. He has also insisted on final approval of the text.

Claude's journalistic instincts rebelled, while at the same time, his curiosity was irresistibly piqued. He wrote a letter to Blessing indicating that he could not continue the project under the terms that he (Blessing) had outlined. He would do the best he could by relying on his own resources, thank you.

Blessing had responded anxiously by dropping his demands for final approval. And though he still refused to meet personally with Claude, he offered to introduce the writer to his oldest friend and lifelong confidant, Haskell Stonestreet, Sr.

"In my discussion with Stonestreet this morning, it didn't appear that he and Blessing were the closest of friends," I interjected.

"It's even more fascinating than that," Claude responded. "I am convinced—although it took a couple of years for me to figure it out—that at the time of this offer, I was no longer dealing with Draper Blessing. I believe that he was already dead at this time."

"I thought he died about two years ago."

"So does everybody else," said Claude. "But they haven't been living and working as closely as I have with Stonestreet. About two and a half years ago, workers installing a sewer system at a site we had previously excavated turned up parts of a human skeleton. They called Stonestreet and he hustled down there. He returned a few days later and announced that the bones comprised a burial site that we had overlooked during our excavation. Well, I've watched Stonestreet work at his profession for several years, and I've learned that he's a thorough and methodical man. It seemed inconceivable to me that we could have missed that burial. So, just out of curiosity, I took a ride down there myself and did some investigating. The skeleton had disappeared. The people down there had just assumed that Stonestreet had taken the bones with him. But he never mentioned to *me* that he had done so. I finally located some graduate student who had assisted Stonestreet in the examination of the skeleton. He told me that the investigation, which by the way, Stonestreet was reluctant to undertake *in situ* so to speak, had revealed that the bones were not the skeleton of a Neolithic man at all. Indeed, it was likely that the corpse was no more than a decade old.

"Now, these sorts of things are supposed to be reported to the authorities, but the graduate student assured me that he had made no such report, having been assured by Dr. Stonestreet that he would do it himself. Needless to say, that report was never made. And as an interesting footnote, I should tell you that the graduate student died about two weeks later when a wall of dirt fell in on him at another excavation site. He had been working alone at the time—late in the evening. His death was listed as an accident."

"And you think that the skeleton was Blessing," I said.

Claude nodded.

"And you think Stonestreet killed him, and that he later killed the graduate student to prevent him from revealing what he knew."

"Right-o," said Claude. "And tonight he tried to pull it off once again with you."

"Jesus, he probably would have gotten away with it, too," I said, the seriousness of my brush with disaster just then beginning to sink in.

"Damn right he would have. If you hadn't sent that kid, or even if you had and Stonestreet had been there instead of me, I never would have arrived in time to save you. You'd be wearing a concrete lid by noon tomorrow."

"But why did he kill Blessing?"

"Well, he certainly had reason enough to. The old man raped his wife, for one thing. And for another, Blessing seemed to have some kind of mysterious enslaving power over Stonestreet, which Stonestreet seems to have resented for years."

"Yeah, I got that impression while talking to Stonestreet this morning," I said.

"In fact," said Claude, "Stonestreet may not have killed him at all. The old man may have died of natural causes, but Stonestreet had his reason for not making the death public knowledge. You see, he knew Blessing better than anyone alive. He knew how he operated, how he expressed himself, how he thought—maybe even *what* he thought. Did you know that no one saw Blessing for the last twenty years of his life? Not even his wife and children. He made Howard Hughes look like Mick Jagger. Not even his business associates ever saw him. Hell, the guy existed on paper and over the telephone lines. I think Stonestreet simply *became* Draper Blessing."

"So then why did he finally kill him when he did, *if* he did?"

Claude shrugged. "Assuming that's what happened, there was no sense in prolonging the impersonation. That was too risky. Even as careful as Stonestreet had been, there was the chance that he would be discovered. He waited just long enough for him to get as much of Blessing's money as possible under his control so that any inheritance would be meager at best. Then he announced Blessing's death. But by that time, he also had control of a huge network of information that Blessing had constructed over a life-time of shrewd business campaigns."

Something still bothered me. "You know, if it was my father who had died, and I was heir to that much money, I certainly would have gotten some official confirmation of his death," I said.

"Where's the problem in that?" said Claude. "The family *did* ask for confirmation. And they got it. They got a death certificate stating that Blessing had died of natural causes and they got positive identification through a comparison of dental records. You must remember, Stonestreet had the bones and he also had enough money to buy legitimate death certificates for every Jew that ended up in an Auschwitz furnace. Christ, he could have *you* certified dead right now as you live and breathe."

"I get the picture," I said. I had almost gotten it all too well. "But why should he want to kill me?"

"Didn't he tell you about the Blessing cipher?"

"Yeah, he did. But I got the impression from what he told me about it that he didn't put too much stock in it."

"That's exactly the impression he wanted you to take away with you," said Stonestreet. "You caught him off guard, I think. He certainly couldn't dispose of you this morning when you showed up at the dig. Too many witnesses around. And like I told you, his style's nocturnal. He had to bide his time and try to get rid of you under more familiar circumstances."

"But why?"

"About a month or so before Leona's death, she announced that Blessing had confided to her that he had drawn up a secret document that was to be made public immediately after her death. This document, she

further stated, would reveal the heir to the Blessing fortune, a secret relative. Because of a story that my father seems to have been the first to
relate, this mysterious heir was narrowed down to a certain graduate student in Detroit."

"I know the rest," I said. "For some strange reason, Stonestreet told me
the whole thing."

"It's not so strange," said Claude. "I told you, he wanted to gain your
confidence in order to stall for time. You see, all indications are that Leona
Blessing was as mad as a hatter for the last couple of decades of her life. It's
more than likely that this improbable story about the mysterious heir was
no more than one of her elaborate hallucinations, to which she was regu-
larly subject. But Stonestreet just couldn't take the chance. Blessing was
eccentric enough to have thought up this scheme just as Leona had
announced it. After all, he had no use for his children and from what I've
been able to determine in the last few hours, Leona died nearly penniless.
As far as Stonestreet was concerned—he had a lot to lose, don't forget—
you just might have been the Blessing heir. As far as that goes, you still
may be. The only thing I can't understand is why he didn't kill you long
before you showed up here."

"It may not have been for lack of trying," I said. "How do the Blessing
children figure in all this?"

"I don't know, exactly," said Claude. "Haskell, Jr. is certainly bloodthirsty enough to kill for money. But he and his father have been
estranged for twenty years. I find it difficult to believe that the old man
would ally himself with the kid. The speculation is, you know, that the
younger Stonestreet is really Draper Blessing's son."

"If you believe Stonestreet, the son, I mean, it's more than speculation,"
I said.

"Miguel is another case altogether. At least outwardly he was devoted to
Leona. Whether or not he was working with Professor Stonestreet, I
couldn't tell you, except to say that he was sure working with him when it
came to dumping you in that hole. The other kids, if you don't count

Crofts, whose parentage is questionable, are dead, and there's always been some controversy about their deaths. In fact, their deaths probably contributed to Leona's insanity."

We were passing through the center of town now, just a couple of blocks from the museum and Stonestreet's apartment. I was getting nervous. I was in no mood to confront a desperate man who had just made an unsuccessful attempt on my life. In his frustration, he might try even harder the second time.

"So, what's our next move, the police?" I asked, silently praying that Claude would find that a first-rate, if not inspired, idea.

But the only thing my suggestion seemed to do was to startle Claude so badly that he almost swerved into a group of pedestrians as we tooled across *Piazza Vittoria* within sight of the museum.

"What the hell would we go to them for?" cried Claude. "I mean, what would we go to them *with*, to be more precise?"

"Well, for one thing," I countered, "the guy just tried to bury me about forty years too early, if actuarial tables are to be trusted at all. And from what you've just told me, Stonestreet's made as much of a career of crime as he has of archeology. Are you kidding or what?"

"Yes, but we have no *proof*," said Claude. "Can you identify the person or persons who tried to kill you?"

"No. I was unconscious. But I could swear out a complaint against Miguel. He was the *reason* I was unconscious. Maybe the police could get him to talk. Anyway, I thought you said you saw Stonestreet dump me in that hole."

"Sure, I know he did it. But there's no way I can prove it. It was dark," said Claude. "And the only thing arresting Miguel is going to accomplish is spooking Stonestreet and his real accomplice, assuming it's not Miguel."

"But it might *be* Miguel."

"No, we've got to be sure," said Claude. "Look, you better scoot down here. We're going past the museum. We don't want Stonestreet to know about your resurrection just yet."

I crouched down on the floor of the van just beneath the dashboard, smashing my forehead in the process. That brought another thought to mind. Not a pleasant one.

"How do I know *you're* not his accomplice," I said.

Claude downshifted to second gear, spun the car around a corner and laughed.

"I guess you don't," he said. "But I didn't see anyone else down there pulling your sorry ass out of that hole."

I had no answer for that, and, in fact, it occurred to me that my show of ingratitude was bad form, to say the least. The van slid to a halt along some gravel and Claude turned off the lights and killed the engine.

"Wait here a minute," he said, and then he was gone. He returned about two minutes later.

"Come on," he said. "The coast is clear. But walk alongside the building and don't say anything until we're inside."

"Inside where?"

"My apartment. It's the safest place right now."

"But what are we going to *do?*" I almost whined.

"Don't worry," he said. "I have a plan."

CHAPTER 26

▼

TAKE MY PLOT, PLEASE?

For my money, the plan was something out of a third-rate TV show. It made a *Charlie's Angels* episode look like pure genius.

I was to wait fifteen minutes—to give Claude enough time to go over to Stonestreet's apartment—and then make a phonecall to Stonestreet. The reason for the time lag was that Claude had to be in Stonestreet's presence so that he would not be suspected of making the call himself. I was to disguise my voice and tell Stonestreet that I had seen him deposit a body at the excavation site and that I would keep my mouth shut for fifty thousand dollars that his accomplice was to leave for me at the Fountain of Neptune in the piazza in the center of the city. Then Claude and I would wait for this accomplice, confront him with our knowledge of what he and Stonestreet had been up to, and by doing so try to force him into a confession implicating Stonestreet.

"It stinks," I said. "You've been watching too many American reruns over here. And something's been lost in the translation."

"What's wrong with it?" said Claude, who had opened a couple of bottles of beer—the big, liter size. He set one down in front of me on the coffee table and took a couple of huge gulps from the other one.

"Well, it's workable up to the point where we insist that he send his accomplice with the money. I mean, what is this accomplice fetish of yours, anyway? We aren't even sure that he *has* an accomplice. And even if he does, how can we be sure that he'll deliver him up to us just because we ask him to? He might send *anyone*. Christ, he might even send you."

"Okay," said Claude after several swigs of beer and a few minutes to think over what to me seemed perfectly obvious. I was beginning to regret having Claude for an ally. "Okay" he said again. "We'll forget about the accomplice for a moment. Chances are he'll have to get in touch with whoever it is anyway. Maybe we'll just get lucky and he'll send his accomplice on his own initiative."

"Sure," I said, feeling more and more forlorn about this plan. "Maybe."

"The plan's still sound," said Claude. "He's bound to try to retrieve your body and he probably won't do it alone. Maybe he won't do it himself at all. Maybe *that's* where we'll catch the accomplice. But no matter how we do it, we've got to learn the identity of the accomplice. It's the only hope we have of getting the police to listen to us. Stonestreet is powerful and respected around here. The police aren't going to listen to a couple of no-account gringos telling bizarre tales about one of northern Italy's leading citizens. This ain't the States. Around here, a Ph.D. can throw his weight around like a Southern politician."

I finally agreed, reluctantly. Claude phoned Stonestreet to see if he was going to be at home, under the pretense of wanting to come over and discuss a geological analysis of the excavation site. Apparently, Stonestreet was not immediately convinced that such a discussion couldn't wait until morning. Claude put a lot of effort into inviting himself over, and, to my mind, he was beginning to sound suspiciously insistent. I tried to wave this message over to Claude, but he just turned away from me and continued importuning Stonestreet, who finally yielded.

"Now, remember," said Claude, as he was about to leave the apartment. "Fifteen minutes. And disguise your voice."

"How?"

"Like in the movies. Put a handkerchief over your mouth."

"I don't have a handkerchief," I said.

"Come on, Fargo. Get in the game, huh? Improvise." Claude stood in the doorway looking at me uncertainly. "Above all," he said, "be *convincing*." Then he pulled the door shut behind him and was gone.

Claude's apartment looked like a way station en route to a transient's version of heaven. The room was painted in faded pastels. The furniture had that tense, utilitarian, Howard Johnson look to it. A few newspapers lay scattered around the room. An overloaded ashtray spilled some its contents over a coffee table from which a strip of veneer had been lifted, revealing a white pine scar. Off to the left of the kitchen table stood a neat phalanx of empty liter-size beer bottles. There was nothing else about the place to indicate that it was home to anybody.

I looked around for a clock, at first leisurely, then more urgently. All the normal places for clock displays were without one. No clock above the sink in the kitchen. No clock in the living room above the couch. There wasn't even an alarm clock on the nightstand in the bedroom.

I started going through all the drawers and cupboards I could find. No clocks. No watches. Goddamn Claude! What was I supposed to use? My metabolic clock? Count to nine hundred (one-Mississippi, two-Mississippi)?

Finally, above the stove, I found one of those hourglass egg timers, a memento, according to the decal on the glass, from Niagara Falls. Hoping that it was a three-minute timer, I turned it over and tried to estimate how long it had been since Claude left. It was more than five minutes, but it sure didn't seem to have been ten yet. I settled on eight. Now, assuming that this was a three-minute egg timer (Do they boil eggs for three minutes in Italy? I wondered), I would let the sands drain through and then turn it over once again. When the sands had run out for the second time, approximately fourteen minutes would have passed. Close enough.

I turned my attention to how I would go about disguising my voice. I could probably handle a passable southern drawl, if the conversation didn't go on too long. In high school I had done a pretty good Foghorn Leghorn. And in a college drama class, I had developed a pretty good Irish brogue in order to play Michael James Flaherty, bar owner in *The Playboy of the Western World*.

I finally decided to go heavy on the hoarseness and light on the English accent. I sounded to myself like a sort of watered down Jack Hawkins, but at least I didn't sound like myself. But then, I didn't think I looked like myself, either, and nobody seemed to be having any trouble recognizing me.

"You pimp!" I screamed at the hourglass, which had run out without my observing it. I grabbed it and flipped it over. This time I watched it closely until the last grains slipped through the tube into the bottom half receptacle. Then I picked up the phone and dialed the number Claude had left for me.

"*Pronto*," said the voice on the other end, surprising me by answering after the first ring. Surprising me so greatly, in fact, that I forgot all about the English accent and growled so deeply that Stonestreet had to ask me to repeat what I had said, which was unsettling enough, and even worse, since I had irritated my throat so badly, I went into a fit of coughing.

"I said," I said, "I saw you dump that young man's body into the hole about an hour ago at the excavation site just northwest of Trento."

"What? Who is this?" asked Stonestreet, sounding perfectly indignant. A remarkable performance, but I wasn't in the mood for conversation. My vocal chords wouldn't stand it.

"If you're interested in keeping your participation in this a secret, leave fifty thousand dollars, uh, in a briefcase at the *Fontana di Nettuno*."

"When?" asked the voice on the other end, after one of those inscrutable telephone pauses.

When, indeed? Claude and I hadn't discussed when. And I had no idea what time it was.

"Eleven o'clock tonight," I said, holding my breath.

"But that's twenty minutes from now," said Stonestreet.

"Make it midnight, then," I said.

"Look here," said Stonestreet. "I don't have American dollars on hand in that quantity. It *is* American dollars you're asking for, isn't it?"

"Uh, yeah. It is," I said.

"Well, in that case you'll have to wait until tomorrow," said Stonestreet.

"I can't wait that long," I said. "Look, just give me all the cash you have on hand—American dollars, Lira, whatever. Just get it there by midnight, or I'm making my telephone call to the cops."

"Is a plastic shopping bag all right?" asked Stonestreet.

"A plastic shopping bag?"

"Yes. To hold the money. I don't own a briefcase." He didn't own a briefcase.

"Oh, all right," I said, realizing that my voice no longer had the same quality that I had begun with. I was almost speaking in my normal tone of voice. "But get it there by midnight. One second after midnight I make my call," I said. Then I hung up. Drops of sweat were rolling from my newly shaven chin, and I had the heart rate of a gnat. I was wishing that I could get my hands on Claude's trowel so that I could carve his liver out of his worthless body, fry it up with onions, and force-feed it to him while the light slowly faded from his baby blue eyes. The plan was turning into a debacle. Even now, Stonestreet was probably paralyzed with laughter. *Ah, I want all of your pocket change and anything else you've got stashed away in the cookie jar. If not, I'm going to tell the police that you buried a non-existent corpse before it was dead, perhaps buried a real corpse after it was dead, and, by impersonating the dead man, swindled his estate and took over the world.*

Jesus!

A few minutes later, Claude stuck his breathless head in the door.

"Come *on*," he said, and then disappeared. I saw the headlights of the van flash on and heard the ignition grind for a couple of seconds before the engine turned over. Claude raced the motor a couple of times about as loudly as he dared. Then, a few seconds later, I heard the door to the van slam shut and Claude was in the doorway again.

"What the fuck are you *waiting* for?" he wanted to know. It had started to sprinkle very gently outside. Droplets of rain clung to Claude's curly scalp. "An engraved invitation?"

"How clever," I said. "You'll forgive me if I find myself unable to summon a worthy riposte. But the fact is, I'm still reeling from the tactical ingenuity of your plan."

"Cut the crap, huh? Stonestreet's ready to move out and I don't want to lose him."

"If Stonestreet fell for one word of that line, he's a bigger fool than he appears to be," I said, still not making any move to leave the apartment.

"Look," said Claude, "can we discuss this in the car? Do you want to blow the whole thing?"

"How come you don't have a clock in this miserable hovel?" I asked. "You tell me to call in fifteen minutes and then leave me sitting here with nothing but a plastic souvenir hourglass."

"Hey," said Claude, "I was just saying fifteen minutes to give you a rough idea. I didn't want you to wait for an hour and I didn't want you to start dialing the minute I stepped out the door. You're making a big thing out of nothing, and the longer we stand here arguing about it, the more chance there is of Stonestreet slipping off to meet his accomplice without our being able to follow him."

"Oh, is that phase two?" I asked.

"Why, hell yes!" said Claude. "Now get in the truck. I forgot something in the bedroom." As bad as he was, Claude was the only person I could trust. He had saved my life, after all. I walked through the door and climbed into the passenger seat of the rattling van. A moment later, Claude mounted the driver's seat next to me and slammed the door shut.

"Here," he said, handing me the item that he had forgotten in the bedroom—a lackluster revolver that looked like something out of the Boer

War. "Put that in the glove box for the moment." When I didn't comply right away, he said: "It's just a precaution."

"Does this thing work?" I asked.

"Of course it works. When I was a kid in upstate New York I got so good with it that I could pick off squirrels at a hundred yards," said Claude. He shifted into reverse and backed the van out into the street. He drove to within half a block of Stonestreet's apartment, pulled over to the curb, shut down the lights and left the engine running.

"I only hope we haven't missed him while we were dealing with your existential crisis," said Claude.

"What the hell are you talking about, existential crisis?" I said.

"Shhhh!" said Claude. "There he is now." I could barely see a figure pull the front door shut behind him and walk to the curb, where Stonestreet's Alfa Romeo was parked. The dome lights in the Alfa Romeo flashed on momentarily as the car door opened, then they blinked out. A moment later the car pulled away from the curb.

"Now," said Claude triumphantly. "On to our accomplice."

Stonestreet began circling without haste and apparently without logic though the narrow streets of Trento. After about ten minutes of this maze-like progress, Claude started to get impatient.

"He's on to us," he said.

"Shit," I said. "A *child* would be on to us. Take me to the nearest airport."

"How easily they lose heart," said Claude. "Look, he's stopping."

We pulled the car up about a block behind the Alfa Romeo. We were on a street that ran along the river. From one of the windows above us a tenor aria from something that sounded like Verdi was blaring away. At a curb-side café just a few feet away, several men sat at an outdoor table squabbling loudly, discussing their interminable politics, no doubt. The street was comparatively well lighted, so that when the driver emerged from the Alfa Romeo, we could see that it was indeed Haskell Stonestreet, Sr. Without even the pretense of caution, he crossed the street and walked into one of the doors that lined the street, using his own key to gain entrance.

"Whose house is that?" I asked.

"Damned if I know," said Claude. "I never knew him to use it before. Maybe it's a safe house. Maybe he's a spy. Maybe this is the real thing. I never did understand how he could live in that economy-size version of an apartment next to the museum." I would have found this amusing coming from Claude and after having seen his apartment, but I was incapable of being amused at the moment.

"Now we wait, huh?" I said.

"Wait, shit," said Claude. "*You* wait. I'm going to make sure he doesn't sneak out the back. If he comes out the front door again, give me a blast on the horn."

I didn't want to tell Claude that I'd had nothing but bad luck with that particular maneuver. He had obviously seen too many cop shows to be dissuaded by arguments that I could offer, so I silently agreed to the plan.

"Give me the gun," he said. But I wasn't quite prepared to go *that* far.

"Hey, Claude," I said. Don't you think we ought to leave the fireworks to the police?"

"Will you just give me the goddamn gun before we lose him?"

Claude was standing in the street with the door open now, and he was talking way too loudly for a stealthy commando. "Jesus Christ!" he finally erupted when it became clear to him that I wasn't going to cooperate. He jumped back into the driver's seat and reached across me to get the pistol out of the glove box.

"If I hadn't dug you out of that hole myself, I'd think *you* were working with Stonestreet," he said. "We got a desperate man to deal with." He slammed the glove box shut, got out of the car, and slammed the door. It seemed to me to be a bad time for such a display of temper, but I could see that Claude wasn't going to be reasonable.

"Now, remember," he said, tucking the gun in his belt. "If he comes out that front door, hit the horn. No. Give me three short blasts," Claude added as an afterthought.

"That ought to fool him," I said.

"Just do it," said Claude. He walked away from the van in the opposite direction of the house that Stonestreet had entered, turned toward the river at the corner, and disappeared.

I waited. I waited long enough for the opera to proceed through a turgid duet, a macho baritone number, a strident *ensemble*, a martial climax, a plaintive soprano swan song, and then an abrupt shift to a Neapolitan love song when someone changed the station. The men at the café had long since resolved Italy's millennium of political turmoil, and were now bantering with a couple of fetching prostitutes. At least they were fetching from where I sat.

This was taking way too long. Christ! It was probably close to midnight already. The men were clearing out of the café and the proprietor was pulling down the shutters. Even the music from the radio had ceased. Enough was enough. I sounded those three short blasts on the horn and waited. Nothing happened. I gave the signal again and somebody yelled something unfriendly in Italian from a window above me—probably the same guy who had been broadcasting the opera to the entire neighborhood only a few minutes before.

Finally, against every instinct for self-preservation that howled through my body, I got out of the van and walked in the direction that I had seen Claude take toward the river. The river was well lighted, even better than the street, and the mosquitoes were out in force. The riverbank was deserted and only once or twice did I see a car go whizzing across the bridge about a hundred feet away. A wall stretched along the river, concealing the buildings from view, so that I could only estimate where the house was that Stonestreet had entered from the front door. I looked around once to make sure that the coast was clear, then pulled myself over the wall and dropped to the ground below.

I hit with a squash, right in the middle of a patch of tomato plants. It was only about ten feet from the base of the wall to the building. Except for palatial villas, official residences, that sort of thing, Italians don't go in much for lawns. I got myself tangled up momentarily in some sort of apparatus for hanging clothes (and unwary intruders, perhaps) and finally got to the entrance. The dwelling was dark and the only sounds I could hear were the steady orchestration of crickets and the occasional, distant barking of a dog, which sounded more like a seal.

And then there was another sound—a sharp, precise slap of flesh against flesh. It came from the courtyard to my left. Another brick wall, running perpendicular to the one I had just climbed over, separated me from the sound. By the light of the moon, I could see a huge reinforced wooden door built into the wall. I moved to it. The latch was closed, but the padlock attached to it was unlocked. As carefully as you might slip a necklace off a pit bull, I lifted the lock from the latch and pushed the door open a crack.

The light wasn't as good there, but I could see enough to know that I didn't like what I was seeing. Two men stood a sort of casual guard on either side of the rear entrance to the house next door. One was tall, pale, with a scalp full of red ringlets. The other was shorter, with a think heavy beard, and much balder. There were the last two visitors that Randi and Randy had ever had. And two less gracious guests it would be hard to imagine. Axtract and Tremble. The Rosencrantz and Guildenstern of the Dark Side.

The tall one slapped his upper arm and let go with some indistinct oath. The mosquitoes were giving him an infinitesimal taste of his own medicine and he didn't like it. His partner paid no attention to the tall one's irritation, but leaned against the house, calmly smoking a cigarette. The only thing I could think of was that if Claude had stumbled into those goons, he was in a world of shit right now. It called for the kind of rescue mission for which I was totally inadequate. Confession or no, it was time to call in the local police.

As I stood there in near jubilation with this decision, my forehead pressed against the wall, the gate flew in suddenly and struck me solidly on the right cheekbone, sending me sprawling into the staked tomato plants.

"*Chi e?*" somebody asked. I looked up to see a boy of twelve or so framed in the doorway. What a time for him to come sneaking home.

"*Nessuno,*" I said. But he wasn't buying that. In a second he had disappeared and was running around to the front of the house shouting "*Papa, Papa!*"

In another second, I had disentangled myself from the mysterious gardening paraphernalia that had seemed to be restricting me with volition of its own. I made the back wall in one leap, scrambled over it, and dropped to the riverside.

I ran as I hadn't run since I was a child. I flew with all the adrenaline my body could produce, until my lungs burned and I couldn't even see straight anymore for fear.

I got to the corner and turned it cautiously, stopping behind a tree to catch my breath. The street was now deserted. Claude's van was still parked alongside the curb, but that was expendable. Claude was expendable. Hell, Valerie was expendable. The only thing I wanted right then was to sob my story out to the nearest cop. But I didn't know where the nearest cop was. I didn't even know where the police station was. I certainly wasn't going back to my apartment. Nor was I going back to Claude's. Those were certainly deathtraps. I thought of Norrod. Where was Giacinto when I needed him? If I had eaten dinner, I would have puked it up right there, just out of principle. As it was, I couldn't even spit.

I sat there thinking of what to do, and, of course, I sat there too long. I didn't hear them approach. But I felt the arms go around my chest, pinning *my* arms and I found another hand clasped over my mouth. Then, for an instant, the hand was removed and I tried to scream. But before I could do so, fabric of some sort replaced the hand. My mouth was open and I could taste something sweeter than anything I had ever tasted. And that was as far as sensory impressions went.

CHAPTER 27

▼

FARGO CURES THE
PROFESSOR'S HAYFEVER

I was getting used to waking up in strange places and to unexpected faces. Only this time, as my head cleared, the face became less unexpected.

"Chloroform," said Stonestreet. We were in a living room. A very nicely, if somewhat archaically, furnished one. There were peacocks on the wallpaper, and crystal lamps, and solid, high-polished furniture—quite a bit of it, although the room didn't look cluttered. I was lying on a couch again. Funny how people seemed to know that it was my favorite piece of furniture. Stonestreet was sitting across from me in an equally commodious armchair.

"What?" I said.

"I said *chloroform*. You're wondering what we used to put you temporarily out of commission, so to speak," said Stonestreet, ever the solicitous host and ever the arrogant presumer of another's thoughts. I wasn't wondering that at all.

"How quaint," I said.

"It's clean," he said. "And elegant. And it's usually quite efficient. I hate the sight of blood."

"So do I," I said. You see, he had this gun in his hand. "But I was referring to the room here."

"Oh, forgive me," said Stonestreet. "I thought you were referring to the quaintness of chloroform. Yes, these are rather charming accommodations," he said, casting his eyes about the room. "Perhaps a bit overly comfortable, but, then, Draper was always sure to provide for his comfort, no matter what the expense."

"This was Blessing's home?"

"It wasn't really home. Draper had no home. It was one of his many retreats."

"Where's Claude?"

"Ah, I presume he's still sleeping. We had to repeat his dosage several times. We didn't expect you to take so long in coming to his assistance. I guess we underestimated your, uh, circumspection. Not to worry. Messieurs Axtract and Tremble are looking after him."

Stonestreet set his pistol down on the shiny oaken coffee table in front of him and began searching his pockets. His face was going through that contorted, anguished look that one assumes just before the discharge. Just in time (it's always just in time; we've got more control that we think) he pulled a red bandana from his back pocket—just in the same way that a magician pulls a silk scarf from his sleeve—and let go with a sneeze that had a certain vocal timbre to it that suggest that Stonestreet was proud of his sneezes. I've always thought that people who call attention to themselves when they sneeze and blow their noses like elephants in heat are the rudest sorts of buffoons. Just why I should worry about the etiquette of sneezing when my life was in great danger is beyond me.

"Bless you," I said. Never was the remark less sincere.

"Hayfever," said Stonestreet. "Or something close to it. It's come over me all of a sudden" He returned his hanky to his pocket, picked up the gun, and tilted his head a bit, the better to scrutinize my face.

"You've gone through a remarkable transformation," he said finally. "I hadn't noticed the extent of it earlier."

"Well, it was dark," I said. "And anyone would look different under a couple of tons of dirt. You should have seen me in my sunglasses."

"A couple of tons of dirt doesn't seem to have been enough," said Stonestreet, just slightly rueful.

"You're probably better at digging up bodies than at planting them," I said.

"Yes," said Stonestreet, amused. "The people I bury do seem to keep turning up. But the truth of the matter is that I'm rather glad that you managed this resurrection. It gives me the chance to celebrate my efforts with someone who can appreciate them."

"I'm supposed to be flattered?"

"You do appreciate a good story, don't you? Maybe I should say a great epic, in all modesty, of course. A professional student of literature like yourself."

"Would it be gratuitous of me to take notes?" I asked.

"I've already told you a good deal of the story," said Stonestreet, ignoring my remark.

"And Claude told me some more of it," I said.

"*Did* he?" said Stonestreet. "I've always suspected him of being more clever than he let on. That's why I let him hang around. You never know what these writer types have lying about in the form of diaries and such."

"Enough to send you away to where the only excavating you'll be doing will be picking your nose as you wait for lights out."

"There's a possibility of that," said Stonestreet, nodding. "But Claude's disappearance will be noticed by no one. *He's* seen to that. I'm more concerned with how *your* loss to the world will be felt. I suspect that your ex-wife will be easy to control. But that cute little co-worker of yours…Aside from some light marijuana use, she's remarkably clean, if you know what I'm saying. Regrettably, she may have to be eliminated."

"You seemed to have learned rather well from Draper Blessing," I said.

"Ah, I've availed myself of his resources and applied his methods, but, if I do say so myself, with a subtlety and scope of which Draper would have been incapable."

"If you kill me," I said, feeling a rush of panic course through me, "how will you get the Blessing document?"

Stonestreet roared at this one. His laughter triggered another explosive sneeze, accompanied by the entire urgent ritual of the handkerchief. Again, he put the gun down.

"Why would you think that approach would work when I've already tried to kill you?" he said when he had recovered from all this. And he had a point.

"Actually, I exaggerated the importance of that document. It may exist, but I certainly have no need of it. I've been getting by very nicely for years without it. You see, my original plan was to fabricate some meaningless document, present it to you in a very solemn fashion, and send you off with your harmless prize. Despite what you think of me, I really don't enjoy killing people. As clever and even as artistic as you try to be about it, murder inevitably renders down to a very squalid act, which not even the most honorable of motives can ennoble."

"Who do you think you are, Hamlet?" I said, getting sick of his bullshit. "You murdered Blessing and you couldn't have cared less about his rape of your wife or any other wound he inflicted upon you. You were his lifelong student and when your greed and envy became unbearable, you killed him and took over. Then, when Leona was on the verge of death, you started to get worried about this document that she had been prattling on about for who knows how many years. And now that I've turned up, you've taken the opportunity to try to kill me, just in case."

"Not bad," said Stonestreet. "But you give yourself too much credit. You are here because I arranged it. I am the one who arranged for the series of events that brought you here. I am the one who has brought *everyone* here—Claude, Norrod, Ultimi, that damn fool Dowagiac—"

"*Dowagiac?*"

"Yes, another potential litter mate. His background is remarkably similar to yours."

"But Norrod was the one who sent me here, if anyone did," I argued.

"To see whom?"

"Claude."

"And how do you suppose that Norrod knew that Claude was here?"

"Are you kidding? He's got an operation back in the States you wouldn't believe."

"Yes, but he won't have it tomorrow. Tomorrow he'll just be another lunatic preacher. And Ultimi will be dispersed. I've allowed them their petty rivalry—their very existence—only as it suited my purpose. They were a sideshow you and others took for the main act, just as I anticipated would happen. It's the way you are made. You are a man who craves significance, and if you find none, you impose significance upon the chaos that you find. Except that what you perceive as chaos has a higher order to it. *My* order, and it has been incomprehensible to you. You are a character, a character who is no longer integral to this production. I am doing you the courtesy of allowing you to be conscious of yourself as a character—the supreme power of the creator. Even the great artists have never been able to do that. Only a god can."

Stonestreet had become very rigid. His posture indicated that he was imagining himself seated at a throne, rather than an overstuffed chair. Then, once again, his face began to anticipate sneeze. This time it seemed to catch him more by surprise. He sprayed out a mist of saliva and I heard the gun pop. Stonestreet rolled to the floor and held his hands over his thigh. For a second we were both motionless. It took that long for both of us to realize that he had shot himself in the leg. Then I leapt off the couch and grabbed the gun, which Stonestreet had dropped to the carpet. I managed to train it on him just as Axtract and Tremble burst through the door, guns drawn. I pointed the gun at the old man's head.

"Call them off," I told him, "before your leg isn't the only part of you with a hole in it." I was so scared that I felt as though someone had shoved is arm down my throat up to his elbow and was trying to eviscerate me via the mouth.

Stonestreet looked at me as though I were a stranger. It took a few seconds for the shock to clear from his head and for him to realize what was happening. I really don't think he believed he could bleed. Sneeze, yes. Bleed, no. He looked calmly for a second at the gun I had pointed at his forehead. Then he turned to his two henchmen.

"Kill him," he said to them without emotion.

When the proverbial hail of gunfire erupted, I shut my eyes and waited for the impact. Hey, I thought to myself, if this is what it's like to get shot, what's the big deal? I didn't feel anything. Or maybe I had been killed instantly, and the transition was too brief to perceive. Maybe I was floating around in some limbo of pure thought that constituted the afterlife. No, it wasn't pure thought, because someone was speaking my name, and then someone was gently prying the gun from my hand.

I opened my eyes to find myself looking into the sweating forehead of Detective Lazard. Behind him, several Italian policemen with Uzis at the ready (like the fulfillment of a private prophecy) were standing over the prone and bleeding bodies of the henchmen. Stonestreet, too, had caught a bullet, square in the forehead. His eyes and mouth were open in surprise. In fact, his eyes almost seemed to be looking up at the black hole in his head, just beginning to brim over with a bubble of blood. It was only several hours later that I learned that I was the one who had fired the bullet through Stonestreet's brain. The act had been as involuntary as a flinch. At least that's what I like to think.

"You're all right, Stephen, it's all over," was all Lazard would say for the moment.

"What is?" was all I could say.

▼

THE GIFT

But, of course, it wasn't completely over. Nothing ever is. Almost a year passed before everything was explained. At least as fully explained as it appeared it ever would be.

First, let me offer a sort of premature appendix, which, for you skittish hypochondriacs out there, is *not* a life-threatening disease, but a symptom, perhaps, of faulty composition.

Haskell Stonestreet, Sr., despite his pretensions to divinity, had never been so far above suspicion as he had imagined himself to be. In addition to testimony from me, Claude Nickle, and Tremble (who, unlike his less fortunate partner Axtract, survived his wounds), there was testimony from several law enforcement agencies regarding investigations of Stonestreet for everything from kidnapping Draper Blessing to fraud, embezzlement, smuggling, drug trafficking, espionage, sedition and murder.

The fact that Stonestreet had been impersonating Blessing (at least it was presumed to be fact) also came as not much of a surprise to the police. They had simply never been able to catch him at it.

But perhaps even more sensational than the revelations about Haskell Stonestreet, Sr. (at least in terms of media attention) were the by-products of the investigation. It was discovered, for example, that Miguel and Stonestreet Jr. had conspired to kill the other two Blessing children at the instigation of the elder Stonestreet. As mere adolescents, they had tossed Benjamin from the ski lift during the holiday trip to Squaw Valley. Later, they had drowned Victor after feeding him nearly enough barbiturates to kill him anyway.

As he had said it was, much of what Stonestreet had told me during our luncheon interview was true. Miguel had killed Minerva after learning that she was a spy for Norrod. Randi, another of Norrod's agents, had been the girl that Minerva had fired for looking at the files. But that had been all for show. It was hoped that suspicion would be diverted from Minerva with this display of her loyalty and devotion. Randi just never realized how extreme her sacrifice would become.

Randy, a bisexual surfer, had been guiltless of everything except having been in the wrong place at the wrong time and of once having briefly been the sexual partner of Millar Crofts. So much for machismo.

Strangely enough, all the really violent and passionate crimes committed *en famille* by various Blessings and crypto-Blessings went unpunished. How or exactly when Draper died was never determined. Since Professor Stonestreet was the only one who had known the whereabouts of Draper's remains, it was impossible to examine them to learn anything about the circumstances of his death.

As far as what was known about the deaths of Benjamin and Victor Blessing, it was Rudy Sultana who had provided most of the damning testimony against his former comrades. Kelly Stonestreet's suspicions about Sultana had, therefore, been justified. Even since before Minerva's murder, Sultana had, in fact, been cooperating with Lazard and representatives of various other law enforcement agencies in return for immunity from prosecution and government assurances that he would not be extradited to various South American countries which were howling for his fat hide.

One of those empty seats I had seen at the dais in Molveno had been Sultana's. His was the seat that had been offered to me.

The other seat turned out, to everybody's surprise but Lazard's, to be reserved for one Vincent Pauling, the same Chief of Detectives who had been so nasty to me on the phone. Pauling pleaded guilty to obstruction of justice and a few other counts of malfeasance. Apparently, the sick bastard had broken the law out of his irresistible sympathies with the policies of the Ultimi organization and he was in no direct way connected to Haskell Stonestreet, Sr. In any event, his career was over.

While Sultana's testimony wasn't enough to convict Kelly Stonestreet and Miguel Blessing of those earlier murders of the Blessing kids, he knew enough about other crimes including gun running, smuggling, heavy trade in cocaine and heroin (Croft's specialties), fraud, white slavery, child pornography, and income tax evasion to put them all away for several lifetimes.

The extraordinary thing was that most of the murder victims were simply casualties of this otherwise laughable organizational rivalry between Norrod's Society of Trent and Ultimi of the brothers Blessing. Professor Stonestreet had funded both of these groups and had encouraged this intense competition between them almost as a lark, but very early on he had seen that he could make use of it by manipulating this war to his own ends, which mainly involved providing a diversion from or a cover for his own activities. Tremble testified, for example, that Midwiff had been murdered because he had learned, through the help of his gossip columnist girlfriend, of the alleged existence of the Blessing document. Professor Stonestreet had ordered the murder. It had been made to look like an execution—a bullet to the head, then an explosion and fire aboard the yacht—in order to make it look as though Midwiff had stumbled into the midst of the war between the Society and Ultimi. Who, after all, would suspect an obscure archeologist thousands of miles away in Italy? That was Stonestreet's style, which he had learned from Blessing. Do things obliquely.

Which brings me to Clifford Dowagiac, connoisseur of the oblique perspective. Dowagiac recovered from his injuries and identified his assailant as one of Professor Stonestreet's Italian helpers at the dig. The attempt on his life may not have been a matter of mistaken identity, as Norrod had assumed. It seems that the elder Stonestreet *did* consider Dowagiac another possible candidate for heir to the Blessing document. The Italian worker who had pushed Dowagiac over the railing had disappeared, however (Dowagiac had identified him from a photo), and, of course, the professor's testimony was unavailable. So there was no way to know for sure.

But, as much as I hate to admit it, Dowagiac's background *was* very similar to mine. He had managed to progress through his academic career by means of performance so mediocre as to embarrass any serious scholar. His parentage was uncertain. His mother may or may not have been his natural mother, but she had had Native American ancestors; his father was almost certainly a stepfather. Stonestreet had lured Dowagiac to Trento with the promise of investiture in the bogus Anamorphosis League, a creation of none other than Haskell Stonestreet *pere*.

When Dowagiac learned of this, he became as intolerable as you could imagine someone with his sort of temperament to be at the prospect of a windfall. He called me a couple of times suggesting that we get together and negotiate a deal—a compromise—should the document surface one day and lead to untold riches. But the great luxury of not having to sit next to Dowagiac on an airplane, or co-exist with him in a small European city, was that I could tell him to fuck off, in so many words. And this, despite my gratitude to his son for indirectly saving my life, is exactly what I did.

Dingo, by the way, remained in Italy, where the last I heard he was thriving as a fashion model, of all things, and was living with that snow queen that he had met on the plane, another of Norrod's ubiquitous spies. Whether she ever got through her "wedding night" intact, I never found out.

Norrod, despite Stonestreet's prophecy that his organization would dissolve without the continued infusion of Blessing money, managed to stay afloat. He did suffer something close to a nervous breakdown, or perhaps it was just a crisis of faith, after he learned that most of his missionary work had been financed by an incorrigible rapist, first, then by a murderer. But he recovered, realizing that God works in mysterious (could I go so far as to say oblique?) ways. Fortunately for Norrod, he had been prudent enough to make sound investments and his organization remained solvent. It did, however, come under intensified scrutiny by the Justice Department and the IRS (and probably the FBI, the FTC, the FCC and the CIA). And the fact that he had cooperated with Lazard also went in his favor.

In fact, Lazard and Stonestreet, Sr. had been engaged in a transatlantic chess game, so to speak. It was Lazard who had given Norrod his "instructions" to send me to see Claude. Lazard had been aware of my activities almost since the day that I had joined the Sultana agency. Apparently, Leona had summoned Lazard a couple of months before her death. She had explained her doubts as to her husband's death and her distrust of Miguel and the Stonestreets. She had also told him about the alleged Blessing document and had expressed her fears about the havoc it might wreak should it fall into the wrong hands. The old girl had not been nearly so infirm as she had pretended to be. That had all been a magnificent performance by an old and disabled Broadway gypsy—a matter of survival, really. Miguel had been as much warden as nurse. Any prolonged indication of lucidity on her part would have endangered her life. This was, no doubt, her conviction.

And I had been introduced as the catalyst. The only trouble was that Leona had died ahead of schedule, so that any help Lazard might have expected from her in the continuing investigation was not forthcoming. Exactly what the plan *was*, Lazard couldn't or wouldn't say. All he *would* say was that he could not have justified sacrificing me. Not that he wouldn't have done so; it just would have left the world that much more out of whack.

I did express my anger to Lazard at his letting things go on so long that I almost got killed despite his ethical posturing, but he assured me that it never would have gotten that far. I had, he explained, been under almost constant surveillance, which probably explained my ongoing sense of being observed. And Claudio and I must have been pretty easy to follow. He had even been in the helicopter with Norrod that day when I had had lunch in Stonestreet's courtyard. The purpose for that rather spectacular display was to dissuade Stonestreet from harming me. He had also had my apartment watched continuously, so that he had known all along about the bodies of the Randies having been deposited there. In fact, it had been Sultana who had removed the bodies at the direction of Lazard, who didn't want bad elements within the force to find them there.

So, everything seemed to have concluded satisfactorily. All the criminals were either dead or in jail. Most of the relatively innocent parties had escaped permanent injury, with the exception of Midwiff, the Randies, and Hugo, and there was a good deal of doubt as to how innocent Hugo was. He seems to have been an independent opportunist who had gotten what was coming to him, in the estimation of Norrod and Lazard. In fact, for a while, Lazard had suspected Hugo in the murder of Minerva Hewitt.

You could even say that *I* was satisfied, at least more satisfied than I had been for many years. I had moved out of my hideous apartment and in with Denise, who, despite some lingering adolescent tendencies and an unnerving hankering for bodice-ripper romance novels, was a joy to live with. In truth, it was probably the joy of having her magnificently energetic and willing body at close quarters that I found so exhilarating, but I was done with analyzing my motives when it came to women. We enjoyed each other immensely and that was enough for both of us.

Each of us had found a new job. (Sultana had vanished into witness-protection nirvana immediately after the legal proceedings, not an inconsiderable feat for a man of his dimensions.) Denise was managing a florist shop. I had landed a job as an editor for a university press. The work was anything but exciting, but it offered a sort of dignified serenity that I found appealing. I guess at heart I had always been a man of contemplation.

Almost a year to the day after I had unconsciously put a bullet through Professor Stonestreet's brain (that was ruled justifiable homicide, by the way), Denise and I were spending a rare weekday afternoon off together at the race track. She had never played the horses before, and after having won a couple of races, she was experiencing the euphoria of the novice gambler. I didn't have the heart to tell her that betting on horses because their names reminded her of her nieces and nephews wasn't going to get her very far. Besides, who was I to argue with success? In the fifth race she decided to put two dollars to win on a horse named Sombrero because she had once passed through Albuquerque and had liked her fleeting glimpse of the city.

I agreed to go along with her on the bet, but on the way to the two-dollar window, I got to thinking about siestas and Mexicans lounging against the sides of adobe huts, their floppy hats pulled down over their sleepy eyes, and I just couldn't go through with it. My fears were inspired by nothing more substantial than the memory of a Hollywood stereotype of the Mexican work ethic, to be sure, but I decided on the basis of my superior wagering skill that I would put our money on a horse called Cheetah. Now there was a horse with a name.

Well, Sombrero came in first, paying twenty-one fifty. Cheetah, for all I know, is still stalking the finish line. Of course, I hadn't bothered to tell Denise that I had switched our bets. I was going to surprise her. And now she was so delirious with excitement that it tore my heart out to tell her that I had changed our minds and put the bet on Cheetah.

"You what?" she cried, taking a swat at my head with her baseball hat with the Jack Daniels emblem on the front. A good-natured swat to be sure.

"You *creep* you!" she screamed. "You Benedict Arnold!"

There are moments of perfection. There are moments of pure truth. There are moments of exquisite clarity. Then there is the one instant in a decade or maybe a millennium when all three converge.

"Jesus!" I said. "He wasn't talking about a man at all. He was talking about his *boat*."

"What are *you* talking about?" said Denise.

*   *   *

"When I was a kid, I used to hang around the Grosse Pointe Yacht Club quite a bit," I said. We were in the car, on the way back to the apartment. "There was this huge yacht that always sat out on the end of the pier all by itself. It was the Blessing yacht. It was off limits to everyone, and it was guarded day and night."

"So what does all this have to do with Benedict Arnold?" asked Denise.

"That was the name of the boat," I said. "Actually, it was the *Benedict, Arnold* with a comma between the two words."

"Geeze," said Denise. "I can't say much for the guy's patriotism."

"It had nothing to do with American history," I said. "It was a matter of convention, more than anything. You know how people have those cutesy names on the transoms of their boats, some kind of pun or something?"

"What's a transom?" said Denise, clearly uncertain.

"On the back of the boat," I said. "Those god-awful precious names they call their boats."

"Yeah," said Denise. "So?"

"This buddy of mine's father used to be the harbor master at the Grosse Pointe Yacht Club. He told us that the yacht had been a wedding present from one of the richest men in the world—Draper—to his wife. My friend's father said that the name of the boat was a private joke between the newlyweds. Then, a few years later, I read a story about it in the paper—you know, one of those offbeat feature stories they run on slow news days. Well, they were talking about how to name your boat. Just like how to name your baby. And they used the Blessing yacht as an example. The speculation was that *Benedict* was a play on the word *benediction*— which, of course, is a *blessing*—and also the word as it refers to a newly married man—a *benedict*."

"You're crazy!" said Denise. "I've never heard anyone called a benedict. They call him a groom."

"No," I said. "It derives from a character in *Much Ado About Nothing*. A *benedict* is a special kind of newly married man, a confirmed bachelor who suddenly decides to marry, which would certainly apply to Draper. You see what spending half of your life in an English department will reduce you to? Anyway, the writer of the article confessed to being stumped by the use of the word *Arnold*, but that was because the writer hadn't done his homework. Arnold was Draper Blessing's real first name. I remember Bill Midwiff telling me that the last time I talked to him before he died. Was killed, I mean. I guess Draper didn't like his given name, so he decided to use his middle name—Draper—which was also his mother's maiden name. Apparently, he managed to keep his real first name pretty much a secret, at least publicly. But, well, Midwiff's girlfriend was a gossip columnist, and she must have unearthed this deep, dark secret somewhere along the way."

Then something else occurred to me.

"*That's* why Midwiff was found on the Blessing yacht," I said. "I'll bet that Midwiff figured it all out about the Blessing document being on the boat, and he went there to check it out. Only he ran into the wrong people while he was snooping around." Something new occurred to me. Things were unraveling so quickly that I could hardly keep up with them.

"And I'll also bet that it was Midwiff that wrote that little note on the inside of the elevator telling me to count my Blessings. I had assumed it was a reference to me. But Midwiff was trying to tell me, as indirectly as his not-very-subtle mind could, that the document was aboard the *Benedict, Arnold.* He didn't know how to get in touch with me. He must have been trying to get into my apartment to leave a note or something when Yolanda saw him."

"If I were you," said Denise, still smarting from her loss in the fifth race, "I wouldn't bet on anything."

*   *   *

Back at the apartment, I hunted up the postcard with Blessing's literary effort on the back while Denise mixed up a pitcher of Tom Collinses in the kitchen.

"This was in the envelope that Leona gave me to give Victor, although her real purpose was to get it out of reach of Miguel, I suspect. Perhaps Stonestreet had been right in thinking that Blessing had told his wife about his suspicions concerning my ancestry." I was explaining all this to Denise, who had joined me on the couch. She picked up the postcard, read the back, then turned the card over to look at the picture of the yacht club on the front.

"It doesn't make any sense to me," she said.

"It didn't to me, either, at least before," I said. "But I had always considered the Benedict Arnold—the traitor—in *human* terms. But see, the mention of *freighter* is important. It suggests a boat."

'I know what a *freighter* is," said Denise.

"This 'key' is the difficult part," I said. "'Opens nary a door, nor a gate e'en.'"

"God, how poetic," said Denise, rolling her eyes and taking a drink from her glass, then from mine, apparently to make sure they were the same, which, of course, they should be, coming from the same pitcher.

"It wasn't meant to be great art," I said. "And see, in this fourth line, he's talking about the manuscript. 'Yet the script by the man you...' *Man-you-script.* Written by 'Arnie.' No doubt that's what Leona called Draper in their more affectionate days."

"'Under both lock and key lies a-waiting,'" said Denise, finishing off the poem. "Well, it sounds simple enough to me. If this traitor is a boat, then the manuscript is locked aboard the boat someplace."

"Yeah, but the key doesn't open anything," I said.

"No, no," said Denise. "It doesn't open a *door* or a *gate*. But maybe it opens a hatch or a cabinet. Or maybe even a safe."

"Safes have doors," I said. "I think you're splitting hairs."

"Maybe it opens a padlock," said Denise, really getting into the mystery now. "It says 'lock *and* key.' Or, hey, maybe it's the key that starts the boat, you know, the motor."

"What does that have to do with the lock?"

Denise thought for a moment. "Maybe the steering wheel locks?" she asked weakly.

"Yeah, okay, so we start the engine up and unlock the steering wheel. Then what happens? The boat drives itself to some deserted island where the manuscript is buried?"

"I'm only trying to help," said Denise, making me feel like the total jerk that I was acting like.

"Maybe Lazard has some ideas on this," I said. "I'll call him."

Lazard did, indeed, have some ideas.

"I have a confession to make," he said.

"That's always refreshing in a police officer," I said, not liking the way this was starting.

"We knew all about the boat," said Lazard.

"How?"

"When you left your things in the hotel in Washington, Norrod recovered them. Before he sent the stuff back to me, he went through it and found the postcard."

"And he called you and told you about it? Why didn't you tell *me*?"

"Hold on," said Lazard. "Let me explain before you get all hot and bothered. Norrod didn't tell me right away. He was cooperating with us, but he also wanted to get his hands on the manuscript, remember? So before he notified me about the contents of the note, he sent one of his agents—a flight attendant—"

"Joanna?"

"Yeah, Joanna, right. He sent her over to the boat to check it out. But when she got there she found that someone had beaten her to it."

"Midwiff."

"Right again. But Joanna didn't know who he was, so she played dumb and retreated, planning to come back later when Midwiff had gone. But sometime after she left, Midwiff was murdered and the boat was set afire. So after that, Norrod thought twice about withholding the information and called me. I had the boat—what there was of it—thoroughly searched in conjunction with the murder investigation, and either the poem didn't mean what Norrod interpreted it to mean, or else somebody got way with the manuscript. Or, hell, who knows, maybe it was destroyed in the fire. The boat was pretty much totaled."

I wasn't bothered so much by what Lazard was telling me as by the style of his delivery. He was speaking like any bureaucrat might be in reciting a regulation. There was no hint of contrition in his voice.

"Lazard, you know, Midwiff was a friend of mine. You could have told me all this before."

"I suppose I should have," said Lazard, softening a little. "But it really didn't seem to be all that significant. Since Norrod had cooperated in the investigation, we all agreed to overlook his little sin of withholding evidence. And we saw no reason to drag Joanna into the thing. Other than trespassing, perhaps, she hadn't committed any crime, not any more than your friend had."

"I would say that Midwiff more than paid for his crime," I said.

"Yes," said Lazard. "I think he paid for a lot of other people's crimes." There was a long silence.

"Where's the boat now?" I asked.

"Scrapped," said Lazard. "There wasn't much to salvage. After the investigation, the owner turned out to be a phantom. Oliver Malvern didn't exist. It was a cash deal. Leona was desperate for money and she sold it without asking too many questions. I think she sold it to old man Stonestreet without realizing it. But there's no doubt that a lot of people were interested in that boat. Nevertheless, as I say, we went over that tub centimeter by centimeter and found nothing. It appears that Mr. Blessing was playing a joke on someone."

* * *

We had finished off the pitcher of Tom Collinses. We had also finished off a prolonged and intense catalog of sexual exercises. Denise reached across my body to the nightstand where half of her marijuana cigarette lay extinguished in the ashtray. The maneuver brought her stunning breast to within a half-inch of my nose. I stuck out my tongue and just touched the nipple, which responded by growing rigid and elongated almost instantly. For such modest breasts they had extraordinarily long nipples when they were aroused, which was frequently. The large aureole surrounding her nipple puckered up right before my eyes, almost comically. God, she was an erotic creature. She fell back to her side of the bed, affixed a roach clip to the remainder of the joint, lit it, and inhaled deeply.

"Let's watch TV," she said, pointing the remote control gizmo at the set near the foot of the bed and punching it with an emphatic gesture, as though it were a weapon of some sort. A real child of technology. She flipped rapidly through the channels, passing by soap operas, commercials, news, a soccer game, "Sesame Street," a TV preacher or two, and a talk show where a panel of women were discussing the male medical community hysterectomy conspiracy or some such thing. Denise finally came to rest on a game show.

"Oh, no," I groaned.

"My God, it's 'Name that Tune,'" said Denise, almost rapturously.

Onscreen, the master of ceremonies was explaining to the two contestants (as jumpy as lab mice on crystal meth) that something was going to happen that I didn't quite catch.

"I can name that tune in one note," said one of the hypercontestants. The audience oohed and aahed.

"What an asshole," I said. "Nobody can name a song on the basis of one note."

"Yes they can," said Denise. "I've seen them do it."

"The fix must have been in, then," I said.

"Shhh," said Denise. Somewhere offstage a single piano key plinked.

"'My Body Lies Over the Ocean,'" Denise screamed, bouncing on the bed.

"Your *what*?"

"'My Body Lies Over the Ocean,'" Denise repeated. "You now, my body lies over the sea?" Denise sang a few bars of the song for me, weaving her head to the beat.

I started laughing uncontrollably. You'd have thought that *I* was the one smoking grass.

"Stephen," said Denise, "I can't hear."

"Your *bonnie*," I cried in the midst of roaring with laughter. "Your bonnie lies over the ocean, not your body. Who the hell do you think is going to bring your body back from over the ocean? I mean, what's it being brought back to?" I laughed until I was weeping.

"Oh, you made me miss it," said Denise, tremendously disappointed. "Now I don't know if I was right."

"I'm sorry," I said. "But you wouldn't have been right if you had said 'body.'" I wiped the tears from my eyes with a corner of the sheet. "It's bonnie. It's a Scottish expression meaning my pretty one, or something like that. The Scots have this weird dialect that only partially resembles English. It's like Gaelic."

Then it hit me. I jumped to my feet and stood naked on the bed.

"It's a *pun*," I said.

"What is?" asked Denise, looking at me, startled a bit by my behavior.

"Blessing was referring to the lake. Loch is the Scottish word for lake, you know, like the Loch Ness Monster?"

"Oh, yeah?" said Denise. 'Well, what is it under, the key of G?"

"No. It's not the musical key. Get dressed. I've got to make a couple of calls. We've got to get to the yacht club before dark."

I called the yacht club first and found to my unbridled delight that Edwin Woodley, the father of my boyhood friend, was still the harbor-master. And he even remembered me—fondly, I think. All of which convinced me that I was still on a roll. He was slightly less eager to oblige when I told him what I had in mind, but he finally consented when I told him that I would be accompanied by a police lieutenant, under whose authority we would proceed. Then I called Lazard and told him to meet us at the yacht club in an hour and a half.

*   *   *

Lazard, Woodley, Denise and I stood on the deserted pier. Just beneath our feet, the bubbles from the divers gurgled to the surface. Beneath the surface, the divers' lights shimmered as they moved back and forth along the pier.

"Is this the only spot where the Blessing yacht was moored?" asked Lazard. He seemed a bit disgruntled and was probably performing this favor only out of a residual sense of guilt for not having kept me fully informed.

"Absolutely," said Woodley. We had already learned that *absolutely* was Woodley's favorite word. He was a very positive man.

"The *Benedict, Arnold* measured seventy foot, stem to stern. It had the whole dock to itself. It hardly ever left the marina after the early sixties. After that, Mr. B used to spend a few days on the boat now and then, although I rarely saw him. He had his own boys to keep an eye on the boat—even had his own crew. He took good care of her," said Woodley, nodding. "Absolutely."

"I don't know," said Denise. Her lips were trembling just slightly. It was a rather cool evening and the breeze off the lake was bracing, to say the least. "It's an awful big lake. Or loch."

"Yeah," I said. "But it's also under a key, remember? Blessing was still punning. He was thinking of the word as a synonym for wharf or pier. A quay. Q-U-A-Y."

"Oh, God," said Denise. "Not another Scottish word. Q-U-A-Y sounds like *kway* to me," she argued, making the word rhyme with play or, depending upon your mental disposition, slay.

"Well, I don't know about the etymology of the word, but I know it's pronounced *key*," I said, beginning to feel a little foolish. Those divers had been down there for a long time.

"He's got that right," said Woodley, nodding his assent. "Absolutely."

I saw Denise turn her attention to Lazard, so I looked at him too.

"Sounds plausible to me," he said without conviction after giving us one of his shrugs.

Just then, one of he divers popped to the surface, raised his mask and dislodged his breathing apparatus from his mouth.

"We got something down here, Woody," he said. "A box or chest of some sort. But the son-of-a-bitch weighs a ton."

"I'll get the winch," said Woodley, as though there wasn't a setback in the world he couldn't troubleshoot. Mr. Woodley was old school.

About fifteen minutes later, as the sunlight was just disappearing behind our backs, the winch, which was anchored to the bed of a pickup that Woodley had driven up to the dock, swung a mucky, oblong object towards the dock and lowered it heavily to the wooden planks. Woodley hosed it down, revealing what looked like an unembellished sarcophagus. Lazard looked at me and raised an eyebrow.

"God," said Denise. "It's just like *Treasure Island.*"

"It's sealed tight," said Woodley, rising from his inspection of the lid. "If you want to take it over to the machine shop, we can take a torch to it."

"Absolutely," said Lazard.

The torch was useless, but a mechanic who was busy reconditioning a propeller managed by a combination of chiseling and prying to remove the lid. Inside, we found another sturdy-looking metal box wound tightly shut with a couple of yards of duct tape.

"Oooo, a Chinese puzzle," said Denise, who was obviously going through some form of regression under the strain of the whole thing. I looked at Lazard.

"It's your party," he said, shrugging. I unwound the box and found a key taped to the top. I unlocked the box and opened it. Inside was a

package wrapped in a bubble envelope and sealed with some more duct
tape. My hands were trembling so badly that I dropped the package to
the floor.

Lazard bent down to pick it up. "I think we're finished here," he said.
"Thanks for all your help, Mr. Woodley."

"My pleasure," said Woodley. "Absolutely."

Lazard walked us back to the car without a word. Only after I had
taken my seat in the car did he hand the package through the window.

"You'll contact me," he said, smiling, "if there's anything in this that I
should know about."

"Sure thing," I said. I was so nervous that I managed to stall the car
twice before I had even cleared the parking lot.

*   *   *

"Congratulations, boy!" read the first line of the manuscript. It had
been handwritten on graph paper, and apparently this was the only draft.
Every other line or so had words or phrases crossed out with a heavy
enough hand to make the obscured material illegible. Words were inserted
between the lines or drifted into the margins, tethered to the text by frag-
ile umbilicals.

"And massive apologies," the text continued. "I suspect, if events have
proceeded as I have foreseen them, that you anticipate staggering disclosures. Well, get used to disappointment. They are not imminent.

"There! Are you composed? As I am probably decomposed by this
time? Ah, the glorious privilege of speaking from the dead! Immune to
rebuke, resigned to the futility of regret, freed from the petty confines of
coherency.

"Life is a lesson, boy, the learning of which affords no subsequent application. I'm sure that this sentiment is not original with me, and yet, all
things are original with me in the Great Pool of the Dead. I am Homer

and Shakespeare, Alexander and Caesar, Jesus Christ and the ethereal mind of God himself. But, before I swoon away under the magnitude of my unqualified liberty, let's have a story, a favorite of your Great-grandfather Emil, my father. He was a bear of a man with a robust disposition, crimson face, a huge gray beard that hung to his belt buckle (I never did learn precisely where my father's mouth was located), and a passion for justice that fairly flamed from his nostrils.

"When I was a mere boy of ten or so, he told me this story, almost by way of formal instruction. It stands out so vividly in my memory because it was the most sustained, the only substantial communications that he allowed me in our relationship. He was a military man, and he conducted himself as one even among his family. He fought under the great General Karl Friederich von Stienmitz at the battle of Weissenburg during the Franco-German War, at which the French suffered a serious defeat. My father was one of a company of dragoons which had distinguished itself mightily during the day's fighting.

"Now, it seems that there was a good deal of celebrating amongst the company one evening soon after this great victory. Too much was drunk, and the bravura of the conqueror began to prevail. During the course of the revelry, an argument developed over whether or not the French, those elegant and fastidious warriors, came equipped with assholes. In order to resolve the dispute (the drunkards proceeded logically, despite the absurdity of their inquiry), a French prisoner-of-war was secured for inspection so that the issue could be decided immediately and publicly. The prisoner was stripped and inspected and found, indeed to possess the orifice in question. Wagers were settled, the merriment, rekindled by this ribald exhibition, increased.

"Yet, the sport with the prisoner was not finished, and, if anything, began to assume even more obscene proportion. Some anonymous provocateur insisted that the orifice be proved genuine, and not a mere cosmetic ornamentation designed to deceive the enemy. So it was agreed that a rifle barrel be introduced an agreed number of inches into this unfortunate knave's rectum in order to verify the previous conclusion. (I do not relate this anecdote with the skill of your great-grandfather, or perhaps my experience of the cruelty of men leads me to forsake all hope that you have not anticipated the culmination of these events. Anyway, I continue. We always continue. It is the curse of mankind.)

"That stage of the proceedings accomplished, it was suggested, again from an anonymous voice from the crowd (Who will claim that the Evil One does not dwell amongst us, bellowing for his sacrifice?) that the prisoner's anatomy might be improved upon by, shall we say, a bit of impromptu surgery. Hardly was this butcherous proposal uttered than the weapon discharged; such is the acceleration of madness. But I tell you, as my father told me (I can hear him now, the resonance of Truth possessing him) that man is the master of almost nothing, and least of all his own headlong folly.

"*But no story ever ends*. Stories swirl around forever, protean and insidious and unstillable, like divine asides. The bullet did not come to rest in the body of that wretched Frenchman (believe me, I still writhe in sympathy with that poor soul, the cramps bringing me to my knees without warning), but deflected off one of his already lifeless bones and out of his body, and thence into the heart of an aghast spectator, a comrade of my father's and his dearest friend.

"Mad with grief and rage, my father fell upon the instrument of this mishap, a veteran Italian mercenary named Sassovia (who was still too dumbfounded—and probably drunk—to resist), took the rifle from him, and, without hesitation, fired a bullet through the prankster's brain.

"Now, my father had influential friends among elements of command, and, in any event, the circumstances of the offense were mitigating. The Italian's conduct had been highly improper, criminal even. He was unpopular among his comrades—untrustworthy and craven.

"But my father, driven by his irrepressible sense of justice, would not allow it to be thought that his act was anything but recompense. To the day of his death, he refused to acknowledge that he had killed Sassovia out of any other motive save justice. He considered it the only response a civilized man could make.

"Now I assume *my* burden of this tale. Unfortunately, Sassovia had a son with his own ideas about justice. When I was thirteen years old, I was walking in the park with my father and mother. Suddenly, a man leapt from the bushes behind us and stabbed my father, wounding him in the shoulder. Despite this injury, my father managed to subdue his assailant while my mother and I looked on in horror. The assailant turned out to be this son of the man my father had killed.

"During the younger Sassovia's trial, my father, who was not a vengeful man (he insisted that the only difference between a savage society and a civilized one was that the latter could distinguish between revenge and justice, a distinction I confess to never having been able to appreciate and a hopelessly naive and romantic contention, I have come to believe), pleaded for leniency for his attacker, whose life my father had no desire to see wasted. (The young man had once been a promising art student in Milan, although he eventually settled for carpentry and woodworking, and as part of his defense, several of his paintings were introduced into evidence to show the disintegration of the man's mind since his father's death. *My* father was taken with these artistic efforts—which even to my young taste were morbid and irredeemably abstract—and even offered to purchase some of them, a prospect which enraged the young artist.) But despite my father's efforts, Sassovia was confined to a mental institution, where he spent the rest of his life doing woodworking by day and literally painstaking monochromatic paintings by night using his own blood as the only medium.

"My father died a year and a half after the trial, and my mother, with the devotion of a suttee, soon followed him. I was seventeen years old, well provided for, and anxious to see the world. I left Germany and never returned.

I pass over a number of subsequent years—almost three adventurous decades—not because I wish to be evasive, but because to dwell on them would expose too many innocent people to distress in some form or another by virtue of their association with me. Enough have suffered and are very likely still suffering. In the mid-thirties, I was living comfortably in Chicago, having made my way only that far west in those turbulent years. I had managed almost effortlessly to increase my fortune. Making money came as easily to me as losing it comes to most people. I had never spent so much as one day in anyone's employ. What I had was a gift for recognizing a profitable idea, even in its most unintelligible form. My instincts in this regard were invariably unerring. As my reputation as a financier spread, I began to be besieged by all sorts of applicants, from the most unbalanced crackpots to the most inspired creative geniuses. It was not unusual, the times being as hard as they were, for me to entertain a hundred such petitions in a week.

"But I remember only one of those courtiers, a young man with eyes like blue stones and a dignified, no, a disdainful bearing. I knew the moment I laid eyes on him that he was a Sassovia, although he had changed that hissing name of menace to its English equivalent—Stonestreet. He was even more Anglicized than that; his widowed mother had married an Englishman. And his much older brother had been my father's attacker.

"He made no secret of his identity; in fact, he announced it. But he was polite…and proud. And though he must have struggled to compose himself against native tremors of vendetta, he made no further mention of the terrible history that linked us. He simply offered his proposition, which I agreed to without even listening to him.

"I tell you, boy, I wish that I had killed him at that moment, or that he had killed me. How is one to rectify the evils and misfortunes that precede him? I had sought to do it through indiscriminate fornication—to dissipate the Blessing line and in so doing to make my pursuer's task hopeless. (Yes, I had always known that there would be a pursuer.) But now I chose accommodation, or, submission (or do I deceive myself? Was it only confusion?). I stole his idea and made another fortune. I took his wife, an act not of lust or cruelty, but of charity—can you understand? I was—and am—a man who wanted to disintegrate, to disperse my corrupt identity beyond recovery. But his wife fell in love with me—*me*! This pile of shit trying to stink itself into oblivion. She fell in love with me, and once again, I was confirmed *me*, and even as I tried to bleed myself away, the white blood of life spilling into her, she screamed my name in her passion that conferred a despicable unity and wholeness upon *me*, a word that I hate with supreme, cool logic, like a drowning man hates moisture. It is God's word alone.

"*Me* is other, separate and distinct. I did not want that sort of privilege of consolation, the sort of uniqueness that invites the identity to exercise authority. But what could I do? I had inherited a dormant vendetta and an instinct for survival that I could neither circumvent nor deny.

"The only course of action left to me was to absorb, to insinuate myself into the interests of my enemy so thoroughly that he would no longer be capable of distinguishing between us. This involved a number of tactics— the repeated inflicting of injury until injury became routine, the domination of will, and, on the other hand, complete surrender, generosity, and devotion to the adversary. Let me give you an example: Once, I convinced Haskell to undergo an examination at a private clinic which I supported. He agreed, as he agreed to everything I suggested, and when he was in the clinic I had him anesthetized without his knowledge and brought to an operating room. He was revived from the anesthetic and as he regained consciousness, I was standing over him with a scalpel. After calmly explaining what I was about to do, I carefully slit his throat across in one smooth stroke from ear to ear. He suffered this action without complaint, and immediately my surgeons, whom I had stationed at my side, sprang to work closing the wound, thus saving Stonestreet's life. I wanted to know what it felt like to cut a man's throat.

"My, my. I have read over the previous three paragraphs and find that my rapture, like the misty, private thresholds of paradise that raptures are, communicates nothing but uncertainty. Let me tell you simply (but inadequately) that out of an eradicable sense of guilt and historical disruption,

I sought to repair the world—to restore that much of it for which I felt responsible. You may disapprove of my methods, but who can question my intentions?

"I had given to Stonestreet almost everything that I owned. I couldn't give him back his father or his brother (who had long since died, spitting out my father's name in a display of such durable malice that even his attendants had been surprised; until the moment of his death, he had not spoken a word for the final twenty years of his life). Nor could I give him back his wife, even though I offered to compensate him by offering him a wife in return. I even sought a woman as close as possible to the original in appearance, intelligence, ethnic background, and disposition. Yet, after I married Haskell's wife, I found it almost impossible to stem the tide of my own affection for this duplicate, who, to my surprise, Haskell apparently found unsatisfactory, since he rejected my offer of her.

"But I did give him money, my influence—my very identity, in fact, asking only to be allowed to observe. But, after all, I decided that that was too empty a gesture, a gift of excessive pride.

"Now I am very old. I used to think that I would die, or that, mercifully, the world would explode in a moment of irrevocable petulance. I no longer have such confidence. The world may endure—or persist—forever, and I am not sure anymore that the realm of the dead is so soundproof that we don't detect frightful nuances of immortality. I intend to arrange my own death. The world *must* be justified. I am sure that Haskell will never *try* to kill me. But I am also convinced that he will try to eliminate my natural descendants. His mode of vengeance is to force me to endure, to witness, my own line's exhaustion. He's a fool to believe that this would distress me, I who have already engraved my life upon this planet with too heavy a hand. He has already convinced Miguel that I intend to transfer my wealth only to my natural progeny. And the only reason that he hasn't killed Kelly is that Kelly was castrated by some leftist guerillas in Argentina. I am sure that it was Haskell who arranged the deaths of my other two sons.

"And, finally, I believe that he intends to kill you, should he learn of your existence and discover your identity. In all honesty, boy, I don't know if you are one of mine. Why I should be so impressed by the claims of a squaw who had no scruples when it came to swindling the white man, I can't exactly answer. But I do *believe* it, boy. And that is why, in order to protect you, I leave you the most precious bequest available to me; I leave you nothing, and thereby you gain everything."

Draper Blessing
4 August 1974

"Do you believe this?" said Denise, looking up from the final page of the manuscript. She was sitting on the corner of the couch, her legs tucked under her, the manuscript in her hands.

"Is that a serious question?" I asked.

"You know what I mean," said Denise. "Do you think this guy was for real?"

"Well, it explains a few things. I mean, Jesus, it gives us the motive for Stonestreet's attempt on my life, if nothing else."

"I liked the other motive better," she said. "At least I could understand it. This is just, well it's raving is all."

"Well, I'm sure Blessing isn't giving the entire picture," I said. "What Stonestreet seemed to be after, or at least what Blessing thought he was after, was not merely one-for-one revenge. He was going all out—the complete extinction of the Blessing lineage. The magnitude of Stonestreet's purpose must have unhinged Blessing a bit, especially since Stonestreet was so methodical and unemotional about it. I know how Draper must have felt. During my conversation with Stonestreet, Sr., I had never had the slightest indication that he intended to do me harm. He was really a gracious and disarming fellow. He must have expressed genuine affection for Draper. On the other hand, that affection didn't deter him from what he must have considered his destiny or duty."

"Well, I don't know how anybody could be so cold-blooded about things."

"Oh, I don't know," I said. "I've come to think of murder as a pretty nonchalant affair for those who are proficient at it."

"I still can't understand why Blessing just didn't do away with Stonestreet if he was such a threat," said Denise. "He certainly had the power to do so."

I shrugged. "Guilt. Or arrogance. Or both. He was undoubtedly subject to both. What amazes me is how similar Blessing and Stonestreet were."

"Similar?"

"Yes. Neither of them could seem to deal with loose ends. Anything left unresolved drove them to distraction. If there was a beginning, there had to be an end. If there was a birth, there had to be a death. If something was opened—whether it was a grave or a jugular vein—it had to be closed. If someone was loved, they also had to be hated."

That's what I told Denise, and I wasn't really lying, but I also wasn't sure that I believed it. I was trying to draw some conclusion from this whole affair, which made me as bad as Stonestreet or Blessing. What I was saying was as inauthentic and rhetorical as Blessing's document had been, which didn't make it any less true.

"Well, what are you going to do about it?" said Denise. "The manuscript, I mean."

"I don't know, destroy it I guess," I said. "Somebody's got to put a stop to things." Denise thought about this for a few seconds, and then I saw her face begin to register alarm.

"You don't suppose there are other Stonestreets or Sassovias or whatever they are out there, do you?"

"I don't know," I said. "That's not what I meant. I was just saying it's time to put this Blessing thing to rest."

I wanted to put myself to rest, too. I wanted to be unconscious for about a year. When you go to sleep, you *have* to wake up, right? Except for the last time you do it. At least that's what my father used to say when, as a child, I was afraid to go to sleep for fear that I might not wake up. (The words "If I should die before I wake" somehow always seemed to make the possibility likely.)

"You *have* to wake up," he would say. "Except for the last time."

So I thought of my father. I tried to think about how his voice sounded, what his minute idiosyncrasies were, how he smelled, but I couldn't summon forth enough of these characteristics to compose a real person. I couldn't even remember exactly what my father looked like, although I had seen his face almost every day for more than twenty years. Christ, I could more easily recall the greasy, soft-jowled face of the auto mechanic who had tuned my car five years ago or the perpetual grimace of my sixth grade principal. And the failure of my memory made me feel unfaithful to his. I could only remember him as a slightly overweight machinist whose style of conversation ran to modest and original aphorisms (a contradiction, perhaps, but true nonetheless), and who always seemed to be observing the affairs of the family, rather than conducting them or participating in them. Maybe I was mixing him up with Ozzie Nelson; I don't know. But I *do* know that my image of him was beginning to generalize right before my mind's eye into Father—the idea of paternity, rather than the fact of it.

But what difference did it make, anyway, whose father was who?

In effect, all fathers were dead once the bolt was shot. Then I remembered Ambrose Jensen. And I thought of his definition for *father*.

Fertilizer.

End

AFTERWORD

As I write these words, it is almost just over two years since Stephen Fargo disappeared somewhere in the Atlantic Ocean between Cape Hatteras and Bermuda during the first week of August 1998. Fargo was 50 years old at the time. He is presumed dead, but there is always something tantalizing about a loss at sea such as this. His body was never recovered. His sailboat was found drifting, its hull intact, its sails serviceable, its equipment, including the radio, in good working order. Was Fargo thrown overboard during a storm? Did he simply slip over the side accidentally while attending to some sailing duty or other? Was he the victim of foul play, modern-day pirates, illness? Or did he commit suicide?

None of these fates would come as a shock to anyone who knew Stephen Fargo or followed the Fargo mythology with any care. First, to say that he was an inexperienced sailor would not begin to describe his incompetence. By all accounts (mine among them), the man could barely hang laundry, let alone maneuver a complex system of sails. He was known to loathe sailing and most other forms of activities on the water. He suffered severe episodes of motion sickness throughout his life and disliked traveling so much that he once told an interviewer how proud he was not to have left his residence for 621 straight days during one stretch in the mid 1980s.

Fargo's paranoia was legendary, which makes his final folly all the more perplexing. No one ever endured celebrity with more reluctance. Several years ago, one enterprising reporter managed to document more than thirty aliases that Fargo employed over the final two decades of his life. Rare visitors to his home (myself among them) have spoken of the elaborate security systems that festooned it and rumors persist of underground escape tunnels running for miles, allowing Fargo to enter and exit unobserved. He frequently confided to me his obsession with being poisoned, so much so that he turned to vegetarianism and grew most of his food on his own property. His needs for water were met by a rainwater collection system, and he even brewed his own beer at home.

The rationale for these eccentricities is clear to anyone who has read *The Blessing Cipher*, but for those few who may not be familiar with that book, some history may help.

It was, in fact, the publication of *The Blessing Cipher* in 1985 that first brought Stephen Fargo to national public attention. I had a small part in *The Blessing Cipher*, Fargo's first-person account of his adventures in search of the truth about billionaire industrialist A. Draper Blessing (a part greatly expanded in length and significance in *Our Father*). The Blessing mystique, along with the publicity surrounding Fargo's exploits described in the book, helped make it a best seller. A fictionalized version was filmed in 1988 as "The Secret War," although the story was ill advisedly and inexplicably transplanted to England in the 1930s (a less stimulating environment would be hard to imagine; rumors held that the leading lady was involved in one of those searing Hollywood romances that last about thirty seconds with a native of Britain and would only agree to that location for filming). The movie bombed, even in video, but a subsequent four-part PBS documentary on the life of Draper Blessing revived interest in the story in 1990.

By that time, however, Fargo had virtually withdrawn from public life. Many have speculated that Fargo fell into a deep depression following the death of his wife, Denise, in an accidental fall while on a retreat in Sedona, Arizona. Fargo himself was rumored to have died or to have undergone everything from a sex change operation to a religious conversion to Buddhism to abduction by aliens to a nervous breakdown. This reclusive period came to an abrupt end in 1993 with the publication of another book on the Blessing affair by Clifford Dowagiac.

Dowagiac's book, *Count Your Blessings: Anatomy of a Hoax*, challenged Fargo's account of the Blessing affair, in which Fargo strongly suggested that he was an heir to the Blessing fortune (although he never did make legal claims on that fortune). Taking his title from an incident in Fargo's book wherein the hero reads a cryptic graffiti message on the elevator door in his apartment building, Dowagiac provoked controversy by claiming that he, Dowagiac, was, in fact, the heir to the Blessing fortune, and that he had the notorious Blessing Cipher to prove it. Many readers will recall the famous Larry King interview with Clifford Dowagiac during which he cavalierly brandished what he called the authentic Blessing Cipher. Eventually, it became clear that Dowagiac had simply been pinning his hopes on the assumption that Fargo was so hopelessly reclusive that he would either be ignorant of or incapable of responding to these charges.

As we all know, he miscalculated.

Fargo emerged from seclusion to counter with his own feverishly hyped appearance on "Larry King Live," bringing with him the actual Blessing "manuscript," as he referred to it, along with certificates of authenticity concerning Blessing's handwriting, and an offer to have both of the documents examined by independent experts to determine which was genuine. He also offered to secure affidavits from some of the key players in the Blessing affair, including Dr. Motherwell Norrod, Rudy Sultana (who remains in hiding as part of the witness protection program) and Jules Lazard, by then retired from the Detroit Police Department. It was a brilliant performance. Bizarre highlights included Fargo referring to Dowagiac as "the Ed Wood of the literary world" and reminding Larry King that Dowagiac shared his given name with another great twentieth-century forger—Clifford Irving.

Fargo's gambit had the desired effect. Dowagiac's publisher pulled the book from the shelves, deleted it from the online bookstores, disavowed its contents, and initiated legal proceedings against its author. And Dowagiac himself slipped back into well-deserved obscurity.

The episode seemed to revitalize Fargo. He became less reclusive. In 1997 he again attracted media attention after he became involved in the conspiracy so well documented in *The Big Island*. So as not to deny readers the pleasure of that adventure, especially its riveting climax, I will not dwell on that episode of Fargo's life.

It is sufficient to recognize that Fargo led a remarkable life, by turns murky and meteoric. Ironically, the more we learn about him, it seems the less we know him as a man.

Only a miracle will return Fargo to us, but through a minor miracle we are now able to understand him better. That minor miracle is the publication of the volume that these words follow, and, no less, the story of how I came into possession of it. On the surface, it seems to be a predecessor version of *The Blessing Cipher*. And it may well be that its composition came before that famous account. However, although *The Blessing Cipher* contains one hundred fewer pages than *Our Father*, it is not what I would call an improvement. More accurately, it is, perhaps, an expedient. I suspect the shorter version represents a capitulation to Hollywood. That version is more cinematic in construction, more action—oriented.

In contrast, *Our Father* has a richness of character development and a sensitivity to language missing in the earlier version. Far more important, however, are the insights into Fargo's psychology that are allowed full expression in *Our Father*, while being almost totally obscured by what one critic called the "chase imperative" that seemed to be the entire rationale for *The Blessing Cipher*. That chase is considerably decelerated in *Our Father*, leaving more room for humor, intrigue and, quaint by today's standards, allegory.

An example may clarify. Readers of *The Blessing Cipher* will recall Fargo's flight to Italy en route to Trento for the showdown with various villains primarily for its comic introduction of Clifford Dowagiac's character. During that introduction, Fargo mentions that Dowagiac's wife and son are also on board, with particular attention given to the name of the son—Dingo. The humor is effective and, of course, these characters are necessary to the plot. However, in *Our Father*, another dimension is added, greatly enriching the story. In this version, Dingo is attempting a graceless seduction of a female passenger. He is disappointed in this effort, so that one has to wonder why the scene is included at all.

To help answer that question, Fargo's marginal notes in the manuscript of *Our Father* are helpful. They suggest a narrative on several levels. First, Dingo's clumsy attempted seduction on the plane prefigures the burlesque and pornographic en masse mock weddings that occur late in the story. Further, the episode provides resonance for one of the book's major thematic devices—the distortion and perversion of sexual love. An earlier canine reference occurs during Fargo's initial confrontation with Minerva Hewitt, one of the secretaries in the office of Rudy Sultana where Fargo finds his first job after leaving his college teaching post. During her ruthless rejection of his request for a date, Minerva suggests that they skip the dating formalities and proceed directly to the sex act. She tells Fargo "…and you will have accomplished your objective without having gone through some extravagant mating ritual, and I will not have been disappointed to find that your attention had been focused on the culmination of the evening's activities all along. I will not feel like a whore, and you will not have had to pay for it. We'll be just like two dogs that happened to bump into each other. We can blame it all on the biological imperative."

This also connects with Ambrose Jensen's account of his father's cruelty to the family dog in Chapter 13, a perversion of love into masochism and abuse.

In fact, the overall rich texture of the sexual metaphor clearly differentiates *Our Father* from *The Blessing Cipher*. A marginal note in the chapter alluded to earlier concerning the Dowagiacs explains that Fargo travels to Europe "like a turbo-homunculus heat-seeking the menopausal Mother Church." Thus entire narrative structures function as steps in an elaborate dance of mating and reproduction, both sacred and profane. Whereas the scramble for the Blessing Cipher as a kind of certificate of legitimacy is the primary driver of that book's narrative, the subtler and grander theme of fatherhood and its responsibilities and consequences is the story of *Our Father*. Hence, the paltry Blessing manuscript aggrandized to the status of The Holy Grail in *The Blessing Cipher* is relegated to the status of no more than one of Hitchcock's MacGuffins in *Our Father*.

These examples are inadequate in evoking the fully realized, multi-layered, subtle, and sophisticated artistic creation that is *Our Father*. This volume is unlikely to be rendered into film. It's also unlikely to become a bestseller. *Our Father* has a different fate.

Finally, I would be remiss if I did not relate briefly the story of how I came to possess the manuscript of *Our Father*.

Stephen Fargo was not a man who ever considered the possibility of a literary legacy. He did not save documents or correspondence with an eye towards posterity. In fact, it is entirely likely that *Our Father* would never have survived had it remained in Stephen Fargo's custody.

For all the intrigue concerning the possibilities of Fargo's heritage in both books, he died a remarkably unattached human being. No family survives. He also had few possessions and little wealth. The money he made from the sale of his books and the movie rights to *The Blessing Cipher* seems to have been spent on the many travels that Fargo made with his wife. Whenever he exhausted his funds, he apparently did work of one form or another—primarily consulting to politicians (at which he was unaccountably successful, inasmuch as he detested politicians and had no political experience of his own) and private investigations—usually for the rich—to finance the next trip or adventure. This cycle continued until his disappearance. Evidently, he used most of the proceeds from the sale of his assets to buy and outfit his sailboat for his final journey.

While Fargo had many acquaintances, he had few friends. He prized solitude and valued a life of seclusion. While I cannot say that I was his friend, I was without doubt his most valued comrade during the events of the Blessing affair. I also acknowledge that Fargo's portrait of me is not always flattering. But Fargo trusted me, probably as much as he trusted any living person. The controversy stirred up by Dowagiac's book had convinced Fargo that other pretenders probably lurked about, and, looking for a place of safekeeping for his manuscript before setting sail for Bermuda, he sent it to me with instructions to use my own judgment as to its disposition in the event of his demise. It was all very nonchalant, and I sensed no premonition of doom in his prose.

Nevertheless, his demise ensued, followed by reckless speculation among the news media regarding his credibility and faithfulness to the truth in the composition of *The Blessing Cipher* (not to mention the tabloid drivel claiming that Fargo was yet another victim of the Bermuda Triangle). It was only at this point that I took up the manuscript and, after reading it, decided immediately to seek its publication. The record needed to be set straight; potential claimants on the Blessing fortune—if it exists—needed to be preempted.

I have no guarantee that publication of *Our Father* will accomplish these objectives. Stephen Fargo's main talent seems to have been elusiveness. Some of the more outlandish tabloids have suggested that he never existed at all. That he was made up by Hollywood and portrayed by an actor in his few public appearances. It is like the contention by a small minority of conspiracy whack-jobs that America never really landed on the moon.

Well, I know he existed. In fact, it is because of me that he had the opportunity to exist as long as he did. While I am compelled to acknowledge his chameleon existence in his final decade, I am equally obligated to testify to the integrity of his life.

He would find any tribute tedious, so I won't offer one. Men *have* walked on the moon and one man, anyway, managed to live an extraordinary life nearly at the heart of obscurity. This is his story, or, at least, one of them.

Claude Nickle
New York City, September 2000